LET EVENING COME

YVONNE OSBORNE

For information contact:

Unsolicited Press

Portland, Oregon

www.unsolicitedpress.com

orders@unsolicitedpress.com

619-354-8005

Cover Design: Kathryn Gerhardt

Editor: S.R. Stewart

ISBN: 978-1-963115-52-9

For My Family

Let the light of late afternoon
shine through chinks in the barn, moving
up the bales as the sun moves down.
From the scoop in the grain
to air in the lung, let evening come.
-Jane Kenyon

The white man is a stranger who comes in the night.
His appetite will devour the Earth and leave behind only a desert.
-Chief Seathl, Suquamish Tribe

PART I

CHAPTER 1

There were some things Sadie Wixom would never forget—her mother's apron smeared with chocolate and blood, riding a motorcycle into the boreal forest with winter coming, and making love in the back of a van with a boy from Saskatchewan.

The first time she saw him, it was from the vantage of height. She was throwing hay down for the horses when she heard a truck pull into the driveway. She leaned out the opening in the side of the barn and watched her cousin, Sam, park his truck by the stable.

He threw her a wave, but her eyes fastened on the stranger climbing out of the passenger side. He wore a flattened fedora and a pair of baggy pants cinched at the waist. An object hung against his leg, and for a second, she thought it was a gun. He looked up at her from under the brim of his hat and tipped it back with his finger.

Their eyes locked for a moment, then he disappeared with Sam into the shadows of the stable, and she stared at the space they had vacated.

She climbed down the ladder through the shafts of light streaming between the rough-hewn planks of the hayloft, jumping off the bottom rung into the cool of the barn below where the cows were contentedly chewing their cuds and the pregnant barn cat padded across the stanchions. She brushed her hands off on the seat of her pants, combed the hay out of her hair with her fingers, and took a shortcut through the side door to the stable that housed her two horses.

The stranger was running an admiring hand over the withers of her favorite, Two Socks.

"This is Stefan Montegrand." Sam nodded at him. "We're going to ride the horses and he's going to show me how to throw that thing." Sam motioned at the wooden object hanging from a braided loop in the stranger's belt.

Stefan gave her a nod from under his hat. He had dark hair and a heavy brow. There was a cut at the corner of his mouth, and he had a Band-Aid over one eye and a bruise under the other. She felt an immediate distaste for him and took offense to his nicked-up face, to the hair that hung lank to his shoulders, and the hands on her horse.

"He bucks," she said curtly.

Stefan studied her with eyes the color of Two Socks', and she shifted uneasily under the weight of his regard. "Ask him." She beckoned at Sam to deflect his attention.

But he was still staring at her. "What's your name?" His Canadian accent was discernible in three syllables.

"Sadie," she said, crossing her arms, newly aware of the thin material of her soiled shirt.

"You got some horse, Sadie." He dragged his eyes back to the horse and stroked his flank. Sadie found herself looking at his hands; brown as Two Socks' withers, brown as the leather reins he gentled across the horse's neck like he needed to get accustomed to them.

"He doesn't like strangers," Sadie said curtly.

"Don't be rude," Sam said.

"He bucked you."

"That was your damn dog's fault." Sam countered.

The dog had been with her for six months, the first thing her father brought home after the tornado zigzagged across the county, sparing one family to flatten another. He was a shaggy, long-haired dog of no discipline or discernible breed, but he attached himself to Sadie and came when she called.

Stefan ran his hands down Two Socks' neck and the horse nuzzled his shirt pocket.

"I think I can handle him," he said.

She pursed her lips. Two Socks was checking his other pocket.

"What's his name?"

"Two Socks. 'Cause he has two white feet," she added, as if he needed an explanation.

"Tussock," he repeated like it was one word. He stroked the barrel chest down to his fetlocks, murmuring his admiration. He was all over that horse, and Two Socks accepted the familiarity, docile as a kitten, belying Sadie's concern. Stefan looked at her from across the horse's withers and the corner of his mouth moved.

"Okay if I ride your horse, Sadie?"

"Just warning you."

He held his hand under Two Socks' nose and whispered words she couldn't understand.

Two Socks nickered and tossed his head, knocking Stefan's hat off with his nose.

Sadie laughed, then covered her mouth.

Stefan plucked it out from under the horse's feet, knocked the dirt off against his leg and settled it back on his head.

"We have come to an understanding," he said with a serious look.

Sam chuckled and threw the saddle on the other horse's back, a plucky little mare, and rocked it into place. The mare that didn't yet have a name shifted her feet and blew. "A companion for Two Socks," her father had said when the horse trailer pulled into the yard a month earlier. First, she got the dog and then a companion for Two Socks. While others tiptoed around her, her father kept bringing things home, and everything dovetailed into *before* and *after*.

Resigned that this galling stranger was going to ride her horse, Sadie lifted Two Socks's saddle off the sawhorse and balanced it on her knee.

Stefan dismissed it with a wave of his hand. "I don't need that."

"Stef rides bareback," Sam said smugly, as though he were privy to all his secrets.

She cradled the saddle against her stomach and stared at the two of them. *Already on a nickname basis.* She looked pointedly at the gelding's length of leg, and then at Stefan.

"How do you plan to mount him?" she asked.

Stefan didn't seem to hear her, immersed in the secret dimension of man and horse, each with clear understanding of the other. His focus

5

was on Two Socks, aquiver with his ears pricked as Stefan ran his fingers under the noseband of the hackamore and spoke to him in soft undertones.

He checked the tension on the horse's face, grabbed a handful of mane, and in a blur of movement, swung himself up. He gathered the reins and put the horse forward, touching the brim of his hat with his forefinger as he rode out of the stable bay.

Sadie stared after his retreating figure in disbelief.

"Who did you say he was?" she asked Sam.

Sam watched as Stefan put the horse into a canter around the circle drive. "I'd say he can flat out ride a horse," he mumbled, as much to himself as to her.

"I didn't ask your opinion of that," Sadie muttered.

"You know the family that moved into Dad's rental house? Well, I'm supposed to show this one around."

She frowned. Her uncle's rental was just down the road. Was this guy going to be coming around all the time, wanting to ride her horse? "Where're they from?" she asked, after a minute.

"Saskatchewan. Be nice. He wanted to ride. Can't you be nice?"

"He's rude."

Sam rolled his eyes. "Ignoring your stupid comments doesn't make him rude."

"He's cheeky and rude."

"Cheeky? Why're you so judgey?"

"What happened to his face? Was he in a fight?"

"Found one on his first trip to town."

"With who?"

"Won't say."

"What's with that thing in his belt?"

Sam laughed. "It's called a boomerang, cuz."

She watched the stranger with his odd attachments bring the horse down from a trot to a walk, leaning over his neck and talking in his ear. "I thought that was an Aussie thing."

"Nah," Sam shook his head. "I told you, Saskatchewan. He's Dené, or maybe it's Denésuline." He weighted the syllables. "And part Maliseet," he added with a shrug. "Something like that."

"Never heard of them."

"Ancient Indigenous tribes." He grinned. "They have secret powers." He wiggled his fingers like they were kids telling ghost stories.

Sadie rolled her eyes. Other than the dark hair, he didn't look like pictures she'd seen at school of Indigenous people. A little too tall and a little too thin, like he wouldn't survive a winter.

All Sam knew was that what was left of the family had recently arrived in Michigan from a troubled area in the resource-laden lands of Canada. He'd been instructed by his mother, Sadie's formidable Aunt Helen, to show this one around. When he mentioned horses, Stefan showed an interest. The family had been sponsored through a cultural exchange program at the Women's Center for displaced Native Americans, and they had needed a place to live until they located their relatives in the Upper Peninsula. So, Sam's dad had fixed the front steps and replaced the hinges on the door, while his mother had cleaned up the rental and put a vase of cosmos on the table the day they arrived.

"You could say they're homeless. So, we have to be nice. I know it'll be hard for you."

Sadie chewed her lip. This homeless person intrigued her, but she would jump off the silo before she let Sam know.

"Maybe you can hook up." Sam joked. "Being new and all, he won't be aware of your personality."

Sadie flung the grooming brush at his head, and dust flew.

Sam ducked. "Watch it!" he growled. "You need to start acting like a lady if you ever expect to get a guy." He mounted the mare, giving Sadie a disapproving onceover. "You know, if you wore something other than those grubby jeans and actually brushed your hair once in a while maybe you could get one. I swear to God you're turning into a slob. Ever since–" He clamped his mouth shut and looked away.

"Ever since what, Sam?"

But he rode out in pursuit of the one he was supposed to be showing around.

She gave the empty water pail a satisfying kick. Like she would wear jeans with manufactured rips and useless pockets you couldn't tuck a marble in. Jeans like the ones the girls Sam hung out with wore.

She looked down the lane to where the horses were galloping into the distance. Heat shimmered the two-track, and the only way to place the road that ran along the back of the farm was by the stray cloud of dust that rolled up from an occasional passing vehicle. A soft cooing drew her eyes to the roof of the barn. A row of doves lined the peak as if waiting for an audition.

She had caught scraps of conversation between Aunt Helen and her father, Henry Wixom, talking about the tar sands and hydro controversies in Canada, the drilling and damming and subsequent displacement of the native population that stood in the way. It was what her aunt called *predatory resource extraction*. A conversation she didn't have to weigh in on. A conversation she could absorb yet walk around without the responsibility of opinion. But now with a face to put with the subject, she wondered.

Why not stay and fight for what was yours? What could possibly be here for them?

She grabbed the handle of the push broom and swept the floor of the stable bay, then carried a bale of hay from below the loft window and tucked it in the corner by the water bucket. She straightened the tack, running her hands over the worn trappings, remembering the way his hands acquainted themselves with her horse, the way his gaze seemed to undress her.

She left her boots on the back porch and washed her hands in the sink with the cake of Fels-Naptha soap. She took down the jar of peanut butter and rummaged through the fridge for jam. The homemade jams were all gone and they were down to store-bought grape. Homemade jam was in the *before* category.

She grabbed a plate and a jug of milk, carrying it to the table where her grandfather sat with a plat map, draft paper, pencils, and his pocket watch. He was one for time and punctuality, and not much for daydreaming, which is where he and her father collided.

The watch was solid silver and as big as the palm of her hand. His father, her great-grandfather, had given it to him before he died. A conductor's watch, he told her. At one time, all the conductors had one and the trains ran on time by pocket watches they had to wind. How a lumberjack-turned-farmer acquired it was never explained.

"What're you doing, Grandpa?" She pulled a chair up across from him.

Simon Wixom, named after his father, peered at her over the top of his glasses. "Just cogitating, Sade."

"Where's Dad?"

"Out with the pickup."

She nodded. Her dad had taken to driving around, but never having been anywhere when asked.

"What are you drawing?" she said.

He tapped the eraser end of his pencil on the table. His hands were leathered, and his nails were ridged by age like the rings in a tree. "House plans," he said.

"House plans?" She swallowed a clump of peanut butter.

"Can't stay here forever. Your dad will meet someone."

"Meet someone?" She snorted. "What's that mean . . . *meet* someone?"

"The man needs a woman."

"What is this, the eighteenth century?"

"It's the way it is."

"You didn't after Grandma died."

"I was seventy years old. Besides, I had your mother looking out for me."

A clock ticked away from the bowels of the house, and she could hear herself chewing.

"He has me," she said, swallowing her unease.

He took his glasses off to better see her. "He doesn't want you looking out for him, Sadie."

"Well, if you move out, so do I." The thought of living alone with the quiet man who looked through her without seeing her was unsettling. What would they say to each other? Her grandfather was the

9

foil against which they balanced themselves on their tightrope walk through the *after*.

"You're his daughter, Sadie. You'll get on."

"Better have two bedrooms in that plan." She took another bite of her sandwich. "What's the plat map for?"

"Looking at the drainage ditches and the buffer zones." He ran his finger along a penciled line. "The drain here behind Bolton's place runs into the creek that forms a buffer zone. But the creek is running slow and foul. I've been meaning to talk to Ronnie at the Drain Commission. Word is Bolton's constructing a dam. Word is they ran off one of Ronnie's boys who came out to talk about drain issues. Some of these guys think they can do anything they want on their property."

"They're always lighting fires at night, and it doesn't smell like wood." Sadie thought aloud.

"If you're burning something you shouldn't, you do it at night. I could probably find him some old pallets that would burn clean and fast if it's a campfire he wants, but I don't think they're roasting marshmallows."

When the neighboring farmer died, the farm across the road fell into neglect. Then strangers from the city moved in with guns and vapor lights. Within a month the shooting range went up, and *No Trespassing* signs cropped up like chickweed.

It hadn't taken Grandpa long to figure them out. "You should've bought that place, Henry, while you could," he'd said. "Never know what's going to move in next door and now look what we have across the road. People afraid of the dark." He spat in the dirt and kicked it dry.

From the headlands there used to be nothing but uninterrupted night. Now a permanent fluorescent glow marked the Bolton residence and silhouetted the human-shaped targets on the firing range.

"Can you check the zoning laws while you're at it?" Sadie asked. "Must be some law against shooting ranges. Destroying the peace."

"Disturbing the peace." Grandpa corrected.

"Whatever."

He squinted at her. "You've been told to stay away from there, right?"

Sadie took a swallow of milk and passed the back of her hand across her mouth with a cursory nod.

"What do you know about the family Aunt Helen and Uncle Larry took in?" she asked.

He leaned back in his chair and tented his fingertips.

"They lost their land through a court ruling. The father was jailed for illegal occupation and a murder charge, drummed up according to Helen." He shook his head. "I understand he died while incarcerated. The older boy's been in and out of jail for blocking roads and destroying property."

"So, a bunch of criminals."

"Some wouldn't say that."

She thought for a minute. "You can't just kick people off their land."

"Been going on forever, Sadie."

"I thought Canada got along with the Eskimos and all."

"They aren't Eskimos. They're an Indigenous people unfortunate enough to be living on oil-soaked sand and caches of uranium. Helen says they have relatives somewhere in the Upper Peninsula. She's helping them make connections down at the Women's Center. You know she'd be all over that, troubled family in need of help."

Helen Vermeulen had made women's issues her life's work. An activist and ardent "women's libber", the affectionate family joke, she said the correct term was feminist, and she used her Flemish maiden name. To Aunt Helen, women were women, none of that lady bullshit. Sadie couldn't figure out why Sam was such a Neanderthal.

"What about the other one?" Sadie asked. "What's he in trouble for?"

He raised an eyebrow.

"The kid that came over with Sam to ride," she clarified.

"He's a long way from home, Sadie. Try to be nice."

Sadie scoffed. Everyone wanted her to be nice. "He's already been in a fight."

"That right?" He picked up the pocket watch, palmed it, and set it back down.

"Is that all you're going to say?"

"It's not surprising. Folks around here are suspicious of outsiders, especially anyone who looks different."

"You mean anyone who isn't white."

He shrugged. "Wasn't always like that. But lately, well, throw in an accent and attitude, and it's like a hand grenade with a loose pin."

"You're saying he provoked it?" Sadie asked, surprised.

"I've heard he's a hothead."

Sadie slouched in her chair and crossed her arms. "He's riding Two Socks."

Simon looked at her with a little furrow in his brow. "And?"

"Sam didn't even ask."

He clucked his tongue, shaking his head mockingly. "Didn't even ask."

Sadie pushed her chair back. Everyone was belittling her concerns. "Well, he should have," she said, dropping her dishes in the sink with a clatter.

She opened her laptop and googled *Maliseet* and *Dené*. The first originated in New Brunswick and the latter in the western provinces. She clicked on a video posted by Greenpeace shot from a helicopter over what was once boreal forest, but now held the largest of the tar sands developments, open mine pits, and tailings ponds. From the window of the helicopter, it looked as barren as Mars.

A gust of wind riffled the papers on her desk and billowed the curtains like a ghostly presence. She replayed the video and turned up the sound. The camera panned down on the desolation. She didn't blame them for leaving. Why would anyone want to stay?

CHAPTER 2

Stefan studied the windswept fields. Storm clouds brewed on the horizon with the low-pressure light that augurs thunder, and redwing blackbirds flitted across the switchgrass looking for a place to hide. The inside of his pant legs were hot and wet, and the horse was lathered. They had covered the length and breadth of the farm twice over, and were back at the top of the lane that dissected the spread, waiting for Sam. A cooling breeze rippled the shirt across his back and lifted the hair from his neck.

Two Socks snorted and tossed his head. Stefan rested his hand on his shoulder and spoke to him. Sam's cousin didn't know it, but her horse liked bareback as much as he did. With bareback, a horse knew what you were about, and you knew what he thought about doing before he did it. This one loved to run. He was broken but spirited.

But then, with the graceful way that girl moved, she would be easy on a horse's back.

Sam rode abreast, fighting the filly who was fighting the bit. Two Socks pranced sideways and Stefan tightened the rein. He nodded at the field in front of them. Left fallow, it was covered with grasses gone to seed, and ragged trees crowded the fencerow.

"Do you ever get grouse out of here?" he said.

"Grouse?"

"Good land for grouse. We used to get them."

Sam shook his head. "See an occasional pheasant, but you can't take them out."

Stefan pointed overhead at a raptor soaring on an updraft. "I see you have redtail."

Sam squinted against the sun's glare. "You must have eyes like one. They're protected."

"Like your pheasants?"

"This is Michigan, not Canada. And it isn't hunting season. Suppose you're used to shooting what you want when you want?"

Stefan watched the hawk glide lower. It circled a bird-of-prey challenge and then banked for the fencerow to settle on the upper branch of the tallest tree.

"We don't shoot hawks," he said finally.

"I wanna see you throw that thing," Sam said, changing the subject.

Stefan dropped his hand to the boomerang. He had tied it to his thigh to keep it from bothering the horse. It was the first time he had it out of his suitcase since they left Rainy River.

Two Socks high-stepped and complained, fighting the rope.

"Hey boy, you wanna run?" He stroked the top of Two Socks' head, and the horse's ears quivered. He looked at Sam. "We'll race you."

They rode at a hard gallop neck-and-neck down the lane. When they rounded the silo, Stefan leaned forward to talk the horse on, and Two Socks pulled ahead with a burst of speed.

They pulled up to the stable in a cloud of dust, horses stomping and doves scattering from the rooftops.

"Not much of a race," Stefan said with a grin.

"Horse just couldn't wait to get out from under you."

Two Socks high-stepped into the stable and Stefan slid off his back.

Sam dismounted with a grimace and loosened the cinch around the mare's belly. "This filly hasn't been ridden enough. That's her problem."

The sudden crack of a rifle split the quiet of the stable. It was followed by six shots from a handgun, evenly spaced. The mare tossed her head and whinnied nervously, and Two Socks' nostrils flared and his eyes rolled.

Stefan held the trembling horse. "Thought you said it wasn't hunting season."

"It's the neighbors," Sam said quickly. "They've rigged up a shooting range back of their place. It's worse on the weekends."

"Sounded close."

"It is. You'd think the horses would be used to it."

"Horses never get used to that."

Henry Wixom pulled up to the farm's gas pump and removed the lock that kept the hose in place. Precautions were taken after the old farm truck disappeared one night. At first Henry blamed Sadie, so Sadie blamed Sam, but that theory was soon discounted, and they reported it to the police. It was discovered two days later parked on the side of the road over by the lake, out of gas. They never found out who filled it up and took it for a joyride but figured it had to be a neighbor kid who knew them and their careless habits.

They had all gotten careless after Sadie's mother died.

He unscrewed the gas cap and the smell of petrol wafted out of the tank. The hose bucked in his hand, and he tightened his grip. His face was leathered and his hair flecked with gray, but he still had his grip. He looked over at Sam and the boy with the horses, but saw no Sadie. He glanced at the dial frozen in time at thirty-two cents a gallon. He listened to the sound of the tank filling.

Gas was thirty-two cents a gallon when he learned how to drive. His dad made him keep a notebook in his glove compartment to keep track of his fill-ups, and he took it out of his allowance at the end of every month. But a tank of gas would last him all week and took him and Jenny down all the country roads and to their favorite parking spot by an inland lake where migratory waterfowl congregated. With the engine idling and the heat on, the trumpeting of geese was their music, and they had nothing to worry about except getting it on without getting caught.

Despite what his friends thought, he paid for every gallon of that gas. They were envious of the convenience—who else had a gas pump in their yard? —but he took it for granted, like her. He had been an oddity among his group of friends, monogamous from the age of seventeen.

Who would have dreamed that thirty years later he would be back living with his dad? On good days, it felt like he was in a time warp. On bad days, he would suddenly forget what he was supposed to be doing.

Now gas was four dollars a gallon, but he was still driving back roads for the hell of it, radio at full blast, parking by the lake to watch the geese fly in and out, the only danger the thoughts in his head.

Cars were coming that would drive themselves, but Detroit would never get him out from behind the wheel. Never turn him on to a smartphone like Sadie had to have, though he warned her about all that screen time, bugs in your ear and in your brain. He knew enough about electronics to disconnect the computerized voice that came with the truck, and muzzle the eavesdropping bitch who refused to say why she was so nosy.

Your question is inappropriate. Would you like to ask another?

It was quite satisfying to pull the plug on her.

Ever since Jenny was taken out by a nail-studded board flying through the air with the force of a two-hundred mile per hour wind, the worm had turned, he envious of the friends who complained about someone waiting up for them and in their business, bitching about the checkbook and the television, newspapers strewn across the floor, and dirty socks under the bed.

He screwed the cap back on the gas tank and checked his tires—force of habit, all these things the old man had him doing. Though he hadn't listened when he'd warned him about the weather system alert on the radio. He was always warning Henry about one thing or another, couldn't let go of the everyday operation and let Henry run things. Worried about the line of credit, worried about the cattle, worried about the boards falling off the side of the barn. Worried about the weather, but off he went to Grayling anyway—regret growing deep and wide—to buy this truck he found on the internet. He was going to drive the wheels right off it.

CHAPTER 3

The sun had hazed over, and the air was thick with humidity. The cloud bank that had hovered on the horizon and caught Stefan's eye was on the move, threatening to take out the mountain he could see in the distance.

"That's Mount Bannon," Sam said, as they finished up with the horses and walked to an open area where they could throw the boomerang. "It's the highest point in this part of the state. The old timers claim it messes with the weather. Storms break up around it, veering one way or the other to miss us entirely. Of course, that only happens when we're in a drought."

Stefan studied the mountain in question. Covered with towering evergreens, it reminded him of home. "Do you go over there much?"

"Nah, it's farther than it looks. Grandpa says if you're up there with a pair of binoculars you can see Lake Huron." He looked off in that direction. "Shoreline is rugged this far north, perfect ports-of-entry for the bootleggers of his grandfather's generation." He laughed. "Great-granddad reportedly supported prohibition—saloons were leading good men astray—but he had a prescription for whiskey he took a shot of every night before dinner."

Stefan looked at him. "Really?"

"That water can turn rough without warning. It must have been a dangerous enterprise. If you go out a hundred yards due east of that mountain—" he drew an imaginary line in the air with his finger— "you can see the hull of a shipwreck grounded in the lakebed."

Stefan followed Sam's finger from the mountain sporting evergreens across a pasture brimming with life to the invisible lake. But in his mind, he was seeing deforested wasteland pockmarked with stumps and ponds of sludge.

'C'mon," Sam said impatiently. "Let's see you throw that thing."

They walked to a level area, and Stefan eyed the throwing field. Sadie's shaggy dog suddenly romped across the field in front of them with his ears flopping. She was sitting against the trunk of a walnut tree at the edge of the field, throwing a stick for her dog to fetch.

He stifled a smile. The dog's attention was about to be disrupted.

He set his feet and held the boomerang away from his body, going through the motions for Sam. He would show her something that came back on its own.

He threw it overhand like he was pitching a baseball, and it flew in an upwards elliptical path. It soared, up and up, and then picked up speed on the turn and spun back like a top. He caught it on a stretch, like a first baseman with a foot planted on the bag.

The dog dropped the stick and bounded across the field, barking with excitement. He circled Stefan with eyes peeled on the boomerang.

"Shut up, you stupid mutt," Sam said.

"What's his name?" Stefan asked.

"He doesn't have one."

"Doesn't have one?"

"Nope. She just calls him Dog. Tell you the truth, she ain't been right since her mom died." He looked over at her for a minute, then lowered his voice. "I think she's afraid to get attached."

Stefan looked back at Sadie leaning against the tree. She looked all right to him. He'd never seen hair the color of hers or a girl who moved like she did, as though she could move right through you without you knowing. A fluid stride that caught and held the eye. He turned the boomerang over in his hands and gazed across the throwing field.

A car passed on the road, and the dog with no name tirelessly circled. He was built like a timber wolf through the neck and shoulders, and in the yellow of the eyes lurked an animal who had known wild nights and hungry times.

Sam frowned. "You don't talk much, do you?"

Stefan wet his lips. He wanted a cigarette, not talk. He pointed across the field like a billiards player calling his pocket, and measured the wind against his cheek the way his grandfather had taught him. He tilted the foil at a slight angle to compensate and launched it with a grunt. He watched it soar, flatten, and curve. He hadn't lost his touch.

The dog circled, confused with this new game of fetch. Stefan threw until his shoulder hurt, but each heave was a release of bottled-up tension—the drive south in a van leaking oil, and a brother left behind.

Sam gave it a try, and Sadie's stifled laugh carried across the pasture. He was on the town's intramural baseball team, but his first attempt was clumsy, and the boomerang took a sharp dive into the grass. The dog bounded forward in excitement, but Stefan shouted, "Leave it!", and he stopped in his tracks, looking back in confusion.

Stefan collected the boomerang and talked to the dog who listened with his head cocked.

Time and again, Sadie's dog circled the spot where Sam's throws landed, but he never again tried to pick it up, his unbridled, if misplaced, enthusiasm for the tossing of sticks reined in.

The setting sun briefly escaped from behind the cloud bank. The full glare of its narrowed beam fell like a spotlight on the walnut tree and the slim girl who suddenly jumped to her feet. She called to the dog, but he didn't budge from Stefan's side, reluctantly looking back and forth between them.

Stefan watched her stomp around the corner of the house.

"Oops, she's pissed now," Sam chuckled. "I told you she weirded out after what happened to her mom."

"What happened?"

"A tornado came through here last March. It flattened Grandpa's house. Her mom was down there making sure he got in the basement. He did but she didn't. Funny thing, the barn wasn't touched. Neither was the attached garage, but there wasn't a stick of that house left standing."

Stefan stared at the spot where Sadie had disappeared. The setting sun tinted the white house pink before twilight dropped like a curtain.

Stefan knew about loss. His oldest brother, Jake, fell through the ice and was never found. His youngest brother, Rory, one day shy of fifteen, died from exposure in a dog sled race when he got caught in a blizzard. And then there was his dad, sending him away with the authority a father never lost, even when he had lost everything else. But to lose a mother? That would be tough.

He threw the boomerang one last time, but as soon as he felt it leave his fingertips, he knew it wasn't coming back. It flew end-over-end and landed in the tall weeds that filled the ditch across the road.

He jogged across the stretch of gravel and walked the ditch, but the light was fading fast and the shadows of twilight played tricks. He crossed into the neighbor's yard and kicked a fledgling pine in exasperation. He walked up and down the edge of the property, swearing at himself. He hadn't thrown as poorly since he first learned at the age of eight under his grandfather's eye, nor had he ever misjudged a landing.

"What's going on out here?"

Stefan raised a hand to shield his eyes from the glare of a flashlight. A blurred figure stood behind the light. Stefan had a vague impression of bulk and animosity.

"You're on private property, boy." The man aimed the beam at one of the *no trespassing* signs that lined the roadway and then back in Stefan's face. "See that?"

"Can't see anything with that light in my face."

"Who are you and what're you doing out here?"

"Lower the damn light."

"Answer the questions, hippie."

Stefan laughed.

"Something funny?"

"That struck me as funny."

The man's mouth twitched. "You think I'm funny? You aren't from around here, are you?"

Stefan frowned at the antagonism. The man was worse than the hardhats at White Lake.

"I'm looking for my boomerang," he conceded. "It landed over here somewhere." He motioned in a circle with his arm and voice of reason.

"Boomerang? What are you, an Aborigine?"

Sam walked to the edge of the ditch. "Hey, Bolton, chill."

Maxwell Bolton swung the beam in Sam's direction, then back on Stefan, playing it over his person, from the flattened crown of his hat to the moccasins on his feet. "Where are you from, boy? You and your *boomerang*?"

"Australia. How'd you know?"

Bolton looked at Sam. "This smartass looks illegal. Old Simon hiding illegals over there?"

Sam made a dismissive noise. "Don't be ridiculous."

"Humph. I don't like the looks of him. So, if his story's true, help him find this, this *boomerang*, and get him off my land." Bolton swung the beam back and forth across the ground.

And there it was, lying in the grass between them, and Stefan felt foolish.

They both reached for it.

"I've got it," Stefan said through his teeth.

But Bolton was quicker than he looked and he had it. He turned the artfully curved piece of wood over in his hand and the etched carvings came to life in the beam of his flashlight. "Well, ain't this fancy." He looked at Stefan. "You wanna sell it?"

Stefan made a noise in the back of his throat. The dog came across the ditch and stood beside him with his ears pricked.

"You look like you could use a few bucks." Bolton continued.

"It's not for sale," Stefan replied. Sadie's dog growled softly in agreement.

Bolton took a step back and flipped his jacket open to reveal a holstered sidearm. "I'll put that mutt down if he bares his teeth at me again."

"Is he reading you wrong?"

"A dog like that can be mistaken for wild. A bullet between the eyes and no one would even question it."

"That'd be a mistake," Sam said.

Bolton licked his lips. "You're on private property. I'd be within my rights."

"You're all about private property in this country," Stefan mused.

"You got something against that?"

"Maybe."

"What are you? A Commie? Here—" Bolton shoved the boomerang at Stefan— "take it. And some advice: lay low with those Commie ideas, and stay off my property, or I'll report you to ICE." He killed the flashlight. Someone inside the house turned the fluorescent yard light on, like they had been watching.

Stefan took a handkerchief out of his pocket and wiped the boomerang off as though he were cleaning fingerprints. The dog followed him and Sam across the road, bearing new allegiance.

"They the ones scaring Sadie's horses?" he asked Sam. "Wasting ammunition?"

"Personally, I think he's all bluster, ignorant stump-jumper belongs in the U.P."

"My mother has family up there."

"It's a big area. Gotta be pockets of intelligence."

"What's ICE?"

"Nuthin." Sam clamped his mouth shut.

"You suppose that gun was loaded?" The holstered sidearm had caught him by surprise. Even the Canadian authorities they'd battled with over land rights didn't carry guns.

"Doesn't take brains to load a gun and anybody can get a permit to carry." Sam glanced at him sideways. "You rubbed him the wrong way. Wise not to throw in that direction again. What the hell happened anyway?"

"Guess I was distracted."

"Distracted? Shit." Sam shook his head. "Like I said, you better wise up."

They drove back to Sam's place in silence. Sam made a few more attempts at conversation, but Stefan retreated back into the refuge of his learned reticence.

CHAPTER 4

The eyes of the barn cat shone in the dark, and the moon was shrouded by clouds when Sadie left the house later that night to take the dog for a walk. Lightning illuminated the thunderheads bunched on the horizon in a holding pattern. The bowl of the Big Dipper, detached from its handle, was still visible to the north where, strangely, the Bolton lights were off.

The presence of the Boltons had changed the dynamics of the neighborhood. Friendly borders and blurred property lines had turned into barbed wire and signs tacked on trees. Growing up, she and one dog or another had traversed fencerows, flushed varmints from brush piles, and explored woods without borders. Farmers shared their fences and drainage problems. The common good was keenly felt in farming communities. What was good for all had been good enough for one.

The proximity of the Boltons and their firing range put her on guard. The fluorescent glow that dimmed the constellations and silhouetted the human-shaped targets gnawed at her psyche.

The Bolton lights were off, and that seemed suspicious. She stood in the familiar field, surrounded by the familiar lay of the land, and was struck by the memory of another summer night, another dog she had as a puppy on a hunt through the clover. With the blood of enterprising rumrunners coursing through her veins, the draw of dusk had always been instinctive, if nameless. Alone in a vast field under a big sky, she had been filled with euphoria, and a sense of being older than she was.

She blinked, drawing herself back to the present. The dog was impervious to human affection for the past, and with his nose to the ground, he was intent on following it. She turned to keep up. He paused with one foot in the air and his hackles rose under her hand.

"What's wrong, Dog?" she whispered.

Gunfire ruptured the quiet and they froze in place. She crouched beside him with an arm around his neck, imagining stray bullets flying overhead, and for a moment the two of them made a tableau molded as one.

A drawn-out howl erupted from across the creek and then another from the opposite corner of the farm. Baying that sounded like a pack of outlaw dogs sounded across the way, and a coyote chorus answered the outlaws, closing in. She would take coyotes over dogs. At least coyotes were shy of man. Having been bitten twice while reading meters the summer before in a short-lived job, she did not trust strange dogs. But these howls sounded more mournful than mere coyotes. The dog was shivering. She told him it was coon hunters, but their walk was ruined. She grabbed him by the collar and started back across the field.

She didn't have to drag him; he dragged her, not stopping until they were back in the yard and safely within the pool of light cast by the bare bulb hung on the side of the garage. Thunder rumbled off in the distance and he ducked into the safety of his doghouse, plopping down on the rag rug she had tucked corner-to-corner on the night Henry brought him home. He said he was a mixture of every dog in the county, but when he brought him home, he didn't have a name.

Dog had carried that rug around in his mouth like a baby blanket, but now he only lay on it with his head on his paws and looked at her with worried eyes until she was safely within the confines of the house.

She stopped Henry in the hallway.

"Dad, something frightened Dog."

"You gonna give that poor mutt a name?"

"Did you hear anything?"

"Like what?"

"I'm not sure. Do you think there could be wolves this far south?"

He snorted. "I don't think there's even any up north, maybe on Isle Royale."

"Wild dogs?"

"Where did you get that idea? Probably coyotes."

"Sounded like more than a coyote. Did you tell anyone they could coon hunt?"

"No money in that anymore." He turned to walk away.

"A storm's coming," she said abruptly. "Think it'll rain?"

Henry looked surprised and turned his ear to the window. "Rain?" He tested the word on his tongue.

"Smells like it."

"It'll wait until we get the hay ready to bale. Then it'll rain."

"Don't be a pessimist. You weren't—Mom always said you were the optimist—" She broke off, not knowing how to continue. She waited for him to hold up his end of the conversation, take her into his confidence. But confidences were *before*. In the *after* he had turned unapproachable and pensive, as though the grief belonged only to him, and he would keep it close.

He muttered goodnight and shut his bedroom door.

Maybe he would sleep in there tonight. Sleep in there with his closely held grief. Leave the television off and the couch could revert back to a couch instead of a makeshift bed for an insomniac. Made it hard to watch a movie or stay up late reading in her favorite chair by the window. It was hard to pretend things would ever be okay again when your own father had turned into a morose insomniac.

But she wouldn't know if he stayed in his room that night because she went back to her laptop to study the place Stefan came from. The fight of the Dené was a futile one. Even from the screen of a laptop, that much was obvious. The Maliseet originated in the New Brunswick area, three thousand miles away. Maybe he did have magic powers. He threw that boomerang like he did. She kept seeing that, how he gracefully landed on the balls of his feet, arms impossibly long and the cadence of his voice—deeper than his frame would seem to support— carrying across the grass.

An email came in from her aunt reminding Sadie to go through her mother's things, this time with a note of impatience. The Montegrands needed summer-weight clothes, and she needed to start sorting through what she wanted to keep and what she wanted to give away.

She closed the laptop, washed her face with a diminished cake of soap, and brushed her teeth, then crawled under the covers with a murder mystery that involved sheepherders, dogs, and a mysterious creature in the outback of Australia.

Rolling peals of thunder woke her in the middle of the night, and she got up to check the windows. She cranked the casements on the porch shut as lightning spiked across the sky and illuminated the trees swaying in the wind. If a tornado formed in the night, how could you see it coming?

It hadn't started to rain yet. A dry storm would be just their luck. The rain would go around them and they would only get wind. It wouldn't be the first time that happened.

The entire sky lit up with a flash of lightning and illuminated the yard. She inhaled sharply. A hooded figure stood next to the mailbox. The sky went dark. Then another flash of lightning illuminated the driveway and the mailbox, and the figure was gone.

She rubbed her eyes. It was a dry lightning hallucination, a natural phenomenon. That's all that it was.

A bolt of chain lightning struck close, funneling nitrogen into the earth as a crack of thunder shook the house. She pulled on a jacket and ran across the yard to the stable. The sweet smell of ozone was in the air and she remembered the day of the tornado—she and her mother in the kitchen tempering chocolate when the alert came over the radio.

The horses were kicking the sides of the stalls, further agitating each other. She flipped the switch inside the door and started talking to them like her grandpa told her.

If they can't see you, they at least like to be able to hear you.

Two Socks's eyes were wild and his withers were wet. She rested her hand on his neck and felt the blood pumping through his veins. She remembered when her father first brought him home as a colt, and she slept in the corner of the stall with a stadium blanket. Now he quivered under her hand like that same scared colt.

"Whoa, boy, it's okay. It's just thunder. It can't hurt you." She rubbed his neck and his shoulder. "See, it can't." The mare in the adjacent stall kicked the sidewall and Two Socks side-stepped and tossed his head.

The mare was the problem. She was a pretty little thing but high-strung, part of the *after* package Sadie had not familiarized herself with. She came with a name but she could not remember what it was. Those days were a blur, her mother fresh in the ground.

She threw a blanket over Two Socks' back and gave him a windfall apple. He scooped it off her palm with his velvet lips. The storm was passing, thunder grumbling in the distance, and combined with the blanket and the apple, he was settling.

She latched the stall and opened the adjoining one. The mare looked at Sadie from the corner of her eye as Sadie leaned against the sidewall. "What're you thinking about? How you liked it better where you used to live? I know horses can think, okay? Grandpa told me so. He knows everything about a horse. Knows every bone you got. Dad thought you'd be a good companion for Two Socks. He's gonna be awfully disappointed."

The mare tossed her head and blew out of the bellows of her lungs.

"I think your name was Nelly, something innocent like that, wasn't it?" The mare snorted. "I agree, totally inappropriate." She pulled an apple out of her other pocket. The mare tested it with her nose and then rolled it off Sadie's palm with her lips.

Sadie threw a blanket over her back and smoothed the corners. The mare chewed the apple and dropped her head, nuzzling her pockets for another. Sadie gave her a final pat and left the warmth of the stable.

She paused just outside the door to let her eyes adjust to the dark. The air had turned cold with the passing of the storm, and the trees in the yard stood limp in the aftermath. The only movement was the rope swing touched by a breeze. Clouds scuttled across the moon. Beyond the yard lay the ribbon of an empty road and nothing more. Lightning streaked the eastern horizon, but the thunder had moved out of earshot and the rain was falling someplace else.

The following morning, low clouds raced overhead. Tattered remnants from the front that crossed the lake into Canada during the night. With no rain of a measurable amount for four weeks, they were officially in a state of drought.

Sadie sat on the front porch of her father's house with a hot cup of coffee between her hands and the morning sun in her lap, thinking about the uncertainty of the neighborhood.

Her radio was set to a station out of Canada and music played softly from the ledge in the corner. Henry used to be first up, but that was before the twister dropped its tail on their section of road to leave him bottled up like corked wine. After the funeral, he sat in a corner of the living room as visitors and conversation flowed around him, like a river around a fallen tree. Aunt Helen had told her that men didn't like to be alone.

Maybe it would be best if he met someone else, someone who could pull him out of the quicksand of abject indifference he was wallowing in. But the thought of someone else made her chest hurt. The thought of someone changing her radio dial, rearranging pots and pans, and throwing out the plaque that said *Jenny's Kitchen* hollowed her out in a different way than watching Stefan ride bareback had. Watching him leap astride the horse who was seventeen hands high and ride off like he was born on the back of one hollowed her out like a plummeting roller coaster. While the thought of her dad taking up with someone else just left her empty.

Sam's pickup pulled into the driveway and interrupted her contemplation. He let himself in the screen door with a bag of donuts.

"Want one?" He asked around a mouthful of fritter, handing her the bag.

"What're you doing here so early?"

"Cutting hay. Gotta get a head start. I might have a date tonight."

She sipped her coffee, looking out at the summer trees, fleshed out and starting to turn.

He picked out another donut from the bag and looked at her impatiently. "Don't you want to know who with?"

She looked at him. Sam had fleshed out in the last two years—muscles in his arms and hair on his face.

"Who with?" she obliged.

"Abby Montegrand, that's who. The hottest new girl in town."

She studied her coffee mug as if she'd never seen it before. The Montegrands were crowding in on her.

"Montegrand." Sam persisted. "As in *Stef* Montegrand. You know—" he smirked— "the one you couldn't take your eyes off."

She looked at him with a flat expression. "He's a showoff."

"You have to admit, the guy can ride."

"He's too skinny."

"You can't be too choosy."

"You sure she's old enough?"

"I had to get Stef's permission. Isn't that funny?"

Sadie didn't answer.

"He rode *Tussock* like an Indian," he said, imitating his accent. "I hear he fights like one too."

She fixed a questioning gaze on him over the rim of her cup.

"Got the low-down from my buddy Sid about that fight. Stef was filling up at Bolton's and went inside to buy smokes. They carded him on principle and he took offense and next thing you know Zender Bolton tells him to buy his smokes somewhere else and all hell broke loose. Sid says he has never seen anything like it. They had to pull Stef off."

"Over a pack of cigarettes? There was more to it than that."

Sam shrugged. "Perhaps. And he might be skinny, but he got his cigarettes."

Sadie watched a pair of rabbits nose their way into the yard and drank off her tepid coffee.

"He'll have to be careful once old man Bolton connects the dots. The way he likes to cut loose with the ammo." Sam said.

"Bolton isn't that crazy."

"Maybe not, but I wouldn't want to get on his wrong side. Speaking of . . . he might already be there."

"What do you mean?"

"After you stomped off last night, he threw that damn boomerang clear across the road, a totally fucked up throw, and it landed right in Bolton's yard. Stef ran over to get it and Bolton was on him like a chicken on a June bug. High-powered flashlight to blind a guy, like it was an immigration roundup. The look on Stef's face, it was kind of hilarious, to think about it now."

She tucked her feet under her lap and waited him out. Sam had a way of circling a story.

"He was as cool as a conservation officer. You know, few words, just that *presence*. 'Can I see your recreation passport please? Can I see your deed to this ditch please?'" Sam laughed and Sadie joined him. It felt strange in her throat. She choked it off.

"He threatened to report him to ICE." Sam continued.

"ICE?" Sadie snorted. "That's ridiculous." But the acronym was like a police car on your bumper.

The immigration enforcement branch of DHS was unhindered by due process and other onerous constitutional requirements. The week before, they had swooped down on a local carrot plant in black helicopters and hauled away half the workforce. There had been reports of them stopping people getting on buses and walking through train cars, demanding proof of citizenship from whomever they suspected of coming up short. They had POLICE stamped across their backs, but Henry said they were misrepresenting themselves.

"Is it? He isn't white and he has that accent. That alone would be enough for Bolton to call in the militia, but Stef didn't bat an eye at the bullying, like he was used to it. Maybe he is. I think his attitude pissed the old man off as much as his outward appearance."

"Did he find it?"

"Find what?"

Sadie rolled her eyes.

"You know what they call a boomerang that doesn't come back?"

"No, Sam. What?"

"A stick." He grinned. "Yeah, don't worry, he found it."

"I wasn't worried."

"Course not." He brushed the crumbs off his shirt. "I better get started on that hay. If you need rain, cut hay. Just wanted to bring you up to speed on my date. Let me know if you want to double up on one. In spite of my best efforts to discourage him, he's interested."

She watched him leave, and twisted a thoughtful lock of hair around her finger.

Bolton's diesel flew by, probably on one of his early morning runs. He floored it in front of their driveway as if he knew they had been talking about him. It was a brand new 4x4 extended cab. He was either making money off his shooting range and the CCW classes he taught in town—everyone wanted to carry concealed—or dealing drugs.

The only range she had ever been on was the golf range. Her mother had been a golfer.

She was reluctant to go through her mother's things. Maybe the place to start would be in the garage with the clubs.

She took a couple of practice swings with the 3-wood, interlacing her fingers the way her mother showed her. *Don't take your eye off the ball.* She immediately took her eye off the ball and topped it. It skittered off the boot of the club like a poorly laid bunt.

She was halfway through the bucket before she hit a good shot. She felt a flush of elation, but with it came a crawling sense of being watched. She turned and caught a shadow at the kitchen window. She felt guilty, like she should have asked his permission to get into her mother's things, suddenly embarrassed at all the topped shots, hooks and pure whiffs.

She gathered up what balls she could find and put the clubs back in the garage, then took down two totes from the loft, went inside to the spare bedroom with the storage closet, and started going through her mother's clothes. Sleeveless dresses with big belts, golf outfits, sarongs that tied on the side, short skirts, and sandals and straw hats. She pressed her face in the crown of a floppy sun hat, and the smell of sunscreen with its attendant memory hit her hard—her mother tanned and smiling behind sunglasses against a big sky. The sound of gulls and motorboats washed over her like the waves that took the sand out from under her feet. Her dad floated with the current to swim his way back, arms muscled from wrestling calves and baling hay, while she and her mother dug their moats deeper and their turrets higher.

Everything was big and blue and wonderful, but the memories were slipping through her fingers, the image of her mother fading like an old Polaroid.

She shoved the sunhat to the bottom of the tote. The funeral had been closed-casket, the source of growing resentment. They should have at least let them see her hand, the scar on her palm; know it was really her inside the box.

She put the sarongs aside, the one her mother bought on Venice Beach, the first time Sadie saw the ocean. It had Che Guevara's mustached face on one end of the wrap and the back of his head, long hair and slouched hat, imprinted on the other, so he was both coming and going, depending on which way you wanted to wrap and tie.

Her legs were too long for the dresses, but sarongs were forgiving of knobby knees and wide hips, and she had always coveted the Che, the rebel on a motorcycle. She held it up, and it occurred to her that that was who Stefan Montegrand reminded her of.

Separating the emotion from the task, she finished the job and loaded the totes in her car. It was an old Duster with cracked vinyl seats and Quick Draw McGraw floor mats. She drove the two miles down the road to the house where the family from Saskatchewan was staying. Parking in the driveway, she lugged the totes to the front step and knocked on the door.

Stefan opened it. He was dressed in an undershirt and a pair of drawstring pants. His hair was damp from the shower and the Band-Aid was still above his eye. The neckline of his undershirt was stark white against his dark skin, and there was a faint bristle of hair above his lip.

She was newly aware of her wrinkled clothes and uncombed hair.

She looked over his shoulder. "Is your mother home?"

He frowned at the totes. "What's this?"

"Aunt Helen said your mom could use a few things."

"Like what?" There was an edge to his voice.

"Clothes."

"Clothes?"

She faltered. "It's just a few summer things . . ."

"We have clothes."

"Aunt Helen said—"

"We don't need handouts."

"Well—" She flushed. "Never mind, then. I'll drop them at Goodwill." She hefted a tote up with her knee and carried it back down the steps.

"Hold up." He walked out in his bare feet. "Wait."

She rested the tote on the hood of her car.

"Wait. Leave it."

She bit her lip. "It's not a handout."

He grabbed one of the totes and carried it back to the porch, held the door with his elbow and looked at her. "Please." He beckoned with his head. "Come in."

She hesitated, but his voice had smoothed over like he had taken an emery board to it, and she found herself inside the house she hadn't been in since her uncle kicked the last tenants out. It was sparse of furnishings, but tidy with the faint scent of vinegar in the air. The tea kettle on the stove shone like a hotspot, and she smelled coffee.

"I was just having a cup of coffee. Want one?"

He poured a cup and motioned for her to sit at the Formica table and then refilled his mug and sat across from her. He was drinking his coffee black, so she did too. The Band-Aid above his eye had a blood spot in the center, and he had picked a scab off the corner of his mouth which left a pink circle of new skin and added contrast to the faint bristle of hair above his lip.

There was an aura of controlled apprehension about him, as if he were readying to meet any hint of trouble. He stirred his coffee with a spoon, though there wasn't anything to stir, and glanced at the totes. "That's a lot of stuff."

"I sorted through the nicer things."

He sipped his coffee with eyes on her.

"I didn't want to give Mom's things to Goodwill." Sadie said.

"Okay."

"It felt . . . I don't know. I just didn't."

"Mom took Dad's things to the council house. Joachim and I each kept a couple of coats but gave the rest away. He was a lot bigger—" He broke off and took a sip of coffee.

"Is that your brother?"

"Yeah. Older. Joachim. He'll meet up with us when we get settled."

"Where will that be?"

He shrugged. "Still working on that."

"I don't have a brother. Sam's the closest thing but he's just a pain."

He almost smiled. "I could see that."

"So, when you get settled—"

"He'll come. He's wrapping things up, selling the snow machine, some power tools, you know, things too big to haul. And then he'll meet us."

She nodded. Her head was full of questions, but all she could do was nod and drink his coffee.

He was waiting for her to say something, evidently comfortable with silence, comfortable with waiting for someone else to speak. She shimmied her legs under the table, jazzed and shaky on caffeine.

She drained the cup and pushed her chair back. "I better get going. Thanks for the coffee."

He walked her to the door. "That your car?"

"Yeah, it's a junker, but it's paid for."

"I like it."

"Are you kidding?" They both looked at the Duster. It was a two-door with a jacked-up rear end and a bad paint job, but ran soft as a kitten.

He leaned against the doorjamb with a thumb hooked in his waistband. "I'm sorry about earlier. You just, well, you took me by surprise."

She glanced at him. Funny how a Band-Aid could make someone look like trouble, and he wasn't really skinny, more like twenty-gauge wire wound tight. With a few more pounds and facial hair, he could totally be Che. "It's okay, I understand." And she thought she did. "See you around."

She backed out of the driveway, and when she looked back, he was still leaning against the doorjamb.

CHAPTER 5

It was the end of the short summer season in Saskatchewan, but changeable air masses often occurred in September and brought back summer. The landlocked prairie province with its semi-arid to humid continental climate received more sunshine than any other Canadian province. The current air mass circling south of the fifty-third parallel between Prince Albert and Moose Jaw—from the Cree word meaning *warm place by the river*— was the hottest on record.

Most of the population lived below the fifty-third parallel, which was where government centers were located and where Joachim Montegrand was headed.

Halfway to Prince Albert he pulled off the road to take the top off his jeep and stuffed his flannel shirt under the seat on top of the sheathed switchblade that had belonged to his father and the sidearm he had acquired illegally. With the sun on his arms and the wind in his hair, he didn't miss his father or his brothers.

He pulled into the parking lot of the Prince Albert government building and untangled himself from behind the wheel. The fancy double doors pushed open hard like they were resisting entry. The air conditioning was on and the cold hit him in the face, raising goosebumps on his arms.

He was directed to an office down the hall with chairs lined up along the wall, but he didn't have to wait. They were waiting for him, eager to close the book on what had been an embarrassing chapter for an otherwise reputable agency which prided itself on equanimity when dealing with the raucous faction of its Indigenous population.

Joachim looked over the list of items no longer considered evidence and signed the release form in the stubborn scrawl his mother had never been able to correct. The keeper-of-the-evidence pushed the shoebox across the desk and wiped his hands of it. Joachim carried it to a side table and checked the contents against the inventory list. Not much evidence in what remained of his dad's possessions. He put the watch in the side zipper of his satchel along with the billfold and the other odds and ends from his pockets: pieces of folded paper with lint in the creases, a little tobacco, and a medicine pouch. All of Sonny Montegrand's personal effects fit in one compartment. Joachim looked at the man behind the desk, who was consciously not looking at him. He didn't know what his father had gone in with, but this was apparently what he came out with.

He left the empty shoebox on the table and took his leave.

He started the jeep and spit a glob of blood in the dirt. He scuffed gravel over it with his boot and felt for the handgun under the seat. It was loaded to capacity for this drive to Prince Albert and back to the cabin his father and the Trappers Alliance had built beside the roadblock they thought would derail progress and halt the devastation. Joachim used to think that too. In the early days, they all thought the First Nation would prevail, and that the companies involved in resource extraction would pull up stakes, leaving for more profitable ventures where there was less resistance, or that demand would dry up like the wash behind their property at the height of summer.

He shifted gears and put the town nicknamed the "Gateway to the North" behind him. He drove down the middle of the two-lane highway the way the oilmen steered their rigs, and headed north for the boreal forest. Land the Montegrands used to call home, land soon to be flooded once Hydro's dam was completed. The needle on the speedometer crept up the dial, and the hemlocks and cedar flew by like the sentinels they were, the Gods of the forest. He believed in those Gods, and had faith that justice would prevail.

Fifty miles north of Prince Albert, the air turned cold, and he put his flannel shirt back on, steering with his knees. An hour later, he passed the newly-erected *no trespassing* signs, and the break in the trees loomed ahead. He downshifted and jumped the ditch to gain the two-track through the forest that few knew about. Savior and Bobby had fashioned a makeshift marker out of two boards nailed like crossbones to the trunk of a tree. It was a longer route but the only way to avoid a glimpse of the newly erected facility, with its towers of billowing exhaust that colored the sunsets made more brilliant by the activity of busy men. He needed to avoid the anthill to keep the blade locked and the gun under the seat on this, his final run.

He had promises to keep, a burial rite to see through to its proper end, and a woman with almond eyes and a place off the map.

He didn't know what day it was, but he was sure to have missed several calls from Stefan. Their father had been right to send him away. Stefan and Abby were young enough to start over, and their mother's heart had never left the eastern part of the continent, but Joachim felt something drain out of him when his little brother pulled out of the yard in the family's beat-up van, like someone had pulled the plug on him. There was Abby waving out the back window, Ma refusing to look at him, while Stef just honked and raised his fist out the driver's side window, their own private goodbye, trying to burn rubber in a van with his fist in the air.

It had recently rained, and the swale of the two-track was muddied and littered with fresh windfall. He hit a rough spot and fishtailed. He slipped the jeep into four-wheel drive and gunned the engine. This was a longer way, but one unmonitored by the intruders with their self-appointed authority. He was going to his father's cabin by the roadblock the hardhats had dismantled. He had promises to keep.

CHAPTER 6

Sadie was awakened in the middle of the night by a current of disturbance. She felt her way to the bathroom to draw a glass of water and pin her hair off her neck. When the lights were off and the house slept, her mother's absence was a weighted reality. It loomed in the hallway and in the corners. It manifested itself in the quiet of the bedroom where her father used to snore, but from where now there was scarcely a sound, as though he wasn't even there.

Ground fog lay heavy across the land, and treetops jutted above it like islands adrift. The mournful sound of a lowing cow drifted from the rear pasture, and unidentifiable sounds from the bordering state forest carried in the fog.

She turned on the overhead fan and slept fitfully with just a sheet. She couldn't sleep well unless she was wrapped up tight.

A rooster crowed in the predawn and diesel engines sounded from the equipment shed. As the fog lifted, the rising sun glinted off the metal roof of the granary, and a second rooster answered the first. Rubbing the sleep out of her eyes, Sadie pulled a change of clothes out of the dryer and made an iced coffee, then went back to sorting her mother's things while she was in the mood.

In a cobwebbed corner of the garage behind the golf clubs, she found another bucket of range balls. She checked the pockets in the golf bag. The league sign-up sheet with team pairings was folded in one of them. Jenny's name was halfway down the sheet with her long-time golf partner, Margie Stillwater.

Margie was one of the women who kept bringing over casseroles and sheet cakes until Sadie finally had to tell her to stop. The freezer was full, and she had grown suspicious of Margie's ulterior motives. She would complain about never again finding a partner like Jenny while dropping a shoulder Henry's way, conveniently dropping a strap along with it.

Sadie slung the golf bag over her shoulder, carried the bag of misfit balls to the edge of the grass, and pulled a wood club from the bag. She set up her tee, laced her fingers around the grip of the club, tucked her chin in, and clenched her teeth. She hit the ball with a solid whack that resonated all the way up her leading arm. The ball sliced for the road at the same time a motorcycle rumbled over the hill. She rested the club on her shoulder and watched as it hurtled on a collision course with the biker. He skidded sideways, as though feeling the displacement of air as the ball flew by his head.

He gunned the engine and turned into the circle drive. The bike rolled past the overgrown rose garden and disappeared behind the stand of scrub pine to reemerge at the edge of the grass where he dropped his feet.

It was Stefan. Stefan with no helmet, on a motorcycle that looked like it could pull a horse trailer. The only person she knew with a bike like that was Uncle Larry, and he never let anyone ride it.

He parked the bike and looked her way from behind a pair of mirrored goggles. He knocked the kickstand down with his heel.

She hauled the bag across the lawn, feeling half-dressed in the cut-offs and frayed blouse she wouldn't normally let herself be caught in. Clothes left in the dryer overnight and thrown on in haste because she didn't expect to see anyone, let alone a stranger from another country with an unsettling gaze.

He removed the goggles and glanced at the club in her hands. "So that was you." His tone was incredulous, yet circumspect, as if nothing would surprise him.

His hair was held back with a bandanna, and he looked different: prominent brows and cleft chin, all sharp angles. He had replaced the Band-Aid above his eye with a butterfly strip, and the bruise on his jaw had faded to the color of a vein. There was a pack of cigarettes in his breast pocket, and he wore a pair of black jeans and scuffed boots.

Sadie made a face. "Horrible shot."

"How about going for a ride?"

She looked at the motorcycle. It was long, low, and reeked of power, like a Corvette with its pipes exposed.

"Is that Uncle Larry's?"

He nodded.

"He doesn't usually let anyone ride it."

"My dad used to have one like it, but it was impounded."

He said it impassively, but there was a metallic hardness in his eyes.

She looked away and kicked at the golf bag with her toe. "I don't know. . ."

"I have experience."

"With what?" She squinted at him. "Getting in trouble?"

A little muscle in his jaw jumped, and he settled the goggles back on his face. "Never mind. I wouldn't want you to get in trouble."

"I didn't say no."

"No?"

"Where's your helmet?"

"I don't use a helmet."

"Like you don't use a saddle?" she said wryly.

He smiled. It changed his face, softened the sharp angles, and made him almost handsome in a bare-knuckled way.

"I have an extra pair of goggles in my saddlebag."

Henry suddenly stepped out on the porch and shoved his hands in his pockets.

"Introduce us, Sadie," he said.

"Stefan—" she motioned him over— "this is my dad."

Stefan held out his hand. "Stefan Montegrand."

Henry gave it a shake. "Thought it was time we introduced ourselves. Name's Henry Wixom."

"Nice to meet you, sir."

Henry looked Stefan up and down.

"You and your mother are staying at my brother's place, right?"

"And my sister." Stefan nodded.

"Looks like you got Larry's motorcycle."

"He told me to take it for a spin," Stefan said quickly. "Said he'd sell it to me if I had the money. Says it's nothing but trouble for him."

"Helen would give it away if she could get away with it."

Stefan didn't say anything.

"Been a while since I've been on a bike." Henry looked at it with an unreadable expression.

"You want to ride?"

He blinked and rubbed his jaw. "Nah, I'd probably dump it. You go on."

Stefan looked at Sadie. "Are you ready?"

"Let me grab my jeans." She turned and headed for the house.

In the silence, Henry rocked on his heels with a raised eyebrow.

"Thought we'd go for a ride." Stefan said, addressing his unasked question.

"That's a lot of bike."

"Dad had one just like it."

"You got a motorcycle license?"

"We get all-terrain and motorcycle endorsements automatically," Stefan said.

"That right? Things easier up there?"

"I wouldn't say that, sir."

"No. I guess you wouldn't." He dug a ring of keys out of his pocket, slung the golf bag over his shoulder, and carried it into the garage.

Sadie was back, and Stefan lifted the kickstand and gassed the throttle. She settled herself on the seat behind him and held on to the backrest as they rolled down the driveway, the rumble of the thunder-stroke engine suggesting all the places they could go.

Once they were on the pavement, Stefan opened the throttle, and the road rushed under their feet. With the wind in her face, she knew why Dog liked to ride in the back of Henry's truck with his head out the window—faster, younger, weightless.

They rode until she wasn't sure where they were, and still they kept going. They rode into a small town with a four-way stop. Stefan downshifted and dropped his feet at the stop sign. There was a bar on the corner with several bikes pulled up to the sidewalk and a neon *Open* sign in the window.

He pulled into the parking lot and turned the key off.

Sadie dropped her feet. "What're we doing?"

"Thought we'd stop and get a beer."

"Are you crazy? I can't go in there."

"Why not?"

"You have to be twenty-one."

"Why?"

"That's the drinking age."

"There's a drinking age?"

Sadie laughed. "You're funny."

He thought for a second, then dropped the kickstand and pushed the goggles up on top of his head. "I'll be right back."

Five minutes later, he came out with a six-pack. He opened the saddlebag and arranged the cans to fit, then re-snapped the closure. He settled the goggles on his face and they were back on the road.

For the next two miles she fully expected to hear a siren. She didn't have her wallet with her. She couldn't even prove who she was. But after two miles of road and heavy forest, she decided it didn't matter.

They came upon a deserted roadside park, and he pulled into the gravel drive, parking the bike. He turned in the seat.

"What do you think? A better place to stop and have a drink than that parking lot?"

She climbed off the bike and stretched her back, breathing in the scent of pine trees and the near-distant lake.

"Much better."

Stefan draped his jacket across the handlebars. Half-moons of perspiration darkened the underarms of his T-shirt. He took the beer and a bag of peanuts out of the saddlebag, and they sat on a picnic table under a tree. He cracked open two cans of beer and handed her one. It foamed up around the top, and she sipped it off. The sun dappled their legs as they drank their beer.

He shook a cigarette out of his pack, tapped it against his wrist, and lit it with a lighter, shielding the flame with his hand. He inhaled and held it out to her.

After a second's hesitation, she held it between her fingers, getting a feel for it. She inhaled the way he had, and the tip flared. The control of fire, the rush, and the burn.

She choked and grabbed her throat.

He rescued the cigarette and watched her with a bemused expression.

"Oh, my God," she gasped. "That's terrible."

He tapped the ash on the ground between his feet. "Didn't know it was your first time. Only burns the first time." He squinted at her. "Are you always so theatrical?"

She made a face. "Are you always such a know-it-all?"

He laughed. "We better stop there."

"I have to pee," she said as it suddenly hit her. She looked around. Not even an outhouse. She stood up and had a head rush, and then she really had to go.

He pointed to a stand of trees at the edge of the clearing.

She considered the indignity of the idea.

"You think I'm going to look?" The corner of his mouth with the pink circle of new skin lifted in a half smile. "I won't if you won't."

She rolled her eyes and brushed off the seat of her pants. When she glanced back, he was studying the treetops and smoking contentedly.

Then it was his turn, and she shelled a peanut and wondered what her friends would think of her now; drinking, smoking, and peeing in the open with a stranger of dangerous looks and troubled background.

He was back and lit another cigarette from his pack. They passed it back and forth. He was right: it no longer burned, just a low-grade fever spreading out from her core.

Emboldened, she said, "So, what was it like up there?"

"Where?"

"Where you're from."

Stefan held the cigarette out to the side and tapped the ash off with his forefinger.

"Fewer people, different climate."

She waited for him to elaborate.

He shrugged. "Wasn't so damn humid. We didn't need what you call summer clothes. And it wasn't as crowded." He motioned around the clearing with the hand that held the cigarette. "It was like this."

She followed his hand, the trailing smoke, and the sun glancing through the dense foliage of late summer.

"I saw pictures of the tar sands online. But you can find anything online. I just wondered if they were accurate."

"Pictures?" Stefan looked puzzled.

"There was a video posted by Greenpeace shot from a helicopter over a tar sands facility."

Stefan nodded. "I've heard of Greenpeace. There was an altercation with security guards not far from us." His eyes had turned cold.

"Is that what it was like where you're from?"

He held the cigarette thoughtfully between his lips; smoke curled around it, and he inhaled it back.

"Where I'm from?" He thought for a minute. "At first, it was just rumors, water diversions draining the wetlands. But it's a big area and people weren't paying attention. Then there was talk of a dam, and they started chopping down trees and dug a road through the forest for heavy equipment. Our people started getting alarmed and tried to stop it. Come to find out, the Provincial Government had negotiated with a hydro company to construct a dam on a tributary behind us. Compensation was offered and agreed to before the elders even knew what the damage would be. By the time they found out there would be serious flooding, the company was beyond the planning stage. It was too long before anybody paid attention, and then it was too late."

"Maybe it isn't." Sadie suggested hopefully.

"Yes," he said in a measured tone, "it is. Tribal meetings, court orders, calls to Ottawa where they only care about building hockey rinks. . . it couldn't be stopped. Then they announced a concession to satisfy the pesky natives. A low-level dam. So, they wouldn't flood us a lot, just a little." He scoffed.

"Dad said it was our own fault. The elders were too trusting. Signing bogus treaties that cheated us out of what is rightfully ours. I call it gullible." He blew smoke out the corner of his mouth and inspected the burning tip of the cigarette.

"Now we have nothing. No access to our traplines, security gates everywhere, and fishing will be ruined by the dam. Shit, upstream even the minnows are already dying. If it's not drilling and mining, it's deforestation and water diversions, and either way we were screwed. We used to eat a lot of fish, but then we started seeing lesions on them, bloody sores, and bloodied eyes, and we were afraid to eat them. Would you eat something like that?"

Sadie shuddered. "I don't even like fish."

"Then a mutant fish with two mouths was hooked from a dock *downstream.*"

"So, easier to hook." she said, trying to lighten the mood.

"We don't rely on store-bought food like you do here." Stefan said coolly. He kept his gaze focused on the treetops overhead. "We started to wonder about everything else that went near that water."

"I'm sorry, that wasn't funny." Sadie gulped her beer, wanting her words back.

He continued as though he hadn't heard the remark.

"Surface roads crisscross the drilling fields to the north of us, roads only they can drive on. Even on public roads the big rigs nearly run you off. In winter, with the snow flying, you sure as hell better ride the ditch because they drive down the center of the road. The big tar sands facilities are to the west of us, over the border in Alberta, but we figure it's only a matter of time. They're already scaring off the wildlife and blocking access to our trap lines. Dad drove out last autumn to check his lines and a helicopter dropped overhead and followed him all the way."

"That's creepy."

He dragged his eyes back to hers. "That's what it's like."

Sadie hugged her knees. "Those pictures . . ."

He looked at her questioningly. "What?"

"Looked like a war zone." Sadie said, completing her thought.

"Sometimes the worst is what you can't see." Stefan acknowledged solemnly. "The tailings ponds are bad but the uranium mines are worse because you can't see or taste what they're putting out—radioactive dust they've reportedly buried, but a group of scientists found traces in moose spoor. Before the mines opened, it was very rare for someone to get cancer. But now, well . . ." He stared at his hands, turning his palms over.

Sadie checked her own, the bisected lifeline. Wondering if it was true it could predict longevity.

"So," she said carefully, "What happened to your dad?"

"He, Joachim, and their trapping buddies set up a blockade to keep the loggers and cement trucks out, but it wasn't long before the Mounties rode in and arrested all of them. They only held them overnight but warned them not to do it again. Of course, they did it again. They set up camp and even built a cabin to stay in because it was winter. Then Dad started having funny spells."

A flock of birds on a whoosh of wing flew out of the tree they were sitting under. He looked up through the branches, and the cigarette dangled from his fingertips.

"He used to be so sure-handed," he said wistfully. "But then one day he dropped his rifle, fell right out of his hand, lost his grip, hand like a claw. I was there, bringing in supplies on a snow machine, scared the shit out of me. Next thing I know, he had some rare form of cancer."

She kept silent, recognizing his need to keep talking. Wanting him to keep talking.

He ground the cigarette out on the sole of his boot and put the butt in the cuff of his pants. "Right after that he was jailed. The authorities closed the public school where Mom taught—one sure way to get people to leave. Dad wanted us out and after the authorities suggested sending Abby to their modern-day version of a residential boarding school, Mom didn't argue. Next thing we know, he's on a hunger strike. Ever hear of anything so stupid? He has cancer and goes on a hunger strike. He thought to draw media attention to the displacement of natives, but he had a fast-growing tumor, and there wasn't enough time to draw attention. The last time I saw him, he asked me to take care of Abby and help Mom find her cousins."

Stefan paused. His face was stoic, yet distant.

"He gives me this dying wish bullshit. But even though he was down to a hundred pounds, I didn't believe it." He brushed some invisible dirt off his pant legs as if brushing away the memory.

"I'd like to go back some day, but part of me just wants to remember the way it used to be."

"You must miss him." Sadie said at last.

He looked at her. "From what Sam said, your mother died about the same time."

She swallowed, waiting for the inevitable questions, but they didn't come.

A pair of chipmunks ran across the ground right in front of them, looking for crumbs. They chased each other around the trunk of a tree, and then sat and looked at them, noses twitching.

"You must miss her," he said after a minute.

"I can't remember what she looked like, can't see her clearly. It wasn't even that long ago."

"At least you have pictures, right? Dad wouldn't let his picture be taken. He believed it would steal his soul."

"So, he wasn't taking selfies?"

"What?"

"Never mind." She thought for a minute. "He was *that* superstitious?"

"What religion isn't? Do you believe in an afterlife?"

The question surprised her.

"There has to be something," she answered finally.

"Why?"

"Why not?"

Stefan shrugged.

"Elders are always talking about the gods of this and the gods of that," Stefan pondered aloud. "I just wonder about these all-powerful beings looking down on us, like they got nothing better to do than meddle in our piddling lives."

"That's a depressing way to put it." She grimaced.

"I didn't used to think about things like that."

Sadie shrugged. "It's comforting to think you might meet up again with the people you love."

"What about the people you don't? Say you and your mom meet up and that's great, but she has someone else with her she loves too but you hate, like an old boyfriend or something—"

"She didn't have a boyfriend."

"I'm just saying."

"Well, she didn't."

Stefan shrugged. "It would be the same old petty jealousies and muckraking. For infinity? That wouldn't be heaven, or whatever you want to call it. That would be hell. Do you believe in that?"

"I don't know. I've never thought about it."

"If you believe in one, you have to believe in the other," he reasoned.

"Maybe heaven isn't a place but a state of mind." Sadie suggested.

"So, there can be the proverbial heaven on earth?"

She took the cigarette from him, needing a diversion. The silence between them wasn't uncomfortable, like it had been at his kitchen table.

He opened the last beer, drank off the foam, and handed it to her. "Last one so I'll share."

"You're driving, better let me have it."

He looked at her sideways. "There's more to you than I thought."

"Oh yeah? What'd you think?"

"A little backwards, possessive of a horse and a dog with no name."

She laughed. "Is that really what you thought?"

"No." He studied her quietly, as though trying to discern his real thoughts.

"So . . ." She held the can in both hands. "Your mom was a schoolteacher. That explains things," she added with a nod.

"She came to Saskatchewan from New Brunswick on a government initiative that paid teachers well if they taught in an underserved area for at least five years. That was thirty-five years ago."

"New Brunswick?"

"Go on. Say it."

"That's a long way to go for a job."

"She used to fly back at Christmas—which we don't celebrate—but she missed the last few years. There was a falling out after her parents died. She won't say, but something happened."

"I understand she's from a *Maliseet* tribe." Sadie pronounced the word as *mal-iz-seet*, and then quickly became aware she might offend him. "Is that how you say it?"

He lit another cigarette, going through the pack, and narrowed his eyes. "*Tribe?* Where'd you hear that?"

"People talk. I'm just curious."

"You've been checking on me?"

Sadie flushed. "No—"

"Matters, does it? Everybody asks that, the first time they meet you. What's *your* nationality, Sadie? Where are you from?"

"My great-grandparents were from Alsace-Lorraine. I'm not ashamed."

"Who's ashamed, Sadie?"

"I didn't mean that. I mean, that doesn't matter to me."

"Where's *Alsace-Lorraine?* Sounds suspicious."

"Stefan—"

"Some *Alsatian* tribe?" he said, raising an eyebrow.

"It's an area in Northern France."

"Humph." He looked at her over the burning tip of the cigarette, and his eyes took on a softer contemplation. "Funny, we could be related—five degrees of separation, isn't it?"

"How?" She didn't want to be related.

"My mother's half Flemish. Then she married my father, so I guess I'm quarter."

"Flemish?"

"Her grandparents were from Belgium. They're all in the same neighborhood: France, Belgium, Germany. . . related."

Sadie considered the logistics. The possibilities were infinite. She studied his face. "Grandpa said you have cousins in the Upper Peninsula and assumed they were Finnish."

"Everybody's trying to figure us out."

"There are a lot of Finlanders in the U.P. It's kind of a running joke, the priest from Escanaba and the Finn from Ishpeming."

"Haven't heard that one."

"Where exactly are they?"

"The priest or the Finlander?"

She smiled. "Your mother's relatives."

"That's the problem. She doesn't know."

"Doesn't know?"

"Like I said, there was a falling out. Her last letter was returned, no forwarding address. Personally, I take that as a *fuck you*. But maybe she's right, maybe it just got lost somewhere between White Lake and Rainy River and—where are we? —Sawyers Pond? She lied on the paperwork to get us here. Maybe they all moved back to Dalhousie."

"New Brunswick?"

He nodded.

"So now what?"

He shrugged. "I don't know. Mom's doing some research at the library. You can find anyone on the internet."

"Even if you don't want to be found?"

He took the beer from her and finished it. A murder of crows inched closer, eyeing their peanut shells, waiting for them to leave. He crumpled the can in his fist and looked at her.

"Do you want to be found, Sadie?"

The space between them was no space at all. He turned towards her, and their knees touched. He draped a hand over her shoulder and dropped it down her back. A tremor ran up her thigh and lodged in the curve of her tailbone.

"No," she said. "I don't."

He leaned over and kissed her, tentative yet deliberate. His lips were firm and warm, and it was nice kissing him, unlike the boys in high school with their wet mouths and fumbling fingers. He shifted his weight and pulled her closer; his mouth covered hers, and his hand gripped her back. Her senses funneled into points of contact—his mouth and his tongue tasting of beer and smoke and the hand splayed on her back—and cradled between the two she knew his loss and his desire. They entered her like the smoke from his cigarettes, burning like an ember at the apex of her sex.

Shocked at the explosion inside herself, she pushed him away.

He sat up, and the muscle in his jaw jumped. "Sorry," he said.

She rubbed her knee, not knowing what else to do with her hands.

He stood up and scattered the peanut shells with his foot. "I should get the motorcycle back."

And she thought of what he had just said. *I'd like to go back some day.*

She picked up the bag of empty beer cans and put them in the saddlebag, and he snapped the straps. She buried her hands in her pockets. Her mouth felt bruised and bereft. She wanted a do-over. As if in sympathy, the sun went behind a cloud and the temperature dropped.

The ride home along the Huron shore was a blur of blue water and tall trees, the gulls scavenging the roadsides replaced by flocks of land birds when they turned inland. With the sun glancing through the trees, they rode in and out of shade pockets. The stroke of the engine paced the rush of asphalt under her feet. She tried to identify the collage of smells the wind picked up on its rush through the woodlands, but they were all mixed up in a primordial stew.

Sadie rested her forehead against his back, the smell of leather and smoke, that which she could identify, and as with a partner on the dance floor—her mother and father who used to draw rapt attention—she followed his lead and leaned when he leaned. They were one with the motorcycle and the swale of the road that rose and fell on the glacier-forged topography.

When he dropped her at the top of the driveway, it was late afternoon, and they were both feeling the effects of the long ride. She climbed off, stretched, and removed the goggles. He tucked them in the breast pocket of his jacket. She waited, but he didn't turn off the key.

"Do you want to come in, get a bite to eat?" She kicked at the gravel.

"No, I better get home." All the sharp angles were back, like a mask he could take on and off.

She stood with her arms cradled across her stomach, elbows in her palms, holding in the feelings for which there were no words. She mumbled something she later couldn't remember, an inanity not worth remembering.

He gunned the throttle, and then he was off. He turned onto the road and put his fist in the air. Was that his idea of a wave? It suddenly seemed important.

CHAPTER 7

By the time Joachim reached the cabin by the dismantled roadblock, the sun was behind the trees. The inside was dark and the hearth cold. He left his gear by the door, lit a fire with the kindling in the wood box, and coaxed it to life before he went back outside.

He restrung the barbed wire across the road with the ghost of his father's hand guiding his, then uncovered the skid steer that Savior had rescued from a salvage yard. Good with mechanics, he and Bobby had gotten the rusted hulk running. It was camouflaged with spray paint and covered with brush.

The machine fired with a puff of smoke and a groan of protest. Working the controls deftly, Joachim stacked nail-studded utility poles across the road with the forks of the machine and built a roadblock Sonny, his dad, would have been proud of. When finished, he parked the skid steer back behind the stand of hemlocks, pulled the brush over it, and hid the key where his friends and he had agreed to hide it. They would never give up the fight.

Joachim walked back to the cabin. He lit an oil lamp and searched inside for anything that remained of his father. On the floor beside a cot there was a cache of pain pills, a box of strike-anywhere matches, a pouch of tobacco, and a box of linen handkerchiefs.

He frowned at the latter and opened the box. An *SM* was monogrammed in the corner of each handkerchief. To the bitter end, his mother had tried to gussy up Sonny Montegrand.

Joachim put the items in his satchel and zipped it shut. He stared at it for a minute, and then opened it back up and stuffed one of the handkerchiefs in his pocket.

Looking around the cabin, he wondered what he was forgetting. His eyes fell on the hand pump at the sink.

He opened his pocketknife and pried open the hidden door under the sink that he and Savior had fashioned when they installed the hand pump. It was their mailbox—his, Savior's and Bobby's— a holdover from their adolescent days of clandestine note passing and distrust of the elders. It was a place to pass messages they couldn't trust to the post, starting with the frivolous (sexual conquests and challenge), and ending with the serious, (coordination of efforts in the resistance).

There was a folded note inside. It was from Savior. Joachim read it over, then gazed out the clouded glass of the window and crumpled the note in his fist. The message changed things, but he still had to eat.

He fired up the gas stove and set a knife and fork beside his sidearm, a place setting his mother would not have approved of. As children they had learned to suppress unseeming shows of emotion. Most of his father's friends were trying to fit in and doing the same. The way Joachim saw it, Sonny's bottled-up hostility had only led to the explosiveness that had landed him in jail.

Joachim looked around the mud-chinked walls. Even in the bone-cracking cold of winter they kept the weather at bay, and with the hearth ablaze, it was comfortable enough. He remembered nights when they were building this cabin. Eight to ten of them would crowd around the table and eat stew out of a communal pot and tell stories. Stefan would sit quietly in the corner, soaking it all in, never wanting to leave, hoping their father would forget he was there. But leave he would when Sonny ordered him out and back to the house. He never let Stefan spend the night. Not once.

Then Sonny started dropping things.

Joachim greased the cast iron fry pan with duck fat, fried a slab of venison along with some old potatoes from the root cellar at their vacated house, and ate what he knew would be his last meal around this particular table. He had originally intended to swing by the council house on his way to the burial site and check for messages. But now, maybe not.

And then there was the woman with Indian Affairs who helped finalize the sale of the property and the transfer of royalty rights that Stefan wasn't going to like. Josie cut her own wood, dressed her own venison, and drew clean water from a deep well as of yet untainted by the uranium mine that had promised good jobs but only left her orphaned and fierce on the cusp of womanhood.

Joachim wiped the plate clean with a piece of bread and washed it down with water in a tin cup from the hand pump at the sink. He opened a package of caribou jerky with his teeth, wondering if the animal had been harvested in the vicinity of a uranium mine.

He turned and spat in the wastebasket. He had started spitting up blood before he'd been arrested, but it had worsened after his stay in a cement-block cell.

Like his father, his repressed anger had found an outlet.

He would conduct the final ceremony and put away his father's name. There wouldn't be another Sonny Montegrand. He sat by the fire, tossed Savior's note in the flames, and watched his words curl and disintegrate.

The fire was a bed of coals when a rig pulled up and blew its air horn. Joachim pulled on his boots and stuffed everything into his pack. The idling diesel drowned out the sounds of night birds, foragers, and the great hoot owls that lived in the forest. Truckers could sleep in those things, run them all night and not have to hear the forest. Collect their pay for helping to besmirch it without ever stepping foot in it.

He zipped his jacket and turned off the oil lamp, and the cabin went dark. The glowing bed of embers marked the rim of the hearth and lit his path to the door.

He stepped into the night and looked at the idling oil tanker. The sound of music drifted from the cab, and a stab of anger shot through him.

He flattened himself against the cabin, pulled the Ruger out of his waistband, and sighted down the barrel, taking careful aim at the rig's front tires. He drew a breath, steadied his elbow with his left hand, and emptied the chamber. In the ensuing silence, he heard the hissing of air and smelled burnt rubber.

He dropped his arm. He'd done it now.

There was movement inside the cab, then the door opened, and a figure with a rifle ducked around the front of the rig. Joachim looked at his jeep fifty feet away, then back at the man who was on a phone. He felt for a stone at his feet and heaved it into the woods. The driver fell for the age-old trick, dropped his phone and fired into the brush.

Joachim tucked the pistol in his waistband and ran for the jeep.

He turned the key in the ignition. The motor sputtered and caught. The crack of a rifle sounded above the engine and he felt the displacement of air along the path of the slug as it grazed his ear. The truck driver wasn't aiming at rubber.

Joachim floored the gas pedal and drove out of the clearing with his lights off. A bullet caught him in the shoulder and threw him against the steering wheel. Another round blew the hat off his head. The baseball cap somersaulted through the air in a whirlwind of leaves, birch bark and broken glass.

Blood dripped from his ear and down his forehead from where the slug had parted his hair, grazing his scalp. He wiped the blood from his eyes and peered out the windshield, wondering what kind of a scope the shooter had.

He steered with one arm for the hidden track through the woods, finding his way by the light of the moon shining through the trees, and then the northern lights fell from the heavens, and the woods were on fire.

Warm blood ran down the inside of his shirt, but he was cold.

He was out of earshot when the first siren sounded across the landscape, the shrill horn a caterwauling in the night, and all the owls turned and blinked.

CHAPTER 8

Stefan parked the motorcycle behind Larry's house and dragged the tarp across the handlebars, thinking about Sadie on the seat behind him.

He hung the key on the hook inside the lean-to and walked across the driveway to the rental house Sam's parents kept apologizing for, but which was bigger than the house back home where he had shared a bedroom with his three brothers, back when he had three.

He grabbed a beer from the fridge, then opened a can of sardines and forked them over the sink, satisfyingly salty and tasting of home where they could no longer eat the fish.

The lethargy he'd been mired in since leaving home had lifted. With his first glimpse of Sadie leaning out the window in the hay loft with that glorious head of red hair, a bolt of electricity had shot through his core and hard-wired his senses. Amplified now by the tease of a kiss she aborted when he was just getting started.

He dropped his clothes by the washing machine in what the Wixoms called a "mudroom". Funny things they had here: mudrooms, family rooms, kitchen nooks, islands. It was enough to make him long for home where things were simple and there were no such things as parlors and islands. If he'd wanted an island, he would have hitchhiked into the Canadian Shield.

There was a small mirror over the bathroom sink, and with one eye closed and the other on what he was doing, he pulled the Band-Aid off the cut above his eyebrow, than ran his fingers over his jaw. The Zender kid had clocked him a good one.

He took another swig of beer and turned the shower on. The showerhead was attached lower than most, and he had to duck to get under it, but the pressure was amazing for a jerry-rigged affair. He backed up to the spray and let it pummel the tightness from his neck. He soaped himself and turned up the heat, luxuriating in the release of tension.

He was toweling off when the front door opened and familiar voices entered the house. He threw the towel over the shower rod, pulled his jeans on, grabbed his beer, and opened the bathroom door.

Abby stared at him. "Where have you been?"

He upended the bottle of beer, then set the empty in the kitchen sink and drew a glass of water from the tap.

His mother set her bag of groceries on the dining room table and sat on the closest chair. "You're drinking too much," she scowled.

"Here, Margaret." Helen took the milk off his mother's lap. "Let me put that away for you."

"Water's safe here, Mom," Stefan said.

"Don't be so smart," she retorted.

He drew a stool up with his foot and straddled it. "No one's ever accused me of that."

"I thought you were just going for a bike ride," Margaret said.

"I did."

"With who?" Abby propped her feet on a chair, all-knowing. "The rancher's daughter?"

"None of your business, Abby."

"Put a shirt on, Stefan," Margaret snapped.

"I wish you'd take that motorcycle off Larry's hands," Helen said. "He's going to kill himself. Too old to be riding around on that thing."

"It's easier to handle than my Dad's." Stefan said.

"Your dad has a motorcycle?"

"*Had* a motorcycle," he corrected. "They took it off his hands."

Nobody said anything for a minute.

He pulled on a clean T-shirt from off the back of a chair and checked the time.

"It's time to call Joachim."

They had set up a coordinated time once a week for his brother to be at the council house where there was a phone with a dependable landline. Stefan would make the call. If Joachim wasn't there, Stefan was to call back an hour later. If he still wasn't there, he was to leave a message and they would try again the next day, same time. In this way they kept in touch, albeit sporadically, but they had not talked to him since they arrived in Sawyers Pond.

Joachim wasn't there, and nobody had heard from him. Silence filled the kitchen, and the hum of the refrigerator grew like a freshly hatched batch of mosquitoes advancing across the marshlands.

"Come on." Helen put her hand on Margaret's arm. "Let's get on my computer and we'll see if we have any leads. We'll be right next door." She looked from Stefan to Abby. "Holler if you need us."

"I'm getting a tattoo," Abby announced after they left.

"You ask Mom?"

"Sam says all the girls have them."

He cracked open another beer. "I've been hearing lots of stories about all the girls. I don't want to hear any about you."

"You're as bad as Joachim." She examined her fingernails. "How is he going to find us if we can't reach him?"

"We'll reach him."

"I dreamt about those fish again." Abby said, changing the subject. "I was with Dad on the dock, and they were jumping out of the water. One landed at my feet, looking at me with its bloody eye." She shivered.

He took a long pull from the bottle. "I remember one time Dad took me fishing in that old skiff with the blue seat cushions Mom always teased him about. He told me there was an outlaw char that couldn't be caught, reputed to be upwards of forty pounds. Stole bait and pulled rods out of boats and swam off with them. I scoffed, but then damn if he didn't hook the biggest damn fish I ever saw. He threw it in the bottom of the boat, thrashing pink and silver, mad as hell. Almost flipped right over the rail, but Dad caught it with both hands and held it up like a trophy and said, Look at this Stefano. Now this is a fish."

"He never took me," Abby said.

"You never wanted to fish."

"I like American food. Pizza and burgers and French fries."

"That'll make you fat."

She cast him a sideways glance. "So, what's Sam's cousin like? What's her name... Sadie, is it?"

"She's nice."

"I bet she eats French fries."

He shrugged.

"Sam told me she has a dog with no name and a horse with no name and never changes her clothes."

"Sam talks too much. And so do you." He opened another beer with a quick twist of his wrist and headed for his room. He wasn't going to talk about Sadie. Not to Abby, anyway.

But that night he thought about the animals and Zender Bolton, and to the last drop from the last bottle, about her changing her clothes.

CHAPTER 9

Blood had soaked through Joachim's shirt, and he tucked a towel under his arm to cushion his shoulder. The needle on the jeep's gas gauge hovered above empty, nudging the red line with each pothole he hit, and the dull ache in his shoulder had turned into a throb.

His mouth was dry, and he felt queasy. He struggled to stay on the roadway as the path through the birch forest narrowed and the white of the trees closed in on him like wraiths in a fog.

He thought of the whiff and suck of the bullet that took his hat. The silent thud of the one that barreled through his shoulder to lodge itself in the dashboard of the jeep. He was shot clean through and he felt the cold entering the space the bullet left as the blood seeped out.

He leaned over the steering wheel and peered out the windshield for the junction that would take him to Josie's. He should have reached it by now, but the trees mirrored each other in the dizzying shimmer of the aurora borealis. He slammed on the brake and the jeep rocked to a halt. He turned on the dome light and tapped the compass with his finger. The magnetic needle was reversed, the electrical disturbance of the night's aurora interfering with the reading. It had happened before to Jake—a malfunctioning compass forced him to hunker down for hours by his snow machine, and he nearly froze to death.

He surely couldn't be going south in the direction of the security guards from the petro company, guards who operated independently and non-judiciously.

The engine idled and he considered the direction he should be going versus the one he seemed to be going. His shoulder had gone numb. He pressed his fingers against the wound below his collarbone. His shirt was wet and sticky, and the entire area hurt like hell. He needed to rest, just for a minute.

He swallowed two of Sonny's pain pills with a bottle of water and turned off the engine. The woods were deep, silent, and safe. An owl hooted in the trees overhead as if commiserating with his predicament. As the narcotic deadened his senses, he fell asleep against the steering wheel with the bottle of water between his legs.

He awoke with a jerk. The shadow of a figure passed by his window.

Joachim tried to gather his bearings. A stabbing pain shot through his shoulder, and it all came back.

The hooded figure tapped at his window, like a crazed bird, and in his dazed state, he fumbled for the ignition key. The battery was dead. He pumped the gas pedal like that would give him a jump.

A familiar voice seeped through the fog in his brain.

"Joachim! Open the damn door!"

He groped for the lock, but couldn't find it. He was trapped against the steering wheel, and panic set in. Now he knew why his brother, Jake, couldn't find his way out from under that ice.

The figure dropped the hood and pleaded with him to unlock the door. It was Josie.

He knocked the water bottle on the floor and found the lock. She opened the door and he swung a leg out.

"Joachim! What's going on? I woke up, saw headlights out here, thought I'd better see who it was. Why'd you leave your lights on? You killed your battery." She leaned over him. "Baby, are you drunk?"

He eased his other leg out and reached up shakily. "I wish I was— thought I was lost."

"You feel hot, Jac. What happened?"

"Been better," he admitted.

She grabbed his arm to help him stand, and he cried out in pain. "What?!"

"Not that one." He winced and stretched out his other hand. "Here, take my hand."

She pulled him to his feet and he leaned against her.

"What's wrong? Can you walk?"

He fell back on the seat. "I don't think so."

"I'll get the truck. Stay here."

He closed his eyes, grateful to let her take over.

Josie grabbed her keys off the table and backed the 4x4 out of the garage, careening down the drive that looped through the trees. She helped him into the front seat, and then drove back up to the cabin. She parked as close as she could to the front door.

With his reserve of strength, she got him down the hallway and into the bedroom where they had spent the better part of spring when the pussy willows were bursting and bees hummed outside the open window. Joachim collapsed on the bed, and Josie turned on the bedside lamp. Her eyes went wide at the sight of his blood-soaked shirt.

"You've been shot! Who shot you?!"

"I don't know."

"Sit up. We have to get your shirt off."

The blood had dried and blackened. She cut his shirt away with scissors and laid him back slowly on the mattress. She slid a pillow under his head and looked at the jagged hole under his collarbone.

She was a midwife and had never had to deal with anything like this. The exit wound still seeped blood, and the edges were raw and ugly. Dirt and bits of matter were stuck to it, and dried blood had coagulated around the torn tissue.

She turned him on his side and examined the entry wound. He gasped and clutched at the air.

"Easy." She coaxed "I know it hurts. When did this happen?"

"I don't know, four, maybe five hours ago."

"How long were you sitting outside? Come on, Jac, think."

"I don't know, Josie. I passed out. Give me a blanket, I'm cold."

She pulled a wool blanket out of her cedar chest. "I have to wash my hands, baby, and then stop the bleeding." She tucked the blanket around his legs and lower torso. "You're in shock, but you're going to be okay. Just hang on."

She pinned her hair up in a bun, rolled her sleeves two times, and washed her hands in the bathroom sink adjoining the bedroom. letting the hot water sluice over her wrists and through her fingers.

What she had feared ever since his father was imprisoned had come to pass. She had to stay calm because he was in shock. She looked at herself in the mirror. Could she do what needed to be done?

She set a stool beside the bed and a basin of hot water on the bedside table, along with soap, gauze, iodine, and tweezers. She placed a sheaf of gauze over the exit wound and applied pressure to the site. She gently touched the area beside it where the skin was blue and swollen, then removed the gauze. The hole yawned like an empty eye socket. A trickle of blood ran down his chest past his nipple. She pressed another layer of gauze over the hole and held it there with the tips of her fingers. It slowly darkened. She replaced it with another.

When the hole in his chest stopped bleeding, she rolled him on his side, tucked towels around him, soaped a clean washcloth, and cleaned the entry wound in the back of his shoulder. She washed his neck where the blood had dried around his ear and examined his head where one of the bullets had grazed him.

"He nearly nailed you, Jac," she said.

"I lost my hat."

She rinsed the cloth and wrung it out.

"It was my favorite."

"We can get you another hat. No more talking now. I need you to hold still."

She wiped the soap off his chest and shoulder, patted his skin dry, and dabbed the area with cotton dipped in iodine. Then she turned him on his side and did the same with the entrance wound in his back.

She worked methodically. Her hands were steady. She shouldn't have doubted herself when it came to him. She cleaned around both wounds and then dabbed them again with iodine. It dyed his skin a rusty brown. His breathing was labored.

She picked up the tweezers and told him to hold the bed railing above his head. She steadied her hand and probed the wound. The tendons in his neck shone taut in the lamplight, and she dropped the bone chip in a dish on the table. She wiped her face on her sleeve, took a breath and fished out another. Small chips flaked off by the path of the bullet.

Satisfied, she swabbed both wounds again with iodine and pressed clean gauze over each one, taping them into place.

He sucked in a long rasping breath. "Done, doc?"

She wiped the back of her hand across her brow and breathed. "I got the bleeding stopped. Should be good until we can get you to a real one."

"You did good, Josie." He smiled faintly. "I know 'cause it hurt like hell."

"We're lucky it's mostly tissue damage, and the bullet passed clean through."

"I reckon it's in my dashboard."

"Lucky it only took some bone fragments with it. I think I got them all."

"It felt like you took out a rib."

She gave him a clean pillow and rested her hand on his forehead.

"You can tell me tomorrow how it is you came to me in the middle of the night all shot up." She handed him a glass of water with a straw and two pain capsules, watching him swallow and drink. She put the instruments in the basin of water with the soap and dirty towels, then draped a clean sheet over him and tucked it around his feet, hands lingering on his person.

"Tomorrow, babe, okay?" But Joachim was already asleep.

She wasn't at all sure she got all the bone fragments, nor was she sure it was a clean wound. The downward path of the bullet worried her. He had no color and a fever, but the closest clinic was some distance, and he needed rest.

She gazed at the length of him, remembering how he had come into her life during a court hearing where she was the Indigenous interpreter for another case. She was captivated by his earnest face and passionate cause and quickly became sympathetic to his self-defeatist standing.

It was time to leave the protests to someone else. Protesting was a dangerous sport. He should have played hockey instead of billiards. Billiards led to talk; all that standing around. Talk led to anger, anger led to action culminating in protest, and protest led to a bullet in the shoulder. Hockey was safer. Hockey afforded acceptable means of venting frustration.

She tiptoed out of the room, put the cabin in order, then went back into the night. She jumped his jeep, parked it inside the shed, and padlocked the door.

CHAPTER 10

After a fitful night with Sadie in and out of his dreams—in and out of her clothes— and a late breakfast of lukewarm coffee and leftover corn bread slathered in maple syrup, Stefan walked the two miles to the Wixom farm with a knapsack strapped to his back. He smoked two cigarettes on the way, pinched the butts out between his thumb and index finger, and dropped them in a pocket. It was low summer fading to autumn but still warmer than it ever got north of the border. He kicked a series of stones down the road aiming for potholes; that much at least was familiar.

He was considering another smoke when the silo came into view. The sound of a tractor came from behind the barn, but there was nobody in sight. A cluster of cars were parked at the other place, the Bolton place, and he noticed the shooting range with the human-shaped targets and heard the *pop, pop, pop* of small arms fire. Part of him wanted to walk over there, find Zender Bolton, and punch his pale face in. It had felt disturbingly good the first time.

He cut the corner, crossed Wixom's ditch, and ducked through a raspberry patch. Her car was parked by the gas pump. He walked up the sidewalk and knocked on the farmhouse door. He knocked again and looked for a doorbell. There was an old-fashioned brass knocker on the door and he gave it a whack.

"Hey." Sadie came out of the stable and walked across the yard, arms swinging, "Did you walk?"

"Yeah, I needed some exercise." He opened the knapsack and unwrapped the boomerang from a towel. "I thought I'd show you how to throw this thing, if you want to try."

Her eyes widened. "Sure."

They walked to the edge of the field, and he tested the direction of the wind.

"I watched you and Sam," she said.

"I know you did. You can't do any worse."

He handed her the boomerang, and she turned it over in her hands.

"It's so light," she said as she ran a finger across the etched markings.

He nodded. The foil was light yet weighted with the sensation of flight, like it would fly off your fingertips if given the chance.

He showed her how to hold it right, how to throw it so it would come back, but her first try duplicated Sam's. Even the dog was unimpressed.

He corrected her hold on the wingtip and guided her arm in a practice throw, breathing in the scent of her hair as it brushed his cheek.

"You have to concentrate," he said. "Think of it as throwing through the eye of the wind. Watch your release point. Here, like this." He adjusted his stance and heaved it into the air. The foil sailed end over end, circled, as if on a planetary orbit, and picked up speed on the return. He caught it between both hands with a clap.

"Catch it like that with both hands, or you'll jam a finger. If it ever comes back, that is."

She made a face.

"Come on," he coaxed. "Try it again."

She nodded and wiped her hands on her pants.

A flock of swallows dipped and swooped across the field, and she waited them out. She took a breath, drew her arm back, and threw overhand the way he had, landing on her front foot. The boomerang spun like a top and flew back at a forty-five-degree angle. It fell short, but she had it, and he told her so.

Throwing something that came back could be addictive, and she was getting better, though it still hadn't come back to her cleanly. The dog was frustrated with being made to stay, and the angle of the sun reminded Stefan of the time.

He pulled out his cell phone to check, then shoved it back in his pocket. "I should get going, Sadie. Time to make a phone call. You did good."

"No service?"

"No, it's not that."

"One more, okay?"

He shrugged. "Sure. This time, I want you to catch it."

She pointed at the trees along the creek and checked her grip. Holding it with a slight tilt, she brought it back behind her ear and loosed it at the same time a rifle shot rang out. The boomerang flew off her fingertips on a doomed trajectory. A volley of gunshots followed the single shot and the dog barked wildly, crazed but not scared, like he was used to it but didn't like it.

Stefan scanned the throwing field. "Did you see where it went?"

She swallowed. "No. Did you?"

The distracting gunshots had drawn his eye from the spinning airfoil. "No," he said.

Even the dog was confused, barking at nothing.

They walked the area where she thought it went, but they couldn't find it. Stefan pulled his phone out of his pocket and swore under his breath.

"What?"

"Look, I gotta go."

"Do you want a ride home?"

"No, I'll run." And he was already halfway across the lawn. He settled the knapsack in the center of his back remembering the look of hurt puzzlement on her face. He focused his attention and jogged down the driveway. By the time he cut through the overgrown raspberry patch, darkness was falling, cloaking the road ahead in shadow.

CHAPTER 11

The next morning, Sadie pulled her work jeans out of the hamper and took up the search for the boomerang with the dog dutifully running circles, nose to the ground. After she lost Stefan on the road, she had walked the field again, kicking brush all the way to the creek, though it would never have gone that far.

She retraced those steps and widened her search. Leaves crunched like parchment under her feet. She kicked them up and walked back the other way. It was as if the ground had opened up and swallowed it.

Empty handed, she returned to the barn and threw hay down for the cattle and some for the horses. Then she rubbed them both down until their coats glistened. She lingered over her work, grooming the horses and arranging the tack, everything where she had left it and where she would find it again.

Her eyes fell on the hackamore bridle and she remembered how Stefan used it when he rode Two Socks. She looped it over her arm and entered the mare's stall. The horse was shorter than Two Socks and smooth-gaited with low withers. Sadie led her out by the lead rope and considered how she might go about what she wanted to try.

With the hackamore in place behind the ears and around the nose, she gripped the mare's mane, bounced on the balls of her feet and prepared to jump, but the feisty filly sidestepped and dropped her head. Sadie grabbed the rope rein and squared her up. "I need you to hold still so I don't fall on my ass. You know what I intend to do. Grandpa would claim you know what I'm thinking, so don't pull a Lucy on me."

The mare tossed her head and nickered.

Sadie laughed. "I agree. Charlie Brown's Lucy suits you." She stroked her neck. "Now hold still . . . *Lucy*."

After several tries, she landed on the mare's back. Sadie hugged her neck. It felt like the first time she landed a backflip in gym class. She wrapped the halter rope around her hand and declared her newfound devotion.

Sadie rode the mare around the outbuildings and down the drive, circled the garden and back around the buildings, getting the feel for no saddle, feet hanging loose.

It was time to put into play the idea that took root round the table with her grandfather and his plat books and magnifying glass. The mare with her smaller stature and sure footing could more easily navigate creek beds, fallen brush, and low-hanging branches. It was time to take a ride around the back of Bolton's place and practice the investigative reporting skills she was supposed to be going to school for.

She turned Two Socks out to pasture, then leapt back on the mare's back, and put her forward on the circle drive.

Meanwhile, Henry had poured a third cup of coffee and took it into his office. He was behind on his paperwork and didn't need his dad on him about that along with everything else. He stood at the window and watched as Sadie rode the mare around the barnyard. She rode well with her elbows loose and her back straight, but something was off. He scratched his neck. It took him a minute to realize she was riding the mare bareback.

He watched her reach down, pull off one boot and then the other, and ride out with no saddle and no boots.

He refilled his coffee cup and added a shot of whiskey. He took out his pocket calendar and it fell open to the circled entry, a dinner date with Margie who had recently lost her spouse, a club he now belonged to.

"Want me to check the hay, Henry?" Simon came out of the bathroom and hooked the suspenders on his coveralls.

"Ah, sure." He rubbed the back of his neck. "Is it raked?"

"Twice through yesterday. Sun's already hot. Reckon it's dry, but I'll go out and check. You were gonna line up some help. Any luck?" His gaze was drawn to Sadie riding past the window, and he craned his neck as she disappeared down the driveway.

"Guess it won't be her, eh? She's never around anymore when we could use a little help."

Henry blinked. "What do you mean?"

"Shirking responsibility, off with the horses, off with the dog, wandering around alone at night. She never has friends over anymore, never goes out with any of 'em."

"What are you talking about?"

"Frankly, I'm worried. Every night after dinner, same thing, off she goes."

"Come on, walking the dog? She likes taking the dog out at night. Always did. That border collie was always more hers than Jenny's."

"I'm not talking about ten years ago, Henry. The neighborhood has changed, don't know anybody anymore. I don't like her wandering around at night, not with those Boltons across the road. I've seen the way the one with the tattoo—" He stopped himself mid-sentence. "I just don't trust them."

"What about the one with the tattoo?"

"She'll listen to you."

"What about him?"

Simon hesitated. "He's on the sex offender list."

Henry scoffed. "Aw, come on. So are a hundred other guys for pissing outside a bar."

"Those have been expunged."

"Because that list is arbitrary and I'm guessing unconstitutional if it's ever challenged in court. You can't lump rape and public urination in one category. Really, Dad, I'm surprised at you."

"I'm surprised you don't care who's living across the road."

Henry passed a hand over his eyes and pinched the bridge of his nose. "I care, he said."

"Just have a talk with her, okay? She needs to go back to school. It's going on six months. You gonna let her brush that off too, like all the jobs she can't seem to hold for more than a week?"

Henry felt himself shutting down like the protective mechanism in an overheated computer. "I don't want to talk about this now." He grabbed a pair of gloves out of the closet where he kept his barn clothes. "I've got a heifer about to calve. If the hay is ready to bale, have Sam round up a couple of guys." He turned and exited the office. The screen door slammed shut behind him, putting an end to their conversation.

Sadie rode to where the stream crossed under the roadway and raged through the culvert in spring, all but disappeared in the drought. Even at the end of autumn when apples lay shriveled on the ground, the creek bed was usually soggy with rotting leaves, a predictable stream of running water following the path of least resistance down the middle of the streambed. Now it was as dry as corn standing in December.

She turned the mare into the wash and followed the dry bed bordered by scrub trees that sheltered them in cooling shade. When the horse started shoeing up mud, they clambered up the bank and ran directly into a *No Trespassing* sign nailed to a tree. They were on Bolton property.

She took the horse forward cautiously. The signs were nailed intermittently through the woods. She ripped one off, dropped it under the horse's feet, and steered the mare toward another. A branch snapped behind her, and she looked over her shoulder. Birds flitted through the dappled light, but nothing else. She shrugged off the feeling and put the horse forward.

They entered a clearing, and the Bolton place came into view. Grandpa was right. A pond had formed in front of a dam and a roughshod jetty stretched out across the water. Someone was swinging a hammer on the end of it, and Sadie pulled Lucy up short. She had come out of the woods closer than she had intended.

A dog started barking from a kennel behind the barn, followed by another. Several were lunging against the wire fencing, crazed to get out. The hammering had stopped, but all the dogs were barking.

She had seen enough and yanked the mare around and dug in her heels, but the horse stepped in a groundhog burrow hidden by underbrush and fell up to her knee. The mare scrambled to recover. Sadie pulled on the hackamore, and the horse screamed and pawed the air in fright. Sadie grabbed for a pommel that wasn't there and somersaulted off the back. She landed on her tailbone, and the impact knocked the breath out of her.

She lay motionless in the dirt, then groaned and opened her eyes. The light hurt, and she shut them again. She rolled to her side and tried again.

The mare stood a few paces off with her head down, breathing heavily. The jetty, the trees, and the sky swayed in and out of Sadie's line of vision, then footsteps rustled through the undergrowth, and two pairs of boots stopped in front of her.

"You all right, girl? Woo-ee, that was quite the tumble."

She rolled to her knees and dropped her head between her arms. It hurt to breathe.

"You want to explain this?" Maxwell Bolton dropped the crumpled sign on the ground in front of her.

"Give her a minute, Pa, can't you see she's trying to catch her breath?"

"I don't have all day. Took me a while to get these nailed where I wanted 'em, special ordered with bold print so any dummy could read 'em."

She straightened her back and looked at the mare, cropping grass as though nothing had happened.

"So aside from ripping my signs down, what are you doing over here?" He studied the mare. "Riding bareback on your little Indian pony."

"She's been hanging with one, Pa. I seen her."

"The one who beat up Zender?"

"There's only one."

Bolton rubbed his chin and looked her over. "Girl, your offenses keep adding up. Why you hangin' with illegals, trespassing, and destroying property?"

"Why are you damming up the creek?" Sadie asked.

"Why?" He raised his eyebrows in surprise. "We ain't damming it up, we're just redirecting it. Got some pooling and erosion needs correcting. We're *stewards* of the land, like they preach down at the conservation office. Ain't we, Danny?" He looked at the boy who was looking at Sadie.

"Piece of advice, little girl." Bolton leaned down to look Sadie in the eye. "Stay away from that Indian. He already has an assault and battery pending."

"He's the one who ought to be pressing charges," Sadie said.

"He started it, busted Zender's ribs, he did," Danny said.

Sadie got to her feet and brushed the dirt off her hands. The dogs had quieted, and the dock lay empty. The mare was grazing contentedly, none the worse for stepping in a hole, but would she be able to get back on her?

"Need help getting in the saddle?" Maxwell started. "Oh, that's right. You don't have one. Don't even have a proper bridle. And barefoot. We have a bunch of fruit loops living across the road, Danny."

"Is there a problem over here?" The man from off the dock joined them, ready to arbitrate the situation. A holstered gun was strapped to his thigh. He was taller than the others, and with his shaved head, he looked like someone out of a Nazi propaganda film.

"Have ourselves a trespasser, Clem, but she was just leaving. Might need help getting on her horse, might have to point her in the right direction."

"Point her?" Clem spat in the dirt. "I can do more than that. I know where she lives."

His eyes were flint with flecks of amber, and up close the tattoo on his neck looked like a swastika. If she'd had hackles, they would've been standing straight up.

The flight instinct triggered a rush of adrenaline, and she grabbed the rope rein and landed on the horse's back, biting her lip as she threw her leg over. Clem Bolton grabbed her by the ankle, but she kicked him sharply in the chest. He flailed backwards cursing, and she put Lucy into a gallop.

Branches scraped her arms and struck her face, but she pressed her bare heels into the mare's ribs and leaned over her neck. She didn't slow the horse until the Bolton signs were behind them, and the road with passing traffic was visible through the trees.

CHAPTER 12

Stefan needed money. He needed gas money, beer money, beating-around-town money. Buying-another-boomerang money?

The weight of the loss had grown through the night, and he'd fought the impulse to traverse the field with a flashlight.

"Her dad needs help baling hay," Sam offered, swinging his legs off their porch railing.

They were hanging out together after dinner, Stefan picking his brain about odd jobs around the area while discretely feeling him out about Sadie. He liked saying her name out loud.

"He pays if you can handle a bale of hay."

He could handle a bale of hay.

He went over early the next morning to first search for the boomerang. Their inability to find it was baffling. On the heels of greater loss—brothers, father, family home—this should be trivial, but it was complicated. Having grown inured to the tragic, he took the loss of a mere object he should have had control over as a direct hit, indicative of a character flaw, a failure on his part to take care of things. How could he lose the one thing of value entrusted to him?

He judged the distance and possible trajectory of a wayward throw. She could only have thrown so far, but the flat surface of the foil, the color of earth, would be hard to spot. He sectioned off the throw area in his head and paced it off. Scanning the ground, like a soldier on point, he tried to remember if it was his grandfather's or his great-grandfather's.

As the eldest son, it became Jake's. But after he fell through the ice, everyone agreed that Stefan should have it because he was the only other one who could throw it the way his father said it should be thrown. Jake had told him it was thought to be the oldest boomerang in the Dené Nation, engraved by an ancestor who came across the Bering Sea.

Regardless of whether or not that was true, the story had taken on myth-like qualities.

The thought of Jake trapped under all that ice haunted his sleep. The loss of his brother at the peak of manhood was harder to take than that of his father.

Stefan walked back in the direction of the outbuildings and began assigning blame: the dog, thieves, wormholes, aliens, dark forces at work in the universe, a crack in time.

Sam's truck was parked beside the motorcycle Stefan had borrowed, and he remembered he had a job waiting that paid.

Sam was sitting in the elevator, chewing a wad of gum and eyeing him with a calculating look. "What're you looking for?"

"Lost the boomerang yesterday."

"How the hell did that happen?"

Stefan shrugged and looked at the stable and the one horse out to pasture.

"She's not here. Out riding the filly."

He took his gloves out of the saddlebag and snapped it shut.

"Dad's looking to sell that." Sam nodded at the motorcycle.

"Yeah?"

"A pretty penny, I'm sure."

"We haven't talked price." Stefan said.

"*We?* Shit, you know how much an old Indian motorcycle in that condition costs? They don't even make them like that anymore."

"Yeah, I know."

"Dude, I can't see any *we* in that transaction. There's a reason you only see old guys riding 'em. Or wealthy sons-of-bitches, and you and me, we don't qualify." He narrowed his eyes, seemingly suspicious of Stefan's noncommittal nature. "Do we?"

"We haven't talked."

"You in on some casino money up there or something?"

Stefan rolled his eyes. "No, Sam. I'm not."

Sam motioned at the load of hay. "Let's get started. I have a date tonight with you-know-who. You can unload, I'll stack. Flip the switch there on the elevator." He pointed in the general direction and disappeared into the hayloft.

Stefan flipped the switch and started tossing bales. It felt good to work, to throw forty-pound bales of hay on a conveyor belt that carried them away and off his hands.

It was good to get out of the house, away from Abby and his mother with her silent accusations. It wasn't his fault that once again Joachim couldn't be reached. That once again the lead on a relative she hadn't kept in touch with for twenty years was a dead end. Like their dead-end family and their dead-end tribe living in the past.

It felt good to sweat it out, like the old guys in their sweat lodges, swatting themselves with birch sticks like a bunch of repentant sinners, flailing themselves for perceived losses— loss of temper, loss of fortune, loss of standing. The art of losing perfected by practice.

He turned to grab another bale, and his thoughts, vacillating from wormholes and thieves to sweat lodges and penitence, were interrupted by the sight of Sadie coming up the driveway on the mare. She was slumped over the horse's neck, clenching her side with the rope rein hanging loose in her hand, the telltale look of a thrown rider.

He braced a hand against the side of the wagon as Sadie reined the horse in beside the stable and slid off her back. The mare stood with her head down, breathing heavily.

Riding bareback and neither of them looking any better for it.

She tried to remove the hackamore, but the mare tossed her head and high-stepped backwards.

Stefan jumped off the rear of the wagon and ran across the drive. He grabbed the halter and pulled the horse up tight. "Whoa, girl, whoa." He loosened the noseband, and the mare shuddered. He talked her down and looked at Sadie. Her clothes were grass stained and her hair was matted with brambles.

"You get thrown?"

She took a shallow breath and nodded.

"You hurt?"

She shook her head.

"What the hell's going on down there?" Sam shouted from the haymow. The elevator was running empty.

Stefan looked from her to the mare. "Let's get her inside. You sure you're okay?"

"Just knocked the wind out of me." Sadie pulled at the rein to lead the mare on, but the horse wasn't having it.

"Here, let me take her." He leaned against the mare to feel her breathing. He wrapped the rope rein around his hands, talked to her and led her into the stable. He removed the hackamore, careful of the swelling around her face and jaw, dropped a halter rope loosely around her neck, and put her in the stall.

He looked over the horse's back at Sadie. "What happened?"

"She stepped in a hole."

"Why were you riding bareback?"

"I wanted to."

"You wanted to?"

"I practiced last night. I was getting better."

"I can tell."

"That's *not* why I fell."

"Why'd you use the hackamore?"

She blinked. "You did. I thought—"

"It puts pressure on the face if you pull up hard. See the swelling here around her nose?"

Sadie chewed on the corner of her mouth, then grabbed a rag. She limped around the horse, and started rubbing her down.

"I'll do that."

"It's my horse."

"You born stubborn?"

"You can't fish if you can't hook your own worm."

"You can't rub a horse down with broken ribs."

She swiped the rag half-heartedly across the horse's withers. "Nothing's broken."

"You mighta cracked one, should get some X-rays."

"Nothing they can do for a cracked rib except tell you that you have a cracked rib."

"Why don't you sit down?" He nodded at the stool by the tack rack. "Let me finish up."

"I'm fine."

"Can't tell you nuthin', can I?" He looked at her feet. "And where are your boots?"

"I took them off."

"You took 'em off?"

"She didn't like them."

"Who didn't like them?"

"Lucy." She glanced at him. "I gave her a name."

"Well, I'll be damned. And she told you she didn't like your boots?"

"Quit making fun."

"You got a special relationship?"

Sadie shoved her hands stubbornly in her pockets. "She might have hurt herself stepping in that hole. Do you think I should call the vet?"

Stefan stood in front of the mare and looked at the leg. He leaned against her, ran his hand down the front of it, and tapped on the back of it. He waited and tapped again. The mare lifted her foot, and he held her foreleg between his knees and her hoof in one hand. He felt around the fetlock and examined the hoof, talking to her in a soft voice, and the mare leaned into him. He took out a pocket knife, ran the tip of it along the side wall of the hoof to clean it, and checked for cracks. He loosened a stone, cleaned out the mud, then let the mare's foot back down, and stroked her shoulder.

"She'll be alright. She's a tough little filly."

"How'd you learn to do that?"

He shrugged. "Like you said, if you want to fish, you have to hook your own worm."

"What the hell's going on?" Sam stood in the doorway.

"She got thrown."

"The God almighty horsewoman?"

"You got some liniment or salve?" Stefan said.

"There's some in the cabinet."

Stefan opened a tube, smelled it, and dabbed some around the mare's nose and jaw. He rubbed some on her knee and fetlock for good measure, then finished rubbing her down. He threw a blanket over her back and patted her rump. "There you go." He looked at Sadie. "A bag of oats would make her feel better."

Sadie didn't answer. She didn't take her eyes off him either.

"You done babysitting?" Sam said.

"Come on now, you can quit pouting."

"I'm *not* pouting." Sadie snapped.

"Lucy will be fine."

"Lucy?" Sam hooted. "That's all you could come up with?"

"Will she let me ride her again?" Sadie asked, ignoring Sam.

"If you don't show her the hackamore." Stefan paused a minute. "Why don't you go get some X-rays?"

"I'm not going to the stupid clinic. I know what they'll tell me. Take some aspirin and go to bed."

Sam twirled his hat in his hand. "So, take some aspirin and go to bed. Come on, Stef, let's get that hay in the mow."

Sadie pulled her hair back in a ponytail and then dropped it again. "You good?"

"I'm fine. Enough with the questions."

"Yes, ma'am." Stefan touched the brim of his hat and walked backwards out the door.

CHAPTER 13

With the last bale of hay tossed on the elevator, Stefan walked across the lawn to the water hydrant. He lifted the handle, and water from the well rushed out in a torrent. He adjusted the flow, ducked his mouth under it, and took long thirsty gulps.

"I'm taking off," Sam said. "You coming back tomorrow?"

Stefan wiped the water off his chin and nodded. "I'll come back."

"If you need the money, he'll pay you now."

"No, I'm good."

"Just saying."

"I'm good." Stefan repeated.

Sam peeled out of the driveway with a wave and Stefan walked to the bike. Two Socks was still out to pasture, and Stefan wondered if she meant to leave him there. The horse approached the gate in the fence and looked at him with his long face.

Stefan took a rope rein down from a hook in the stable and coiled it around his shoulder. He looped it around the horse's neck and led him to the water tank. He stood patiently while the horse drank. The sun rested at the horizon and cast elongated shadows across the field. The same setting sun, yet foreign to him. He wondered if he would ever fit into the narrow confines of this structured world.

The horse lifted its dripping muzzle, looked about, and then sunk his lips back into the tank. Stefan could stand all day and watch a horse drink.

When the gelding had his fill, he put him up and latched the stall door. The mare was looking over the top of hers and Stefan gave her a nod good night. He started to pull the stable door shut along the overhead track when a soft moan emanated from the mare's stall. He turned into the dark interior of the stable and heard it again. He crossed the bay and opened the stall.

Sadie was curled in a ball on a blanket in the corner. He pulled the cord on the overhead light and she rolled over and knocked the stool under the horse. The mare kicked out and caught Stefan in the shin.

"Sonofabitch!" He hobbled backwards and grabbed his leg. She kicked out again in retaliation for some equine-perceived wrong and hit the sidewall with her hoof. "Settle down, you sumbitch." He glared at the horse and her sides heaved.

Startled awake, Sadie sat up and rubbed her eyes.

"What are you doing out here?"

"What are *you* doing out here?"

She looked at the horse and then looked at Stefan. "What time is it?"

"Near dark."

"Oh." She tried to get up. "Oh, I'm so sore."

"I imagine. Sleeping in a horse stall . . ."

"I wasn't asleep."

"You do this often, sleep in the barn?"

"I just thought I'd stay out here a while, talk things over with her."

"Yeah, how'd that go?" Stefan retorted.

"Here, help me up."

He pulled her to her feet. Her hair was full of straw, and she smelled like horse and hay.

She cricked her neck and grimaced. "I feel like I got run over."

He dropped his hand down the center of her back and rubbed her tailbone.

She closed her eyes and leaned against him. "Ohh," she moaned, "yes, that's where it hurts."

A pair of preening doves looked down from above and softly cooed as he found the place where it hurt. The call of the doves was hypnotic, and the rafters went opaque as a state of fugue as his hands familiarized themselves with the enticing flair of her hips.

Sadie stepped back abruptly, and they dropped uselessly to his side. "It's late," she said hoarsely. "I better get inside."

He exhaled. *Right, probably should.* He limped across the stall and motioned her out ahead of him before latching the gate.

"Why are you limping?"

"Your horse kicked me," he said matter-of-factly.

They walked across the yard and Dog circled, thinking something was going to happen.

"Go to bed, Dog," she told him. "No walks tonight."

"You walk him at night?"

"Only time I don't feel like someone has a bead on me."

The dog licked Stefan's hand, and he squatted down and rubbed his ears. "So, what's his name going to be?"

Sadie shrugged. "Haven't thought of one."

Stefan tilted his head and looked the dog in the eye. "He might have some retriever in him but I'd bet a steak dinner he carries a strain of wolf."

"Really?" She looked at him, amused. "So, give him a wolf name."

"There are a lot of words for *wolf* in my people's language." He stroked the dog's head and jowls. "Why not just call him Wolf?"

The dog sat like he was under a stay command and stared at Stefan with his ears pricked.

"Wolf?" Sadie said with a smile. The dog looked back and forth between them and barked. "I think he likes it."

Stefan held his hand out and the dog licked his palm and his fingers, then his wrist and the back of his hand like it was a soup bone. Stefan laughed, grabbed him by the nose, and wrestled him into the grass.

Sadie squatted on her haunches and looked at the two of them, the dog in heaven with someone who would get down on the ground with him. She scratched his belly and his leg thumped. "Okay, your name is Wolf, and don't forget it."

Wolf lay between them with his paws in the air, content just to be there.

"So, tell me how you got in that fight," she said abruptly.

"Who said I was in a fight?"

"Come on, Stef."

He rested his elbows on his knees and considered her. "It was all over a stupid pack of cigarettes. Asking for ID and I only had my territorial health card and since when do you need an ID to buy cigarettes? They're giving me a hard time, and I mighta said something I shouldn't have, but the next thing I know someone has me around the neck."

"The Bolton kid says you started it."

"That's a lie."

"But you finished it?"

He shrugged.

Henry banged the screen door open and looked at the two of them. "So, there you are. Thought I was hearing things."

Stefan jumped to his feet and brushed off the seat of his pants.

"I got a deluxe meat lovers pizza about to come out of the oven."

"Did you burn it again?" Sadie turned to Stefan. "It's Dad's specialty. Are you hungry?"

The buzzer was going off on the oven and smoke drifted across the stoop. It smelled burnt but good, and Stefan realized he was famished.

He washed his face and neck in the bathroom sink, and finger-combed his hair. Sadie threw a quick salad together and set a jug of milk on the table. Henry sawed off the burnt edges of crust with a long-handled bread knife and they ate off paper plates.

"Where's Grandpa?" Sadie said.

"He took some muscle relaxers and went to bed. Said his bursitis was acting up. Probably from driving that tractor all day, but you can't tell him anything."

"So, you come by that honestly." Stefan looked at Sadie.

Henry popped the tab on another beer, leafed through a stack of papers at his elbow, and threw a ripped *no trespassing* sign in the center of the table.

Sadie looked at it and swallowed.

"So," he said, "tell me about your day."

"Sign looks familiar," Stefan said dryly.

"What were you doing over there?" Henry demanded.

Stefan darted him a look. "Over where?"

"She took a ride over Bolton's way, being neighborly, I guess. Was that it, Sadie?"

Stefan set his piece of pizza down and felt the muscle in his jaw jump.

"Dad, you've been drinking."

"Yes, I have." He looked at Stefan. "She's been tearing signs off trees, destroying private property, gets herself thrown riding bareback, *bareback*, and God knows what else. Bolton stops me on the road and throws this cheap piece of cardboard in my truck and goes on and on about all of it with other lewd comments I won't give legs to by repeating. And when I get home her grandpa says he has no idea where she is, which sounds about right."

He stopped and threw back a slug of beer from his can.

"Don't talk about me like I'm not here."

"Go ahead," Henry continued. "Since you're here, tell me your side of the story. I'm dying to know what in Sam Hill you thought you were doing."

Stefan picked up another slice of pizza and set it back down. What he really wanted was a cigarette and one of those beers. He knew trouble when he saw it, and the bunch across the road was trouble.

"Grandpa told me the creek was dried up, and we might be in a drought, but there's always water in that creek. It smells like they're burning tar over there with roadkill for kindling, and I just thought I'd ride over and take a look, do a little investigating. I followed the creek bed. You always said waterways are public property."

"You can't go tearing down people's signs."

"I don't like them."

"And you want to go where you want to go."

"And what's with all the dogs?"

"I could've warned you about going over there," Stefan said. The thought of her *over there* by herself had stolen his appetite.

"And I could've warned *you* about getting in a fight with one of them." She looked at Stefan. "They've got you pegged."

"Pegged for what?"

Henry looked at them both. "That place and a mile behind and either side is off limits. Thought I'd made that clear. The amount of gunfire I hear over there, cutting loose like a war zone, makes me nervous. They don't even have a bank back of those targets." He looked at Stefan. "Care if I give you a piece of advice? Stay clear of the whole bunch. They'll make nothing but trouble for you."

"You can't always avoid trouble."

"I can tell you've had some acquaintance."

Sadie motioned at the ripped sign. "Can we get that off our dinner table?"

Henry tossed it over his shoulder.

They finished the rest of their pizza in silence. Stefan pushed his chair back and settled his hat back on his head. "Thanks for supper. Hit the spot."

Sadie stacked their paper plates. "I'll walk you out."

They headed for the bike sitting in the driveway. Stefan straddled the motorcycle, shook a cigarette out of his pack and placed it in the corner of his mouth. He looked over the end of it at her.

"Well, that was interesting." He lit it with his lighter and offered her a hit.

"You're getting me hooked."

"So, you gonna follow your dad's advice?"

"Are you?"

"It's my vocation, staying out of trouble."

"Dad exaggerated, or maybe Bolton did. The horse reared and I fell. Okay . . . I tore a sign off a tree. I'd do it again. But that's all that happened."

"Who'd you have the conversation with?" he asked.

"The younger one, Danny, I guess his name is. Said you broke what's-his-name's ribs. Zender?"

"Zender was the one who caught me from behind. The one with the tattoo was behind the counter running the show."

"He had a gun."

Stefan drew slowly on the cigarette with narrowed eyes. It flared and faded, and still he held it to his lips.

Wolf came out of his doghouse with his tail wagging and heeled at Stefan's boot.

"Dammit, Dog—I mean Wolf—quit hounding us."

Stefan smiled and scratched his floppy ears. "Good dog needed a good name."

She kicked at the ground. "I looked for the boomerang."

"I took a walk around earlier too. It's out there. Couldn't go anywhere on its own."

"Wolf wouldn't have picked it up."

"Didn't say he did."

"We'll find it, Stefan."

"Sure, we will." They smoked the cigarette down to the filter. He ground it out on the heel of his boot and put the butt in his shirt pocket.

"Why do you do that?"

"What else should I do with it? Don't see an ashtray. Besides, wouldn't want him to think you've been out here smoking. He already has a low opinion of me."

"Why do you say that?"

"I can tell."

"He hasn't exactly been inspiring high opinion of himself lately."

"He reminds me of my father." Stefan looked down at the bike. He was getting attached, and it wasn't even his. "I should get going," he said.

He turned the key in the ignition and revved the throttle.

Sadie stepped back. "See you tomorrow?"

He gave her a nod, lifted his feet to the pedals, and rolled down the driveway, wondering exactly where the hell he was going.

Sadie watched him disappear over a rise in the road and went back inside. Henry was still sitting at the table with his hand around an empty beer can and looking out the window at nothing.

"Dad—"

He looked at her and blinked.

"I want to invite them all over for dinner on Sunday, roast a stuffed chicken, you know, like Mom used to do."

"Dinner?"

"She would've already done it. We're forgetting our manners."

Of late, it seemed manners were in the *before* category. As were Sunday dinners and roast chicken, but she suddenly had a powerful urge to put on an apron, stuff a chicken, and look up old recipes.

"You like this fella?"

She was surprised. "Yeah, I do."

"We don't know where he and his family will end up, do we?"

She didn't say anything, but it wasn't like she hadn't thought about that.

"What's the deadline for fall registration?"

The abrupt change in topic caught her off guard. "I missed fall."

"Winter, then."

"I don't want to go back." She had lost all interest in higher learning.

He cracked his knuckles.

"You'll need help around here, and there won't be anyone to ride the horses and take care of the house and—"

"We don't need taking care of."

"I just want to be here. Here with you and Grandpa."

"A couple of old farts."

"You aren't old. But I'd rather a couple of old farts than a dorm full of girls I don't have anything in common with. Girls who hang used rubbers on their closet doors."

"*What?*"

"Yeah, my roommate did that."

"You never told us."

"Not something I wanted to share."

"You should have told us *that*," Henry said angrily.

"It's okay. I got over it."

"I thought you wanted to be a writer."

"I don't have to go to college to be a writer. I can sit in the haymow or your deer blind and do that. More inspiration there than at Severn, and it doesn't cost anything."

"What about the community college? Keep your feet in the water."

She chewed on a fingernail. "I'll check into it… if it'll make you happy."

He poured himself a finger of whiskey and swirled the glass. It changed color in the light. He fastened his eyes on her. "Yes, it would."

Excusing herself, Sadie left the kitchen and headed for the bathroom. She drew herself a tub of hot water and lowered herself in.

The water eddied between her legs, an ebb and flow. She closed her eyes and thought about the intimacy of a shared cigarette—the heat and the flame, the passing back and forth over the dog at their feet. She had already been hooked, hooked from the moment he looked up at her from under the brim of his hat. Hooked on a transient who was only passing through.

CHAPTER 14

Nobody was home, so Stefan didn't have to worry about arranging his face or measuring his words. He showered, washed the chaff out of his hair, and combed it back in a tight ponytail, then wrapped a towel around his middle. He checked the refrigerator out of habit and settled on a beer.

There was mail on the table, the first since they'd arrived in Sawyers Pond. He leafed through the stack—advertising flyers, sales catalogs, and what he would come to know as junk. But at the bottom of the pile were two personal pieces. The first was addressed to Margaret Montegrand, and he recognized Joachim's handwriting. He hefted it and tried to decipher the date on the smudged postmark. He propped it up against the salt and pepper shakers, then looked at the other; an airmail envelope from the Department of Indian Affairs in Ottawa.

It was addressed to a Mr. Stefano Montegrand. It took him a second. Other than his father, nobody ever used his given name. There was a "forward" stamp in the corner from the Women's Center in Rainy River.

Nothing good ever came out of Ottawa. He drank his beer and lit a cigarette, forgetting his mother's admonition about smoking in the house. He slit the envelope open and drew out a sheet of heavy bond paper with a raised seal. He read it through once, then read it again.

It was an official notification of a pending wire transfer of funds from Joachim Montegrand to Stefano Montegrand. The Dené Nation Bank of Shipyard, Saskatchewan, would initiate the wire transfer upon notification of the recipient's account information, the receiving bank's routing number, and officer signature.

The transfer involved mineral royalties paid out to the eldest sons of Dené elders as defined under the treaty signed in 1989. A copy of a statement relinquishing any and all future royalties as bequeathed to him by treaty signatories and assigning them to Stefano Montegrand was signed by Joachim and notarized by a bank official.

What the hell? He dropped the documents on the oilcloth and tipped his chair back on two legs. The clock on the wall ticked the passage of time. The chair creaked.

His eyes fell on the other envelope addressed to his mom. He needed an explanation, and with no compunction, he opened the envelope with his penknife.

It was a cashier's check for the proceeds from the land settlement. Joachim had included a note.

Dear Mom,

I kept out what I needed, like you asked. This should be enough to get you settled wherever you decide to go. I'll keep the jeep. After I go to Prince Albert and finalize things, I'll head to Black Bay for the ceremony and then I'm going up to the Churchill River area. I'll call you from there. Tell Stef I'm not going to need the royalty money, but I have a feeling he will. He will understand.

Joachim

What was he supposed to understand? That his older brother was disengaging himself from his family? Where was his, *Stefano's,* letter of explanation?

It all became clear. Joachim wasn't meeting up with them like he had promised. It was all a ruse to get them to leave.

The cigarette was dead in the ashtray. He was out of cigarettes and out of beer.

He pulled on a T-shirt, a clean pair of jeans, and yanked the tarp off the motorcycle parked behind the adjacent house.

"Stef, is that you?" Larry Wixom was at the back door.

"Yeah, hey, I was gonna ask—I need something in town—if it's okay."

"I put some mail on your table that was mixed in with ours. Did you get it?"

"Yeah. Thanks."

"Come in when you get back. We'll have a beer."

"Okay, sure. Thanks, you know, for letting me use the bike."

Larry nodded, and waved him off.

The convenience store at the edge of town sold cigarettes and beer. They were loose with ID and it was a safe distance from the gas station. He parked in front of the door.

He bought two packs of cigarettes and a tallboy of Canadian Moosehead lager.

The girl at the register snapped her gum and looked at the dusty can of beer. "Where'd you find that?"

He jabbed a thumb over his shoulder. "In back. Top shelf."

"Is it any good?"

"Yeah, it's good. I'm surprised you carry it."

She trailed a finger through the coat of dust on the top of the can. "Me too." She wiped her finger on her pants and looked him over. "You new in town?"

"Yeah."

She looked out the window. "Is that your bike?"

"Yeah," he lied, and put the cigarettes in his pocket before grabbing the beer.

"Whoa, gotta put it in a bag. Take-out law." She opened a paper sack and dropped it inside. "Wanna drop the smokes in here too?"

"Naw, I'm good."

She leaned over the register as if to get a better look at him. He felt the probe of her perusal down to his boots.

"I'm Nan," she said.

He wet his lips. No one had ever come on to him so blatantly, and it took him a few seconds to process.

"Name's Stef."

"I'd love a ride on that bike, Stef. It's an Indian, isn't it?"

"Yeah."

"Are you?"

There was music coming from the back room and the sharp clack of a break announced the pool game in progress behind the curtain draped across the doorway.

"An Indian, that is?"

"What's back there?" he asked.

"Pool tables. Dad's trying to expand his business, make enough to support me and my extravagant habits." She rolled her eyes and looked at her nails.

"You mean billiards?"

"Fancy." she said.

He crossed the floor and pulled the curtain back. There were four full-size tables with a light over each one. Smoke drifted in the air and high-top tables with stools were set up along the wall. The scene called to mind a different place, a rough-hewn room with tar paper walls and dim lights, the shuffle of men moving about with low voices, and the click of the billiard balls. He was back at the council house where Jake taught him how to hold a cue stick longer than he was tall. He never got as good as Jake. Jake used to play for money though their father frowned on it. Said it was for hustlers and white men.

"There's an open table," she said over his shoulder. "Do you play?"

Her breath smelled like bubble gum, and the timber of her voice, the way she leaned against him—the soft thrust in the small of his back—reminded him of a girl back home. He missed a lot of things about home. He missed Rory, Jake, and now Joachim. Joachim the loner, always off the rails, always impulsive.

He wasn't stupid. He knew what the wire transfer meant. It meant responsibility, for Abby, Mother, and oversight of mineral royalties. It wasn't fair. He wasn't even twenty-one and he didn't want any of it.

The player closest to them leaned over the green with a cigarette in the corner of his mouth and took aim at a corner pocket. The targeted ball ricocheted off the felt and ended up back in front of him.

Nan laughed. "Oops," she said.

The player turned and stared at them. It was Clem Bolton. He looked at Stefan.

"You again?"

Stef dropped the curtain. He had what he came for and didn't need this.

But Clem followed them to the front of the store. "What's in the bag?"

"It's none of your business, Clem," Nan said.

"Obvious what's in the bag. Did you card him?"

"Why do you care?"

Clem wielded the cue stick like a javelin, blocking Stefan's path. Nan stepped behind the register and picked up her cell phone.

"Put it down, baby. Check his ID before your daddy loses his liquor license."

She looked at Stefan. "You got one?"`

"He don't. He's illegal." Clem grabbed the paper bag and set it back on the counter.

Stefan looked at the bag holding his dusty can of beer. It wasn't worth it. Larry had beer.

Nan leaned over the counter. "I owe you money."

He backed away. "Run me a credit, okay?"

"Yeah, run him a credit, like the Indos do at their casinos. Yeah, I've been there, seen how you people operate, drawing us in with drinks and lights, ATMs and credit vouchers."

Stefan felt his jaw clench. "I don't know what the hell you're talking about," he said.

"This ain't Indian country." Clem said, pointing the pool cue at the door. "I suggest you get back to it."

"He lost a bundle at the casino," Nan told Stefan. "Lost your car, didn't you, Clem?"

"You into him? A dirty Indian that smells like jerky?"

She laughed. "I love jerky."

Stefan turned for the door. He had more important things on his plate, a beer with Larry, the problem Joachim had presented, a talk with his mother—

"Seen you hanging around those Wixoms. You like the way that chick rides bareback? She was over my way today, little titties loose and bouncing."

Stefan knocked the cue stick out of Clem's hand with a lightning-fast reaction and drove his fist into the center of his smirk. Blinded by anger, he threw a follow-up punch from off the balls of his feet, but Clem jumped back in time, and Stefan's momentum landed him on the counter. A display of energy drinks crashed to the floor, and Nan screamed. Clem grabbed Stefan by the neck and threw an uppercut that cracked his head against the register.

He was falling through a dark whirl of space but sensed the knee coming at him, like a torpedo through water. He twisted to the side, but it caught him in the groin and pain exploded through his middle. Laughter came at him through the dark, and all the snide remarks and disparaging looks of the past few weeks coalesced in his gut like a brick.

On a rush of adrenaline, Stefan landed a punch to the side of Clem Bolton's head that dropped him like a broken zipline.

"Shit." Nan stared wide-eyed and snapped her gum. "I think you killed him."

Stefan hunched over, protecting the hurt and gasping for breath.

Nan nudged Clem with her foot. "He's dead."

Stefan spat blood on the floor. "He ain't dead," he croaked.

"Shit, you're a mess." She handed him a tissue.

He pressed it against his mouth. He'd bitten his tongue, and a throbbing pain emanated from the back of his head. His nuts were on fire.

The back room had emptied at the commotion and a silent circle gathered around them.

"Cops ain't gonna like this, Nan. It's that same guy."

"He didn't start it, Eddie," Nan said. "I'll vouch for that. And put that fucking cell phone away. Any of you assholes call the cops—" she swung her eyes over the lot of them— "you'll just get me in trouble and shut us down. Y'all like shooting pool and smoking in a public place?"

There were mumbles of agreement.

"Then get back to it, all of you."

Clem rolled to his side and groaned.

"Here," she said quickly, "take this." She handed Stefan the paper bag. "Go on, git!"

He pushed the door open with his elbow and limped to the bike, fumbled with the snaps on the saddlebag and dropped the beer inside. He adjusted himself with a wince and threw a leg over the saddle. The street lights were distorted, and the lines on the pavement wavered in front of him. He gunned the throttle, lifted his feet to the pedals, and took aim at the center of the road.

When he cleared the end of town, the street lights fell off behind him, but the high beams from tailing traffic glanced off his mirrors and blurred his vision. He yanked the bike off the highway at the next crossroad. He hit a patch of loose gravel and skidded sideways. He dropped his foot, and the drag of the road tested the well-nailed heel of his boot. He found the foot pedals and eased the bike back to center.

His vision cleared, but his head hurt from the impact with the cash register. He should go home, but he couldn't go home. He didn't know where he was going. He needed to think, but images of Nan snapping her gum—there would be no conflicting signals from that one—crowded out constructive thought.

Then there was Joachim, signing away royalties in his scrawl of a signature and driving his beat-up jeep into the wilderness of the Churchill River area, which was about as far north as you could go while still being in habitable lands.

He didn't know where he intended to go. He just knew he needed to *go*.

CHAPTER 15

Sadie was turning off the lights and locking the doors when she heard the motorcycle. She opened the back door and watched Stefan climb off the bike and limp up the walk.

She dropped her eyes down the front of him, taking in his disheveled appearance.

"What happened?!"

"Is there someplace we can talk?"

She led him through the house to the front porch and slid the door shut on a silent track. She sat beside him on the wicker settee, tucking her feet underneath her.

She took in the abrasion on his chin and the gravel caught in the lacings of his boots. "What happened?" she said again. "Did you dump the bike?"

He wiped his hands on his jeans. "No. Close, but no."

She waited him out. He rested his elbows on his knees and then looked at her sideways. "Remember how I told you we were waiting for my brother to meet up with us? How he was supposed to be coming? Well, he isn't."

He told her about the letter, and Sadie let out a soft whistle.

"Maybe I'm a little dense but it sounds like winning the lottery to me." Sadie said.

"It's not that simple. He was supposed to join us once things were settled back home. This means he's not."

"How do you know?"

"I just know. I don't like it. I knew we shouldn't have left without him. I just knew it."

"He must have a reason."

"The way I look at it, he's the oldest. He should handle it."

"The way I look at it, this means he trusts you and wants to empower you. What's wrong with that?"

"Empower?" He scoffed. "What a word."

"You can go to school, do anything you want."

"You sound like my mom. That's the last thing I want."

"Well—" she lifted a shoulder in a half shrug—"I get that. Guess you could call me a dropout."

He looked around the porch. "Can we smoke out here?"

She pointed at the ashtray on the wicker table, and he struck a match. The flame flared and the tip of the cigarette glowed in the dark.

He felt the back of his head with his fingers again and winced.

Sadie rocked back on her heels. "Did you hit your head?"

"Something like that."

"Something like that? You either did or you didn't." She leaned over him and felt the back of his head with her fingers. His hair was wet and sticky, and he had a knot like a duck egg. "Geez, what happened?"

He shook his head. "Nothing."

"Nothing," she mimicked. "Right, well, you should put some ice on it. Hold on." She untangled her legs. "I'll get some."

She tiptoed through the kitchen, knocked some ice cubes in a baggie, grabbed a towel, and went back to the porch. With the towel wrapped around his head like a turban, she sat back and considered him.

"So, Stefan, tell me again what happened."

He shrugged and smoked his cigarette.

"I mean, you were just starting to look normal."

"Humph." He tapped the cigarette over the ashtray.

"Let me guess. You were in town raising Cain again."

"Doing what?"

"Never mind." She shook her head. "It's just a figure of speech."

"I needed a cigarette, but I guess this *free country* isn't so free. Think I've seen enough of this free country."

She pursed her lips.

"Go back to *Indo* country and see what big brother is up to," he said.

"What are you talking about?"

"Here—" he handed her the cigarette— "hold this. I'll be right back."

She took it and placed her lips where his had been, the heat from a draw warming her from the inside.

He went out the side door, disappearing in the dark. She held the cigarette between her lips, wanting him back.

When he returned, the towel was still wrapped around his head and she laughed. "If Bolton saw you now, he'd really be alarmed."

He popped the tab on a can of beer and handed it to her. "Here, have a drink of Moosehead."

She took a sip and wiped her mouth on the back of her hand. "About what you were saying—you weren't serious, were you?"

"About what?"

"About leaving."

"Nobody harasses you back home because you want a beer and a cigarette."

"Bolton again?"

He studied the burning end of the menthol. "Do you know the girl who works at the party store?"

Sadie frowned. "In town?"

"Yeah, name of Nan."

"Nan? Everybody knows Nan. She was a year ahead of me." She paused. "She hit you?"

Stefan laughed. "No, she knows Indian bikes. I guess that surprised me, and something about her, I don't know, she reminded me of Joachim."

"Nan reminds you of your brother?"

"Calling things what they are."

A kernel of jealousy seeded itself in the bottom of her gut. She changed the subject before it could take root.

"What's this brother of yours like anyway?"

He took a drag on the cigarette and touched his chin.

"He has this bristly little beard he keeps trying to grow, and his hair sticks out all over." He smiled. "He had a beat-up skiff he called his *rez* canoe. He'd putter around the watershed, always knew when the salmon were starting to run before anyone else. Then they started floating. He was one of the first to raise an alarm. He sold the skiff and the outboard motor and got himself a beat-up jeep. Turned into a landlubber. Started poking around the works of the *trespassers*, he called them. He helped Dad supervise the building of the cabin they erected by the roadblock, you know, the one I told you about."

He tapped the ash off his cigarette and gazed at the rope swing swaying in the moonlight.

"Joachim's holding something back. I can feel it. And the money is a way for him to convince himself that we don't need him. Maybe I don't."

His mouth stitched itself into a thin line. "Maybe I don't, but I warrant Abby does. She always listened to him."

"Is she still out with Sam?"

He shrugged. "I suppose so, probably getting tattooed up, even though I told her not to."

"Don't you think she's too young for him?"

"I think age matters more here than it did back home."

"Oh?"

"First thing everyone wants to know—after your nationality, of course—is how old you are. Like then they can judge if you can buy a beer, or drive, or get a job. Or date a girl." He looked at her. "How old are you, anyway?"

"How old are *you*?"

"Twenty-one in October."

"So, you fooled them back at that bar."

"It means nothing, this magic number you have here."

"It's just a benchmark. Don't be so critical."

"I suppose you think I'm too old for you?"

She laughed. "Hardly."

He dropped his arm around her shoulder. "I don't think so either," he said.

He ran his thumb across her bottom lip and lowered his head to kiss her, but the towel, wet with melting ice, slipped off his forehead. Sadie tossed it aside, took him by the collar and kissed him on the mouth.

Having replayed the amateur moment at the roadside park *ad nauseam*, she was determined to not make the same mistake. She kissed him the way she should have kissed him then.

Stefan groaned and draped his leg over hers. He nuzzled the soft skin below her jaw and ran his tongue around the lobe of her ear. The probing warmth dropped a sinker through her middle. He loosened the drawstring on her lounge pants and slipped his hand between her legs. His fingers inched under the elastic of her panties, and she froze under the paralyzing flood of sensation. She wanted to rid herself of her onerous virginity, but this was too much too fast. She thought of her insomniac of a father with his penchant for wandering around. The image had the effect of a wet towel.

"Don't," she whispered, forcing his hand back. "Dad . . . he's always walking around."

Stefan sat up with a mumbled curse. "So, lock the door." He looked at the one in question. "There's a lock on that slider. Lock it."

Sadie took a deep breath to settle the turbulence in her center. *God.* Kissing him the way she wanted to had rapidly led to more than she was ready for.

An owl hooted from the pear tree to echo her whispered, "We can't. Not here. I can't."

He was silent, and she clasped his hand, needing him to understand.

"I'm sorry, Stefan. It's just, I've never, you know—" she broke off, measuring her words, trying to explain. "I've never been with a guy."

He sat up straighter. "Never?"

"Never."

He didn't say anything—he of already few words—and she wondered what he was thinking. It was a rude thing to ask someone, her mother had always said, prying into someone's thoughts.

"I'm sorry," he said finally. "Sorry for pushing you. I assumed you had. That you wanted what I want."

"I do. Just, not yet. Not *here*."

He ran his fingers through her hair, and a smile touched his lips. "I can wait if you can. Just tell me when, baby."

It was the first time he had called her that, and a warm feeling filled her like a mug of hot cocoa. The *when* wasn't far off. But there was still so much she didn't know about him.

In a backdoor way of combing his thoughts, she steered the conversation back to him. Back to their conversation at the roadside park and the subject he had touched on about his own societal differences; the tug-of-war between the old and the new, the mysticism of the elders versus the obsession of the younger generation with personal possessions fostered by the progress introduced to natives in the north by the missionary schools and then carried into their homes by electricity, electronics, and gadgetry.

"Tell me more, Stef, what you touched on at the roadside park. Tell me about *your* Canada."

And he did.

Safe from marauding insects in the seclusion of the screened-in porch, it was easy to lose track of time. She relaxed to the soft murmur of his voice and sensed he was telling her more than he would normally speak of. From the day he lost his younger brother, Rory—just shy of fifteen—to his father's incarceration and their land's imminent flooding.

"So, we have color TV," he said, finishing on a somber note. "But we don't hear the ducks singing anymore."

"That's a sad way to put it," Sadie said.

"Yes." His eyes were dark orbs in the night. "I suppose it is."

Within the context of the safer subject, Sadie shared her own concern with the hypothetical—what if one day the moon went off track? How would that affect the lakes, the tides, and the wildlife? What about the rising sea levels and the melting ice caps? All the *what-ifs?* And he told her of the star knowledge passed down through the generations, the folklore associated with the aurora borealis, the tsunami in the sky.

"I don't know about the ice caps, but the moon will always be there," he said.

She turned her face into the fabric of his shirt, the drum of his abdomen, and the whisper of his reassurance caught in the whorls of her mind, like his fingers in her hair.

Later, after he left, she was filled with regret. After he left, she only wanted him back and wondered if she had imagined what he had whispered in the dark. *We'll always be here.* What he had whispered conflicted with what he'd said, his obvious yearning for home. She wondered whether he would stay or whether he would go.

A morning ground fog hung over the fields as Stefan lifted his feet to the pedals and rolled down the driveway. It burned off in reluctant degrees as he took the long way home.

He eased himself in the door and hung his hat on a peg. Coffee brewed on the counter, and his mother sat stalwart at the table wrapped in a throw with a stoic expression, looking more Native than she ever had at White Lake.

"Abby get home?"

"Abby did." Her eyes followed him as he gimped stiffly across the room and poured himself a cup of coffee. "What happened to you?"

He adjusted himself, still sore from Clem's knee in his scrotum. "Just a little stiff," he said.

"Where were you?"

"At Sadie's," he said.

She raised an eyebrow. "All night?"

It wasn't what he wanted to talk about. He pulled a chair up to the table and looked at the letters propped against the salt shaker. "Did you know about all that?" He waved a hand in their direction.

"Some of it. I knew about the treaty, of course. But I didn't—"

"I don't understand," Stefan said, perplexed. You're Dad's heir."

"It was a separate issue, something that was negotiated for future generations."

"Why doesn't he want it?"

"It's complicated."

"Complicated? Then why doesn't the sonofabitch call?"

"When did you start cussing so much?"

"I don't want it," he said.

"I don't think you're in a position to refuse it."

"He won't take it, but he expects me to?"

"He's afraid the account could be garnished if it's in his name," she said.

"By who? The outfit that had to pay out?"

"No, not them."

"What'd he do now?"

"I don't know." She rubbed her hand across her eyes. "I'm afraid for him."

"He needs to get out of there and meet up with us like we all agreed."

"I can't make him come if he doesn't want to," she said.

"This isn't what we agreed on. All this—" he waved his hand across the table— "it's too much."

Her eyes settled on him, assessing the musculature of his shoulders and arms. They were defined and articulated. No longer those of a boy.

"You're almost twenty-one," she said.

"I know how old I am."

"He trusts you to be in charge, to do the right thing."

He drummed his fingers on the table. "Larry wants to sell that bike."

"Don't talk crazy," she snapped. She wrapped the blanket tighter around herself.

"I'll need my own wheels if I'm to be in charge. I'm gonna buy it and then I'm going back home."

"You know what Joachim would have to say about that."

"He doesn't have much to say about anything anymore, does he?"

"He trusts you to be responsible, not go off on some crazy road trip."

"Crazy?"

"You think he wants you tracking him down?"

"I know where Churchill River is."

"Running the breadth of the province? On a motorcycle? With winter coming?"

"He's probably holed up with that woman from Indian Affairs. He's wanted in her pants for a while now."

"I wish you wouldn't talk like that."

"It's the truth."

The silence stretched out between them and Stefan let out a sigh.

"Look, Mom. There's plenty of time before winter comes."

"You're being unreasonable." She put the coffee cup down on the table and folded her hands in her lap, a mountain of reasonableness. He pushed his chair back, picked up the letter from the bank in Ottawa, turned it over in his hands, and dropped it back on the table.

"I'm tired, gonna get some sleep."

"It's morning and you need to sleep?" She studied him with the wisdom of one who has raised four boys and lost two. "You need to go to the bank," she said.

"It can wait a couple of hours, can't it?"

"I suppose it can."

"Wake me if he calls." He pulled his shirt off and headed for the bedroom.

He dropped his pants by the bed, pulled the window shade down, and climbed between the cool of the sheets, stretching his legs and curling his toes over the end of the mattress. He hadn't pulled an all-nighter since the time he and Joachim drove through the night to watch the salmon run. That was a long time ago.

He tucked his hands between his legs and fell asleep.

CHAPTER 16

Stefan stood in the doorway of the office the bank teller had directed him to and waited for the loan officer behind the desk to acknowledge him.

The man looked up and motioned Stefan to a chair.

He took a step forward and twirled his hat.

"Sit down, son."

His name was Goudy, according to the plaque on his desk.

Stefan sat.

Goudy folded his hands on the desk. "What can I do for you?"

Stefan handed him the letter stamped with the government seal.

The man settled a pair of glasses on his nose and read it over. He looked up. "Well..." It was all he could seem to say. Time slowed. Stefan loosened his collar and resisted the urge to check the egg-sized knot on the back of his head. It seemed to have swelled in the night.

The bank officer was talking and Stefan blinked.

"Pardon?"

"I said, do you have an account here?"

"No sir. I need to open one."

"Yes, you do, son. Do you have identification?"

Stefan handed him his territorial card. The man frowned and turned it over, looking for more information.

"What else you got?"

Stefan handed him a copy of the electric bill. "I understand this will work for proof of address."

He studied the bill, Stefan's ID, then read the letter again. He tapped his finger on Joachim's signature. "This a relation?"

"He's my brother."

Goudy picked up the phone, then hesitated. "You understand we've not dealt with this before?"

Stefan nodded and twirled his hat.

The process took an hour.

The Xerox machine pumped out copies while distant phones rang intrigue and finance through the bowels of the bank. A clerk in spiked heels wobbled in and out. Stefan lost track of the number of forms but the figures stayed the same. There was a signature line at the bottom of each one, and with every stroke of the pen, it started to sink in. Joachim was passing control of a sizable fund.

By the time Goudy stood and shook his hand, he had become the object of attention—various bank employees walking by the glassed-in office, whispering conjecture in the hallway and casting glances at the dark-skinned stranger with a ponytail.

Stefan left the building with advice on CPAs and IRAs, and an account in his name which would hold the funds by the end of the business day. He slipped the bankbook in the inside pocket of his jacket, climbed on the bike, and revved the engine, empowered.

The bell tinkled above the convenience door and echoed in the empty store. He set a beer on the counter with his territorial card and drummed his fingers.

Nan came out of the restroom wiping her hands on a paper towel. Her eyes widened and she tucked a strand of hair behind her ear.

"Well." She took a stance behind the counter. "You are a ballsy one."

"Slow time?"

"Very. The gang doesn't start dropping in 'til after three. What's this?" She looked at his ID card.

"That's my ID."

She turned it over. "Might as well throw down a library card. How am I supposed to know how old you are?"

"Guess you'll have to take my word."

"That'll go over with Liquor Control."

"It's good enough for banking. Oughta be good enough for drinking."

"This ain't a bank, sweetie." She snapped her gum. "I get off at nine. Why don't you stop by, meet me out front and give me a ride on that bike of yours?"

He ignored that. "If I shoot some pool, can you sell me some beer?"

She looked at the clock behind his head. "You have until five. Trouble never comes in before five." She opened the register. "Need quarters?"

He knew all about trouble, and he had a score to settle. But right now, he needed to relax and think. He needed a game of pool.

She pulled the cord on the light hanging over one of the pool tables. While she racked the balls, he selected a cue and chalked it.

He hadn't played since leaving White Lake, but everything was the same. The tables were the same size, the balls were the same color, the weight of the cue was true, and the chalk was blue. Even the pool of light cast over the green was the same.

He moved quietly around the table, finding his rhythm, feeling at home. She poured the beer into two steins and watched until the bell on the door called her to the front.

They played two games and then the rubber match down to the eight ball. Nan missed her shot, setting him up, and he knocked it into a corner pocket.

He hung his cue back on the wall rack and she pulled the light cord.

"Shark," she said as the room went dark.

"You should see my brother."

"Yeah? He around?"

"No." He shrugged his jacket on. "I'm outta here."

"See you at nine?"

"Not sure about that." And he wasn't.

"I'm not waiting around. If you want to give me a ride, be here at nine."

He followed her to the front, let a customer pass at the door, and touched the brim of his hat with his finger. He straddled the bike and opened the throttle, feeling empowered by the thunderstroke engine, the bankbook in his pocket, and discovering himself to be the object of desire.

He accelerated into a sharp curve on a tilt that defied gravity. He looped back and forth across the center line, nosing on and off the gravel berm, testing the bike's readiness for a trek into the boreal forests of Saskatchewan. And like a robot gone rogue—a flash of chrome, oiled pistons, and spacious saddlebags—it flew past the Wixom farm on a mind of its own.

The wind in his hair soothed the ache of homesickness, his bone-weary companion. But the glimpse of her car sitting at the top of the driveway as if about to depart, slowed his hand, an inanimate object governing the animate as he circled back in her direction.

CHAPTER 17

Sadie awoke from her own late morning nap to a lingering sense of regret. She rolled over, hugged her pillow, and thought about the night before. The ebb and flow of his voice, and the smell of denim and cigarette smoke.

Had she imagined a connection, a settling in? As dawn broke, he had left so abruptly—as if coming to his senses—she wondered if she was mistaken.

She pulled on a clean tank top and went downstairs to make an iced coffee. The maple tree outside the kitchen window was full of clamoring sparrows. A pair of raucous blue jays perched on top of the empty bird feeder while finches pecked away at hulls on the ground. She tapped on the window and the jays flew off.

She rummaged through the broom closet intending to fill the bird feeders, but came across the car wax and changed direction. She gathered up a handful of clean rags, and filled a bucket at the hydrant. She turned the Duster's key to auxiliary to play the radio, leaving the trunk open to the speakers.

She started on the roof and worked her way down the hood, applying the paste in overlapping circles to the beat of the music. Wolf lay in the grass with his head on his paws and followed the hypnotizing movements with his eyes.

After coating the roof and hood with paste, she knelt in the grass to do the quarter panels when Henry walked out of the tool shed and stopped to watch.

"Sounds like a party out here." He wiped his hands on a rag.

She looked at him. "There's an idea." Her mother was always the initiator of parties. Parties were in the *before* category.

"She running okay?"

"Unfortunately."

"You don't need a car payment, going to school," he reminded her. "You remember to check the oil? Keep an eye on your tire pressure?"

She laughed. "Really, Dad . . ."

"You won't be laughing if you end up on the side of the road."

"That's why they invented cell phones."

He snorted.

"When you get done there, how about washing my truck?"

She stopped to look at him. His jeans were cinched on the last hole of his belt and bunched around the tops of his boots laced halfway. He needed a haircut.

"Remind me tomorrow," he said. "I'll change your oil." He headed for the porch and paused at the door.

"Hey, Sade, vacuum it out while you're at it, okay?"

She stared as he disappeared behind the screen door.

The Duster shone like a new penny and the truck was as clean as it had ever been. She rolled up the garden hose and hung the floor mats across the fence to dry. The shop vac was full of loose gravel, screws, pennies, and all sorts of rattling nondescript debris from under his seat. She emptied it into the trash barrel.

Finished, she drove into town for groceries. Without thinking, she walked through the beer and wine and found herself looking for Moosehead. On her way out of town, she noticed a motorcycle parked in front of the party store. She slowed and craned her neck.

From the saddlebags to the slope of the handlebars, it looked dishearteningly familiar. She drove around the block for another look, not believing he would go back. But then, the party store was the only place in town where a guy could get Moosehead.

She parked across the street and pried her hands off the wheel. She wanted to go inside, see what Nan was up to. Practice her nonchalance, maybe even play some pool. But she knew she couldn't pull it off. The confidence that girls like Nan exuded had never been something Sadie could master.

Besides, she couldn't play pool.

She sped out of town with the front end of the car shaking, making a mental note to get her tires rotated. After she put the groceries away, she caught her reflection in the hallway mirror. She was in obvious need of a makeover.

She wet her hair over the bathroom sink and trimmed her bangs with her mother's sewing scissors, then rummaged through her vanity for makeup. She experimented with the eyes and the lips, blotting and redrawing. She pulled on a spandex tank, shook herself into the built-in bra, wrapped the Che sarong around her hips, and stood in front of the floor-length mirror.

Her father appeared behind her in the mirror, and their eyes met. His hair was slicked back and he had donned a starched shirt from the *before* part of his closet. His shoes were polished and the shirt was tucked in.

They were unfamiliar to each other.

"Your grandpa fed the horses, threw hay down to the cattle . . ." His voice trailed off as he looked her over. "You forgot about that, did you?"

In fact, she had.

"Where are you going in that get-up?"

She flushed and tightened the knot on the sarong. "Nowhere. What about you?"

He looked down at himself. "Going out to dinner. Do I look okay?"

"Where?"

"That new seafood place over on the lake."

She raised an eyebrow.

"I'm taking Margie. She asked me." He grinned sheepishly, which dropped years from his face. Sadie felt a twinge through her middle as the recognition of what should have been apparent all along reared its head.

"The truck looks good. You did a good job."

"Thanks," she tilted her head.

His collar was up in the back. She smoothed it down, gave his shirt pocket a pat, stepped back, and smiled.

"You look great, Dad."

When Henry left, she studied herself in the floor-length glass again. In the Che wrap with her newly crafted bangs and mascaraed eyelashes, she looked like someone who wouldn't be afraid to stand up for what she wanted.

The rumbling sound of an approaching motorcycle echoed through the house, interrupting her critical self-assessment. She felt it in her gut and tightened the sarong around her hips. The fabric draped her legs in a seductive whisper as she glided across the wooden floor.

As she walked through the dining room, the motorcycle coasted by the window with Wolf nipping at the tires. She adjusted herself into the built-in bra that was suddenly too small as the dog followed Stefan to the stoop, barking for attention.

He crouched beside him and scratched his jowls. Wolf rolled over on his back with his legs in the air, and Stefan rubbed his belly, the muscle in the dog's leg gyrating like a jackhammer.

Sadie smiled at the sight of him on the ground with the dog and opened the screen.

"Hi," she said.

He jumped to his feet and her confidence soared at the look on his face when he saw her. She motioned him inside and led him through the kitchen, aware of his eyes on her backside, and she, holding the upper hand.

She opened the refrigerator and casually said, "So, where've you been?"

"I, ah, I was at the bank."

"Oh, yeah, the bank. Want something to drink? I don't have Moosehead," she added quickly.

"That's fine, whatever. What's that you have on?"

"This silly thing?" She looked down at herself. "It's a sarong. It was my mom's."

He opened his bottle with a twist, lit a cigarette without asking, and shoved the lighter back in his pocket. He held the smoke in the bottom of his lungs, and his eyes moved over her.

She sat at the counter and tucked the sarong around her legs. "What?"

"You look . . . different."

She touched the hair on her forehead. "I cut my bangs."

He took a pull from the bottle. "No, it's that gunk around your eyes."

"It's called *makeup*, and you shouldn't smoke in here."

"You don't need makeup."

"Is that your idea of a compliment?"

"But I like the sarong." With his accent and syllabic emphasis, it came out *so wrong*.

She looked down at herself, wishing to God she hadn't seen him at Nan's place because now that was all she could see. She couldn't control the petty line of questioning she hadn't wanted to get embroiled in.

"I saw you in town."

"You did?"

"Parked out front of Nan's."

"You mean the party store?"

"Same thing."

He peeled the label on the bottle. "Why didn't you stop in?"

"Not old enough."

"To play billiards? There's an age requirement on that too?"

"I suppose you're going to say that's all you were doing?"

He nodded. "That's all I was doing."

"Humph." She opened the liquor cabinet, took out a bottle of Irish Mist, pulled the cork, and upended the bottle. She wiped her mouth and set it down with a thud.

"Whatcha got there?"

"Moonshine. Totally illegal." She pushed it across the table. "So, you'll want some."

"What's wrong with you?"

"You like being on the wrong side of the law, don't you?"

"Not necessarily."

"I'm just trying to get to know you, figure you out."

He handled the bottle and looked at the label. The gold filigree and the genie-shaped fluting. He pushed it away. "I don't drink liquor," he said flatly.

"I'm surprised."

"They have a billiards room in the back of the store. I miss that and felt like a game."

"There's billiards where you're from?"

"Billiards was actually very popular in White Lake."

"Where's that?"

"The closest town with billiards."

"You are full of surprises."

"Why? Because I can do more than ride a horse? I'm not as good as Joachim but I'm good enough to beat your friend."

"She's not my friend," Sadie said quickly. "She was ahead of me in school. She was always bad news."

He drew on his cigarette. "Teachers used to say that about my brother."

Sadie chewed on the side of her mouth.

He nodded towards the porch.

"Why don't we go out there, have some more conversation? You can get to know me." He grinned. "I'm not hard to figure out."

But Sadie was stuck in a rut. "Nan not much of a conversationalist? No, she wouldn't be. Not known for her performance on the debate team."

His smile faded. "What's that?"

"She's known for other things."

"Like what?"

"Are you dense?"

"What're you trying to say?" he said, eyes narrowed.

"Nan's a whore."

"Whoa, she charges?"

"You don't have to be paid to be a whore." Sadie felt hot and hollow.

"I get it, you're jealous."

"Don't be ridiculous."

"You don't have to be jealous."

"Good, 'cause I'm not. I just know what she's like."

Stefan leaned in, as if secrets were being confided. "What's she like?"

"You tell me."

"She's good at pool."

"Then why don't you go back and play some more?" Sadie knocked her chair back and jabbed her thumb at the door. "Go on, get out!"

"Hey." He grabbed her wrist and set his cigarette on a saucer.

"Hey, come on now. Why are we arguing? I don't want to argue." He clasped her other hand and rested his forehead against hers. "I don't want to play pool."

He had persuasive ways, and why drive an argument her heart wasn't in? She didn't want him to leave. She had *never* wanted that.

Sadie thought of a poem by Mary Oliver she had memorized in high school: *What is it you plan to do with your one wild and precious life?*

He tasted like hops and tobacco, all of it bad and all of it good. He lifted her up on the table and her prior reservations were gone. Her doubts dissipated on the breeze that swirled through the open window. It blew papers off the table and ashes around them, like leaves before a storm, and all the birds were singing.

CHAPTER 18

It had been two days since Joachim arrived at Josie's in the middle of the night.

He'd only been half asleep when she'd finished bandaging him up and left the room, but with the click of the door latch, he succumbed to the luxuriant narcotic wave.

He'd dreamt he was in his father's boat with an old man of indeterminable age. The old man was speaking in the language of the Denésuline that had been beaten out of Sonny Montegrand and his friends at the residential boarding school. Though their native tongue had been forbidden, squashed and ridiculed, remnants remained, spoken in secret to pass down to their sons.

In the dream, Joachim understood every word the old man said. He talked of the Bering Sea, the ice ridges, and the bison they hunted and ate. Of the salmon and how they dated back to the woolly mammoth. The old man claimed to have hunted one of those great beasts, rolled underneath its legs, and thrust his spear deep into the animal's entrails. Joachim knew it was true.

Then they were paddling through a sea of floating fish. The old man threw ashes into the water, and then it was his brother floating under the blade of his father's oar, suspended under the surface, face swollen and blue, hair grown long and floating about him like a veil.

Joachim shouted at the old man to stop, but he said it was no use, Jake was dead and should be left like the mammoth fossilized in mud and ice. Joachim knew that also was true.

He awoke in the morning with a dull feeling that echoed the hollowing in his chest. He was cold and troubled by the dream.

Josie was sitting in a chair beside the bed, and she told him his fever broke in the night. She had jotted his temperature readings on a log sheet periodically using an old-style glass tube instrument, but he didn't remember any of that either.

She brought him in a tray of light breakfast.

As the day progressed, the feeling instilled by the dream faded, and he thought the worst was behind him. But that night, his fever again spiked. He fell in and out of coherent thought—his brother again floating in a sea of ash, mammoths, and ice ridges. He awoke in a sweat of delirium.

Josie turned on the light and probed the skin around the bandage. He could feel the heat, and knew by her expression that the redness had spread.

She tried cold compresses on his neck and forehead but couldn't get the fever down. When morning broke, it finally abated, but she assured him the relief would be fleeting. She changed the dressing and helped him dress for the drive to the clinic as he talked more sensibly of his brother, Stefan, and the transfer of royalties she had helped him draw up.

She reclined the front seat, brought along a pillow for his head, and eased the 4x4 through the trees toward the main road.

He emerged from sleep clear-eyed and thirsty, and opened a bottle of water.

"How are you?" Josie asked, glancing at him sideways.

"Stiff," he said, trying to crack his neck. "Sore," he added.

"There's aspirin in the glovebox."

He dug through it for the bottle, tossed three back with a gulp of water, then shifted his position. He put the pillow between his head and the window and watched the sun dance across Josie's profile as they drove in and out of pockets of sunlight. She still bore the scars of an exceptionally hard case of chickenpox. The small white circles stood out on her dark skin like white spots on a fallow deer. Her nose, long and straight, conflicted with her square jaw and broad forehead, competing ancestry splayed across her countenance.

He put his hand on her knee and ran it lightly across the top of her thigh. "I think I'm better, babe. What do you say we skip the clinic, find ourselves a little motel?"

She snorted. "Fevers come and go. Don't be fooled."

"Always so serious."

She looked at him sideways. "Have you talked to Stefan?"

Joachim looked out the window at the scenery. Every hemlock was different, each evergreen a varied shade of watercolor, more shades than there are days in a month, constellations in the sky. Sameness only in the eye of the unschooled.

"No," he said. "He wasn't there."

"Think he'll be okay? Not do anything rash?"

He would explain things to Stefan. Details he had left out of the conversation with his mother. Stefan was good with figures and frugal with money. The only kid who didn't touch his piggy bank.

"He's not a rash kind of kid," he said finally.

The sun was casting shadows across the parking lot when they pulled up to the after-hours entrance.

They were ushered into an exam room, and a nurse took his vitals. The on-call doctor did not make them wait.

"Hey, Murph," Joachim said, "you haven't moved on yet to the big city?"

Charleston Murphy sported a braid down his back and wore a flannel shirt under his lab coat. They went back a long time, back to a one-room schoolhouse, youthful antics, and blood secrets.

"Dr. Murphy." Josie smiled. "I was hoping you'd be on."

"Josie, Joachim." He nodded gravely at each of them in turn. "What brings you two in?"

"It's a shoulder wound. I'm afraid it's infected," Josie said in a rush. "I can't get the fever down."

"A shoulder wound?" He looked at Joachim and shook his head like a disappointed father. He checked his pulse with two fingers and listened to his lungs with his stethoscope. He opened Joachim's shirt, felt the bandage with his fingers. Joachim sucked in his breath. Murphy removed the tape and released the dressing; it came away reluctantly, having grown attached.

He rocked back on his heels and blew out a deep breath.

No one said anything.

He looked at Josie. "You mean a bullet wound."

She dipped her head in a small nod of agreement.

"Did you do the bandaging?"

"Best I could, cleaned it and removed some bone fragments."

"A couple of ribs, you mean," Joachim quipped.

He rolled Joachim on his side and looked at the entry wound, measured entry to exit with a practiced eye.

"Anyone else know about this?" Murphy inquired.

Josie shook her head.

He traced the faint mustache above his lips. "When did this happen?"

Joachim blinked. "When what?"

"When'd you take the bullet?"

Joachim looked at Josie. "Josie, when did it happen?"

"Two nights ago. I'd say around nightfall." She took his hand. "Right, baby? Early evening?"

"Yeah. He had a rifle. Wasn't aiming at my tires—"

"I don't want those details," Murphy interrupted. "I didn't hear that. I just need to know when."

Josie nodded. "Forty-eight hours ago, no more."

"Okay, good. I'll send an order over for a CT scan and have my nurse start an IV. Then we'll talk."

The nurse was deft with the needle. She got a vein on her first try, admiring his "good veins".

"You're good," Joachim said.

"Great veins make my job easy. You should see some of the old codgers we get in here, veins slippery as overcooked noodles." She adjusted the drip of intravenous fluids, electrolytes, and antibiotics, and tapped the line with her finger. "There we go, a good steady drip."

She looked at the clipboard and frowned. "Looks like he wants a CAT scan . . . a puncture wound—" She shot a look at Joachim, and he looked away. She dropped the sterile wrappings in the waste can. "I'll get Dr. Murphy back in here."

Murphy closed the door and pulled a stool up between them. "I trust Susan, but I asked her to leave because I don't want her compromised. A call came in last night warning us that a fugitive, armed and dangerous, could be heading in our direction." He waited, letting it sink in. "Then, this morning, two guys with badges came in around ten o'clock asking questions, wanting to know if we'd seen any gunshot wounds."

Josie bit her lip. "Local police?"

"No, they weren't local."

"So, we need to leave."

Murph looked at the intravenous bag hanging from the pole. "You aren't going anywhere. My diagnosis will be—" He looked at his clipboard, then at Joachim, "I think you got some kickback from a chainsaw. Probably hit a nail trying to chop up one of those old fence posts, didn't you? A rusty nail and wood splinters somehow embedded in your chest. Happens, Joachim, doesn't it?"

Joachim coughed, and Josie handed him a tissue, and he wiped a fleck of blood off his lips.

Murphy crossed his legs and considered him for a minute. "The bullet could have nicked your lung," he said.

"It's not from a bullet, doc. But I'd rather die from one."

Josie handed him another tissue. "Who said anything about dying?" She looked at Murphy. "We were getting ready to start an herbal regimen before this happened."

"Herbal regimen? How long have you been coughing up blood, Joachim?"

"A few months."

"A few months." He repeated the words like a death knell.

"You're sounding like a cuckoo, doc," Joachim said with a faint smile.

"I can't endorse that plan of treatment."

124

"I got enough poison in me already." Joachim attempted a shrug with the uninjured shoulder.

"Are you trying to speed up the process? Putting yourself in harm's way?"

"Just tryin' to live, that's all."

Murphy heaved a sigh and climbed to his feet. "I'm ordering a throat culture and a tech will be here in a minute to wheel you down to X-ray. Then we'll move you to a different room." He looked at Josie. "One a little more comfortable."

"We don't want to make trouble for you. We'll leave as soon as possible."

"You'll leave when I say you can leave."

She pinched her lips and nodded. "Thanks, Murph."

He closed the door with a soft click.

"He was always bossy," Joachim said.

She sat on the edge of the bed and leaned over him. "You do what he says. You'll get better."

He tucked a strand of hair behind her ear. "I do what you say."

"Remember the friend I told you about?"

He traced the curve of her jawline with his finger. "What friend?"

"The one who supposedly only had six months to live?"

"That old Navajo with the scar from chin to ear?"

"He's not old," she argued. "I saw him last week. He and his girlfriend are planning a trip to Hawaii this winter. All he needs is sunshine."

"Hell with Hawaii. Everyone goes to Hawaii. I wanna go to Cuba."

"*Cuba?*"

"Hole up next to the ocean, drink rum and smoke some of those cigars." He pulled her closer with a reservoir of strength. "Do it on the beach, rinse off in the ocean . . ."

She laughed, ran her hand under his chin, and kissed him on the mouth. "You dumb Indian," she whispered. "How you talk. You could've sold sunscreen to my mother."

"Does that mean yes?"

A radiologist came in unannounced and she got off the bed. "Ready for a ride, my man?" he addressed Joachim.

"We were just discussing our trip to Cuba."

"Really? Cuba? I'll be lucky to make it as far south as Montana." He took the brakes off the bed and secured the IV. Josie followed them out the door as they discussed their travel plans.

Turning a corner, the tech pointed out the room they would be returning to, and Joachim noted its proximity to an exit and the forest beyond.

CHAPTER 19

Murphy clipped the X-ray film on the wall-mounted viewer, and showed them the path the bullet took as it ricocheted off bone, and exited above Joachim's nipple.

"You can see here," he said, pointing at a cloudy area on the film, "bone chips still embedded next to the clavicle. They need to come out."

Joachim squinted at what looked to him like innocuous specks of lint.

"Looks like nothing."

"They can cause trouble."

"I say do it," Josie said.

"You won't feel a thing."

Joachim snorted.

"We're short right now on scrub techs, but we'll schedule you as soon as we can. If not later today, first thing in the morning. Once you're under, it won't take more than an hour, and if all goes well, we can have you out of here in two or three days, as long as you continue to respond to the antibiotics."

"You're the man," Joachim nodded. "I'm just a dumb Indian."

True to Murphy's word, the next day Joachim woke from the anesthesia having not felt a thing. He regained consciousness to emerge from another dream of drowning, hanging by his nails to the underside of a dock slick with algae.

His eyes snapped open.

Everything was white: the ceiling, the walls, and the nurse by his side.

"Hello, Joachim." Peppermint breath and white teeth. "How do you feel?"

The monitor behind the bed beeped, and he considered the question. "I have a headache."

"That's normal."

He looked down at his chest and hands that appeared to be his own. He spread his fingers and inspected his nails. He could still feel the wood, wet with decay. "I guess I'm alive."

"Very much so. You did great. Doc will be in shortly, but I'm telling you, you're a champ."

A champ. He rolled the word around in his head. He smiled at the nurse with peppermint breath. He was a champ.

Joachim stared wide-eyed at the ceiling and listened for the noise to repeat itself. After several days of hospital food, open-back gowns, and interrupted sleep, he was ready to leave the sterile environment of the clinic and get back to wood-fired stoves, wild game, and blue jeans.

The room was dimly lit by the monitor, and a light shone under the door. Even with it shut, the lights in the hallway bothered him. He turned on his side to look at Josie. She was curled up in a chair beside the bed with a blanket under her chin.

He threw his legs over the edge of the bed, running his hand along the bandage wrapped around his chest and across his shoulder. He dropped his feet to the floor and tested his weight. A shadow crossed under the door. He sat back on the edge of the bed and breathed.

He was still hooked up to the IV tree that nurses kept hanging bags from. Swaddled in a hospital gown open in the back and attached to an umbilical cord, he felt as vulnerable as a baby.

Headlights streaked across the window pane and swept the parking lot. He stared out at the night with a bad feeling. He looked at the wedge of light under the door and nudged Josie.

"Josie! Wake up."

She sat up with a start. "What's wrong?"

"Get this off me." He lifted the plastic tubing connecting him to the bag of fluids hanging from the stand.

"Are you nuts? Lay back down. What's wrong with you?"

"I think they're here."

"Who's here?"

"The cops. I saw lights."

She threw the blanket on the floor and rushed to the window. "It's an ambulance, Jac."

"They're turning me in. I know it."

"Nobody would do that. It's an ambulance." She shut the curtains, sat beside him, and pulled the gown back over his shoulders. "You saw an ambulance."

"You sure?"

"Yes, I'm sure. Come on, lie back down." She checked her phone. "It's three in the morning. Murph said the IV can come out today, and then we'll talk about going home, okay? It's still dark. People are sleeping."

"They aren't sleeping out there." He nodded at the door.

"*They* aren't supposed to."

She pulled the blankets over him and placed her chair closer. "It's three o'clock, Jac. Let's get some sleep."

Joachim pulled the covers over his head to block the light streaming in from under the door. Bolstered by Josie's confidence and the reassuring murmur from the nurse's station, he fell asleep.

He was jostled awake by a frantic hand. "Wake up!" Murphy whispered hoarsely. "You have to get out of here."

With a penlight between his teeth, he pulled the IV and taped a wad of gauze over the puncture wound.

"What?" Joachim was groggy and rubbing his eyes. "What's going on?"

"Get him dressed," Murphy told Josie. "You have to leave. No questions. You only have a minute."

She nodded mutely and pulled his clothes out of the closet—tee shirt, flannel shirt, shorts and jeans. She rolled his socks on, and he wiggled his feet into his boots.

"Cops are here, aren't they? I knew it. I told you, Jos."

She threw on her jacket and grabbed her handbag.

"Here." Murphy handed her a small pharmacy bag. "Three a day until they're gone. No booze, lots of water. There's extra bandaging in there. You know to keep it clean. You can call me on my cell. It should be secure. Number is in the bag. There's an unmarked SUV parked across the street. They're waiting for their backup and backup is taking their time, but you don't have a lot."

"How'd you know?"

"Doesn't matter. Go!" He pushed them to the rear exit. "Your vehicle is outside. Keep the lights off, and take the service drive. Make sure no one is following you before you head for home."

Joachim clasped his shoulder. "You gonna be okay here?"

"There's another number in that bag I want you to call. Promise me."

Joachim looked at the bag in Josie's hand. "Sure. Sure, I will," he said.

Murphy checked the hallway and motioned them out. He held the exit door with his shoulder. "Remember, Jac, no lights, and watch your ass."

Joachim nodded and the door shut softly behind him with a click.

As Josie steered them down the service drive and into the embracing darkness of the forest, he watched for lights in his side mirror. The bandage around his chest pulled up tight under his arm, and he was short of breath from the dash to the jeep.

Josie leaned over the steering wheel. "I can't see the road."

"Slow down." Joachim's eyes darted between the road and the side mirror.

"I need lights."

"No." He stared at the side mirror. "Not yet."

A deer bounded across the road in front of them, then another, and she hit the brakes. In contrast to the silent passing of the herd, the sound of their engine seemed deafening, but it was muffled by the forest and swallowed by the weight of the evergreens.

The highway gleamed ahead in the starlight. When they reached the pavement, Josie stepped on the gas. The aspens overhanging the road trembled in their wake. A helicopter flew overhead with blinking lights and an emergency vehicle flew by in the other direction. Everyone seemed out to get him. But they couldn't all be after him. He wasn't that big of a fish.

Then he thought of the message Savior left for him at the cabin. If they tied him to everything, he was a pretty big fish.

"Next crossroad, hang a left," he said.

"The highway will get us home faster."

"I don't want them following me to your place. We can go to Savior's cabin, hole up for a while, let things settle."

"That shack?"

"It has water and a woodpile. I've got my drugs." He kicked the bag under his feet. "What else do we need?"

"Electricity, cell service . . ."

"Take a left. It's all back roads." He knew a road within a road that couldn't call itself a road. It was nothing more than an old snowmobile trail, but with a 4x4 it could be navigated.

Headlights appeared in the rearview mirror, coming on fast.

"Hurry! Floor it!" He leaned over the dash. "There on the left. That dirt road. *Crank it!*"

She spun the wheel and their rear end fishtailed as they hit the gravel. Tree branches scraped his window. She steered them clear of the ditch and straightened the wheel to rock back on four tires.

Josie shut off the engine, gripped the steering wheel, and breathed. The engine ticked and settled. Joachim turned in his seat, eyes glued to the highway behind them.

"I don't think they saw us. I don't see how they could have."

Their breath steamed the windshield as the tailing vehicle flew by on the highway behind them. It was followed quickly by another, and sirens sounded in the distance. They watched while another vehicle with flashing lights and blaring siren followed the others. The darkness and quiet returned. They looked at one another for a long minute.

Joachim shifted in his seat.

Josie was quiet, but he knew a reckoning was coming.

She took her hands off the wheel and turned to face him. Her features were white in the dark confines of the vehicle and her voice was strained. "Tell me exactly what you did."

"I told you."

"You did more than shoot out some trucker's tire. I need to know what we're up against. You need to tell me everything, and I don't want any lame made-up stories."

He took a deep breath and shimmied his leg, recognizing the need to come clean.

"There was an accident up by the mine a few weeks ago—maybe you heard about it. A guy ended up in the hospital, but we didn't think he was seriously hurt. But I found out from Savior that he's back in critical care."

"Oh, Jesus." Josie dropped her hand on the steering wheel. "Don't tell me—"

"It was an accident, Josie. I didn't mean for any of this to happen."

"If it was an accident, what did you have to do with it?"

"We got so sick of all those damn *no trespassing* signs and blocked roads—no this, no that, no access to our own trap lines and fishing holes. We'd had it. Then one night we had a few drinks and decided to put up our own signs. We had lifted a couple of their 'detour' signs a few months back. So, we hauled them out and placed them on the logging road up by the uranium mine, directing their truck traffic down a shit dirt road to nowhere. We thought it was funny.

"But it's one of those roads that hug the edge of the Vernier Ridge, and there'd been a washout with the heavy rain that we didn't hear about until the next day. We went back to pull them, but it was too late. The signs were gone, and then we heard over Savior's CB that a trucker went off the cliff.

"We got the hell out of there as fast as we could. We didn't think anyone saw us, but something broke. They pulled Savior in the next day

132

for questioning. But his sister got him a lawyer from Indian Affairs and they couldn't hold him because the connecting evidence was inconclusive. He followed legal advice and kept his mouth shut.

"The trucker had multiple injuries but it looked like he would pull through. As long as he did, we figured that would be the end of it. But if he doesn't . . ."

"And they're connecting you and Bobby with Savior?"

"I'm not sure, but they know we're close. His sister says they're putting a case together, manslaughter charges if the guy doesn't pull through."

"We can fight this, get a lawyer."

"I'm guilty. What's to fight?"

"We can try for a plea bargain, reduced sentencing with community service or reparation."

"I'm not going back to jail, Josie. The last time—did you know I had to sleep on the cement floor? The *fucking floor* for three nights in winter, listening to the faucet drip, scratching in the walls. Place was filthy, probably had rats."

He stopped to adjust the bandage wrapped too tight, choking him off. "Maybe it was a coincidence, but that's when I started spitting blood. I'm not going back. They take me . . . it won't be alive."

"This is why you wanted to get that money out of your name, isn't it?

He didn't answer.

"You were afraid something like this would happen over your protest activities. I warned you guys to let it go. I would've thought that after your father—"

"What? That I would go meekly along? Put on a shirt and tie?"

"You signed off on the settlement."

"Did we have a *choice*? I never wanted the money. I just wanted to fish."

"Does your family know any of this? Stefan?"

He shook his head. "Absolutely not."

He was right to send Stefan away. Stefan was crazy enough to get himself involved. He was impulsive, immature, and placed too much merit on an older brother's activities. He had never done anything to deserve his unflagging regard.

"What about Savior and Bobby? Where are they?"

"Bobby left for the Narrows. We don't know where Savior is. I stopped by the garage last week. His cousin is running things. Savior wouldn't say where he was off to, just that he was going fishing."

"All this over a stupid stunt. We knew this takeover was inevitable. We knew we'd have to get out of the way, but my house is out of the way. We had a plan, dammit!" She slammed her fist against the steering wheel. "We had a plan. Now what? If that wasn't enough, you show up in the middle of the night all shot up after another stupid stunt, and now we have to hole up in a shack with no toilet, winter coming, all over, over—"

"A stupid stunt. I know it, Josie. You don't have to keep hitting me over the head with it."

They sat quiet, neither looking at the other.

She glanced in the rearview mirror. "What do you think? Safe to go on?"

He looked over his shoulder at the empty road. "Yeah, and I need to get this binding off." He twisted side to side. "It's too tight."

It was late when they pulled up beside the one-room hunting cabin. It was nothing more than a shanty, Josie was right about that, but it was remote and solidly built. In the beam of a flashlight, he brushed the cobwebs away from the door and pushed it open with his good shoulder. The musty smell of mice and neglect met them, and Josie hesitated on the stoop.

"When was the last time anyone was here?"

"I've no idea." Joachim made his way through the gloom to the wood stove in the corner. There was an oil lamp on the mantle and he got it going with a match. The light cast shadows across the beamed ceiling. Pots and pans hung overhead along with tackle and assorted bamboo poles. A shelf of canned goods and utensils lined the back wall. There was a stack of dry wood and kindling beside the pot-bellied stove. He filled it and coaxed it going with another match, blowing softly on the fledgling flame.

The heat rose and Josie inched closer with her hands out.

He sat back on his haunches with his hands between his knees, feeling vindicated. Feeling safe for the first time since he'd taken a bullet through the shoulder.

"It smells like mice. I'm not staying here."

He looked at her with an idea. "You don't have to. No, wait. Hear me out. I'll be fine. You go back, take care of things at your place and go back to work. If you don't, they might connect your disappearance to mine. You need to go back. I'll be fine here for a few days."

"What about food?"

"Look at the stash of canned goods." He pointed at the wall behind them. "You can always make a run back. I'm not suggesting you leave me high and dry." He suddenly remembered his jeep. "Shit, is my jeep still sitting out front of your place?"

"I jumped it that night and put it in the shed."

"I left my gun on the seat. Did you get it?"

"A gun?"

"It shouldn't be loaded, but be careful. There should be a box of ammo in the back."

"Wait a minute."

"Make sure it's not loaded, Josie."

"You can take care of it when we get back."

"You're going back tonight and you need to take care of it."

"I'll leave this mice-infested shack when you do."

"What about Casper and Bigfoot? They gotta be getting lonely."

He shamelessly played the cat card. The two cats had been with her since her parents died. She had a pet door and cats were self-sufficient, indolently indifferent to human activity, but she had never been gone this long.

"They might think you aren't coming back and take off, decide they need to fend for themselves."

She pursed her lips and looked out the side window, and he thought he was getting close.

She walked gingerly around the cabin, watching where she stepped in the dim light from the oil lamp. "Where's the bed? I know you don't like sleeping on the floor."

He walked over to the back wall, loosened a board to uncover a hidden handle, and gave it a tug. A neatly made bed fell out of the wall.

Josie gasped. "Well, I never."

"Cool, eh? Savior got the idea from an old apartment building he helped renovate. It's called a Murphy bed." He smiled. "No, no relation. But I won't have to sleep on the floor."

Josie ran her hand over the coverlet and then sat on the edge of the mattress and bounced on it. She lifted a pillow and looked underneath it, then lifted the sheet and inspected the mattress. She looked up at him. "I'll be darned. Seems mouse-proof."

"Yeah, it's pretty ingenious."

"I have to say," she said, looking at the framed-in closet that the fold-up bed had fallen out of, "to find something like this out here is remarkable."

He looked at the wall unit, the cove molding, and the mitered corners. "Savior's good with wood. Good with his hands." He looked around the shack with its hidden comforts and thought of the one he had helped his dad and his buddies in the Trapper's Alliance erect at the roadblock. It was erected before the authorities even knew they were there by men who were good with their hands descended from a people of historical significance who had systematically lost everything, from the native tongue the missionary took, to the hunting grounds that companies devoted to resource extraction took with government collusion.

Josie wrinkled her nose. "Maybe I'll bring Bigfoot back with me. He's a good mouser, and he was always partial to you for some reason." She smiled. "I think that after I had him neutered, he lost his male identity." She took her cell out of her pocket and looked at it. "Just like I thought, no signal."

"Try by the door."

She walked to the door with her phone outstretched and lifted it to the ceiling, as if that could help. She even stepped outside to no avail. "This is a dead zone. I don't like it."

"Maybe that's the beauty. Look at it that way."

She looked at him for a minute, trying to see things his way. "Let's take a look at that bandage. You say there's water?"

There was a pitcher of water with a film on it beside the hand pump. He primed the pump, and a gush of cold water flowed into the basin. He carried it to the table, set the oil lamp beside it, and draped his jacket across the back of a chair.

Josie helped him off with his shirt, then washed her hands and unwound the ace bandage.

The surgical incision was still red, but looked clean and healthy. The wound in his back was growing a scab, and even the exit wound in his chest was beginning to heal. She dabbed antibiotic ointment on it the way Murphy instructed, then taped on clean gauze, wrapped the ace bandage around his chest, and crisscrossed his shoulder. He flexed his arm and twisted side to side. "Better. Thanks, babe."

She leaned back and looked at the bandaging. "You can't do that by yourself. I'm not leaving. Murph would have my head."

"Yes, you are. I can change a bandage."

"He said to change it every day for a week."

"Sure, I'll do that."

"If you're staying in this mouse-infested shack, then I am too."

He shook his head somberly. "Some animal lover you are, not to mention your unexplained absence from work, house dark, gun left on the seat of my truck . . ."

She chewed on the corner of her mouth. "You'll remember to take your pills? You, who never even liked to take an aspirin?"

"Come on, give me a little credit." He took the pill bottle out of the pharmacy bag and shook one into his palm. He threw the capsule back with a sip of water, then wiped his mouth and grinned. "Three a day, I know. And look," He lifted his elbow, "I'm already getting some range of motion back. Be reasonable, Jos, they won't be looking for a lone woman and there's no way they can trace your vehicle to me. Wait about five days, but keep an eye out." He ran his eyes along the shelf of canned goods, heavy on the beans and corn. "Come back in five days and bring me some meat."

She rested a hand on his stomach, gone concave with weight loss. "I'll bring you some bread and butter is what I'll bring you."

"See if you can catch wind of Savior and Bobby."

"I'll check in at the Center. Gossip flows through there like it's the Ottawa Gazette."

"Call home for me and get Stefan's cell number. Mom said he bought one of these pay-as-you-go phones. Tell him I'm fine and I'll call him in a week or so." He looked at her for a minute. "Don't tell him too much."

"I'm not stupid, Jac."

The fire had knocked down the chill and the oil lamp cast a soft light. They had run out of words, but an air of hesitation hung between them.

"I don't like this," Josie said. "Leaving you with no cell service."

"So, no tracking devices. Besides, how did people used to survive?"

"I don't care what people used to do. I don't like leaving you."

"I'll be fine. You need to get home, go back to work, act normal."

"Right, act normal."

He took her hand and led her to the door. "Remember, if Savior or Bobby get in touch, tell them to use our backup drop point. They can't leave messages at the roadblock anymore. It's not safe." He kissed her on the mouth and then stepped away from the door. "Five days, baby, okay? And don't forget about the gun."

She nodded and turned abruptly for the jeep.

He shoved his hands in his pocket and stood in the doorway long after she was gone, long after the sound of the engine was swallowed by the forest. The stillness was set in relief by the song of a night bird singing his coda from a branch overhanging the roof.

CHAPTER 20

All the birds might have been singing, but Stefan was deaf to everything but the beating of his heart—near leapt from his chest—when Sadie wrapped her legs around him and the sarong fell open.

For weeks, her mere presence had been an aphrodisiac—the sway of her hips, the dimple in her chin, the brilliance of her smile and the flush of her anger. From their first kiss on a picnic table under towering pines he had wanted her. Bound by restraint, the sexual tension between them had built to a crescendo, abstinence a torment constantly at war with desire. So, when he lifted her on the table, and she took him in her arms, he thought he would explode.

He was impervious to the outside world. It was as irrelevant as that birdsong on a wire, until the slam of the back door made it rudely relevant.

"Shit." He pressed his fist against his mouth, biting his thumb. "Someone's here."

Sadie gasped and scooted off the table, yanking the sarong down around her legs.

Stefan adjusted himself and found his composure as Simon rounded the corner of the kitchen and threw a clipboard on the table. Sadie smothered her hair. "Grandpa . . ."

"Where's your dad?"

"Out."

He rifled through the papers on the clipboard, looked up at her, and then at Stefan, seeing both for the first time. "Montegrand . . ." He paused with his hand in mid-air. "Did I interrupt something?"

Stefan swallowed, called to account. It was the first time anyone had called him that.

"No, sir," he said.

Simon's eyes flicked from Sadie's flushed face and choice of dress to Stefan's disheveled appearance, which colored him interrupted. He pulled up a chair and took a cigar out of his breast pocket and a book of matches from somewhere. He struck a match and lit the cigar, rolling it between his lips and puffing to get it going.

Stefan took a second to straighten himself and wrap his head around the interruption.

Sadie secured the knot in her sarong. "What's going on, Grandpa?" she asked warily.

"Bolton's filed a false lien on our property."

"A false what?"

"Against us and Ronnie Cummins." Simon threw a folder on top of the clipboard. "And nuisance complaints on the cattle."

"What's that mean, Mr. Wixom?" Stefan said.

He rolled the cigar and leaned back in his chair to consider him.

"It means we have a headache to deal with. Can't renew our line of credit at the Land Bank if we have another lien on the property. If we can't renew our line of credit, we can't take care of fall planting, equipment repair, the shed that's falling down that her father keeps ignoring." He pointed the cigar at Sadie.

They both stared at him, and he set the cigar in the ashtray. "You know what a lien is, right?"

"A loan?" Stefan guessed.

"It's security on a debt. Bolton's lien says we owe him and we used our property as security. Like collateral. You see that?"

Stefan frowned. He recognized a patronizing tone when he heard it. While he himself had never borrowed money, he knew Jake had gotten in some trouble for the same. He knew the whole business could be dicey, and he knew he wouldn't want to cross this man.

"Why us?" Sadie said.

"I testified at the last Drain Commission meeting. As a neighbor with conjoined property, they needed my collaboration with Ronnie's report, which I was damn happy to give. My testimony is a matter of record, but this, this—" He separated a piece of paper from the others. "This complaint about the cattle is ludicrous. We were here before he was."

"What's wrong with the cattle?" Stefan asked.

"They offend his sensitive nose."

Stefan snorted.

"He can't get away with that," Sadie said. "Can he?"

"No, but it'll take time to clear up, and we'll have to hire a lawyer, more money out the window, even though Bolton has no standing, and stink is subjective. Some people don't like the smell of gunpowder."

"Or the sound of gunfire," Stefan interjected.

Simon considered him through a puff of smoke and rolled the cigar between his lips. He looked at Sadie. "Your dad say where he was going?"

"He has a date."

"A date? Boards falling off the barn and Henry has a date." He shook his head, put the cigar back between his teeth, and thumbed through the phonebook. He found the number he was looking for, dialed it, and covered the mouthpiece. "With who?" he said.

"Margie."

"He could do worse."

"Or better."

"Go in the office," he said, pointing a finger as if she needed direction, "and find the most recent survey for me, and I need last year's income tax and the LLC folder—"

His party picked up, and he put the phone to his ear.

Stefan saw an out and jabbed his thumb at the door, but her grandfather was motioning urgency at Sadie, and she gave Stefan a helpless shrug.

He made his escape out the back door and took a gulp of fresh air. *Jesus, he hurt.* The old man had terrible timing. He walked across the grass to where he had parked the motorcycle and threw a leg gingerly over the saddle. He revved the engine, and the gauges settled. He peeled his sleeve back to check his watch. It was end-of-business-time.

Speed-shifting through the gears helped release the pressure built up through sexual frustration. By the time he pulled up to the ATM on the edge of town, the tension along the conduit from his groin to the area in the brain that processed desire and sent it out to the furthest reaches of the body had eased.

He punched in his pin and studied the options on the touch screen. As he suspected, he would have to go to the main branch to withdraw what he needed and the main branch was closed. He opted for the maximum amount possible, and the machine spit out crisp twenty-dollar bills along with a printout to complete the transaction. He tucked the bills inside his wallet and read the printout. The money was there, an astounding amount for one who had hoarded nickels and dimes and rolled pennies.

He tracked Larry down at the construction site where he was running electrical.

Larry tucked his hard hat under his arm and motioned him to a picnic table where a water cooler sat on one end and an over-sized Stanley thermos sat on the other. "Which do you want, lukewarm coffee or lukewarm water?

"I'm good, thanks."

Larry poured black coffee in a mug and straddled the bench. "What's up, kiddo?"

Stefan straddled the other end and got right to it. Joachim should never have expected him to be responsible. "How much you want for the motorcycle?"

Larry paused with the mug halfway to his mouth. "You want to buy the motorcycle?"

"Yes," he said.

"I figured that was just a pipe dream."

"What do you want for it?"

"Well, I'll have to think about it." He took a sip of coffee and looked at Stefan for a long minute. "Think you can get financing?"

"I don't need financing."

Larry was silent.

"I have cash."

"You aren't in any trouble, are you?"

Stefan breathed. The familiar expectation was starting to grate. "No, sir," he said.

"Blue Book price is nine thousand."

"Sounds fair."

"You're supposed to haggle, son."

Stefan shrugged. "You say it's fair, it's fair. Besides, you've been loaning it out for weeks."

"You talk this over with your mother?"

Stefan looked at him from under a steady brow and Larry dropped his eyes.

"Sorry, that was unnecessary. I'll let it go for eight."

"I'll need the saddlebags."

"Included."

"I can give you a down payment now—" he peeled off the roll of twenties crisp from the ATM— "give you the rest tomorrow."

Larry nodded, but his eyes were puzzled.

The unasked questions hung in the air, and Stefan felt the weight of his gaze as he walked to the bike and palmed the key. The bike roared to life, and he released the kickstand with his heel. The air was as heavy as the weight on his back as he rode out of the drive.

When he pulled into the shared driveway between Sam's place and their rental, there was a strange car parked in the way, strange yet familiar. He rolled around it with his heels dragging the ground, eyeing the ride, sassy, foreign, and in the way. He knocked the kickstand down and rested his hands on his thighs as the engine cooled. He had already grown to think of it as his, as retribution for the one taken from his father. It connected them in an abstract way. The gods had intervened on his behalf; he was meant to acquire a cycle that matched the one seized through laws fashioned after arbitrary drug decrees and seizure authority.

He made a mental note to ask Joachim about their dad's leather gloves, chaps, and motorcycle boots. He suddenly wanted more than a boomerang he couldn't find.

He swung his leg off the bike and stretched his back. He was still tense from his close encounter with Sadie's grandfather, tense from yet another interrupted moment with her.

Sam hailed him from the middle of a group sitting around the picnic table. He strode across the lawn, planted a foot on the end of the bench, and looked around the table. Nan was seated next to Abby.

"I think you know Nan, and this is my buddy, Sid." Sam motioned between them.

Sid gave him a nod. He had a thatch of blonde hair and an open face. "I was there," he said.

Stefan raised an eyebrow. "Where?"

"At the gas station. You ever need anyone to vouch for you."

"Trouble always starts at the gas station," Nan said.

"You all know each other?"

"Coincidentally, she just stopped by to see if I knew you, my man."

"Seems everybody knows *of you*," Abby said.

He grabbed her arm and looked at the fresh tattoo on her wrist, still wrapped in protective film.

She yanked away and tucked her hands between her legs. "Leave me alone."

"I told her next time she should add color," Nan said.

"I thought you worked until nine," he said.

"Got out early, so I could warn you."

"Warn me about what?"

"You have everyone stirred up."

"Who?" Abby asked.

"Zender and Clem for starters, and that's not a good place to start."

"Clem fancies Nan," Sam explained. "And Nan fancies your brother."

Stefan looked at Nan who hadn't taken her eyes off him. She was unabashedly forward, uncomplicated in her intentions.

"Where's Sadie?" Abby asked pointedly.

Nan flipped a hand dismissively. "Riding horses, shoveling manure . . . something wrong with a girl never wants to go to the mall."

"She's helping her grandfather." Stefan challenged her gaze. "There's some legal trouble with Bolton, false loans—I mean liens—something like that. She's helping him find paperwork."

"First you beat up Zender, and then you beat up Clem." Nan stayed on track, not interested in false liens or the like. "I just wanted to warn you. Next time it'll likely be two on one. That's not fair, but that's the way they roll."

"I mind my own business. They should mind theirs."

"But they've made you their business."

"Maybe you should listen to her." Abby worried her lip.

"I just want that bike ride he promised."

"I did?"

"I heard you're buying it," Sam said.

"You heard right."

"How can you do that?"

"Wait, you said it was yours," Nan said.

Stefan looked at her stone-faced. "Did I?"

"I'll be damned." Sam shook his head. "Hell, he could've put me on a payment plan."

"When're you starting the charcoal?" Sid asked. "I'm hungry."

Sam looked at Stefan. "You like hot dogs?"

"He'll eat anything," Abby said.

"I need some buns. Why don't you give Nan that ride? Coals will take thirty minutes."

Stefan shrugged and looked at Nan. "Sure, let's go." He took the key from his pocket and they walked across the lawn.

"I need a helmet," Nan said as he threw a leg over the saddle.

"I don't have a helmet."

"Isn't there a helmet law?"

"Another law?" He revved the throttle. "Are you coming?"

She hesitated, then climbed aboard, wrapping her arms around him.

"Give me some elbow room."

"Sure, honey." She shifted her hips side to side and hooked her fingers inside his belt loops.

He inched the bike backwards, dragging his heels.

"How fast you had this baby?" she asked in his ear.

He looked at the speedometer. It went up to a hundred miles per hour, but he hadn't come close to that. He shrugged. "Maybe seventy on a straightaway."

She laughed. "Pussy."

He turned into the road and opened the throttle. The bike lurched forward with the power that satisfied a guttural craving he couldn't name or describe but knew to be a part of him.

Pussy. He accelerated into a curve and wondered if anyone had ever dared call any of his brothers that. He watched the needle inch up the speedometer, suddenly wanting to go faster and harder.

Nan was in a full body press, fingers in his belt loops, then below his belt. *Lord.* He was being felt up in full view of the traveling public. She wasn't the one he wanted, but his duplicitous body was betraying him. With self-deprecating thoughts, he swerved to take a shortcut out to the main highway, concentrating on gears, balance, and just *getting there.*

He turned into a headwind, felt the hiccup in the guts of the engine, and looked down at the needle on the gas gauge fluttering above the red line.

He was low on gas and had known it, but forgotten it.

"Where's the closest gas station?" he yelled over his shoulder.

"What?"

"Gas. I need gas."

She put her mouth next to his ear. "There's a four-corners up ahead."

"How far?"

"Couple miles."

He looked at the needle flirting with the red line. His dad always said an Indian bike had hidden reserves.

"I'm not walking." Her bubble gum breath was a warm contrast to the air rushing over him.

A blinking caution light appeared ahead, and he eased off the gas. He coasted into the station that doubled as a grocery and parked beside one of the pumps. The sign advised *pay inside.*

He stuffed the buns and cigarettes in one of the saddle bags, and pumped the gas. The smell of petrol wafted from the tank while Nan leaned against a display of firewood stacked in ten-dollar bundles, plaited her hair in a thick braid, and secured the end with a covered rubber band.

The pounding in Sadie's head grew exponentially with the sound of Stefan's leaving. The small office was crammed with filing cabinets, shelves of books with worn bindings, agricultural yearbooks from the 1800s, and atlases of the world beyond. The stabbing headache had centered behind her temple. She rubbed her eyes and considered a good starting point.

She was thumbing through manila folders, through the S's and the T's, but she wasn't there. She was behind him on the bike in the forced intimacy of a shared-seat embrace. He, straight-backed in front of her, gunning the throttle yet careful on the curves, leading with his head and a dip of his shoulder, which from the first curve in the first mile she had found curiously endearing.

She finally found the survey and legal property description misfiled under the T's. She threw the documents on the desk and inched her way to the door. "Do you need anything else?"

He looked pointedly at the clock on the wall. "You do chores yet?"

She smoothed the sarong, the sensual feeling long gone. Chores? Of course, she had not done chores. "I was just getting ready to when . . ."

"When what?" He waited and followed her glance out the window. "He'll be moving on, you know. I think that's probably a good thing."

"What do you mean?"

"Not much work ethic in that young man."

Sadie frowned. "I don't understand."

"Go on, get your work done."

"He wasn't keeping me from it, Grandpa."

"No? Well, I think he was."

She was surprised at his sudden accusatory tone, not sure what he was accusing Stefan of, or what she needed to defend him for. Had he seen something? She blushed at the possibility. He couldn't have, but if he hadn't seen anything untoward, what had Stefan done to warrant his dislike? She had never been on the wrong side of Simon Wixom, and had no experience with standing her ground on an opposing side.

"They need bedding too," he called after her.

It was late before she finished in the barn. She walked the short distance to the stable through the gathering dusk and turned on the interior lights. The horses hung their heads over their stalls. Tomorrow, she would turn them out to pasture. Tomorrow, she would take Stefan horseback riding and show him the hidden grove at the far corner of the farm next to the creek where the ground was cushioned with pine needles and the sun didn't shine. Where the only sound that encroached was tinkling water and the wind through the firs. A place where she could take her one precious life by the horns.

With the horses settled, she checked for messages and missed calls. It'd been over four hours since her grandpa had barged in on them and Stefan escaped on the motorcycle. She left him another message, and then called Sam.

He picked up right away. "Hi, Sadie. What's up?"

"Have you seen Stefan?"

There was a pause along the line and he cleared his throat. "Ah, yeah, he's here, um somewhere. We had a cookout."

"Is there anything left?"

Another pause. "A couple over-cooked brats and a blackened hot dog."

There was background chatter and a burst of laughter.

"Who's there? Sounds like a party."

"I'll tell Stef you're looking for him."

"No, don't do that."

There was a muffled sound, and the call dropped.

Sadie frowned at the screen. He needed an upgrade. Sam's calls always dropped. She grabbed a sweatshirt and her keys. Sam had a fire pit, and sitting around a campfire with Stefan while making plans with fall in the air was a good way to close out a day.

CHAPTER 21

Five days in, the pills in the bottle were a third gone and there was a sizable dent in the shelf of beans, squash, and corn. The air turned cold, and Joachim kept a fire going through the day, banked it at night, and slept in his flannel shirt, hoping Josie would think to bring back blankets and coffee.

There was an old bow and a cache of arrows in the rafters with the fishing gear. His wounded shoulder was still stiff, but he was ambidextrous and practiced drawing the bow and aiming at various trees around the clearing with his opposite arm. He took walks along the road, into the woods, venturing further and further from the cabin. He kept the cell phone in the inside pocket of his vest and periodically turned it on in different locations to check for service. On the fourth day, he made it all the way to the running water he had heard on the third. The creek ran fast and cold, and he looked for traces of trout. He followed it for a hundred yards, then backtracked across fallen limbs, and under low-hanging boughs that cast the shade trout loved.

Today was Josie's scheduled return, and he planned to take out one of the rabbits that frequented the clearing. They would have roasted rabbit, along with whatever else she might bring to the table.

He made the bed and tucked in the corners, remembering the first time they had lain together; how she had thrown her bedroom window open to the chorus of spring peepers, turned down the covers, and climbed on top of him.

He stood in the doorway with a cup of water warmed over the stove and breathed in the air. He felt strong in himself. He had not spit blood since the first day at the clinic with Murphy watching. He tamped down the hope, tamped it off the step and into the dirt.

The sound of distant trains carried at night, like the whistle of the train across the six miles between home and the tracks that ran east to west across the province. But in the light of day, there were no sounds other than which he could see and recognize, and he wondered if the search was still on. The forced period of inactivity had started to grate on him. He longed to sit down with Savior and Bobby, to get behind the wheel of his jeep, or out on the boat. Thoughts of Stefan and the others nagged him. He had insisted their mother give up the search for distant relatives, buy a house, and encourage Stefan to make friends and fit in. He needed to talk to Stefan. He owed him an explanation.

Relieved at the strength returning in his shoulder, he shot an arrow through the head of a snowshoe rabbit. He salted the meat the way Josie liked it, and roasted strips on a spit over the coals. He found a pouch of stale tobacco and papers, rolled a cigarette, and smoked it while the rabbit roasted and the sun fell behind the trees. There was a bite in the air and the aspens were dropping their leaves.

He sat there until dark.

A restless owl hooted from its camouflaged perch and shuffled along a branch with blood on its mind, and he felt the extent of his isolation. He tamped down the worry where he had tamped down hope, went inside, and closed the door.

She could have had car trouble, or been called away on a midwife emergency. Or they found his jeep in her garage.

He lit the oil lamp and knocked back two pills, having forgotten his noon dose. He checked the bandages and slapped new sterile gauze on the exit wound. It was still sensitive to the touch but the redness was all but gone. He dropped the bed out of the wall. It stretched out before him like the night ahead.

Back in Michigan, where autumn's encroaching darkness had crept in an hour earlier, Sadie peeled out of the driveway with escape in mind. Behind the wheel was the only time she felt free. And while she was sitting on the cold vinyl seat of a Duster, it was his hands on her, warm and sure of purpose.

The fire blazing in Sam's fire pit was visible from the road and lit the shadowy group of figures surrounding it. She parked at the end of his driveway, turned the engine off, and canvassed the group for Stefan's familiar figure. A couple walked out from the shadows behind the house and joined the others around the campfire. She recognized him by his height and carriage, and let herself out of the car, remembering the first time she saw him with the boomerang hanging from his belt, a wide-brimmed hat shading his face.

He wasn't wearing a hat. He crouched beside the fire, and it illuminated the checkered headband tied around his head and the hair hanging loose to his shoulders.

At first, she didn't even notice who he was with.

Sam saw her first. "Hey, Sade—"

Stefan looked up, but all she saw was Nan, pressed against him in a possessive posture, and Sadie knew why he had not answered his phone.

She processed the scene with flashpoint precision. She had overplayed the significance of the intimacy they'd shared a few hours earlier. His singular affection was a figment of her imagination. He wasn't particular; he was already with someone else.

"Hi, Sadie," Nan said, drawing him closer, staking claim.

"Sadie?" Stefan was on his feet. "Sadie, wait!"

She sprinted for the car, but tripped and fell in the gravel, scraping her hands and twisting her ankle. There was muffled laughter and she scrambled to her feet, wanting to make a clean exit, not this clumsy laughing-out-loud display of leaving. She ran around the front of the car, then was fighting him for the door handle.

"Sadie, slow down! What's the matter with you?"

The alcohol on his breath amped up her anger.

"You're drunk. Let go of me!" She wrenched her hand away, got the door open, and fell sideways onto the seat. She dropped the car keys on the floor, like a feckless heroine in a horror movie, and cursed herself, fingers fumbling over the floor mat.

"I'm not drunk." He leaned against the door, holding it open.

She jammed the key in the ignition and cranked it.

"You aren't leaving." He crossed his arms. "You just got here. What's wrong?"

She stared at him. Could he really not know? She was suddenly tired, and her ankle throbbed. She licked the blood off her lip. "Go back to her." She nodded in the direction of the campfire. "I'm going home."

"Get out of the car."

She grappled for the handle in frustration. "Move, Stefan! Get out of the way."

He dug in his heels.

She turned sideways and kicked him. He caught her foot and held on.

"Let go!" She kicked at him, infuriated.

He tightened his hold. "You're acting like a child."

"A child?"

"Only children stomp and kick, Sadie." He eased her foot down on the floorboard and squatted beside her. He suddenly seemed cold sober. "So, let's talk, okay? Get some coffee. Have a conversation." There was a note of humor in his voice.

But she was crying with the humiliation and the hurt. She slapped his hand away. "Don't touch me."

"You think you saw something you didn't see."

"I know what I saw."

"What, Sadie? What did you see?"

"How long has this thing been going on with her?"

"There is nothing going on."

She scoffed in exasperation. "Are you going to get out of the way, or do I have to walk home?

"You can't walk home."

"Watch me."

They were at a stalemate, and he tried a different approach. "Come in the house. I'll make us some coffee. Mom has probably gone to bed and Abby, well . . ." He glanced back at the firelight. "Abby will probably stay out there all night. He lowered his voice and he almost had her. "Come on Sadie, let's go inside and talk."

She considered his reasonable tone and sobering persona, how much she wanted to sit at his table, drink black coffee, and believe him. How much she wanted to stay, but pride stood in the way.

"I'm not the one who needs coffee. I'm leaving. Now get out of the way." She shifted the car into reverse and swerved recklessly out of the driveway. The road was blurred, as if in a downpour. She turned on the radio, blasting her speakers and crying freely.

CHAPTER 22

Henry arrived home from his dinner date to a houseful of lights. Simon Wixom III was waiting up for him as though he had broken curfew, and the irony struck him in an almost wistful way.

"You didn't have to wait up for me, Dad."

"We got a mess." Simon motioned at the papers strewn across the table.

Henry kicked off the dress shoes. He felt altogether loose, and he didn't like his dad's tone or the implication that any mess was a shared mess.

But Simon proceeded to tell him about the false lien and the nuisance complaint.

Henry loosened his shirt and cracked open a beer, his first of the day. It was the farm that drove him to drink. Get an evening away and he hadn't had a one. Just a civilized glass of white wine with Margie's knee against his under the table, her bare foot inside his trouser leg, up and down his calf. That bare foot got him to thinking how much he missed female company, someone to talk to, go out to dinner with, someone to, yes, have sex with. And contrary to Sadie's opinion of Margie, he found it comforting to talk to someone who had known Jenny, known her idiosyncrasies and her habits, someone who had known her and missed her.

Now here he was, one minute home and needing a beer. And his dad was still talking.

"The odor nuisance complaint is a joke. We can counter with all kinds of complaints associated with that place. The lien is another matter. We'll need some legal advice."

"How the hell did he do that?"

"Forged our signatures."

"Well, that's just plain stupid."

"Has anyone accused Bolton of smarts?"

Henry rubbed his brow and drummed his fingers on the table. "Call Mike. He had some experience with false liens last winter. I think the guy ended up in jail."

"I thought Mike retired."

"Does anyone retire anymore?"

"Jail, eh?" Simon squinted at him. "Wouldn't that be a gift."

"He thinks cows stink? We should get a batch of piglets. Pasture them on the other side of the barn, right across from their house. Give him something to complain about."

"We could counter with a noise complaint on that shooting range."

"Yeah. . ." Henry looked at him. "That might be easier. I really don't want to mess with pigs. Fuckers are too smart by half and I'm too old to chase them around the yard." He stood up, downed the beer, thought about another, and decided against it. "Think I'll head off to bed. This can wait 'til morning, right?"

"Another thing I want to talk to you about."

"Yeah?" Henry hesitated, not liking the tone.

"I don't want Sadie seeing the Montegrand boy anymore."

Henry's eyes widened. "Why not?"

"I went back to the courthouse just before they closed to see how to go about filing a rebuttal and I found out that Montegrand has an assault and battery charge pending. And where does he come up with eight thousand dollars to buy a motorcycle?"

"Who filed assault and battery charges?"

"Dick wouldn't say who, doesn't matter, he thought we should have a heads-up, knowing the kid is staying in Larry's rental."

"You're wrong, Dad. It does matter."

"Too many things aren't adding up on Montegrand."

156

"He seems like a good kid."

"In danger of deportation."

"Who said anything about buying a motorcycle?"

"Larry stopped by earlier. The kid has cash, Henry. *Cash.*"

"Why you telling me this? Who doesn't want cash? It's better than an IOU or a payment plan. If Larry's okay with it, I'm okay."

"You know Larry, always giving someone the benefit of the doubt."

"And you consider that a character flaw?"

"The boy's no good, and he has a flash-pan temper."

Henry rocked back on his heels. "That's a pretty harsh statement."

"I don't know how else to put it."

"I think you're wrong."

"We don't know these people. I don't care what Helen says, we don't know them, what they've been up against, or what they're about."

"Sadie likes him."

"He's trouble."

"He works hard. How many kids you know nowadays who are okay with baling hay for ten dollars an hour?"

"He didn't get eight-thousand dollars baling hay. You don't know where he'd get that kind of money, especially to buy something illogic like a motorcycle. She needs to go back to Severn, not the community college. It'll be better for everyone."

"Look, Dad, it's late. We'll talk tomorrow, okay? I'm beat."

He set his bottle in the sink and walked down the hallway before the old man could come up with more problems.

There was a light shining underneath Sadie's door. He raised his hand to knock, then dropped his arm and moved on down the hall.

CHAPTER 23

Sadie was steering clear of her father and grandfather, and staying away from Sam's place, and any chance glimpse of Stefan. She wisely steered clear of the Bolton's and Bolton doings. She traversed trails deep into state land alone with her anger astride Two Socks, avoiding any place where she would meet up with the expectations of others, the imagined pitying looks, as if the whole world knew she'd been jilted.

Evenings, she sat out of sight on the west side of the house against the cement block foundation warmed from the setting sun, nursing her hurt self-esteem, and watching the sun set over the adjacent field to leave tendrils of color across the sky. She walked the field with the dog, kicking clumps of dirt and dry grass on the stray chance of unearthing the lost boomerang. *Why the hell did she care about that?* The events surrounding it and the days of late summer seemed to have happened to someone else. It couldn't have been she who got tangled up with a transient, faithless cad. Someone who would hook up with the likes of Nan.

It was a cool morning, so she put on lined flannels, a hat with ear flaps, and shoved gloves into her back pocket. She put the mare out to pasture and saddled Two Socks. He liked the cooler weather, and when she settled the blanket on his back, he whinnied and tossed his head. She remembered Stefan's hat in the dirt, how he had ridden bareback out of the stable bay with his hands loose on the reins and a smile teasing his lips. That he would have ended up with Nan, of all people, had hurt more than anything. But he had never made any promises. It was humiliating to have acted as though he had. Like the child he said she was.

She rode to the grove of evergreens that bordered the creek at the corner of the farm and ducked the low-hanging boughs to enter the clearing blanketed with pine needles. She dismounted and led the horse down the bank to drink. Bolton had been forced to dismantle the dam, and the creek was running free again. The nuisance claims and false lien were running their course between two sets of lawyers. Henry told her Bolton was being forced to withdraw the second, while they were fighting for legal fees and a fine for wrongful action. But Bolton was throwing out bizarre charges the court couldn't outright dismiss without the obligatory examination.

She watched the horse drink. He raised his dripping muzzle to look about and then sunk his mouth back into the water. Watching a horse drink could give a person a sense of rightness in the world when everything was wrong.

According to her cousin, Stefan was looking at used boats, and she remembered how he had spoken fondly of his brother, his penchant for motoring around the waterways of home in his "rez" canoe.

"Boats aren't cheap, even used," Sam had said, joining her in the stable earlier when she was readying Two Socks for the ride. "The guy must be loaded." He went on to speculate about his casino theory, and Sadie interrupted him.

"Trust me, Sam, that isn't it."

"Then what is it?"

"It's none of our business."

Sam squinted at her. "I saw him yesterday. He asked about you."

Sadie pinched her lips together. She wasn't falling for it.

"You know he didn't come back to the campfire that night."

"Do I care?"

"I think you do."

She grabbed the push broom, filling the air with chaff and dust.

"You wanna hear about the boat he's looking at?"

She shook her head, sweeping out the corners, dust flying.

"An old wooden one. He says he'd paint it blue like one his dad had. Corny, eh?"

"Look." She leaned on the broom and brushed the hair out of her eyes. "I don't want to hear about it. I don't care what he's doing."

"Liar."

"Tell someone who cares, Sam. Tell Nan." She took up her sweeping, pushing a pile of stable debris to the doorway where a gust of wind swirled it into a dust devil and whisked it away.

"Nan?" He shook his head in disgust. "Look, Sadie, I don't know what happened between them that night, but it couldn't have amounted to much. You know, living next door, I see things. She came around a few times this past week—who could miss that car? —but never stayed long, last time left in a huff, shit flying through the air."

"Whatever." Sadie dismissed Sam and his speculatione with a wave of her hand. She turned her face toward the sunlight, absorbing the end of summer, fleeting warmth from a retreating sun. She wasn't falling for it. Not again.

"I just thought you should know she's back with the Bolton boys, one or both, who knows. I think they're more her speed."

Deep breaths of fading summer, a blue boat on still water.

"His mother told Dad last night that they might be moving. She finally connected with the relatives. They're in the Soo, Canadian side."

The broom stabbed at a stubborn piece of straw.

"I have an idea. Why don't you go out with me tonight?"

"Out with you?"

"There's a band playing at the marina, last outdoor event of the season, they're supposed to be good. They have horns. Abby's going, Sid and a couple other guys. Come on, it'll be fun."

"I'll think about it."

"We're leaving around eight, could squeeze you in."

"If I go, I'll drive myself."

"Sure, okay." He waited a minute. "How about I tell Stef?" He grinned. "You can pick him up."

"How about you don't?"

"Okay, I won't."

160

She had saddled Two Socks and rode him down the lane with no destination in mind. But here she was, watching him drink from the creek that had reclaimed its path across the lowlands.

Stefan was drawn to the boatyard, not knowing what he was looking for until he spotted the fourteen-foot wooden boat in need of attention. He envisioned Joachim at the rudder and he in the bow, fishing side by side like they used to. As though all he had to do was buy a boat.

Sadie was screening calls and not taking his. He regretted giving in and letting her drive away. From eating a burnt hot dog at Sam's to the moment he saw Sadie staring at him in disgust, the night was a blur. The sight of her had jarred him awake, as if from a deep state of fugue, but then what? He had let her leave, that's what. Watching dumbly from the center of the road as her taillights disappeared over the hill. Waiting for her to make a U-turn and reconsider, willing her to come back and let him explain that things had gotten away from him. The tequila, the campfire, and the smoke had all gotten away from him. Yes, he had been with Nan, but to what extent, he honestly couldn't remember.

He drove by her place, but her father and grandfather were out front, and he kept going. He couldn't deal with those two, especially not together. He wasn't even sure how to deal with her. The thing with Nan was an embarrassing blur of urgency, alcohol, and guilt. Boats were easy. He needed some easy.

He had dropped the motorcycle off at the shop for brake work the morning after the debacle at Sam's, and he was reduced to driving the van, which was as clunky as a Conestoga in comparison.

The horses were grazing in the front pasture and the herd of cattle stood in the distance, black behemoths dotting the hillside. He slowed on the edge of the road, considering the idyllic scene, not so different from the prairielands of Saskatchewan, and thought again of Joachim, who seemed to have fallen off the rim of the Canadian Shield.

There were so many things he wanted to tell Sadie, the only person he had been able to talk to since arriving in Sawyers Pond, starting with the news out of Sault Ste. Marie. His mother, with Helen's help, had finally found the erstwhile cousins. They weren't living in the Upper Peninsula of Michigan. They were living in Canada.

So back they were going, or so she said.

He pulled back on the road, unaware he had stopped on the side until a vehicle honked and passed, giving him a wide berth. He left the tranquil scene in his rearview mirror and rang up the boatyard, phone in one hand, wheel in the other.

Sadie pulled into the marina parking lot and parked in the back where she wouldn't get hemmed in. Lights were strung around the outdoor patio and twinkled in the breeze. Music drifted across the gravel lot; the distinctive sound of a saxophone accompanied by a keyboard. Sam was right: a band with brass. She grabbed her handbag off the seat and locked the door with her key.

She walked through the throng, looking for him. The five-piece band was set up on a stage under a covered area in the corner. She had to turn sideways to inch through the crowd and was beginning to doubt the wisdom of arriving late when he hailed her from a table in the far corner of the deck.

He pulled a chair out of nowhere and motioned her to it. Sam always found an empty table, an extra chair, an empty barstool. They opened up for him as if he were a celebrity. He knew how to work a room.

Abby looked at Sadie quizzically "Did you come by yourself?" She looked older than her years with a bob haircut and dark eye makeup.

Sadie nodded and took her wallet out of her purse.

Sam flagged the waiter down. "Bring her a tonic and lime and I'll have another beer. Here." He put a twenty on the tray. "Make it a round for the table."

"Since when do I drink tonic?"

He opened his jacket and flashed the pint of gin in the inside pocket. "Since it goes with gin."

"And no one is going to know?"

He looked at Abby. "I don't know, does anyone know?"

She took a sip of her tonic and lime, eyes wide and lined in black. "You're a bad influence."

"I'm a good influence." He looked around the table. "Right, guys?"

They all laughed. The band was going on break, and the waiter brought their drinks.

"Come here." Sam pushed his chair back and motioned to Sadie. "You ever check out the lower deck?"

She followed him down the steps to the newly hewed lower deck, and they leaned against the railing. A fine mist was in the air and carried a faint odor of mildew. The marina had expanded in sprawling fashion, gobbling up public beach, and dozens of sailboats corralled in their slips bobbed on the water. The moon came out from behind a cloud and cast a silver sheen over the masts, the sun-bleached moorings, and creosoted pilings.

He opened the gin and poured a splash in her glass. "There, that'll lighten you up."

Sadie took a sip and grimaced. "It tastes like pine needles."

"Dad says it's medicinal."

"I thought that was Grandpa."

"Medicinal needs run in the family."

"Is that where he was looking at boats?" She nodded at the adjacent dry dock and boatyard, filled with trailers and boats of various sizes and condition.

He cast her a side glance. "Thought you didn't care."

She watched the waves of Lake Huron lapping the abutment. The breeze picked up on an easterly and carried the smell of fish, sand, and grit. The twinkling lights of a lake freighter steaming for the straits of Mackinac crawled along the horizon.

He poured another measure of gin in her glass. "There, topped off. Let's get back to the others."

She fished out the chunk of lime and rubbed it around the lip of the glass the way she'd seen her mother do in the *before*.

They climbed the stairs to their table, and there, front and center, was Stefan Montegrand.

CHAPTER 24

He wore a brown homespun tunic, and a silver chain with a blue stone set in the pendant hung around his neck. His hair was pulled back in a ponytail, and he was nonchalantly stretched out in a chair. She swallowed and looked at Sam. He had lied to her, and she was unprepared and disadvantaged.

"Hey, my man." Sam clapped him on the shoulder. "What brings you out of hiding?"

"I was over at the marina, heard the band you talked about, and thought I'd check it out."

"Tell us about this boat you bought."

"Who said I bought a boat? I'm just looking."

"Sit down, Sadie." Abby slid over. "Sam, find another chair."

The sight of Stefan looking relaxed and comfortable angered her. The flush that flooded her face angered her more.

"What are you looking at?" Sid chuckled. "Pontoons?"

"A fourteen-foot peeler."

"What the hell is a peeler?"

"Little faster than a pontoon," Stefan said.

"Wooden boats are too much work," Sam said.

"There's no sign of rot but it's been out of the water for a long time. My brother had a wooden boat. Once you've been in a wooden boat, well, there's nothing like it."

"Like an Indian motorcycle, right, Steffi?" Abby said with a smile.

Steffi? Sadie laughed in spite of herself.

"First a motorcycle, now a boat." Sam pulled up an extra chair. "How about a round, Steffi?"

"Knock it off."

Sam flagged the waiter. "Bring us a round. What are you drinking?" He looked at Stefan.

"I'll have a beer, and bring us a couple baskets of fries. I'm hungry." He looked at Sadie. "Are you hungry?"

"He didn't ask for your ID," Sam observed. "I don't know what it is about you."

"What are you drinking, Sadie?" Stefan hadn't taken his eyes off her. His presence was devouring her.

"Tonic." She took a gulp of her drink.

"No moonshine?"

"Moonshine?" Sam said. "Grandpa into that again? Last time he nearly blew up the kitchen."

"He makes moonshine?" Abby asked.

"Criminal activity runs in the family."

Sadie kicked him under the table. "That's ancient history." The family had indeed turned respectable after Simon Wixom II acquired a chunk of bottomland and a herd of dairy cows. With the exception of a great-uncle who absconded under pressure in the dead of night for undisclosed reasons, the rest of the family had since engaged in legal activities.

"Sounds like a noble profession," Stefan said.

"Where's your girlfriend?" she heard herself ask.

He rested his hand on her knee. "Right here," he said.

She was a sap. His slightest touch melted her. She should shove him away. She didn't move. She could barely breathe.

"Hell hath no fury like a woman scorned," Sam remarked. "Especially when said woman is Nan Murkowski."

"I'm surprised you didn't hear her all the way to your place," Abby said. "Oh, she was mad. Kicked his boots off the porch and heaved them right into the road."

"She has a good arm," Stefan remarked dryly.

166

The waiter was back with their drinks. "Fries will be up in five," he said, setting ketchup and malt vinegar on the table.

Stefan put a fifty-dollar bill on the tray.

"Throwing marked fifties around?" Zender materialized from out of the crowd and stood over their table. Clem followed arm-in-arm with Nan.

"Oh, great," Sam said under his breath.

"Hi y'all," Nan said. Her eyes flicked back and forth between Sadie and Stefan.

"Hey, y'all," Zender mimicked. He wore a Michigan ball cap turned backwards. Unlike his brother, he had hair and a two-day growth of beard. "Hey, Montegrand, heard you bought a motorcycle."

"And did I hear something about a boat?" Clem added.

"Rich man's sport." Zender rocked on the balls of his feet and glanced across the sea of masts bobbing in the moonlight.

"Where you getting all this money? You obviously ain't working."

"Freeloader." Zender spat to the side.

"If it ain't casino money, what is it? Somebody die? Leave you a pile of money?"

Sadie felt Stefan stiffen beside her.

"Hey," Zender prodded, "if that's it, just say so."

"Go on, Bolton," Sam said. "Find your own table."

Clem turned to Zender. "Didja hear about the bank robbery down in West Branch?"

"There was one just north of here too. Rash of 'em."

"They suspect the same guy," Clem said. "Law enforcement's all over it."

"That right?"

"They got a whole team studying the tapes from those security cameras. Don't mess with the banks, man." Clem looked at Stefan. "Mom and pop stores are one thing, but don't mess with the FDIC."

"Get lost," Sam said.

"You Wixoms have your own legal problems, should be careful who you hang out with. Just warning you. The old man ain't happy, getting a permit denied over outdated drainage rules. Just because you've been here for a hundred years doesn't mean you own the county. Maybe your rich Indo friend here can help you with legal fees."

"You don't know what you're talking about," Sadie spoke up.

"Why Sadie," Clem turned his gaze on her in mock surprise, "I didn't see you there."

Zender's smile didn't reach his eyes. "You still got that mongrel dog?"

Stefan draped a possessive arm around the back of her chair.

The waiter was back with the fries and a stack of plates. "Can I get you guys anything else?"

"Thanks," Sam said. "We're all set." He looked up at the Boltons. "Excuse us, wouldja?"

"Sure," Clem said, "Enjoy yourselves." He steered Nan away from the table, but she pulled back and dropped a hand on Stefan's shoulder.

"You still owe me a game of pool, baby."

Clem yanked her by the arm. "Don't be a slut."

She threw a glance back at Sadie. "*You* wouldn't know it, but he's good."

Sam broke the silence. "C'mon, let's eat." He took a handful of fries and passed the basket. "They're getting cold."

Stefan helped himself with one hand, the other firmly around Sadie's shoulders. "Want some?" he asked her.

"No." Her voice was clipped.

"Don't worry about them," Sam said. "Eat."

"I'd rather drink." She pushed her glass across the table, and he splashed a furtive shot of gin in it.

Stefan raised an eyebrow as she squeezed her chunk of lime and ran it around the lip of the glass. She stirred the drink with her finger and put it in her mouth.

The breeze had picked up off the water and the lights danced along the railing. Clem and Zender stood in the corner by the stairs, heads together, while Nan drank from a tall glass festooned with chunks of pineapple and blood-red cherries. Laughter carried above the mournful sound of a saxophone solo.

Sam pulled Abby out on the dance floor while Sid and Stefan ate the French fries. Stefan doused his with malt vinegar and extra salt, and leaned over his plate.

She watched him eat. "First time you've had French fries, *baby*?"

He wiped his fingers on a napkin. "When'd you start drinking gin?"

"Since tonight."

"I've been trying to call you." His voice strummed the air between them, and the others receded. He sopped up the vinegar with the last fry, then wiped his mouth on a napkin, balled it up and dropped it on his plate. He paused a moment and then looked at her. "I'm sorry. About the other night."

Sadie gripped her glass, hanging on.

He threw back his beer and stood up. "Let's get out of here. I have Mom's van. Motorcycle's in the shop."

"How about I give you a ride in my car?" she heard herself say. Where was her anger?

"How many of those you had?" He nodded at the now empty glass.

"Two."

"Two too many. I'll drive." He pushed his chair back.

"Leaving?" Sid asked.

"Leaving," Stefan said.

She grabbed her purse, and just like that, she was leaving with him. A sap.

Clem stepped in front of them at the top of the stairs, eyes fixated on Sadie.

"Leaving, Cherry?"

Stefan stepped in front of her. A vein pulsed on the side of his forehead. "Get out of the way, Bolton."

"Make me, pretty boy."

"You want that?"

Zender glanced from Stefan to his brother and grabbed his arm. "Cool it, Clem. Not here."

Stefan took a step forward. "Do you?"

Sadie tugged his hand. "C'mon. Let's go." She pulled him down the stairs and into the parking lot.

The gravel crunched under their feet and the music faded. He opened the passenger-side door of the van, saw her inside, and slammed it shut, glancing over his shoulder. He jumped in the other side and revved the engine. It backfired, sputtered, and he tapped on the gas. "C'mon girl, act right."

Sadie took a deep breath. The interior of the van smelled like Armor All and the bench seat was spacious. The instrument panel was barebones with a push button radio. The gear shift was on the steering wheel, and the windows were roll-down.

The engine coughed, settled, and he looked at her for a long minute.

"Why'd he call you that?"

Sadie swallowed. "I've no idea."

"I should've punched him in the mouth."

"That's what he wanted. We were smart to leave."

"Maybe." He dropped the gear shift into drive and maneuvered out of the parking lot. "Where do you want to go?"

"Somewhere we can talk."

"Okay." He swung out on the lakeshore drive.

She rested her hand on the vinyl seat between them. "I've never seen a van with bench seats. And roll-down windows."

"It's a relic, pushing two-hundred thousand miles."

"Then you've taken good care of it."

"Had to."

She glanced over her shoulder at the space behind them. "It's huge."

He grunted agreement.

Sadie looked out the window at the woods rushing by. Beyond the trees she knew Lake Huron stretched to the horizon. Even from miles away, its presence was a barometer, a ruling force of nature. It was the way Michiganders gauged the seasons, like the passing of migrating waterfowl.

They passed a sign for a roadside park and Stefan tapped the brake. The lot was empty, and he parked the van in the far corner.

He turned off the key and looked at her. "So, here we are."

Yes, here they were. She suddenly felt awkward, wanting to hold on to her anger, but it no longer held its edge, a knife that needed to be sharpened.

"What do you want to talk about?"

She didn't know where to start, so she started off slow. "I understand your mom found the relatives you've been looking for."

"*She's* been looking for. Yeah, a branch of the family is living in Ontario, a few miles from Sault Ste. Marie.

"That's not far."

"They're family, but they aren't Montegrands. I mean, we're related, but I don't know them. Don't know that I *want* to know them."

"Have you heard from your brother?"

He looked out the window as though Joachim was pulling in beside them. "No," he said. "I haven't."

"Aunt Helen said your mother likes it here."

"She's always felt out of place here. No—" he held up his hand— "your family's been great, but there's no escaping prevailing attitudes."

"When are you leaving?"

"Who said *I* was leaving?"

She bit her lip. "I always knew you would."

He tapped his fingers on the steering wheel. "Haven't exactly seen the welcome wagon—whatever that is— the one your aunt talks about skipped us. Least I ain't seen it."

"They don't do that anymore."

He considered her. "You don't want me to leave, do you?"

She looked out the side window, the hooked moon breaking free from a fleece of cloud. No, she didn't want him to leave.

"Do you?"

"What do you want?" she whispered.

He took her hand, pressed his lips softly to the back of it, then turned it over to kiss the inside of her wrist. "I want you to know that I'm sorry. About the other night. It didn't mean anything, and I'm sorry."

Anger was a safer stance, but she couldn't hold onto it with his mouth and lips at her wrist. No, she didn't want him to leave, but the other night was the problem, because if it happened once. . .

"They were drinking tequila."

"*They*? You smelled like a booze hound."

"There's a reason I don't do liquor. It turns me into somebody I don't much like."

"Then why do it?"

He cast her a questioning glance, as if she could help him decipher his vices and pinpoint the weakness in judgment his father had alluded to. Why he couldn't stay at the cabin by the roadblock, traverse the trap lines alone, take the snow machine across ice, why he drank when he knew he shouldn't. He shook his head. "I don't know. I honestly don't remember much."

"Bullshit!" Sadie said angrily. "That's a cop out."

"I know it sounds like a cop out, but it's the truth." He looked at her pleadingly. "It's the truth, Sadie. Hell, I don't even like Nan that way." He rubbed his eyes with the heel of his hand. "The night got away from me. It's embarrassing, but I don't know how that happened. I just know that I'm sorry. I was sorry then and I'm sorry now."

His voice had dropped to a whisper, and he raised his hand haltingly to brush his hair back, and she wasn't angry anymore.

Cradled in the intimacy of a deserted roadside park with the luxury of a bench seat, kissing him was easy. Anger took such an exacting toll on a person. It was good to let it go. He pulled her across his lap, but the steering column was in the way, and she winced when the gear shift caught her in the ribs. He let go of her and opened his door, swung his legs out and looked back at her. "Come with me around back."

"What?" But he had closed the door. She got out and walked around the side of the van. The crescent moon had cleared a path across the sky and cast a muted light about the clearing. The sound of the waves eroding the shore drifted over the ridge of the embankment, the big lake tirelessly changing the face of the shoreline.

He opened the cargo doors and climbed inside the van. She hesitated, but he held out his hand, and she took it. He aimed the beam of a flashlight around the interior. The back seat was folded down into a bed. Side shelves lined one wall of the van and checkered curtains hung over the windows. There was a built-in magazine rack stuffed with maps and travel logs, an overhead rack for storage, and a tiny fridge tucked in the corner.

"Well?" There was a smile in his voice. "What do you think?"

She followed the beam of the flashlight. "It's like one of those tiny houses on wheels."

He kicked off his boots. "Take your shoes off," he said.

He was getting ahead of her.

"Come on, Sadie." He grinned and it transformed his face, like it had the first time she'd seen him smile. "Take your shoes off and stay awhile."

She set her sneakers beside his boots and pulled her knees into her chest.

He turned the flashlight off, and ambient light illuminated the trees that stood tall around the parking lot and blocked the road. It illuminated the shape of his shoulders, the contours of his face and the smoldering depth of his eyes. He leaned against the seatback, crossed his legs, and waited.

She was nervous and heard herself make an empty comment, something to fill the silence he was always okay with.

"Come here," he said. "I can't hear you."

She gathered her hair off her neck and dropped it again in an anxious gesture. Without the confines of seats and armrests, dash and wheel, there was too much space.

"Come on." He patted the sleeping bag. "Sit beside me."

She couldn't *not* do it. She scooched back beside him, knee to knee, thigh to thigh, and it was easy to slip into the crook of his arm, easy to lie beside him and pick up where they had left off.

"I just want to be with you, really with you," he whispered. "But nothing you don't want, okay?"

His hair smelled like shampoo and was soft under her fingers. She wasn't a child, and there wasn't anything she didn't want.

He undid her blouse, one slow button at a time, then unhooked her bra, and the air touched her skin. He trailed a finger between her breasts, cupped one in the palm of his hand, and rolled the nipple under his thumb. She gasped at the sensation, then he took it in his mouth, and his desire became hers.

They unzipped their jeans and were rid of them. She ran her hands inside his tunic and pulled it over his head. The muscles of his back and chest were smooth and defined, and there was nothing between them but a blue stone on a pendant shining in the moonlight, like the eye of the world. She pulled his head back to her nipple because it had turned cold with his neglect.

He rested his hand on her stomach, then lowered it between her legs. She shuddered with surprise, then leaned into it, wanting more. Mindless with wanting, with how good it felt.

He was hard against her leg, but in his urgency, she felt hesitation. "What's wrong?" she said.

He drew in a ragged breath. "Are you okay?"

"Yes," she whispered against his mouth.

Still, he hesitated. "Are you sure this is what you want?"

Her whole life had led up to this moment for which there could only be one answer. "Yes. God, yes." She moistened her lips, holding onto a shred of sense. "Do you have a condom?"

He nodded and took a minute. The separation was torture. Then he lowered himself between her legs, and the breadth of his erection felt impossible. She bent her knees, thinking that would help, thinking it was a good thing he was slim-hipped, but then— dear God! —how could that help? The pressure was intense, as if there was nowhere for him to go. How humiliating would it be if she couldn't even do it?

But with single-mindedness, he pressed himself forward, gently rocking himself in, finding a way. *Slowly, too slowly,* for she suddenly wanted him with all the strength of her being. She arched her back and wrapped her legs around him, locking her ankles, should he ever try to get away. But with a final thrust, he was effortlessly inside her, and nothing was impossible.

He pulled a blanket over them, and the rest of the world fell away, like a receding shot of Google Earth.

CHAPTER 25

Cold breached the mud-chinked corners of the cabin, and Joachim pulled the woolen throw he'd kicked off in the night around his shoulders. He was alone. For ten days he'd been alone, but the remnants of a dream peopled the room. The gray light of dawn wafted through the window, and he tried to separate the dreamscape from reality. The dead from the living. The pane was covered with frost. The cold cracked. The fire was down.

He pulled a flannel shirt over his T-shirt, socks on his feet, and stoked the embers in the wood stove. When he had a lively flame, he threw in a log from the bottom of the wood box. He hadn't felt up to swinging an axe, or the need to do so. But the woodpile was depleted, and now the wood box sat accusingly empty. He stood in the doorway and studied the frost-covered ground. Winter was coming.

He glanced at his shelf of diminished goods. After he'd taken out two rabbits with the bow and arrow, the rest had disappeared, as if the matriarch from *Watership Down* had come to life and raised the alarm. He'd tried fishing off the bank of the stream, casting everything from worms and grubs, to a clump of rabbit fur and a scrap of red cloth. The trout weren't biting.

Drawing a basin of water, he considered the twenty-mile walk out to the main road to thumb a ride. If he left early enough, he could make it before dark. But then who would pick him up? He could see himself with his thumb out, a bedraggled, indigent-looking native. Anybody who'd picked *that* up couldn't have good intentions.

At least the gunshot wounds were healing. The exit wound was slowest to heal but had finally closed like an eye, and the surgical incision had healed to a puckered slit below his collarbone. He washed himself with a bar of soap, then rinsed his undershirt out in the soapy gray water and hung it on the back of a chair in front of the stove. He locked his fingers behind his back to loosen the tightness in his shoulder. It was two weeks since the bullet plowed through him. He had healed fast and hadn't coughed up any more blood. Maybe it was the beans, squash, and corn. Even so, if he made it out of here, he would swear off the three sisters of Indian agriculture.

He pulled a blanket off the bed, wrapped it around his shoulders, and ate his beans from the can. He turned on his cell phone, part of his morning ritual, set it on the table, and drank a cup of water. At least there was plenty of that, cold and sweet from the bowels of the earth.

The phone beeped, and he stared at it dumbly. He had service, two bars of service. He rushed outside and it went to three. He pulled up contacts, scrolled down to "Josie" and tapped *call.*

It rang. He sat on the stoop and pressed the phone to his ear.

"Hello? Jac? Is that you?"

"Josie! Where the *fuck* are you?"

"Baby, are you okay? Jesus—" There was the sound of breaking glass.

"You okay? What was that?"

"Nothing. It's nothing. I've been worried sick. How are you?"

"I'm about out of food and wood and it's cold and where the fuck are you? Hello? Are you there?"

"Yes, I'm here. Did you finish the antibiotics?"

"Yes, I finished the damn pills and kept the incision clean and it itches like hell and I need some coffee. It's damn cold up here."

"Okay, good. That's good, Jac . . ."

There was a pause along the line, and he pictured her thinking with the little vein on the side of her forehead throbbing in overdrive.

"They towed your jeep," she said finally. "Impounded it as evidence. I got ahold of Savior and met him at the Council House last night and gave him some of your things. He said he'd get up there first thing this morning."

"They took my jeep?"

"Louise thinks she can get it back."

"Louise's a rookie."

"She's the one got me out. After they found it in my garage, they pulled me in for questioning and kept me on some blown-up charge."

"You were in jail? Jesus."

"Briefly. Louise's a rookie, but she has methods. They're still poking around, asking questions. She warned me to sit tight, they have me under surveillance."

"Did you get my gun out of the jeep?"

"Yes."

"Did you give it to Savior?"

"Yes."

He rubbed his mouth and the whiskers on his chin. It itched. Everything itched.

"How'd they connect us? They must have someone on the inside."

"Murphy—"

"Murphy would never do that."

"No, but maybe someone who works there."

"You say Savior's coming?"

"He should be there anytime."

"I was ready to start walking."

She exhaled in exasperation, and he pictured her formulating an argument.

"Josie, when are *you* coming?"

"Talk to Savior, okay? He has a plan."

Savior the Sane, the guy with a plan. His was the plan that had landed him here.

"Jac?"

"Did you get ahold of Stefan?"

"No. They confiscated my phone while I was in custody. I just got it back. We probably shouldn't even be talking. Louise is getting me one of those throwaway ones that aren't as smart. Then I'll call him, okay?"

He nodded.

"Jac? I figured that was what you'd want."

"Yeah, okay."

"It's such a relief to finally talk to you . . ." Her voice faded out and there was interference on the line.

"Hello! Hello? Jos, when are you coming?"

The phone went dead. He looked at the screen. The bars were gone. But if it happened once, it could happen again. The battery icon indicated another problem, and he turned it off. A pair of cardinals skimmed the clearing, and he kicked at the ground, digesting the call.

He hung his shirt on the railing outside to dry, then made the bed and hefted it back into the wall unit. He pulled the chair up to the window and rested his feet on the sill to wait for Savior. He had a little tobacco left he was saving, but with more coming he rolled his last cigarette and thought of all the trouble he had brought down on Josie's head. He couldn't go back there, not now. But Savior was coming.

Roberto was Bobby and Josephine was Josie, and he was Jac, but Savior was always Savior.

CHAPTER 26

In the predawn hours, Stefan dropped Sadie off beside her car at the marina. She'd ridden next to him on the bench seat with their legs touching, thinking it a shame they didn't make them anymore. Bucket seats were so . . . *cold.*

He took her hand and brought it to his mouth. "I'll call you later, Sadie."

She hesitated, reluctant to leave, then dug her keys out of her purse and slid across the seat to open the door.

She drove home thinking how everything between them had changed in a mere eight hours. She swung around the circle drive to park where she always parked, but Margie's Honda was in the way. She pulled in beside it and examined her feelings about that. She eased herself out of the car; she was stiff and sore, and looked in the passenger window. There was mail on the floor, cigarette butts in the ashtray, and a pine tree deodorizer hanging from the rearview mirror. She felt a resurgence of the old feeling of superiority her mother had instilled in her from an early age, correcting everything from her grammar and table manners, to her friendships and what she wore out the door, because Wixoms were better than others in the rural community and needed to act it.

On the other hand, Henry didn't care what she wore, if she used double negatives, or ate over the sink. He hadn't suggested she stop seeing Stefan like her grandfather had, and she wondered whose side her mother would have been on.

The old adage that opposites attract was the only explanation for Margie and her mother's friendship. Margie smoked, wore crop tops, watched reality tv shows, and drank the soda pop Jenny never allowed in the house. Maybe it was golf, the great equalizer. They wore proper attire, repaired their divots, and counted every stroke as well as those of their opponents.

She let herself in the back door and tiptoed through the dark kitchen, glancing at the digital clock on the oven in passing, and walked on down the hall, pausing for a moment outside his bedroom door where he was no longer alone. She waited for the old feelings of jealousy and betrayal to rear their conjoined heads, but a shift in mindset had occurred in the back of a van on the edge of the lake.

There was nothing as profound as what she had just discovered with Stefan, and she couldn't fault her father for finding someone again. It took nothing from what he and her mother had shared.

She undressed, remembering the way Stean had done it, as though he had forever to loosen a button and find the pull on a zipper. How what had seemed impossible was easy, and seated in the midst of remembrance was the knowledge that her time in the house she grew up in was ending. It was fitting for someone else to be moving in.

As she drifted off to sleep, she wondered what her mother would have thought of him.

Stefan was in a dream and fighting to stay there when sunlight fell across his face and flickered behind his eyelids. He buried his face in his pillow, but a breeze wafted through the open window along with the sounds of the day and pulled him into wakefulness.

He was sweating under his covers and he kicked them off.

There was a quick tap on the door and Abby opened it.

"Gross!" She averted her eyes. "Cover yourself!"

He swung his legs out of bed and rubbed his eyes. "What do you want?"

"You're disgusting."

He pulled the sheet across his lap. "Don't barge in on a person."

"Mom wants you. She's next door at Helen's." She paused for a second. "Where did you and Sadie go last night?"

"Nowhere."

"Hmm." She tapped her lip with her index finger. "Sam says the hotel has bedbugs."

"Get out of here." He reached for his shorts, and she slammed the door.

He pulled on his jeans from the night before and slipped his feet into the moccasins beside the bed. The events of the past twenty-four hours were a blur, except for one thing, the clear component on which everything else hinged. Just thinking about the night before quickened his pulse. It wasn't his first time, but it dwarfed any others, from embarrassing adolescent episodes to a more serious but brief relationship with Savior's sister.

His mother was on Helen's phone and Helen was on the computer. She motioned him to a chair. He spun it around backwards and straddled it, draping his arms across the back.

"Hello, Stefan," Helen said without taking her eyes off the screen.

Margaret hung up the phone, looked at him for a long moment, and he shifted his feet.

"Were you at the marina last night?"

He frowned. "Yeah, I was there, looking around, thinking about putting a down payment on a boat."

"You bought a boat?"

"Thinking about it."

"Why?"

"Because I want a boat."

"It's hardly the time. Don't be rash."

"I'm just looking. Is that rash?"

"There was a break-in there last night."

"You're kidding."

"That was the police. They wanted to know where you were last night." They were both looking at him. A hint of suspicion lined Helen's brow and agitated his mother's hands.

Stefan leaned back, coming to grips with the line of questioning.

"Someone reported you at the scene, said there was an argument, shouting and big voices, what all. Big argument."

"That's a lie."

"But you were there."

"Yeah, but there wasn't any argument, just haggling the price." He looked at Helen. "Like Larry told me to. He wouldn't come down, so I left. Who said there was an argument?"

"An anonymous informant."

"They just want your help, Stefan." Helen looked at him over the top of her glasses. "See if you know anything, or saw anything untoward."

"What was stolen?"

"Boat motor, cash box, various boating incidentals off the yard. This informant says there was a van backed up to the side door late last night."

"They described ours, Stefan," Margaret said in a soft voice.

He stood up, spun the chair around, and slid it back under the table. "This is crazy."

"Detective Evans is on his way over to talk to you."

"Oh, is he?"

"Just be straight with him," Helen said. "He's a good cop. He'll get to the bottom of it."

"I'd like to know who's making these accusations." He looked back and forth between them. "I'll bet it was one of the Boltons."

Margaret followed him out the door. They walked across the yard, and he looked at the van. There weren't many like it.

He made a pot of coffee, and Margaret told Abby to go to her room. "And stay there. Someone's coming to interview your brother, and I want you to stay in your room."

"Interview? He's getting a job?"

"No, Abigail," Stefan said sarcastically, "It ain't a job."

"Never mind. Go." She pointed at Abby's door, and Abby went, throwing a worried glance Stefan's way.

"Change your shirt," Margaret told him.

He poured himself a cup of coffee. "What? To talk to this copper?"

"It won't hurt to present a clean appearance. That one looks slept in."

He looked down at himself. It had been, more than once. He carried his cup of coffee into the bedroom and opened the folding door on the tiny closet. He couldn't imagine what this was all about, but from witnessing his father and brother's interactions with the law, a clean shirt wouldn't help.

A sharp knock sounded on the front door. Stefan strode across the room and threw it open.

The police officer was tall. He had to duck to come through the door, and Stefan had to look up to meet his eye.

"I'm Deputy Evans from the Sheriff's Department, just talked to your mother." He threw a quick glance at Margaret, and then back at Stefan. "Are you Stefan?"

Stefan nodded and shook his hand.

Margaret waved him in to the kitchen table. "Come in, please sit down. We're happy to help, aren't we, Stefan?"

"Sure, happy to help."

They sat down, and Evans opened a small notebook, taking a pen from the slot in his shirt pocket. "Like I told your mother, there was a break-in at the marina last night and we hope you can shed some light on what might have happened." He glanced at his watch and jotted down the time. "Can you spell your last name for me?"

Stefan spelled it.

"I understand you were there around closing time. Is that right?"

Stefan took a sip of coffee and composed himself.

"You were there, right?"

"I was looking at some of the used boats."

"If you'll just recount for me what happened, if anything, while you were there."

"Nothing happened."

Evans peered at him intently. "If you'll just give me a rundown of the conversation, son."

"Conversation?"

"You talked to someone, didn't you?"

"Yeah, I had some questions about a wooden one. I wanted to check the hull for rot. They weren't going to include a motor, and I questioned that. You ever hear of buying a boat without a motor?"

"Like buying a car without an engine?"

"They were asking too much, and I was trying to get him to come down, but all he'd do was throw in cushions."

"And oars?"

Stefan looked at him, feeling like he was being led. "Don't need oars."

"What time was this?"

Stefan squished up his mouth. "About eight o'clock."

"They close at eight."

"Maybe he was making a concession, thought he had someone on the hook that didn't know boats."

"But you do." Evans rested his elbow on the table and jiggled his pen between his forefinger and index fingers. "Did that make you mad?"

"Mad?"

"Being underestimated."

Stefan snorted. "No, sir. I'm used to that."

The pen was back on paper, scratching a note. He looked at what he had written and then back at Stefan. "So, when did you go back to, ah, just look at the boat again?"

"Who said I went back?"

"Did you?"

"They close the gates after hours, so what would be the point?"

"Right, they close the gates and lock things up."

The atmosphere had turned frosty.

"Your van was reported inside those gates about three this morning."

"How do you know it was my van?"

"That's what we're investigating."

"Reported by who?"

"Can't divulge that right now."

"Check the damn cameras. Everybody has cameras around here. Check them."

"Jerry's cameras are out of commission." He shook his head in disapproval. "Said he was working on upgrading security. A day too late, appears."

"Well, it wasn't me. I can damn well guarantee my van wasn't there at three o'clock in the morning."

"Can someone vouch for your whereabouts at that time?"

Stefan sat lockjawed. This was going nowhere fast.

Deputy Evans looked at Margaret. "Mrs. Montegrand?"

She looked away.

"What was stolen?" Stefan asked.

"A motor, fish finder, cash . . ."

There was silence around the table. Stefan drummed his fingers on the oilcloth.

"How long you folks been in the country?"

"Eight, nine weeks," Margaret said in a rush. "Helen and Larry sponsored us through a program at the Women's Center. She's helping me locate family."

"Hmm, right." Evans read through his notes.

"We were thinking to stay but now, well, we're moving back to Canada." She looked at Stefan.

He sat immobile and uncommitted.

"Mind if I take a look in the van?" Evans said.

Stefan clenched his fists under the table. He wanted to kick him out of the house, along with his notes and insinuations.

They walked across the gravel drive. Stefan threw the cargo doors open and motioned Evans to look inside.

"You don't lock it?"

"Who'd want to steal it?"

He stuck his head inside, and Stefan saw what he saw: slept-in sleeping bags and flattened pillows. Evans gave the sleeping bags a shake, then lifted the foam pad underneath them, and ran a hand over the flooring of the van.

Stefan clenched his jaw. "What're you looking for?"

Evans hefted himself up on the bed of the van and ran a hand along the sidewalls. He gave the interior another onceover and then climbed back out. He walked around the side to the passenger door, lifted a hip on the seat, opened the glove box, and rifled through the contents.

"Don't you need a search warrant?"

Evans cocked his head and looked at him. "Not if you're cooperating. Are you cooperating?"

"So, if I say you can't take this any further, you'd have to get a search warrant?"

"But why would you do that if you've nothing to hide?"

Stefan again felt like he was being led around by his ignorance. What would Joachim do?

Evans went back to his search, as though the matter was settled. He felt around the dome light and pressed on the sagging fabric of the roof. Stefan had tacked it back up, and Evans looked at the repair job without comment. He got out, walked around to the other side, and settled himself in the driver's seat. He looked at the console and in the rearview mirror. "This is quite the ride. How'd you come by it?"

"It was Dad's," Stefan said.

"Where you from in Canada?"

"Saskatchewan."

He looked in the general direction, mulling it over. "Long ways away."

Stefan folded his arms, waiting for him to get on with it. What was his point?

Evans swung himself down and stooped to look under the seat. He grunted, tugging away at something, then straightened his back and pulled a crowbar-type tool out from under the seat. It was two feet long with a pick on one end and a claw on the other.

He set it on the driver's seat and pulled a pair of gloves out of his pocket. "What're you doing with this?" His eyes had frosted over, and his tone was as deadpan as the expression on his face.

Stefan found his voice. "That's not mine."

"Whose is it?"

"I've no idea. What is it?"

Evans turned it over in his hand, testing the weight. "It's a forcible entry tool. They're usually used by firefighters and law enforcement—" he fastened his eyes on Stefan— "to force doors and break locks."

Stefan felt sweat break out under his arms, and a cold weight hung loose in his belly. It was a setup. "It isn't mine," he said quickly. "I've never seen it before in my life. Someone planted it."

"Maybe it's been under there all along and you didn't realize it. Maybe it was your dad's."

There he went again, trying to lead Stefan down a path he knew he shouldn't go.

"No, sir, it wasn't."

"Okay, son, I need to make a call. Why don't you go back inside, and we'll talk." Evans had a hand at his elbow, guiding him.

Margaret was standing on the stoop. She looked at the bar in the detective's hand and then at Stefan. "What's going on?"

"He found that under the seat."

"What is it?"

"A burglar's tool," Stefan said in a flat voice.

Her eyes widened and Evans quickly interrupted. "Ma'am, we appreciate you folks cooperating with us. I need to radio in, and I'll be right back. We'll talk this through, okay?"

They went inside and Stefan kicked a chair out of his way and slammed his fist against the wall.

"Where did that come from, Stefan?"

"I have no idea."

"What does it mean?"

"It means someone is setting me up."

"Who would do that?"

"I could venture a guess."

Margaret paced the floor and then Abby was in the hallway.

"What's going on?"

"Nothing, Abby. Go back to your room. I'm talking to your brother."

"I'm not a little kid. I want to know what's going on." Her eyes were too big for her face and she looked like a little kid.

"Abby, please, don't argue."

"Are you in trouble?" She looked at Stefan.

"It's just a misunderstanding, Abby. Do as Mom says."

"You aren't going anywhere, are you?"

He looked out the window and then back at her. "It'll be okay. Go on now."

She hesitated and her lip quivered.

"I'm *not* in trouble. I'm not going anywhere," he said, placating her, as one would a little kid.

But it worked, then Evans was back at the door, and Stefan let him in, struck again by his height disadvantage.

"I need you to come down to the station with me," Evans said.

"Why?"

"We need to get your statement on record."

Stefan cracked his knuckles. "I just did that."

"No, you didn't." There was a line of tension between the two men and Margaret put her hand on Stefan's arm.

"Do we need a lawyer?" she asked Evans.

"That isn't necessary." He held her gaze. "He isn't being charged."

"I'll come with you."

"No, Ma, stay here with Abby. I won't be long, will I?" He looked at Evans.

"No, we won't be long."

They sat him in a tiny room devoid of furniture except for a table and four chairs, and closed the door. He looked at the four walls and drummed his fingers on the table. It felt like a jail cell. There was a camera in one corner of the ceiling pointed at him, and he itched to give it the finger.

Evans entered the room with two detectives. One wore a macho shoulder harness that secured his gun under his right arm, and the other had a belt clip. Evans sat across from him and introduced the other two.

They grilled him about the night before, but there was no accounting for the time between his departure from the marina and six the next morning.

"I took a drive up the lakeshore, pulled into a roadside park and slept in the van."

"You make a habit of sleeping in the van?" Detective One with the macho shoulder harness asked. His hair was feathered with gray, but there was no stomach over the belt.

Stefan looked at his badge. His name was Pickens. "Something wrong with that, Officer Pickens?"

"Detective."

"Something wrong with that, *Detective?*"

"You didn't see anyone? Stop for gas? Food?"

Stefan suppressed a sigh. "No," he said.

"Can you think of anyone who could collaborate your whereabouts or activity?"

He felt the muscle in his jaw jump. "No," he said.

"You a bit of a loner?"

"What do you mean?"

"Driving around by yourself, sleeping alone in the back of a van. You must have made some friends while you've been here, young guy with wheels."

Detective Pickens had subtly taken over the questioning.

"Did you make any phone calls?"

Stefan shook his head.

"Do you have a cell phone?"

"Yeah, I got one."

"Can I see it?"

"Not on me."

Pickens looked at Evans who was writing everything down and back at Stefan. He cleared his throat and set the forcible entry tool in the middle of the table.

"So, tell us about the Halligan."

Stefan looked at the centerpiece of the conversation. *A Halligan.* "Nothing to tell. It ain't mine."

"They dusted it for fingerprints. It was clean." He squinted at Stefan with one eye. "Someone was very careful about that."

"Maybe someone was."

"So, let's get this straight—" he spread his elbows on the table— "you're claiming that someone planted this in your van. Is that right?"

"Only explanation."

"Why would someone do that?"

"You tell me."

Detective Two with the belt clip made a noise in the back of his throat and put his feet on the corner of the table.

"You've been here, for, what—" Pickens consulted his notes, "over two months and made an enemy like that but no friends?"

Stefan held his gaze.

"There've been reports of altercations in town, an incident at a gas station and another one at the party store." Pickens glanced at his notes again. "Reported as a drunken brawl." He rapped his knuckles on the table and studied Stefan like a rare sort of bird. "You do a lot of drinking?"

Stefan pinched his lips white, and they all but disappeared.

"Come on, son," Evans said, "help us out here."

"I've been trying to mind my own business here. Smoke a cigarette, buy a beer, stay out of everyone's way, that's my mission here."

"Okay, back to the van," the detective said. "How and when did this *enemy* plant this, this—" He motioned at the steel bar, "this *tool* under your seat if you were sleeping in it?"

"I was sleeping in the back."

"Heavy sleeper, are you?"

"I didn't lock it. We never lock it." He looked at Evans for confirmation, but Evans was looking at an invisible point of interest on the wall. "Look," he said, resting his hands on the table, palms down, "they could've done it earlier at the marina—it wasn't locked— or there would've been time to do it after I got home this morning. It was still dark. Someone could've done it then."

"So, you parked the van and went inside and went back to bed?"

"That's about right."

"Didn't talk to anyone?"

"They were sleeping."

Pickens pushed his chair back and picked up the steel bar and handed it to Detective Two. "Go down to the marina and check for a match against the scratch marks on the gate and the lock, both ends of this thing." He eyed it admiringly. "Pretty handy tool if you're a fireman." He looked at Stefan. "Any firemen in the family?"

"Am I done?"

"Yeah, you're done."

Evans guided him to the door and they stepped into the hall. "We'd appreciate you making yourself available should we have any further questions."

"There weren't any fingerprints on that thing?"

"Wiped clean."

"So, it's just my word."

"It's an unusual tool. We'll find out if any have come up missing from local fire departments. But if it was an online purchase, it might be hard to trace."

"He thinks I'm guilty."

"Pickens has been around a long time, getting a little cynical. Just don't let your name come across his desk again, if you know what I mean."

Stefan thought for a minute. "What all did you say was taken?"

"Cash, fish finder, an outboard motor—"

"Did it look like I had an outboard motor in the back of that van?"

Evans looked away, made a study of extracting his keys out of his pocket, and then motioned at the squad car. "Come on, I'll take you home."

They drove back to the house in silence. Stefan knew the Boltons were behind this, and he wanted to confront them, but keeping his name off Detective Pickens' desk limited his options.

Evans was reading his mind.

He threw the car into park at the top of the driveway and rested his wrists on the steering wheel. "Leave this to us now. Don't be taking matters into your own hands, playing private eye."

"No sir, I would never do that," Stefan shut the door and walked around the front of the car. He leapt the three steps on the stoop feeling the weight of suspicion that followed him into the house. Much like the weight of Larry's gaze on his back when he'd left the construction site.

CHAPTER 27

Sadie poured the dregs of the coffee pot into a mug, stepped out on the porch, and turned the radio on, unconsciously following her mother's routine—drinking coffee and listening to the local weather, Tiger box scores, and the farm report. The sky was dark with the storm clouds that refused to develop into promised rain and the wind was riffling the leaves on the cottonwood tree—already turned yellow—that Henry kept threatening to cut down. The messier the tree, the more her mother had seemed to admire it: the willow, the black walnut, and the prickly pear. Now the pear and the willow were in the *before* category, and she sensed the cottonwood was next, the trees in the yard dropping to her father's industry like white pine to the lumberjack.

She had slept late, having only dozed in the van after they'd made love a second time. She cradled herself with the memory of what that was like: the first time, the second time—better than the first time—and now all she could think about was the next time. She tucked her feet under her legs; she was still a little sore, and newly aware of herself.

She checked her phone for messages. There was one from Sam but nothing from Stefan. She rang him but it went to voicemail. She listened to his voice and settled deeper into her chair.

The ringtone on the phone jolted her, and she looked at the screen. It was Sam.

"Have you seen Stef this morning?" he said.

"No. Why?"

"Abby called, upset about something. I was working with Dad. She said the police were at the house. She tried to listen in on the conversation but only caught bits and pieces. They took him into town for questioning."

"Questioning for what?"

"I thought you might know."

"I just got up."

"With the day half gone?"

"Questioning for what, Sam?"

"Did he get in another fight last night? The Boltons left right after you guys did. Where'd you go?"

Sadie thought for a minute. "No," she said, "there weren't any fights."

"Where'd you go?" he asked again.

"Nowhere, really."

"Really? Nowhere? Well, I have to get off here."

She sat with the phone in her hand. The day had taken a turn that matched the clouds on the horizon. She drained her coffee cup, grimacing at the burnt taste, and set it in the sink.

After three more tries to reach him on his cell, she grabbed her car keys and headed for the Duster. Henry caught her midway across the lawn.

"Morning, or should I say good afternoon?"

He looked rested and happy. His shoulders were unbowed and there was a spring in his step, like he had dropped ten years overnight. He even had on a clean work shirt.

She felt his ten years.

"Where you going?

"I'll be right back, just need to check something out."

As she drove out of the drive, he stood motionless in the rearview mirror.

When she pulled into the Montegrand drive, the van was gone. She climbed the three steps to the door and knocked lightly with her knuckles. His mother opened it a crack then threw it open. Her face was lined and her hair was loose.

"He isn't here," she said before Sadie could ask. "They took him."

"Who took him?"

"The cops. They took him in for questioning, brought him back after about an hour, then this policeman came back again, name of Evans, with another charge."

"What are you talking about? What charges?"

"They're accusing him of a burglary at the marina, and, and—" she wrung her hands— "sexual assault they called it."

Sadie clenched the doorknob. "Sexual assault? Says who?"

"Helen is calling a lawyer." She glanced over Sadie's shoulder at the house next door. "My boy didn't do any of that. I know it. I don't understand this place. We should never have come. Joachim was wrong."

"When was all this supposed to have happened?"

"The burglary was last night. The other . . . I don't know."

Sadie had one foot out the door. "Where'd they take him? Evans, you say?"

"I don't know—they should have told me, shouldn't they? — they handcuffed him." Her voice broke and she crossed her arms, gripping her elbows.

"They *cuffed* him?"

"It all happened so fast. Then a tow truck came and took the van."

Sadie took a breath. "Don't worry, Mrs. Montegrand. He's innocent, and I can prove it."

"Were you with him?"

"Yes."

His mother studied her, eyes blue as bell flowers. "Good," she said. "I knew he wasn't alone last night, but he wouldn't say who he was with."

Of course, he wouldn't. Sadie backed out of the driveway, feeling sick to her stomach. But she knew Officer Evans. He'd come out to the farm before to hunt, a regular. He and her dad weren't friends, but they had a history of mutual respect. She had some news for Officer Evans.

"You can't see him," the desk sergeant said. With his ruddy face and swelled-up chest, he reminded her of a little red rooster. "Not without arresting officer's approval."

She considered his likeness to the rooster that fluffed his feathers and came at her with his spurs when her back was turned, the same rooster that ran into the coop when a hawk flew overhead.

"Then get it. I'll wait."

"These are serious charges."

"The charges are a sham and I can prove it."

"Which one, the burglary or the rape?"

Sadie bristled at the word. "Rape?"

"Yeah, rape."

"Says who?"

He shook his head. "That's confidential. There's special protection for sexual assault victims in this county."

"I want to see Officer Evans."

"Not here."

"Then I'll wait." She took the nearest seat and stared at the door which she assumed led to one of the cells where Stefan was being held.

The sergeant shuffled his papers and played with his computer mouse. He glanced at the clock on the wall behind her head. "Might be a while."

But it wasn't. A car door slammed, and Evans walked in, stooping through the doorway.

Sadie stood up. "Officer Evans? I need to talk to you."

He frowned. "And you are . . ."

"Sadie Wixom."

"Thought I recognized you." He hesitated. "What's this about?"

"Stefan Montegrand."

He loosened his collar and dropped a folder on the desk. "Call Pickens, Dan. Tell him to get over here. Come on back." He motioned Sadie to follow him through the closed door to the inner sanctum of the county jail.

His was the first office, and there was a window facing the parking lot.

"Sit down." He motioned to a chair. "How's your dad?"

"Fine." She sat on the edge of the chair.

"I take it you know the Montegrand boy?"

"He's innocent, and I can prove it."

He raised an eyebrow. "Go ahead."

Sadie swallowed. "I was with him."

He pushed a stained coffee mug out of the way and tapped his fingers on the desk.

"*All* night. And we didn't go anywhere near that marina."

Evans narrowed his gaze, weighing her words, then picked up a pen. "Give me the details and a timeline, as accurately as you can."

She did, up to the time Stefan dropped her back at her car and she drove home. "I remember because I looked at the digital clock on the oven when I walked through the kitchen." She stared at him intently. "I remember clearly. It was five-forty in the morning."

"So, you last saw him at…?"

"It takes ten minutes to drive home from the marina."

He finished writing with a flourish and slid the statement across the desk. "Read that over. If it's accurate, sign the bottom and I'll date stamp it." He leaned back in his swivel chair and rocked. "That'll help his cause on one matter. The other might be more complicated."

"What other matter?"

"Someone just came forward with an accusation of sexual assault against your friend."

"An *invented* sexual assault, you mean?"

The door opened and Detective Pickens came in, and Evans motioned him to sit down. He explained the situation while Pickens stroked his mustache.

"It's an ironclad alibi, far as I'm concerned," Evans said.

"I just got done taking the victim's statement." Pickens steeled his eyes on Sadie. "She claims he raped her."

"Whoever it is—and I think I know—it's a rotten lie."

"Almost a week ago, is the problem, Pickens. One has to wonder why she didn't come forward earlier."

A week ago? Sadie's mind raced.

"The usual reasons. You've heard them all before."

"There'll be no DNA evidence, a classic 'she-said, he-said,' and now with this—" Evans handed Pickens Sadie's statement— "I'm inclined to drop everything."

Pickens read it over and then tossed it back on Evans' desk. He rested his hand on the strap of the shoulder harness and studied Sadie closely as though questioning the veracity of her statement. "Can you vouch for him last Friday?"

Sadie narrowed her eyes. The night of the bonfire.

"No," Pickens said. "I didn't think so. It might be 'he said-she said' but maybe it's time we gave some weight to 'she said'."

"It's a lie!" Sadie spat. "There's no proof and you can't hold him without it."

"I can hold him for forty-eight hours. It's my call. And I'm not done."

"We gotta post bail, Pickens."

"Sure, after forty-eight hours, but it can't be no measly thousand-dollar joke bond. I've already talked to the judge."

Evans rolled his eyes.

"He's a flight risk. You said his mother already admitted as much."

"He's not! What if you released him to us?" Sadie looked at Evans. "You know my dad, my grandpa. Like a house arrest."

Pickens snorted.

"We don't do that, Sadie. Besides," he said, looking at Pickens, "it's his call."

Pickens nodded. "The judge will set bail tomorrow." He settled his hat on his head and pulled the door shut behind him.

Sadie stared at the door and then at Evans. "Can I at least see him?"

He drummed his fingers impatiently on the desk.

"Someone is obviously setting him up. The two charges are so blatantly related. Surely, you see that."

Evans tilted his swivel chair back and rocked.

"Don't you?"

"Look," he said, rocking forward and settling his elbows on the desk, "we're going to sit on this until tomorrow. And I'll give you the advice I gave him. Don't go playing Nancy Drew. It could only make matters worse for him."

"We're getting a lawyer."

"He can talk to a lawyer. But he can't talk to you. Now go home." He escorted her to the door. "Tell Henry hello."

Sadie took it to Henry, telling him more than hello. He sat with his elbows on the table up to the point where she explained why Stefan had an alibi for the burglary. He pushed his chair back, made his way to the window, and stood there for a long moment.

His silence worried her. "Dad . . ."

"None of this is what I wanted to hear, Sadie."

"He didn't do it."

"And you in the middle of it."

"He's innocent, and he needs our help."

"Our?"

"You've known Evans a long time. Can't you talk to him? Stefan didn't do any of this, and you know it. The criminal sexual misconduct charge is ludicrous. I know it was Nan, and it wasn't rape."

"How do you know that?"

"Because I know it. He was with her, briefly, but called it off. Nobody calls it off on Nan. She's the one who calls it off. I remember that from high school," she finished with a note of bitterness.

"Old man Murkowski handles the police fundraiser every year. And Pickens—you say he's in charge of the investigation?"

Sadie nodded.

"That's another problem for your friend." He drew a glass of water and stood at the sink. "His daughter was assaulted a year ago. Worse, he was undocumented, big buzz around town. You were at school. So, you see where he's coming from. Where he's going, right?"

"That's not fair. It has nothing to do with Stefan."

"Doesn't matter. Pickens wanted him tried here but he was deported, which might have been worse, but we don't know, do we? I expect he envisions his daughter's attacker living on a white-sand beach, drinking beer, and harassing young girls. You get the picture?"

"What happened to fairness and impartiality?"

"He isn't judge and jury. He doesn't have to be."

"It was the Boltons, Dad. Stefan had a run in with Mr. Bolton the first time he was here. Sam can tell you. I'd bet my saddle that they put Nan up to this other shitty claim."

He looked out the window across the fields, as though considering the ways of the world, which, in a way, one could say he was.

"What about planting false evidence in someone's vehicle. What's the penalty for that?"

He selected a ball cap off one of the hooks by the door and settled it on his head. "I'll take a drive into town and see what I can find out. You stay put, understand?"

Sadie sighed and ran a hand over her eyes. "They wouldn't let me see him." Her voice broke. "Why won't they let me see him?"

Stefan was wondering the same. When he heard her voice through the thin walls of the office adjacent to his cell, he ran his fingers through his hair and waited for the door to open, for the clank of steel, for locks giving way.

The voices faded and doors slammed. The jail fell silent. He was obviously the only misfit in this county lockup, and she obviously hadn't put up much of an argument. He sat on the edge of the cot and dropped his head in his hands. He hadn't even been home an hour before Evans was back with another charge. A sickening charge. It floored him. Could it be true?

He ran his tongue around the inside of his mouth, remembering the odd, chalky taste, like baking soda. *Where had that come from?* He strived to remember, but beyond the memory of taste, the bulk of the night at Sam's was a brick wall.

He had an alibi for the supposed theft, if he chose to use it, but nothing for this other bombshell. Still, they had to post bond, and as soon as they did, he would pay it and leave. They thought he wouldn't be able to. He would find Joachim and disappear. He never would've left in the first place if not for Abby and their mother.

But then he wouldn't have met Sadie.

He stretched out on the bunk, lodged the pillow behind his head, and looked at the shaft of light streaming in from the window overhead. It was swimming with dust motes, and he cradled his head in his hands, mesmerized by the swirling particles. Then it was another window streaming light—*streaming moonlight*—and Sadie was cradled in his arms after they made love the second time under a window in the back of the van.

He was lost in the memory, cloaked in the feeling.

He sat up with a jerk. It was the same dissociative sensation he'd had at Sam's after sharing a drink with Nan. Oh! How it all came back. He'd left the campfire with her, shared a bottle with her, and smoked a cigarette with her. All harmless. But then what?

He rubbed his eyes, trying to recall more. There was a tequila blur of heat and urgency. That bitter chalky taste on the back of his tongue accompanied by a weird euphoria, the sensation of being outside of himself, floating in utter detachment from his surroundings. *A hammock.* There was a hammock and the blur of a struggle—to get out of that hammock or out of his clothes? He searched his mind. What then? Did they have sex? They must have, it was a blur—*couldn't have been very good*—but they must have, but was it rape? Not exactly the way he remembered things, but what did he remember beyond that loss of awareness and a disquieting fugue? How could he explain *that*? Was there any point in trying to reason with any of them? If Nan wanted to call it rape, the law would run with it, and he would never get out of this hellhole.

Was it one hour? Two? Before he came around to the hammer of a headache and a hammock he couldn't get out of with the lingering taste of bitterness on the back of his tongue? Coming around to full awareness at the campfire. Coming around to Sadie, looking at him as if he'd grown horns.

He'd been drunk before but had never experienced such oblivion, such a black hole of memory loss. All he knew was that the sun was resting on the horizon, then it was pitch black, and now he wondered about the drink. Was it the second or the third? The packet Nan had slipped back in her purse when there was still light with which to see, something about the powder of an agave worm, how she'd laughed and said it was just a muscle relaxer as she pulled her shirt off, arms pale and languid in the dark.

He paced the cell, trying to remember what else she'd said, but his mind went blank.

On impulse he searched his jean pockets. In the bottom of the right-hand pocket there was an unfamiliar aluminum foil fold. He smoothed it open in his hand. There was a sheen of residual powder on it and a tiny blue star stuck in the corner.

What the hell? He smelled it and the chalky taste was suddenly back on his tongue.

Relax baby, it's a kick.

The sudden memory was a jolt. He looked at the wrapper in his hand. Why was it in his pocket? Whatever it was, he'd been walking around with it for days. What if it was trace of an illegal drug and they searched him? A pile-on of charges? He would never get out of this godforsaken place. He shoved it back in his pocket, not knowing what else to do with it. He wracked his brain, trying to remember the night with Nan, trying to fill in the blanks.

He *had* been intrigued by her, from the first time she snapped her gum and brazenly looked him up and down. Girls didn't do that back home. They hid their glances, their smiles, and their intention. If he were honest, he had been side-swiped by the boldfaced desire that triggered reciprocity, like a speeding train jumping the tracks and pulling freight with it. So, how to defend himself against this charge of taking her against her will? Could that be in him? Regardless of any alcohol or drug—a cop out like Sadie said—could it? How could he be sure it wasn't when he didn't remember?

They'd had a row the next day. Seeing her had brought back that bitter taste, and he hadn't been very nice but, still . . . could she have stooped so low as to charge him with this? She was pretty tight with the Boltons—seemed to get off on their bravado and influence in the growing community of carry-conceal activists. Had they put her up to it? There was a level of animosity with the Boltons that he still couldn't wrap his head around.

They had to post bail. He would pay it; dutifully recite any promises they wanted him to repeat and get the hell out of—where was he? Yeah, the hell out of Sawyers Pond.

The turnkey brought him in a dinner tray consisting of canned vegetables that, had he but known, was in communion with his brother's fifteen hundred miles away.

That night he dreamed about him.

Joachim had fallen through the ice and he couldn't get out. In characteristic dream fashion, Stefan was frozen in place. All he could do was watch him struggle, grasping for a handhold with one arm, his other sleeve dangling empty, like a flag on a pole. Water was everywhere, lapping his boots, pulling them both in. He was paralyzed, and his brother was flailing in a foaming sea.

His eyes flew open. He didn't know where he was. He was clammy with sweat and tangled in a blanket. He focused his eyes on the beam of light shining through the bars of the cell from under an outer door. Was he looking in or looking out? The muffled sound of a radio drifted from another room, and he remembered where he was and the mess he was in.

He rolled over, listened to the low-level hum of the radio, and calmed the urge to rattle the cage, to shout at the top of his lungs. He thought of the elders at tribal meetings sitting around a fire, seemingly sleeping, but never sleeping, sitting around the fire, soft voices, and slow movements. He timed his breaths to the mantra in his head, a song from boyhood. An ode to spring, to the horn of the moon, to the water running in the creek and the Sockeye salmon that swam determinedly to their death.

He pulled the scratchy blanket over his head and reached with his mind for the hand in the dream.

Henry exited the judge's chambers at the back of the county courthouse to corner Detective Pickens in the hallway.

"You got a minute?"

"I'm late, Wixom. What do you want?"

"I spoke with Judge Hudson. Don't you think a thirty-thousand-dollar bail is a little steep?"

"For a flight risk? No."

"He won't be able to post that and you know it."

Pickens flipped a hand dismissively.

"As a Native American, he has protection against unreasonable incarceration. If this isn't unreasonable, I don't know what is."

"You lawyering now? I don't care who he is. He's been accused of criminal sexual conduct."

"Falsely, some say."

"Whose side you on?"

"Look, I'm sorry about what happened to your daughter. But do you think you're being fair to Montegrand?"

Pickens eyes turned opaque, like a pane of frosted glass. "Fair? You're worried about *fair?*" He turned on his heel, then paused at the door and looked back at Henry. "How old's your girl?"

Henry blinked. "What does she have to do with it?"

"I'd say quite a bit, from the sound of things."

They stared each other down across the width of the hallway. Pickens rested his hand on the grip of his revolver, a habit that didn't go unnoticed.

"You take these people into your home, don't know a blasted thing about them."

"These people?"

"He comes into our community and been nothing but trouble; your brother is responsible for that, and I intend to keep an eye on Montegrand until I get a handle on this. It don't gotta be fair."

The door swung shut and Henry watched him peel out to the street and disappear around a corner. Well, that didn't go very well. Pickens had always been a hard nose for the book and Hudson, the presiding judge, threw it wherever Pickens directed him to throw it, dating back to their little Municipal Court gig in the eighties, padding the court's coffers with traffic tickets and impound fees netted through speed traps and overly zealous traffic cops. Ruled unconstitutional at the state level in the late nineties, the money-making scheme had evaporated in front of their eyes. But they maintained their office and their taxpayer-funded automobiles. Judge Hudson had just been reelected, but by the slimmest of margins. Henry would bet a crop of beans that he would retire rather than risk putting his name on the ballot again.

The criminal sexual conduct charge bothered him. These things did not come out of thin air, a byproduct of complicated situations and relationships, the kind Stefan would attract. He liked him all right, but he was wound tighter than a pocket watch. He remembered what that was like, being that age, hair on fire.

CHAPTER 28

Joachim recognized the sound of Savior's pickup approaching through the trees, and he went out on the stoop to watch him coast into the clearing. He had one arm hanging out the window, and the stained J.B. Stetson with the gentle curl at the brim shaded his face.

He cut the engine, climbed out of the truck, and gave him a hard hug. "Hey, Jac, you okay?" He stepped back and looked him over.

"Been better." Joachim clasped his shoulder. "Man, it's good to see you."

They were the same height, but Savior had his father's hook nose, high forehead, and was darker skinned than his two friends. He claimed to be the only one who was full-blooded.

Savior's eyes canvassed the roofline of the cabin. "You taking good care of my place?"

Joachim laughed. It felt good to talk to somebody. "I was about ready to climb the walls."

Savior rocked back on the heels of worn-out boots the color of his hat. "Hear you took a bullet."

"It's in my dash." Joachim grimaced. "Doc pronounced me lucky."

"Why'd you risk going back there? That was beyond stupid."

"Why'd you suggest we move those signs?"

"I guess we're both stupid Indians."

"You bring some food?"

Savior dropped the tailgate and dragged a cooler to the edge of the bed. "Give me a hand."

They walked the cooler into the cabin and set it by the door. Joachim opened the lid and hunkered down in front of it. There were packages of venison jerky, smoked fish, and meat wrapped in white butcher's paper. He slit open a package of jerky with his pocket knife.

"I'll grab my backpack and sleeping bag," Savior said. "Fry us up some chops. How's the propane holding out?"

"It's not," Joachim glanced at the banked coals in the fireplace. "I'll get the fire going."

"There were backup canisters in the lean-to."

"They're empty, and I'm about out of firewood. Do you know how long I've been here?"

"I got here fast as I could, Jac."

"So, what's the plan?"

"Let me get the rest of my stuff and we'll talk." Savior paused at the screen door. "We'll stay the night."

Joachim added some kindling to the hot coals, hung the cast iron pot from the tripod, and dropped a chunk of lard in the center. It popped and sizzled. He opened a zip lock bag of cut up onions and mushrooms and dumped them in the hot grease. He stirred them with a long-handled wooden spoon as the onions browned and the mushrooms released their juices. He pushed them to the side and plopped the chops in the center to brown.

Savior dropped his duffle in a corner, hung his hat on a peg by the door, and squatted beside him. They watched the meat cook and let the talk wait. In the middle of forestlands bordering prairie far from the steam shovels and earthmovers, the silence was as it should be.

Joachim flipped the chops and piled the mushrooms and onions on top. Savior put a loaf of bread on the table along with their coffee mugs. Joachim sprinkled the box of salt over the contents of the pot a second time. "I think I'm suffering from a salt deficiency," he said at Savior's expression.

"Is there such a thing?"

"That and canned vegetable overload." He forked the chops onto plates, and they ate in silence. Joachim concentrated on chewing with his mouth closed as the sensation of strength blossomed out from his center.

Savior pushed his plate back, pulled a satchel out of his duffle and tossed it to Joachim.

"That's from Josie."

Joachim unbuckled the straps and opened the interior zipper. The smell of old leather and gun oil filled his nostrils. He gripped the handle of the revolver, pointed it at the floor, and spun the cylinder.

Savior slid a cell phone across the table. "This is for you too. It has a powerhouse battery, good for forty hours. Your contacts are loaded, clean slate, new name."

"New name? What's my new name?"

"Eddie."

"Eddie? That's a lousy name. Sounds like a pervert."

"Josie says there are a million white boys named Eddie."

Joachim wiped his mouth on the back of his hand and picked up the phone. He turned it on and the device chimed. He scrolled through the contacts until Stefan's name came up. "Are these the right numbers?"

"You can't use it yet."

"Why?"

"Why do you think? You been in the woods too long."

"Okay." Joachim threw his hands up in surrender. "Okay! Relax, wouldja?"

"Relax? I think I'm pretty relaxed considering the shit I had to go through to get here—roadblocks, detours, hard hats with badges ordering my window down so checkpoint pricks could make sure I wasn't hauling your ass out of the province." He lit a cigarette and blew a thin stream of smoke at the ceiling. "Relax, he says." He took another drag and looked at Joachim, opened his mouth to say something else, then looked away.

"What, Savior?"

"That trucker . . . he didn't make it."

Joachim's chest clenched like a fist. He fumbled with the lighter to get his own cigarette going. The flame caught and flared.

"Go on," he said.

"It was on the radio."

"Josie know?"

"She does by now."

"Any word from Bobby?"

"No." Savior stroked the thin line of his mouth and looked at the rough-hewn beams of the ceiling. "That isn't all, Jac. The company that owns the truck you blew the tires out on is charging you with a firebombing that happened earlier that evening. Someone set off explosives at a storage facility in Beaverton next to the airstrip put in for drilling crews."

The remaining color drained from Joachim's face.

"I heard it set off a fireball you could see for miles." He gave Joachim a speculative look. "You didn't see it on your way to the cabin?"

"I took our detour, you know, the one you and Bobby marked with crossbones." A fleeting smile touched his face. "It's still there."

Savior nodded. "Josie and I figured as much, but they're targeting you as the mastermind, have you connected to The Brotherhood. I'm your accomplice."

"And Bobby?"

"His name hasn't come up. I've been thinking—" he paused to knock the dangling ash off his cigarette— "we need a change of plans, and it's best Josie don't know. Fewer people that know the better. And no fuckin' calls to the kid brother until we're clear."

"Where's clear?"

"I had intended to hole up at the Narrows, see if we could find Bobby and hole up until this shit blows over. Now that's not far enough. Now it's not a misdemeanor. Manslaughter and jail time, lengthy for you if these new charges aren't dropped."

Joachim examined the burning tip of his cigarette.

"I'm thinking Clearwater, Jac. There's a First Nations government office there, tribal council with backbone, policing authority, and legal aid—"

"You fuckin' kidding me?"

"You discounting tribal authority?"

210

"Come on Savior. They don't have any. I don't care what Josie says. They don't even have their own fucking horses."

Savior snorted. "Oh, that's good."

Joachim chucked his heels on the table, settled the ashtray in his lap, and knocked the ash off his cigarette with his forefinger. "Clearwater is too far. I wouldn't trust your truck that far. How about Elk Creek, remote yet within distance of the Narrows; First Nations land, hunted there with Dad. There's even cell service coming out of Manitoba. In fact, if we had to make a run for it . . ." The thought dangled between them.

Savior stubbed out his cigarette and shook another one from the pack, tapping it against his wrist. "I just changed the oil in the truck, checked the belts, and greased what needed greasing."

"I wish I had my jeep. Sons of bitches."

"We could always get us a nice roundabout and navigate a tributary into the Saskatchewan River and hide out with some friendly natives."

"I was supposed to head south, meet up with Stefan."

"Into the arms of the border patrol? You don't think there'll be an all-points out on you?"

The thrum of a helicopter rotor suddenly cut the quiet of the cabin and they both looked in the direction of the approaching sound. Savior rushed to the door and Joachim pushed past him onto the stoop. The *thrump thrump* of the blades grew louder and Savior grabbed him by the collar. "Get back!" He slammed the door, leaned against it, and neither of them breathed as the blades whipped the air overhead, seemingly forever before the chopper finally moved off in the distance.

"My truck—" Savior turned stricken eyes on Joachim. "They would have seen the truck."

"So? It's just like a thousand others in this neck of the woods."

Savior started scooping up belongings and throwing them in his duffle bag. "Gut the fire, grab your shit. We're gettin' out of here."

Joachim stood frozen and confused.

"Jac! Move it!"

He threw water on the fire, grabbed his coat, and looked around the cabin. Savior slung his duffle over his shoulder, grabbed a handle on the cooler, and dragged it to the door. Joachim shouldered the satchel and took another look around the place he'd called home for two weeks, then grasped the other handle on the cooler, and pulled the door shut behind them.

Savior wedged the cooler in next to his tool box, climbed in the driver's side, and gunned the engine. It sputtered, caught, and they peeled out of the clearing.

Joachim leaned against the seat and caught his breath. A fresh ache had taken up residence in his shoulder and it hurt to breathe. He coughed, opened the door, spat a mouthful of phlegm, and slammed it shut again.

Savior glanced at him. "You okay?"

Joachim wiped his mouth and looked at his hand. "Yeah." He drew the seat belt across his lap. "Road out's the other way."

Savior shifted gears, fishtailing through a gully and a bank of brush, and a two-track opened up in front of them. "I know which way the road is and which way it ain't."

"That helicopter could've been on a routine flyby. Probably headed down to Saskatoon, nothing to do with us."

Savior shook his head. "It's the decal. I should've removed it."

Joachim turned to look out the back window. The Dené Nation emblem: arrows, blue water and a rising sun covered the glass. *Land of The People* was etched in black lettering across the top of the decal.

"I remember when you got that. It was in Yellowknife at the annual Beer Barge. Took us three days to get home."

"I don't know anyone else who has a full window decal. Do you?"

"That's why we admired it."

"Yeah, well, I think it was included in the description of a vehicle seen in the area before the accident. They already suspected someone in the native community and that was all they needed to zero in on us."

"I thought it was fingerprints."

Savior shrugged. "That's the rumor."

Joachim thought for a second. "If you knew that, why didn't you take it off?"

Savior thumbed his hat back. "Guess I forgot about it. Had it a long time, just part of the truck, you know. But then that helicopter—I thought about the snide remark one of those pricks at the checkpoint said, and it dawned on me: we're fish in a barrel." His voice trailed off as he concentrated on the road that wasn't a road. They bottomed out and Joachim braced himself against the dash. Savior gunned it and his snow tires caught and held. He left the snows on year-round.

After another minute he said, "We'll grab our emergency funds from the drop point at the Narrows, leave a note for Bobby. If he ain't there—I have a feeling the ex ain't totally ex—ditch the truck for something else if we have to."

"I want my jeep."

"Forget the jeep. It's probably gone to auction."

"Sons of bitches."

"If we keep our heads down for a while, maybe the coppers will give up. They don't want to give this too much press. With the latest pipeline ruling—Arctic Gas got their alternative line—too many young guys are losing their tempers."

"Our fathers warned us about losing our tempers. Then they lost theirs."

"Even the animals are acting funny. It's rumored they won't cross a pipeline."

Joachim gazed out the window. "I wasn't anywhere near Beaverton."

"We can get over by—Elk Creek, you say? —inch into Manitoba, leave the Churchill basin, leave the province, and wait for this case to drop into their cold case file."

Joachim shook out another cigarette, lit it, and set it in the ashtray. He pulled the satchel out from under his feet and took out the revolver. He spun the chamber and opened a box of ammo.

They drove in silence along the rutted road the width of a railroad bed, and he kept the reassuring weight of the gun under his arm.

They came to a gravel crossroad and Savior parked the truck. He opened the glove box and pulled out a map cross-folded to the legend showing road classifications and access. The light was fading and he turned on his dome. "Gimme a pencil," he told Joachim.

Joachim watched him trace a line through an area shaded in green. "I think we can take this road to the left and get into provincial parkland, stay off the map, hit Elk Creek on the other side and find your Indian land."

Joachim looked doubtfully at the penciled route. "You think?"

"Yeah," he said, chewing on the eraser end of the pencil.

"You don't know where we are, do you?"

"I know where I am."

"Okay."

Savior flicked the dome light off and looked at him. "I know where I'm not. I'm not in Prince Albert, and I'm not hanging out in places that have been compromised, and I'm not shooting out tires on petrol trucks."

"It was a quick stop. It was on my way."

Savior looked out at the encroaching night. "Yeah," he said softly. "I know."

"I missed the burial ceremony."

Savior didn't say anything.

"What all happened in Beaverton? Any idea?"

"No. Josie's trying to find out. They hung it around your neck pretty fast. No need to waste time and money on an investigation."

"Who do you think did it?"

Savior looked at him for a long minute. "No *one* person did it. A lot of young guys are being radicalized by Ottawa, by what's happening in the northern tier, foreign companies breathing down their necks with bulldozers, guys your baby brother's age." The idea swung between them, a pendulum gaining weight.

"I need to talk to him." Joachim drew on his cigarette, the tip glowing in the dim of the cab. "I need to do some normal things. Can't remember what it's like to do normal things—fish, run a trap line, cut some wood, play pool, have a beer and a shot." He cracked his neck. "Fuck."

Savior snorted. The truck was idling rough and he tapped the gas pedal. They sat and looked at the dash, the vibration in the hood.

"You got any WD-40 on you?" Joachim asked.

"What for?"

"It'll take that decal off."

"How about lighter fluid?"

"Hate to waste my lighter fluid."

"We get caught, you ain't gonna need lighter fluid."

Working together on opposite sides, they loosened the corners of the decal, and the rest peeled off easily. Savior crumpled it in a ball and looked around, at a loss as to what to do with it.

Joachim grabbed the shovel off the bed of the truck and passed it over the tailgate. "Bury it. It doesn't have to be six feet."

Finished, they brushed the dirt off their hands and Joachim measured the length of shadows cast over the road by the watchful forest. He flicked his cigarette end-over-end into the fresh dirt and ground it out under his boot.

"Let's go. See if we can find us some normal."

CHAPTER 29

The metal door clanged open and the desk sergeant flipped on the lights. "Wake up, Montegrand," he said. "Someone's here to see you."

Stefan rubbed his eyes against the glare and swung his legs off the bed. After two nights on a shelf bunk, it took him a minute to stand up. He looked at the man in a suit standing in the doorway of his cell with a briefcase.

He extended a hand. "My name is Ben Morgan. I'll be representing you in your bail hearing this morning, and I need to go over a few things with you."

The few things didn't take long. He snapped his briefcase shut and gave Stefan a long look. "The burglary charge was dismissed. You evidently have a flawless alibi."

Stefan darted him a look.

"The judge is reviewing the alleged criminal sexual conduct charge. I'm sure bail will be approved after the robbery exoneration, but it will be substantial." He cleared his throat. "If you can't cover it, we can get a bondsman."

Stefan shimmied his knee. "What's that?"

"You only have to pay ten percent; they guarantee the rest. But I have to say, with your non-resident status that might be tricky."

"I can cover it."

Morgan narrowed his eyes. "You sure?"

"Yeah, I'm sure."

"Okay. We're done then." He waited by the door. "Anything else I can do for you?"

Stefan cleared his throat. "Who hired you?"

"Mr. Wixom."

Stefan shot him a look. "Henry Wixom?"

"You have friends of some standing, and they're on record as character witnesses. If things go well, this won't take long. You should be out of here by noon."

There was a fine mist in the air when Detective Pickens escorted him out of the jail and across the street to the courthouse. It chilled his manacled arms and the steel of the cuffs cut into the bony part of his wrists. Pickens grudgingly removed them when Attorney Morgan met him out front with an exchange of words, and Stefan rubbed his wrists wondering how he'd gotten so squarely on the wrong side of Pickens.

The courtroom was small, and the only person inside was the court stenographer. Judge Hudson entered with a swoop of robe, followed by another officer of the court, and Morgan motioned for Stefan to stand. Hudson appraised the small group assembled and read the brief in front of him. He glanced over his glasses at Stefan and then back at the brief. Pickens approached the bench, and they conferred in hushed tones.

The judge studied Stefan for a moment and then addressed his attorney. "Does your client understand bail proceedings?"

"Yes, your honor."

"The penalty for not showing up when called before the court?"

"Yes, your honor."

"Bail has been set at thirty thousand dollars." He banged his gavel for emphasis and the sound echoed through the empty chamber. "Does he have it, Mr. Morgan?"

The courthouse clock struck the hour with a heavy gong that echoed the gavel.

"Yes, your honor, he does." He glanced over his shoulder at the empty room, and the clock chimed its way through the twelve o'clock hour.

The judge leaned forward impatiently. "Mr. Morgan?"

"His mother is posting it, your honor."

The judge raised an eyebrow. "Anytime soon, Mr. Morgan?"

Detective Pickens pushed his chair back. "Your Honor, this is a farce. I request that the defendant be remanded to custody until our investigation into this other matter can be completed."

Judge Hudson tapped his ink pen and looked at the clock, ticking time with rhythmic precision.

"I don't have to remind you, your Honor, these are serious charges and he's a flight risk."

"Pickens, sit down."

Just then the door opened, and Stefan's mother made her way up the center aisle. She had donned a wide-brimmed hat and a regal bearing. Behind her, Sadie slipped into a seat at the back of the room. She wore a blue scarf knotted at her throat and gave him a little finger wave.

The rest of the proceedings were a blur, the blue scarf bookending his racing thoughts, but the ending instructions and admonition from the judge resonated with him long after the hearing adjourned—he was free to go, but he was not free from suspicion.

The attorney escorted them out of the courthouse and Sadie waited by the car while Stefan helped his mother into the backseat. She turned to Morgan.

"I have a question about this sexual assault charge."

"It's an ongoing investigation, as the judge said. We'll have to wait it out."

"What are his chances?"

He glanced through the window at Stefan sitting in the front seat. "As long as there's no corroborating evidence or other, shall I say, unsavory history, his chances are good."

"How good?"

"Your family's support helps. A little."

"What if she's lying?"

He smoothed the lapels on his jacket and shifted his briefcase to his other hand, training his lawyerly gaze upon her. "If she is, that's another issue. Can you prove it?"

Sadie pursed her lips.

"Call me if anything changes. But you should know, Judge Hudson is not going to be sympathetic towards your friend."

No surprise there. She bit her tongue. "And the bail money?"

"If the charge is dismissed when he shows up in court, they'll issue a notice to release."

"Thank you." She held out her hand. He hesitated for the briefest of seconds and then shook it. She climbed behind the wheel, and Stefan leaned his head against the headrest and closed his eyes.

She put her hand on his arm. "You okay?"

He looked at her. "I'm sorry you were dragged into this."

"I'm sorry *you* were."

He looked out the window at the law enforcement comings and goings. "Let's get out of here before they change their minds."

They drove to the impound lot and she pulled up to the office door. A dog barked. She looked in the rearview mirror and met Margaret's eyes. "Should we wait?"

"We'll wait," Stefan said.

It was only a minute, though it seemed longer, before Margaret opened the door and gave them the okay.

Sadie licked her lips and glanced at Stefan. "I want you to know..."

"Drop me at McCabe's. I wanna see if the bike is ready."

"I know it's not true."

He rubbed the redness on his wrists and looked at the dog barking on the end of his chain, at the ground fog moving in.

Sadie swallowed the knot in her throat.

"Stefan . . ."

"Let's get out of here."

No place was suiting him. She turned the car around and drove them back through the chain-linked gate and into town. The silence in the car was as thick as the sudden fog that dimmed the vapor street lights coming on in confusion.

The neon *McCabe Motorcycles* sign glowed iridescent green in the mist. He opened the door and got out, disappearing through the service door.

She turned the radio on, skimmed the dial, then turned it back off. She watched the door, hands wrapped around the steering wheel.

He was back and slid into the passenger seat. "It's ready," he said.

"Okay . . ." The word dangled on a question.

He cracked his window, lit a cigarette, and blew smoke out the corner of his mouth. He looked at her for a long moment. "I've been thinking about that night at Sam's." He took another pull on his cigarette. "I blacked out. Near as I can figure, lost a couple of hours. I might not do well with liquor, but that was super strange."

"How do you mean?"

"I think she drugged me."

"*Drugged* you?" She searched his face. "Did you say anything to anybody else? Sam? Abby?"

"No. I wasn't sure. I've been trying to sort it out in my head. I vaguely remember her giving me something. I didn't think about it until I was in jail. I found this in my pocket." He handed her the aluminum foil fold. "I don't know where it came from."

She opened it. "What's with the star?"

He shrugged. "No idea. Smell it?"

Sadie held it up to her face and wrinkled her nose.

"Kinda leaves a taste on your tongue, doesn't it? Like I said, that whole night was super strange." He described the dissociative sensation he recalled, the dark hole in the events of the night. "Now I have that on me." He looked at it with distaste. "I do remember something she said, though." He looked up at Sadie. "I think that smell brought it back."

"What?"

"She said, Relax baby, it's a kick."

"She said that?"

"I remember it, yes, clearly. Then nothing. Who would ever believe that?" he finished with an exasperated sigh.

Sadie was thinking. "I have a friend who's taking pharmacology. I'll talk to her, see if she has any ideas." She rested her hand on his knee. "This could make a huge difference, Stefan."

He looked at her over the burning tip of his cigarette.

"If it was any kind of an illegal mood enhancer or some sort of hallucinogenic, and she gave it to you, it changes everything."

"Nothing will change," he said glumly. "How would I prove it? It doesn't matter, Sadie. I'm leaving."

A stabbing pain hit her behind the brow. "Jumping bail, you mean."

"If you want to call it that."

"It'll only make you look guilty."

"I'm trying to tell you; I don't know that I'm not."

"What if she takes it back? Tells the cops it was consensual."

"Why would she do that?"

"If it's what we think it is, something illegal—" she looked away for a minute, thinking. "How'd she come by it? Maybe, if pressed, she'll want to drop the whole messy thing. I mean, what could be in for her?"

"Revenge."

Sadie raised an eyebrow.

"I said some pretty harsh things the next day. Plus, I can't help but think the Boltons had something to do with it. Don't know what I ever did to them," he muttered as an afterthought.

Sadie squished up her mouth. "Beat the shit out of them."

"It's not just this, this *rape* charge." He spat the word like bad chew. "I think something's happened to Joachim. No, I don't know what. It's a feeling, can't explain it. I had this awful dream." He recounted it as best he could, and they were silent for a minute before he picked up the conversation. "I need to go back. I never should've left in the first place. Not a choice though. They didn't give me a choice." His voice trailed off like the distance growing between them.

"You can't leave like this. You need to clear your name."

"I don't care about my name."

"I do," she said.

He gave her a quick hug, hard and tight against his chest. Then, as quickly, let her go. "I have to hurry," he said. "They're closing in a few minutes." He opened his door, dropped the cigarette on the pavement, and stubbed it out under his boot.

The damp entered the car with his leaving, and she watched as he disappeared into the shop.

CHAPTER 30

It only took one phone call for Sadie to locate her old high school friend who was enrolled in the pre-pharmacy program at the university. Annie was just getting off work at the drug store in town, and they arranged to meet in the coffee shop next door.

They caught up over coffee—day growing long—before Sadie steered the conversation to what was important.

"I need a favor, Annie," she said.

She described the situation Stefan was embroiled in and the symptoms he had described: the euphoria laced with an out-of-body sensation and then loss of memory. "Can you think of something that could have caused all of that?" She studied Annie for a minute, gauging her attitude. "I know this might be asking a lot, but we really need your help."

Annie frowned. "There's a whole host of drugs that could cause any combination of those type of reactions. You trust this guy? Think Nan really could've dropped something in his drink? Usually, it's guys who do that to girls."

"I know, but yes, I do. They might've had sex but there's no way he forced her."

"It's a shitty thing to falsely accuse someone of."

Sadie slid the aluminum foil fold across the table. "This was in his pocket. He doesn't know where it came from or have any recollection of why it was in his pocket. I figure she probably did that, you know, like it was his in the first place." Sadie cradled her coffee cup between her hands, trapping the warmth.

Annie fingered the foil for a minute and traced the little blue star. "We see packaging examples in class. This looks like the foil folds ketamine can come in. It's a big thing right now. It's known for causing that feeling of euphoria and detachment from the user's environment, kind of a slow burn without a hangover. Readily available and relatively cheap compared to other club drugs. I guess that's why it's popular. It's sometimes called Special K on the street."

Sadie's eyes widened. *Special K?* The term jolted her memory, and her mind raced to place the connection. It was Nan with the Boltons in a tight little circle, cigarette butts dropped under bootheels, a clutch of snide remarks and laughter over—cereal? She had naively thought that's what they were talking about.

She pushed her coffee cup back and slid out of the booth. "Coffee's on me, Annie. Thanks."

"Sure. Let's keep in touch, and let me know how this turns out."

Needing to satisfy her own curiosity, Sadie rushed home and took the stairs two at a time. She opened her laptop and typed *Ketamine* into the browser. There were several links and she opened one that looked like a legitimate medical resource. Paging down, she zeroed in on:

Feelings of unreality; a distorted feeling about one's body, euphoria or a buzz . . . same hallucinogenic effects as mescaline and LSD . . . the user feels disconnected and not in control, detached from their environment . . . Exactly what Stefan had described. And further down—*An infusion therapy approved for treatment of depression but used illegally by people to get high.*

Then below in the packaging descriptions—*Powdered ketamine is typically packaged in small plastic bags or aluminum foil folds.* There was even a picture of one with blue stars adhered to the foil.

She took a screenshot of it with her phone, then closed the laptop, and shut off the lights.

Armed with the leverage and guts to confront Nan, she entered the party store, holding back while other customers paid for their cigarettes and lottery tickets, waiting her turn.

The door jingled shut and Sadie flipped the sign to *Closed*.

"What are you doing?" Nan said.

"I need to talk to you. It won't take long."

"I've been advised not to talk to any of you."

"I'll do the talking. All you have to do is listen. You're going to the police station and recanting your charge against Stefan."

"Why would I do that?"

"Because you had to drug him to get him to have sex with you."

"Are you kidding me? As if!"

"I agree, beyond pathetic. Not something one would want bantered about."

"Banter it about all you want. Nobody would believe it. You want pathetic? The fact that your boyfriend has to go elsewhere. Now that's pathetic. Truth is—" She opened a lipstick, did her lips in the mirror of her compact, blotted them on a tissue, and snapped it shut. "He came onto me the very first time I saw him. Standing right where you are, coming on like the horn dog he is."

Sadie laughed.

"You think it's funny? I have witnesses."

"Who? Clem Bolton? Zender? The two biggest troublemakers this town's ever known?"

"Lately, they've had a lot of competition."

"Not in dealing drugs, they don't." She took a gamble. "Did they sell you some Special K, Nan? And I don't mean cereal," she added.

Nan's mouth dropped for the briefest of seconds before she recovered.

"What are you talking about?" she asked innocently.

"Ketamine, a so-called club drug. Or maybe you know it by its street name, Special K."

"You know all about it, eh?"

"No, but I have a friend who's a pharmacology major."

"Well, I've no idea what you're talking about."

"It's what you gave Stefan, so don't play stupid."

"Is that what he told you? You're both crazy. Get out of here, or I'll call the cops."

"You sure you want to do that? I bet they could search your purse right now and find more of that shit."

Nan's eyes darted to her purse on the floor. She picked up her phone and then set it back down. "I did *not* give him anything." She tossed her hair. "It was hardly necessary."

"You did. It's why he can't remember having sex with you, or even believe he did."

"I didn't!"

"So now you're saying you didn't have sex?"

"Don't twist my words."

"The cops here are as strict about drugs as they are sexual assault. Selling alcohol underage is nothing compared to dealing drugs."

"I'm not dealing drugs! You're twisting everything around." She narrowed her eyes. "He was the one in possession. Maybe *he* gave it to *me*."

"Oh, so there were drugs involved."

"Did I say that?"

"Do you really want to hash this out in court? A full-blown hearing with *publicity?*" Sadie took a flyer out of her purse and set it on the counter. "I see your father is running for state office." She glanced at Nan, satisfied to have finally struck a nerve. She'd taken it off the bulletin board at the coffee shop where people thumb-tacked business cards, lost pets, and used appliances.

She tapped a finger on the handbill, and Nan stared at her father's smiling face. "There are two sides to every story and this one will be front-page, because your dad is a big name around here. It'll be embarrassing if he can't win his own district. My grandpa always said more churches than bars per square mile makes for a sanctimonious citizenry."

"A has-been booze runner."

"A tough district to win if you don't toe the party's moral tightrope and hold forth a perfect family. Political campaigns have gone down for less"

"What're you going to do? Join the Altar Society?"

"I'm surprised you'd joke about something so serious. You know what they call lying under oath in front of a judge?" She leaned across the counter. "Look, Nan. All I want is for you to go down to the station and tell the truth about what happened."

"We had a good time. That's what happened."

"No, *you* had a good time."

"Oh, believe me, he had a good time too, once I got him to lighten up."

Sadie clenched her jaw and breathed. "How'd you do that, Nan?"

Nan laughed. "You have to ask?"

Sadie worked the clench out of her jaw and said, "We both know Stefan Montegrand did *not* rape you. Why do you want to ruin his life? If you recant now—you know, faulty memory, or whatever—it won't go any further, but if you lie before a judge . . ." She let the thought dangle for a second.

"You have no proof. Where's your proof, Sadie?"

Sadie stared at her. "Who put you up to this?"

"Nobody put me up to anything. It was just him and me, my word against his, and who would believe him? Besides, everyone does it."

"No, everyone doesn't. Come on, Nan. I know you didn't come up with this criminal assault idea on your own. Who was it? Does your dad know?"

"He didn't have anything to do with it." She looked down at the handbill of her father's shiny face and chewed her lip. "It was Clem," she blurted. "After that night at the marina, he went bonkers, hates the guy. He said I had to go to the police, tell them I'd been forced, he almost convinced me I had. I'm not taking it back now. He'd kill me. Besides, why else would I have been with someone like Montegrand? He was a real prick the next day. Acted like *I* had dirtied *him*."

Sadie could have sworn her lip almost quivered.

Nan lifted her chin. "No judge would take your ragtag boyfriend's word over mine."

Sadie took a deep breath and went a step further. "There's one more thing I'm curious about. That forcible entry tool they found in Stefan's van that cops and firefighters use, did Clem plant that too?"

"I don't know anything about that." Nan shrugged indifference. "But it's common knowledge that Clem's a volunteer fireman at the Sweetwater Fire Station."

Sadie nodded. "You might want to go down to the police station on your own recognizance. Ask for Officer Evans, tell him you were mistaken about the encounter with Stefan and alert him to that *common* knowledge, and maybe they'll go easy on you for lying in a criminal matter."

Nan snorted. "You are batshit crazy if you think I'm doing any of that."

"Suit yourself." Sadie flipped the sign on the door to *Open* and the bell jingled.

"He wasn't that good," Nan called after her. "Hardly worth the effort."

Sadie closed the door and leaned against it, breathing in gulps of air. She took her phone out of her pocket and turned off the recording.

That night, while walking the dog and replaying the recording to make sure the entire conversation saved, she found the boomerang.

CHAPTER 31

Speed shifting through the gears with the wind in his hair, Stefan was on a tear. The wind watered his eyes and cleansed his senses of the smell of disinfectant, the taste of metallic water, and his two nights on a shelf-bunk. The brakes were tight, and the worrisome wobble in the back tire had been corrected. It would take him as far as he needed to go.

Back home, things seemed normal, as if the past two days had never happened, and he took a long shower scrubbing the jail smell from his hair and out of his pores.

His phone vibrated on the bathroom sink and he squinted at the display. An unknown caller was ringing in. He wrapped a towel around his waist and picked it up.

"Hello?"

"Stefan? It's Josie."

"Josie?" He clenched the phone. "Josie, hello!"

"Jac asked me to call you to let you know he's okay."

"Where is he?"

"He's fine, but he can't call out. He asked me to do it for him."

"Why can't he call out?" There was a pause along the line. "Josie, you there?"

"Don't worry. He doesn't want you to worry. Listen, use this number if you need to reach us. I had to get a new phone."

"What's going on? It's been weeks since we've heard from him."

"I can't say anything else now. We have to be careful. He's safe and he'll call you as soon as he can."

"He can call you, but not me?"

She heaved a sigh of exasperation and he pictured her tossing back that head of hair. He had always been in awe of Josie, the only woman who had ever been able to entice Joachim into a measure of domesticity—dinner around a table, sheets on a bed.

"Trust me," she said, "he has his family's best interest at heart. You just have to believe that and know he's in a safe place."

There was an undertone in her voice he didn't like. "Where's this safe place? And why does he need one?"

"He's staying low for a while. That's all I can say. Don't try to call him, Stefan. He has to get another phone and when he does, he'll call you."

"Lots of phone problems up there, eh?"

"I should get off here."

"Wait. This safe place, I need to know where it is."

There was silence along the line.

"Josie?"

"Savior was taking him some supplies and a better phone." She paused for a minute, as though weighing her words. "That was a couple days ago, but service is spotty. You should be hearing from him. We'll be in touch. Goodbye, Stefan."

He looked at the disconnecting icon. *We'll* be in touch, but she wasn't with Joachim. Savior was, and that was no consolation.

Joachim was in need of supplies? Well, so was he. He needed decent rain gear and cash for the trip because he had suddenly made the decision. He could make it to White Lake in twenty-four hours, but nobody could ride a motorcycle for twenty-four hours and be able to get off and walk. He would have to hole up somewhere and wait to hear from him. Get safely away from here and these maniac cops, hole up halfway. Maybe Minnesota, land of lakes, and close to the border.

Maybe Sadie could get Nan to take back her accusation, but he didn't trust the likelihood any more than he trusted his memory of what had happened. He looked at himself in the mirror and considered a more recent memory, one untainted by alcohol, one as sharp as his reflection in the mirror: Sadie's legs wrapped around his hips with moonlight in her hair.

Why not take her with him? Twenty-four hours on a motorcycle would be like nothing with her behind him, twenty-four hours with nothing between them except the sensory rush of the woodlands. And as they crossed the Saskatchewan prairie with autumn coloring the boreal forest in the distance, like a mountain range across the foothills, she would understand why he wanted to go back.

He was gripped by a flood of homesickness. It was a land and a way of life he missed, as much as he missed his brothers, as much as he wanted another night with her. But he couldn't have both, and the time for making a choice was quickly approaching, like two tectonic plates creeping together on a collision course. They couldn't coexist; one would come out on top to bury the other.

CHAPTER 32

The "normal" Joachim was looking for appeared through the trees in the form of a four-corner settlement on a graded crossroad. A cedar cabin with a metal roof sat on one corner and a general store with beaver pelts hanging by the door sat on the other. Kitty-corner to that was a hardware store with a sign swinging loose in the wind. A newly constructed (and thus out-of-place) pole barn and expansive dog shelter stood a short distance away.

Other than the latter two, the four-corner enclave could have been a photograph of a nineteenth century fur trappers' outpost captured by a wooden box camera and a puff of smoke.

Savior parked in front of the general store and turned off the key. The truck backfired and settled. Two old Indians with hooded stares sat in observation on a bench outside the store.

"I'll be damned," Joachim said, "looks like your grandfather."

Savior snorted.

Joachim looked at the sign over the door and the one across the road. "This place on your map?"

Savior crooked his neck for a better view out the side window. "Looks like a dog shelter over there. Could be a stopover for the Iditarod qualifier to Stanley Mission."

"They have beer," Joachim motioned to a sign in the window.

Savior smiled. "Smokes and lighter fluid."

Making a list, they disembarked at Luca, Saskatchewan.

The first thing they saw upon entering the store was the wanted poster tacked to the wall behind the counter next to a flyer announcing sign-up for the qualifier.

The man behind the counter was a younger version of the two men sitting outside. He wore a ball cap backwards like an American, and a Montreal T-shirt underneath a leather vest. He glanced up from his newspaper, folded to the sports page. "Can I get you guys something?"

Savior pulled his hat down over his eyes and turned sideways, as though studying the contents of the half-empty shelves.

Joachim dragged his eyes off the poster and pointed at the cigarette display. "I'll take a couple packs of Camels and a pouch of Copenhagen and some Scripto, and throw in a couple of those nugget bars." He pointed at the assortment of candy bars.

The clerk took the cigarettes from the rack with a glance at the posters, taking his time over the tobacco and searching for the lighter fluid. He set the metal can of Scripto on the counter with the cigarettes and eyed Joachim for a speculative moment, recognition spreading over his face.

"You gonna rob me?" he said.

Joachim looked at him with wide-eyed innocence. "What gives you that idea?"

He jabbed a thumb over his shoulder at the wanted poster. "Says you're armed and dangerous." He glanced at Savior, absorbed in the beer display. "You armed and dangerous?"

Joachim studied the poster in question. Where did they get such an unattractive picture of him? He wouldn't want to run up against that man in the dark. Savior looked like Savior while he looked intoxicated and unhinged. But he hadn't looked at himself in a while, so it could be an accurate depiction. "There an award out?" he said.

"Yeah, but it doesn't specify, which makes me suspicious. What'd you do, if you don't mind me asking?" His eyes were bright with the asking.

"We killed a man."

Savior hefted a case of beer onto the counter. "It was an accident."

Montreal looked back and forth between them. "I shouldn't be selling to you, turn me into an accomplice."

Savior lit a cigarette, shook out the match, and blew a puff of smoke across the counter. "We won't hold you up if you answer a couple questions."

"You don't look dangerous to me. You look like a couple of flunkies."

Joachim dropped his hand to the ivory grip of the revolver. He wasn't a fucking flunky. He was tired, sore, and coming unhinged.

Montreal's smile faded. "Whoa. . ."

Savior said, "What's your name?"

"Tommy."

"Tommy, let's all relax here. What's the name of this place?"

"Luca. Named after that guy out front, Lucas Yendo. Gets busy about first of January." He darted a nervous eye at Joachim. "You wouldn't believe the mushers."

Savior smoked his cigarette and tapped his ash off in the coffee can on the counter. "Who gave you that wanted poster to tack up?"

"Flashy sorts, driving one of those big SUVs with a rack. Waited to make sure we got it up the way they wanted. Acted like they owned the place." His mouth tightened with dislike, and Joachim knew he was on their side.

"How long ago was this?"

"Early this morning."

"The graded road out front," Joachim interrupted. "Does it head into Elk Creek?"

"Yeah, but that's the way those bounty hunters were heading."

"Bounty hunters?"

"That's what Mr. Yendo called them."

"That's illegal."

He shrugged. "I wouldn't know. We don't usually have this much excitement."

"Is there another way to get to the Narrows?"

"Depends on what you're driving."

A girl came out from behind a beaded curtain in the back and walked behind the counter. She wore a pair of bib overalls and a piece of red fabric was woven into a braid that hung over her shoulder.

Savior straightened his back and grew an inch.

She looked them over with dark, almond-shaped eyes that reminded Joachim of Josie.

"Is there a problem, Tommy?" she said in a melodious voice.

"I don't think so. I think they just need directions."

She looked at the wanted poster and back at them. "We don't need any trouble," she said.

"No, ma'am." Savior touched the curled brim of his hat. "Neither do we."

"We'll just pay for this here." Joachim spread his hands. "And be on our way."

Savior was looking at the girl all the while, spellbound by that piece of red fabric, and Joachim groaned inwardly.

"Tommy," he prodded, "you were saying— about the road?"

"If you have four-wheel drive, you can stay on the rutted track you were on, actually turns into a real road before you reach the Narrows. Those suits were clearly staying on graded road. Head guy complaining about the dust and the grime and losing the shine on his shoes."

Yeah, they had him, but the girl?

She was perusing the poster. "Which one of you is Savior?" She looked at Savior, clearly knowing the answer, and the corner of her mouth moved. "What kind of a name is that for a criminal?"

"My mother's idea. I've been trying to live up to it."

Her eyes sparkled.

"What about a gas station?" Joachim said. "Anything of that sort around here?"

Tommy shook his head.

The girl was still looking at Savior, with him looking back. "You got a gas can?" she said.

"Sure, I do. For the outboard we don't have."

She tossed her braid behind her back. "Grandfather says they don't have jurisdiction outside of the province, but they'll be leaving posters up and down the 106 to the border. Avoid the 106 and you'll avoid those two. We didn't appreciate their attitudes. In fact—" she ripped the poster down, crumpled it in a ball, and tossed it neatly into the garbage can in the corner— "we don't know who did that, do we, Tom?"

Savior smiled with growing appreciation. "What's your name?"

"Sammy."

"What kind of a name is that?"

"My daddy's idea. I was supposed to be a boy. Ring 'em up, Tom. Come with me." She motioned to Savior.

Tom keyed amounts into the register and the drawer popped open. Joachim placed a bill in his hand and dropped the change in his pocket.

Outside, he doffed his hat to Lucas Yendo and his companion, took a beer out of the carton and opened a candy bar. He leaned against the truck, crossed one scuffed boot over the other, and ate his lunch. The two stoic individuals watched from their bench. They reminded him of his father's friends, the ones who never talked.

He crumpled the wrapper, popped the tab on the can, and drank it half down. And still they watched.

"This your town?" he addressed the one on the right, the one who sat a little taller with an air of ownership.

"No, it's my store."

"Nice. Real comfortable spot you got here."

"You should be on your way before they come back."

"I agree. My friend seems to be taking his time." He craned his neck to see around back.

Just then, Savior and the girl rounded the corner with the gas can.

Savior topped off the tank.

"You giving them gas, Sammy?"

"We can spare five gallons, Grandfather."

"We appreciate it—" Savior touched the brim of his hat, turning on the charm.

"Appreciate it on out of here." Yendo waved his arm in a not-so-subtle gesture.

"Maybe I can help you later with your qualifier," Savior said, nodding towards the dog shelter, drinking in the girl. "Things blow over, maybe I'll come back."

Yendo aimed a stream of tobacco juice at the coffee can between his feet. "We never seen you boys. Don't expect to, either."

Joachim crumpled his empty and tossed it in the back of the truck. "Let's go, Savior." But Savior was torn between leaving and staying, and Joachim turned the key in the ignition.

Savior had final words with the girl named Sammy and climbed reluctantly behind the wheel. He turned the truck due east, leaving the settlement and the girl in their rearview mirror, the false front of the general store disappearing last as the woods closed around them.

"We need to get to somewhere we can hole up," Joachim said. "Got a couple hours of light is all, and I ain't sleeping in here with you, acting like you never seen a girl before. Christ."

Savior gave him a lazy smile. "But wasn't she a honey?" He pulled a piece of paper out of his shirt pocket. "I got her number."

CHAPTER 33

Joachim woke, chilled to the bone and needing to pee. He put on his jacket, which had served as a pillow, and climbed out of the truck. Savior was in his sleeping bag on a bed of leaves. He stepped around him and walked into the early dawn of the woods.

They had driven as far as they could in the dark, pulled off the rutted two-track shortly after midnight, and tossed a coin for the sleeping arrangements.

He zipped himself back up and stretched the kink out of his back, thinking Savior got the better end of that toss. He started back for the truck but hadn't gone two paces when a branch cracked in front of him.

He stopped with one foot in the air. "Savior?" he whispered. "That you?"

A flock of startled blackbirds flew out of the tree above him as something heavy crashed through the brush, and he dropped a hand to his empty gun belt.

A moose stepped gallantly through the trees with a mouthful of lichen and likewise froze at the sight of him. She was so close he could see the steam coming off her, standing full-bodied between him and the truck. Her nostrils flared, smelling the air as Joachim took a step back and looked for the calf.

She was luckily without one, for having decided that the strange creature in front of her wasn't a danger, the moose moved off in the direction of another low-hanging hank of lichen.

Joachim let out a lungful of air. He would take the sighting as a lucky sign, his father's take on such things. Moose had retreated in the face of progress, and it was rare to see one, especially one that was fat, healthy, and beautiful.

He watched as the heavy animal shouldered her way leisurely through the undergrowth, the aspens seeming to part of their own accord at a nudge from her nose, holding sight of her until the forest swallowed her up.

He walked back to the camp, sealing the encounter in his mind. He nudged Savior awake with his boot, took the revolver out from under the seat, and put it in his belt.

They ran into a real road as Tommy had predicted and entered the Narrows with the sun behind them. It was a thriving community with sidewalks and pavement, a gas station, kayak handlers, bait and tackle, and a rambling dry goods store. The most prominent building was the Indigenous Affairs government office.

"You know where Bobby's camp is?" Savior said.

"I thought you did."

"Try your new phone, *Eddie,* ring him up."

"I got permission, do I?"

They pulled into the gas station and while Savior pumped, Joachim tried Bobby's number.

"He didn't answer," he told Savior. "Now what?"

He nodded at the government building. "Let's see if someone from there can help us."

The woman behind the reception desk wrinkled her nose at the sight of them.

"We're looking for someone." Joachim said, trying to remember the last time he'd had a bath. "Bobby Clay-Benton. We're cousins, need to find him, family emergency."

Her nose was in a permanent scrunch as she considered how to proceed with the two of them. She directed them to another desk and that desk directed them to a bespectacled man who walked with a cane.

He suggested they review church records.

"Church records?" Savior frowned with confusion. "I don't see how that could help us."

"He has a small hunting camp," Joachim said.

"Why didn't you say so?" The man pushed his chair aside with his cane and made his way to a voluminous book open on a back table. "Land claims—" he tapped the book with his multi-use cane. "If he owns property, he's in here."

Two miles out of town, they spotted the cabin on a hill in the distance.

Joachim chewed the toothpick in his mouth and moved it from one side to the other. "There's someone there," he said.

Savior took his foot off the gas and pulled to the side of the road.

"Doesn't Bobby still have that beat-up jeep?"

"So, he has company. I told you that the ex wasn't."

"I don't see his jeep." Joachim tried his number again. "It's ringing..."

"Still not answering? Man, I don't like this."

"We can't just sit here. Let's check it out."

They parked beside the unfamiliar pickup. It had a flat tire and a crumpled front end. A snowmobile sat on a ramp in front of it with its engine exposed and the skids off.

"Place is a junkyard," Savior said.

Joachim checked the load in his pistol while Savior opened the passenger door of the wrecked truck and rifled through the glove compartment. He found the registration. "Yup, Camille Bridgewater. That's her." He put it back in the envelope and slammed the box. "He said she was a bad driver."

Savior knocked on the cabin door, waited a minute and knocked again. He tried the door handle. It was locked.

Joachim's phone rang, startling him. It was Josie.

"Jac, where are you?"

He hesitated.

"Jac? The trucker died."

"I know. Savior told me. Look, we think it's best you don't know."

"Best I don't know what?"

"Where we are."

"This is a secure phone. You can tell me where you are."

"I'm not tellin' you, Josie. You need to stay put."

"Oh, is that right? I'm sick of people telling me that, sick of people looking at me with suspicion, ever since the cops held me overnight and impounded your jeep, even at work. And after this news broke, well, I'm closing my place up for winter."

"What do you mean? You're talking crazy. Why you talking crazy?"

"I already have the jeep packed, just waiting to hear from you or Savior."

"What jeep?"

"I got a clean plate, transferred under the table."

"How'd you get it out of hock?"

"That's another story."

Joachim ran a hand through his hair till it was standing on end.

"There's ten thousand dollars on your head."

"Is that all?"

"Jac."

"What about your job?"

"I'm taking a leave of absence, health issues."

"What health issues?"

"You tell me." They waited each other out, and finally Josie said, "Did you call the number Murphy gave you?"

"I lost it."

"Really?"

"Have you heard from Bobby?" He changed the subject.

"Bobby? No, why?"

"Just wondering where he is, if he knows the latest."

"Whoa," Savior said under his breath. "Speaking of . . ."

Bobby's jeep swung into the drive and rocked to a halt beside Savior's pickup.

He climbed out before it had settled on its wheels, and slammed the door. He wore a headband and fringed buckskin with a knife in his belt. He didn't look happy.

"Nice to see you too, Bobby," Savior said.

"I knew it," Josie said angrily in Joachim's ear.

"I'm hangin' up, Josie. I don't wanna see you, jeep or no jeep." He hit the side *off* button with his thumb and shoved the phone in his pocket.

Bobby strolled to the stoop in his slim-hipped swagger and unlocked the cabin door with his key. "I'd say it's good to see you both, but I'm not sure."

Savior nodded at the pickup with the banged-up grill. "The girlfriend have another bang-up?"

"She dropped it off a week ago, hole in the radiator, expects me to fix it. I told her I'd sell it to the junkyard before I'd fix it, second time in two months she's run into someone." He pushed the door open with his elbow and waved them inside.

"If you'd consort with someone your own age, you wouldn't keep having these problems."

"Consort?" Bobby flashed them a grin. "I like that word. Who needs a beer?"

They cooked up two packages of venison backstrap from Savior's cooler, and then caught up with each other over an after-dinner smoke.

Bobby worked at getting a cigar going. "What happened to your arm?" he asked Joachim.

"Long story. What've you been doing?"

"Shooting ducks out of season."

They looked at him in confusion.

"I just got back from Elk Creek, had to pay a fine."

"Wait a minute," Joachim said. "Since when is there a season?"

"Local game warden doesn't feel the Indian should get preferential treatment on ducks."

"So now they set their own rules?" Savior said with a sour look.

"Maybe I should call Josie back." Joachim mused. Josie was an interpreter for Indigenous speakers, but she was also good at interpreting legal jargon.

"She still working at the court? Thought she retired to deliver babies."

"Midwifery is a part-time job."

242

"Thought she might be delivering yours by now," Bobby said with a smile.

Joachim smoked his cigarette, not wanting to get into that subject.

"You should know," Bobby added, as though it were an inconsequential detail, "there are wanted posters in town."

Joachim and Savior exchanged a glance. "We've seen them," Joachim said. "At least they don't say 'dead or alive'."

"How'd this happen?"

Savior told him how it happened.

"Don't worry, Bobby." He looked at him over the end of his cigarette. "Seems they don't want you. Must be that guardian angel you picked up at the church school."

Bobby made a face. "Smartass. What's your plan?"

"Shit, guess we'll have to turn ourselves in."

"Shut up, Savior." Joachim looked at Bobby. "We thought we'd take out those emergency funds and head over towards Indian land, but we weren't expecting to deal with wanted posters. Where's the jurisdiction?"

"Nobody's had a chance to challenge them," Bobby puffed thoughtfully on the cigar and rolled it between his lips. "But about the money, there isn't any."

"What do you mean?"

"She did leave me a love note."

"What does *she* have to do with it?" Suspicion creased Joachim's brow.

"She took it."

Joachim closed his eyes.

"She took it?" Savior deadpanned.

"How'd she know about it?" Joachim said.

"Snooping through my phone, thought I was cheating on her but found something better."

"There's no Indian in that woman," Savior drawled. "I could've told you that."

"Then she wants me to fix her radiator, *pro bono*, on account I kicked her out without notice."

"Wait." Savior held up his hands. "She steals *our* money and then wants you to fix her truck for *nothing*?"

"After I told her I was scrapping that shitty little pickup, she stole the money and took off, told me we needed to grow up and find real jobs, join the real world."

Savior blurted a vulgarity. "I never liked that girl."

"What does *she* know about the real world?" Joachim wondered aloud.

"She had some attributes," Bobby said softly.

"We have twenty thousand attributes on our collective heads," Savior said. "Me and Jac, that is. Not you, of course."

Bobby blew contemplative smoke rings and Savior lit another cigarette off his first one, the air in the cabin hazing up.

"The deal with the detour signs was clearly an accident," Bobby said after a minute. "With all those people Josie knows at the Bureau, I would think—"

"Jac has another problem," Savior interrupted. "He shot an oil rig's tires out at the roadblock and took a bullet. Long story short, that's what happened to his shoulder."

"You shittin' me? You can't leave those rigs alone, Jac?"

"That ain't all. There was an explosion at a storage facility they've pegged him with."

"I can't take credit for that one." Joachim raised a palm in denial.

"The same night. You would've had to been busy."

Joachim stifled a cough in his father's handkerchief.

Bobby squinted at him. "You still have lead in you?"

Joachim shook his head, and Bobby waited through another coughing attack.

"You coming down with something?"

"It's these unfiltered cigs."

Bobby gazed at him quietly, and Joachim dropped his eyes.

"Okay, listen." Bobby leaned in closer as if there were others in the room. "I was planning to leave in the morning. Jeep is already packed, just had to tie up loose ends, pay my fines, no reason to have warrants out for stupid reasons. Trying to set an example for you. I really am going fishing this time, meeting my cousin over on Gullet Lake in Manitoba, way south of here, damn straight balmy, angler's heaven. Close this place up for winter—" he held up his hands, forestalling the question— "I was going to leave you a message at the drop. My cousin's place is remote, way off the tracks, plenty of room, room for all of us. We'll ride this out."

"I don't know." Joachim rubbed the ridge of his knuckles.

"Can we agree this is not the best place for you to be?"

"Sounds good to me. It's not like we have a lot of resources." Savior nudged Joachim. "Hell, Jac doesn't even have a change of clothes."

"I have money."

"How you gonna access it without leaving a trail?"

Joachim ground his cigarette out and pushed his chair back. "Is there a Western Union in town?"

They took Savior's truck into the village incorporated as the Narrows.

Outside the market that included a wire service, Joachim said, "You two go on in, pick me up some aspirin and cough medicine. I have to make a phone call."

He paced in front of the store, thinking about what he wanted to say, and then dialed Stefan's number. The phone rang and Stefan's voice came on the line advising the caller to leave a message, short and brusque, and *have a nice day*. Then he was suddenly live.

"Hello." His voice was laced with suspicion. "Who is this?"

"Hey, kid, it's Jac. How you doing?"

"Jac? Where you calling from? I can't believe it. How the hell are you? Why haven't you called, worrying Mom to death. Where *are* you?"

"Sorry, little brother." Joachim cleared his throat. "Out of the call zone for a while, that's all. Did Josie get ahold of you?"

"Yeah, a couple of days ago, said you'd be calling from your *safe* place."

"Listen, I need a favor."

"Sure, anything."

"Sorry I have to ask you this, but I need you to wire me some money."

There was dead silence along the connection, as if the call had dropped.

"Stefan, you there?"

"You need money?"

"Sounds crazy, I know."

"After all this time, you call because you need money?"

"Look, bud, it wasn't my choice, believe me."

"You transfer royalties I don't want without telling me, and now *you* need money?"

"Look, I can explain later, but right now, we're in a bit of a hurry. It needs to be cash. A few hundred is all— make it five."

"Who's we?"

"Savior and me. And Bobby."

"The Three Horsemen."

"Look, Stef, I'll pay you back."

"You're missing the point."

"I'll call right back and let you know where to send it. Everything okay there? You good?"

"Sure, just great."

"Give me a few minutes. I'll call you back."

"I'm not going anywhere."

At the Western Union counter, Joachim jotted down the information Stefan would need, then sat in an alcove that used to be a phone booth, and rang him back.

"How soon can you wire it?" Joachim said, trying to quell the anxiety.

"There's a Western Union in town."

"Okay, any fees, whatall, I'll pay it back."

"I'm worried about that."

"Look, I'll be in touch. Tell Mom I'm fine. How's our sister?"

"Growing up fast."

"Yeah?"

"When are you joining us?"

"I've run into a bit of a problem."

"Go on."

"You ever hear of Gullet Lake, over in Manitoba?"

"No."

"Bobby knows someone with a place there, good fishing, he says."

"So . . ."

"Yeah, going south for winter, don't know why I didn't think of that earlier."

"This is south, brother."

"Getting over the border might be tricky."

"I thought Indigenous were supposed to have freedom of movement."

Joachim snorted.

"Throughout North America, you said."

"As long as you keep your nose clean." He clamped his mouth shut, having said more than he meant to.

Stefan breathed into the receiver. "I figured as much. Knew I shouldn't have trusted you." And then in a rush, he said, "I knew you were in trouble. What'd you do now? Is that lake another so-called *safe place*? Fill me in, I might need one too."

"What are you talkin' about?"

"You heard me."

"What's going on down there?"

"Nuthin'. Never mind."

"You aren't in trouble, are you?"

"I'm okay. I got a girl."

"That could be trouble."

"No, no, man, not her."

"So, you got a girl, chance at a new life, why you talkin' crazy? Buy a boat, like we talked about, get your own place. I'll come down as soon as I can. We'll go fishing."

"It's complicated here."

"Well, work it out. And stay put, hear? I wouldn't be good company at present."

"We can be bad company together."

"Look, I gotta go. The boys are flagging me down. How soon can you send that wire?"

"I'll do it now. I'm ten minutes from town."

"Okay, great. Hey, thanks, bud. I'll be in touch."

Bobby and Savior were waiting for him. "It'll be a few minutes yet," Joachim said.

"What's going on?" Bobby said.

"Stefan's wiring me money."

"Whoa," Savior said. "You sure that's a good idea?"

"I need cash. It's the best idea I can come up with."

"What'd you tell him?" Savior asked.

"Don't worry about him."

"I never knew your little brother to keep his mouth shut," Bobby growled.

"Yeah? Well whose fault is it that we don't have our money? Huh? *Emergency monies,* Bobby. Where the fuck is it? You and your underage dimwit girlfriends!"

"Never knew you two to make exemplary—like that word? — exemplary choices when it comes to women."

"Look, enough," Savior said. "We'll gas up, come back, and get you. Anything you need at the filling station?"

"Yeah, some hand grenades." Joachim shrugged a step back. "More smokes if they have them."

The money was there, and Joachim showed the Western Union agent his ID. The man looked at him for a few seconds, and then placed the laminated picture under a loop.

Joachim shifted his feet. "Something wrong?"

"No, not at all. I just want to make sure I'm doing everything right." He handed the envelope of cash to Joachim, holding onto it a second too long for Joachim's liking.

Joachim counted the bills and then gave him a nod, "Just making sure you did it right."

Savior drove up to the curb, Joachim jumped in beside Bobby, and they careened out to the street.

"I don't like the way that guy looked at me."

"What guy?"

"That Western Union guy. He put my ID under a magnifier."

"Making sure it's not fake." Bobby gave him a look. "It isn't, is it?"

"So, what all did Josie say?" Savior said. "She got your jeep out of hock?"

"Evidently."

"But you don't want it, or her?"

"It's not that simple, is it?"

They were silent for the duration of the trip. As they rounded the last hill on the down slope to Bobby's place, Savior suddenly hit the brakes and they all lurched forward.

"What the—" Joachim grabbed the handle over the door.

Savior threw the pickup into a U-turn and they were heading in the opposite direction.

"Motherfucker! You trying to kill us?" Bobby braced both hands against the dash.

"What's the matter?" Joachim threw a look over his shoulder as Savior's eyes darted between the road and the rearview mirror.

"Coppers."

"Where?" Bobby asked.

"In your fuckin' driveway!"

Joachim cradled his shoulder, having felt the jolt all the way down his arm. "Did they see us?"

Savior downshifted and swung off on a side road. "I don't know."

"Probably heard us."

Savior straightened the wheel and cut the engine, and the silence swelled.

"Are you sure you paid all your fines, Bobby?"

"They don't send coppers out for traffic tickets."

"They do for poachers." Joachim was grasping for a reason that didn't involve them.

"Only two reasons for a copper to come knocking, and I'm stuck between them."

Savior stared at the rearview mirror. "Maybe they aren't looking for us," he mused. "Maybe they got the wrong address."

"And maybe the drillers will decide tar sands aren't worth the work, and Hydro will abandon their flood plans," Joachim rebutted.

They were all quiet for a space of seconds.

"Nobody followed us." Joachim turned to Bobby. "So, who connected us to you?"

Bobby stared blankly at the dirt slog of a road ahead.

"The girlfriend, my guess," Joachim said, trying to quell the anger. "Am I right?"

"You and your white trash bimbos," Savior said.

"Cammy ain't white."

"*Cammy?* Cute."

"What is she?" Joachim snapped.

"Why are we talking about this?" Bobby had turned sullen.

"Honestly," Joachim said, adjusting his elbow in the sling, "I don't care if she's fucking Chinese, would she have called the tip line on us?"

"Damn straight, she did," Savior said. "I'm guessing she saw the wanted posters and called in to see what the award was. Would've given us up for a lot less than twenty thousand dollars."

Joachim ground his cigarette out in the ashtray with a methodical corkscrew motion. "Let's sit tight, give them a chance to poke around. There's nothing for them to find, right, Bobby?"

Bobby was thinking.

"Right, Bobby?"

"They can't just barge in. Can they? Without a warrant?"

"You need to get ahold of Josie," Savior offered, "get her down here with your jeep. This truck is hot."

"We agreed not to involve her."

"Things have changed."

"Not that," Joachim said. "But we have to assume our position here is tenuous."

"*Tenuous?*" Bobby grunted. "You two crack me up."

"You should've graduated your church school."

Joachim tried to light another cigarette, but his hands were sweaty, and the striker kept missing the flint.

"Thought you were quitting," Bobby said.

"Why don't we get serious?"

"Okay," Bobby said. "Here's my serious. We split up. If I get questioned, I haven't spoken to either one of you in weeks. We get the plate off Camille's truck and put it on yours, far as I know, she's not wanted. We'll meet up in Manitoba, outside the reach and jurisdiction of your wanted posters."

"That's a horrible idea," Savior said. "You think I look like a girl?"

"It might work—" Joachim managed to get his cigarette going and massaged his thumb with his index finger— "from a distance."

CHAPTER 34

Outside the Western Union office, Stefan saved the number Joachim had called from and checked the transaction on his bank's app. He was keying Gullet Lake into the GPS on his phone when a police car pulled up to the curb with a chirp from the siren.

Detective Pickens rolled down his window. "Get in the car, Montegrand," he said.

Stefan slipped the phone in his pocket. "Why?"

"I need a word."

Stefan glanced around the suddenly empty sidewalk. The police radio crackled, and the hair on the back of his neck stood on end. He had made a vow to never cross this man again. Yet, here they were.

"Go ahead," he said. "I'm listening."

Pickens turned the radio down and motioned him in. "Get in. I need a word, that's all. Can't talk like this, can we?"

Stefan hesitated, but opened the door. He sat on the edge of the seat with the door ajar.

"Have you been in contact with Nan Murkowski?"

The question startled him. "No, of course not."

Pickens adjusted his shoulder harness, high and tight, and all Stefan could think of was how uncomfortable that must be.

Stefan dragged his eyes back to his face. "What'd you say?"

"I said, not a word?"

"No, sir." Stefan frowned with confusion. "Why are you asking me this?"

"I thought you might need your bail restrictions reiterated. You can't talk to her, or go anywhere near her."

"I'm not stupid."

Pickens looked at him sideways like, *Remember who you're talking to.* The little red eye on the dash cam blinked and his radio squawked.

Stefan shifted in his seat. "Was there something else, *Detective?*"

Pickens' nostrils flared. "You're on thin ice, Montegrand. I'm just making sure you understand the court's order and stay clear of her."

"Trust me," Stefan held his hands up. "I wouldn't go within a mile of her."

Detective Pickens nodded at the motorcycle. "Is that yours?"

"Yes."

"I need to see your registration and proof of insurance."

"Why?"

"Because I asked for it, that's why."

"I don't have that on me."

"You got a driver's license?"

"So, this is a traffic stop?"

"An Indian *status* card . . . something?"

Stefan cracked his neck, searching for his calm. It was in there somewhere. He worked the ID free from his wallet and passed it over.

Pickens held it under his pocket flashlight which highlighted the Canadian hologram and then handed it back dismissively, losing interest. "You can go." His radio crackled, and he picked up the mouthpiece.

Stefan shoved the door shut, and Pickens peeled away from the curb, tires squealing, not worried about traffic laws. Now that would be nice.

He climbed on the bike and gassed the throttle. He needed to get out of this town, but first, a little research.

He found an empty computer at the library, googled Gullet Lake, and there it was, just to the north of Winnipeg. He palmed the mouse, checking mileage. By his calculations, he had just shaved off ten hours of travel time from his original destination.

He printed out the directions to the marshy area in southern Manitoba advertised online as an "angler's paradise", and jotted notes in the margins. He searched the memory of their conversation for further details, but Joachim had been deliberately vague.

He accidentally came upon a link for Greenpeace and the tar sands controversy, and he remembered what Sadie had told him about the pictures.

Shadows lengthened around the building and darkened the sills as he scanned page after page. Whatever Jac was involved in, he wanted to be a part of it. He wanted to help.

The bustle amongst the shelves slowed and voices faded, none of which registered with Stefan until the lights in the library were dimmed.

"Excuse me, young man, but we are closing." The librarian's glasses hung on a chain around her neck, and she spoke with a lisp. She tapped the face of her watch. "Library is closed. Are you checking out materials?"

"Ah, no." He exited the search engine. "Sorry." He smiled apologetically. "Guess I lost track of time."

The air had cooled with nightfall, and he braced himself as he turned the bike into the wind. He couldn't get Joachim and whatever trouble he was in out of his head. If Joachim was asking for money, the trouble was serious. It wasn't like he didn't have any.

By the time he pulled in the driveway, he was chilled to the bone and thinking of something hot to eat, but his mother was waiting with more news.

"Sadie was here earlier, looking for you."

"When was this?"

She shrugged. "An hour ago, or so."

"She was *excited*," Abby piped up. "Like out of her skin."

Stefan made a face.

"Where have you been?" Margaret asked.

"I had a call from Joachim."

Her hand went to her throat. "How is he? What did he say?"

"He sounded busy." Stefan had a sudden thought. "Where's that letter from him?"

"It's in my bureau. Why?"

"Can I see it?"

"Right now?"

"Please, yes."

He read it under the kitchen light. *I kept back what I needed, like you asked.* He folded it and put it back in the envelope. So why was money a problem?

"What are you two up to?"

"Nothing. What's to eat?"

"Nothing until you tell me what's going on."

"He, um, said to tell you hello. He and Savior, hell, I don't know, they're going fishing."

She planted a look on him.

"Honestly." He put a hand over his heart. It helped to be telling a half-truth. "Someplace called angler's heaven."

"He was supposed to sell the boat. Didn't he sell the boat?"

"We didn't talk about that."

"It would appear you didn't talk about much."

"Where have you been? Like, *all* afternoon?" Abby said.

"I was at the library."

She laughed out loud. "Oh, that's good."

"There's a ton of information online about what's going on back home. All kinds of environmental groups are fighting for Indigenous land rights. Here and in Canada, lots of support for us and what's going on."

Margaret tucked the letter in the folds of her skirt. "We left that behind. It's over. Why are you worrying up trouble?"

"And we left him behind too, didn't we?"

They stared each other down across the room.

She pushed her chair back. "You've made enough trouble here without worrying about what's going on back there. Joachim will be fine. There was business to take care of, and you know it. Your father wanted you out and you're out and you're staying out!" Her chin quivered and Stefan looked away.

"There's stew on the stove, Stefan. Let's see if we can get through the night without any more drama."

He ate his dinner with no drama and then cracked a beer in front of the television. It settled his stomach and one tasted like more.

A nature show came on about wildlife in the Arctic and he thought about home. He thought about the conversation with Joachim, falling asleep to the mournful cry of a wolf and the murmur of the narrator.

He awoke at three in the morning with a kink in his neck and the urge to pee. He drew a glass of water and glanced at the number of empty beer cans looking at him from the dish drainer. He drew another glass of water in the bathroom and set it on his bedside stand. As he drifted off to sleep, his final thought touched on what Abby had said about Sadie, *out of her skin*. All thought of Sadie had been hijacked by the patrolling Detective Pickens, the conversation with his brother, and a six-pack of beer.

He hugged himself as he slipped into unconsciousness. He only wanted her out of her clothes.

CHAPTER 35

It was with relief the next morning that Sadie saw the motorcycle parked in his driveway. He hadn't defied court orders. So, why wasn't he returning her calls?

For now, it was enough to know he was home. Another matter was more pressing.

Evans waved her into his office before the desk sergeant could grill her.

The little red rooster looked peeved to have been stepped around as she stepped around him.

Evans pointed her to a chair and settled himself behind his desk. "What's going on, Sadie?"

"Has Nan Murkowski been in this morning to recant her charge?"

He frowned. "No. Why?"

"I figured she wouldn't. I think she's afraid of coming forward with the truth." She set her cell phone on his desk. "It's all on here, the truth, that is."

He looked at the phone as though it had grown legs and was coming for him.

"Michigan is a one-party consent state, right?"

He leaned back in his chair and tented his fingers over his chest. "I heard you were going to school for investigative reporting."

Sadie was surprised. "Yeah, I *was.*"

"Well—" he propped his feet on the corner of his desk— "let's hear what you got."

She tapped the playback control and turned up the volume.

At first there was only background noise, the sound of a door closing, and then Nan's voice.

What are you doing here?

Evans was quiet as the conversation played out, ending with the *common knowledge* of Clem's volunteer firefighter experience and Nan's final statement: *He wasn't that good, hardly worth the effort.*

Sadie tapped *Stop* and looked at Evans over the cluttered expanse of his desk. He rubbed his chin and stared at the phone.

"Well?" Sadie said impatiently. "Is that enough to prove she was lying?"

Evans pulled a USB cable out of his side drawer, plugged it into his laptop, and gestured at her. "Transfer it. I expect you know how to do that too."

The transfer was complete in a matter of seconds. Sadie had already secured a duplicate copy at home, becoming proficient with the tricks of modern technology.

He saved the file on his desktop with a couple of clicks, then unplugged the USB cord, and chucked it in a drawer. "I'll get ahold of Pickens. We'll handle it from here."

Sadie looked at him questioningly, wanting more.

"He'll want to have a talk with Ms. Murkowski, but the conversation is pretty clear on intent."

Sadie shouldered her purse and rose to her feet.

"Young Montegrand might be out of a jam this time, but just between you and me—" he hesitated for a moment, then said, "As regards Pickens, he needs to be *very* careful in the future."

She weighed his words and wondered if Stefan was right in his inclination to leave.

Stefan ransacked the house for his phone before finding it wedged behind the couch cushion, out of juice. He plugged it into the charger on the counter, poured a cup of coffee, and contemplated a plan of action.

Abby shuffled out to the kitchen rubbing her eyes. "What was all the ruckus?"

"Can I use your phone?" he asked her.

"I'm almost out of minutes. What's wrong with yours?"

"It's dead."

"So, charge it."

"It's slow to charge, and I need to call Sadie."

"And your point?" She threw up her hands in acquiescence. "It's on my dresser. And you can buy me minutes." She shouted after him.

He scrolled through her contacts as he walked back to the kitchen. "Don't you have her in this stupid thing?"

"Why would I? You mean you don't even know your girlfriend's number?" She rolled her eyes.

"Fuck!" He threw the phone on the couch. He pulled on his boots and grabbed a shirt on his way out the door.

"You're a hot mess, *Steffie!*" Abby shouted after him.

He threw a satisfying spray of gravel on his way out of the driveway, irritated with himself on multiple levels. He rolled up Wixom's drive on the distinctive rumble of the thunder stroke engine. Henry walked out of the shed wiping his hands on a rag.

Stefan knocked the kickstand down with his heel.

Henry tucked the rag in his back pocket and stuck a hand out. "Glad to see you."

Stefan climbed off the bike and shook his hand. "I meant to thank you," he said, "for, you know, for getting that lawyer."

"I want you to know that we never believed any of it."

"Thanks. That's, ah, that means something. What do I owe you?"

"We'll worry about that later."

Stefan shoved his hands in his pockets, and then glanced around the drive and the stable.

"She must've left while I was in the barn. Do you want to come inside and wait?"

Going inside would mean rubbing shoulders with the old man. No, he didn't want to go inside. He climbed back on the bike and turned the key. "No, I have to go. Tell her I was here."

He gunned it down the driveway and out on the straightaway. He accelerated on a curve, rear end fishtailing and skimming the berm.

Cruising through town, he looked for the Duster. As he coasted by the party store, he couldn't resist a roll of the throttle. He pulled into the gas station, topped off his tank, and went inside for a pack of cigarettes. Someone new was behind the counter and he was on his way without incident.

Back home, he was riffling through his closet with a knapsack at his feet when the freshly charged phone rang from the bedside table.

"Have you heard from Jac?" Josie cut right to the chase.

"Hello to you," he said impatiently. "What's up?"

She breathed through the line. "Have you heard from your brother?"

"Yeah. He needed money."

"When was this? Where is he?"

Stefan frowned to himself. Why was Josie in the dark? Josie always knew everything. "He's with Savior and Bobby," Stefan blurted out.

"I know they're with Bobby. But where? What did he tell you, Stefan?"

"He, um, not much." He pressed the phone to his ear, thinking. "It sounds like they're planning to go south, some lake he called angler's heaven."

"What was the name of it?"

He thumbed through his closet with one hand, mind racing.

"I can't remember," he lied.

"Think."

He threw his lined flannel on the bed, followed by long underwear and thermal socks. He *was* thinking. "He was in a hurry. Needed money and I wired it to him."

"What was the name of the lake, Stefan?"

He felt the bite of her gaze through the phone at his ear. A flash of movement caught the corner of his eye and he looked at the blackbird looking at him from the branch of a linden tree outside his window. Did the mysterious spirit bird portend ill will or good? He stared into the piercing yellow eye. His breath fogged the glass, and the bird flew.

Josie was one of them. He could surely trust Josie.

"Somebody Bobby knows has a place on Gullet Lake, way south, he said." He threw another pair of socks on the bed. "Gullet Lake in Manitoba."

"Manitoba? You sure?" The rustling of papers, wheels in motion. "Okay, I'll find it." She paused. "Let's keep this between us, okay? I'll find him, get him to a safe place. Don't you worry, sit tight, and I'll be in touch."

He hung up and stared at the screen. There she goes again, talking *safe* places. Sit tight? She didn't know him at all.

Sadie hurried home from the police station to collect the boomerang, and then drove back to Stefan's.

His mother let her in and pointed her down the hallway. "He's in his room," she said.

Sadie held the boomerang behind her back and opened his door. He was standing in front of his closet with a pair of jeans over his arm. He had donned his old fedora and she had a déjà-vu moment.

"Sadie—" He let the jeans fall, "there you are."

She dropped the boomerang on the bed, took him by the collar, and kissed him on the mouth.

"Whoa, baby." He held her. "You happy to see me?"

She hugged him, toe to toe with the length of him.

"Where've you been?" He held her at arm's length, a question in his eyes.

"*Me?* I've been trying to call you for two days."

"My phone stinks, no battery life."

She kissed him again, not done with him. "We'll get you a new phone," she whispered.

"Things have been crazy, Sade, I'm sorry."

"I was worried about you."

"I was just out to your place."

"Then I just missed you."

"I wanted to thank your dad for getting me that lawyer. Did you, ah—" he licked his lips— "ever have a chance to talk to, you know . . ."

"Nan? Yes, I talked to Nan last night." She leaned back to look at him. "The charges will be dropped."

"Dropped? How do you know?"

She pulled her phone out of her back pocket. "Do you know you can record conversations?"

Stefan frowned. "Guess I've never had a reason to."

"I confronted her, and she admitted it but refused to recant. It doesn't matter—" she held her phone up— "it's all here. I played it for Evans. He downloaded it on his computer so he can play it for Pickens."

Stefan looked doubtful. "How'd you know—will it hold up?"

"I have a friend who's into pharmacology. She made the drug connection for me. I dug a little deeper and decided to run with it. I might've helped Nan see a way out of a perjury trap. You were right. Bolton was behind it. She got the ketamine from them. I looked it up, symptoms identical to what you described, and it sounds like he was behind that tool you found in the van. Nobody wants to lie in front of a judge. Or have any involvement with drug use brought up when their daddy is running for office."

He raised an eyebrow. "He is?"

"Oh, yeah. A kingpin."

He searched her face. "How'd you—shit—you're amazing, Sadie. I don't know how you figured all that out." His voice cracked and his eyes were hooded with emotion. "I don't know what to say."

"I have something else for you." She clasped her hands in excitement and turned him towards the bed. "Look what I found."

His eyes fell on the boomerang, and she smiled at the look on his face.

He picked it up and turned it over in his hands, the intricate engravings that told a story of a long-ago passage, his ancestral history carved out on a curved piece of wood.

"You found it." His eyes moved in wonder over her face. "How did you find it?"

"It was Wolf." She laughed. "Lucky, I guess. Something spooked him, and the big lug tried to climb in my lap, practically pushed me on top of it."

He pulled her down on the bed and lowered himself over her. "Like this?" His voice was husky, and the springs creaked. He held her face between his hands and kissed her long, slow, and in control.

His bed smelled like him, and nothing mattered but the give and take, his scent and his weight. It grounded her. She welcomed it, all of it. And it came to her that this was what she wanted. Whatever the cost.

I wake to sleep and take my waking slow.
I feel my fate in what I cannot fear.
I learn by going where I have to go.
                                    -Theodore Roethke

PART II

CHAPTER 36

In the solitude of predawn, Stefan packed what clothes he could fit in the saddle bags along with a rain suit, his phone, and a clear vision of intent.

Knowing the sexual assault charges would be dropped was a relief, but he also knew the reprieve was temporary. Pickens was never going to leave him alone. He needed distance to fall off that man's radar. He could still feel the bite of the manacles. Even when his hands were tucked between his legs, the cold was there, penetrating his psyche and firming his resolve to leave while he still could.

But his concern for Joachim was the deciding force. It had worsened after he called asking him to wire money, and he regretted the conversation with Josie. He felt like a snitch. *Let's keep this between us.* If Jac had wanted her to know where he was, he would have told her.

He penned his letters, one for his mother and one for Sadie, the harder one to write, taking the coward's way out because he would have faltered if he'd had to tell her goodbye.

But he left the boomerang as proof he'd be back.

He rolled the bike out of the drive as the sun cleared the horizon and was approaching the Mackinac Bridge before Sadie had breakfast.

She came awake slowly, holding him in her mind, planning a future free of legal entanglements and cultural differences. Over their dinner with Margaret and Abby around the oil-clothed table with frybread and a spicy meatball soup, she had already started planning it, not noticing how Stefan skirted the issues raised by Abby surrounding the brother he referred to affectionately as Jac. Not noticing how he skirted any talk of "tomorrow" and a Sunday dinner, how he walked her to her car and kissed her with a cryptic goodbye, tracing the line of her jaw with his finger before letting her go and walking away.

It was a normal morning: coffee, bagels, feeding the horses, throwing hay down for the cattle. She made a grocery list for her chicken dinner and stopped at his house to see if he wanted to go with her.

The absence of the motorcycle didn't raise her alarm, but then Abby opened the door with a tear-streaked face. His mother was chopping vegetables on a cutting board with a butcher knife and pieces of minced food were flying across the counter.

Sadie glanced down the hallway at his door standing open, and a knot formed in her stomach.

Abby spoke first. "He didn't even say goodbye. He lied. I hate him!"

Sadie swallowed the lump climbing up her throat. "Lied about what?"

"About leaving, he said he wouldn't."

"How do you know he's left?"

Margaret set the knife down, which Sadie was thankful for, and reached in her pocket and pulled out a piece of folded paper. "He left us a letter. Told us not to worry, everything will be just fine."

Sadie stared at the incriminating evidence. He left them a letter.

"Did you know?" Margaret searched her face. "What he was planning?"

Sadie shook her head. "He talked about wanting to go back, worried about Joachim, but, no, I had no idea."

She nodded at an envelope on the table. "He left you one too, so maybe you didn't."

Sadie looked at the envelope propped up against a vase of wilting flowers. She couldn't move. She didn't want it.

"Go ahead. Take it."

"What time did he leave?"

"He was gone when I got up."

"I hate him," Abby punched the pillow in her lap. "He's a liar, and I hate him. I hope I never see him again."

"Be quiet, Abby." Margaret's voiced softened. "Sadie? Look at me. If he says anything about his plan, where exactly he's going, will you let me know?"

She nodded mutely. What else could she do?

She took the letter and escaped into the outside air. She drove home on autopilot, parked where she always parked, and then opened it.

Sadie,

Jac's in trouble and I need to find him. He's hooked back up with his two crazy friends and I have a bad feeling about that. Plus Josie is hiding something, they both are. I can make Manitoba in a day, but I'll stop halfway and stretch my legs. I'll call you then and explain. No explaining last night. I knew you'd do something crazy. Don't worry. I have what I need. I love you. The one thing that isn't crazy.

Stef

p.s. I left the boomerang in your car. Take care of it for me.

He was going to—where? *Manitoba?* — and she wasn't supposed to worry?

She crumpled the letter and slammed a fist against the steering wheel. Like stages of grief, denial came first. *Fucking Manitoba?* She balled it up and threw it on the floor. Why Manitoba? Disbelief crowded out other emotion. He couldn't be serious. She scooped the balled-up letter off the floor, smoothed it open on the dash with the palm of her hand, and read it again.

I love you.

He had a peculiar way of showing it. She chewed her fingernails, turning into her mother. Had she ever told him that? Three little words. Why were they so hard to say? The saying was bottled up inside of her, ever since the day her mother died, balled up like a wad of paper, layered in sorrow and hardened like paper mâché. She had never come to terms with the grief. She had never cried.

It's in your car.

She found it on the floor behind her seat, neatly wrapped in the towel, and how he'd managed that sneaky maneuver, she'd never know.

She traced the engraved surface with a finger, then wrapped it back in the towel with the memory of many things and hid it on the top shelf of her closet. The heartbreak of a letter was concealed in her bedside table.

By slow degrees, disbelief turned into anger, and she went about her day, bolstered by its protective edge. But the sun wasn't shining, and the air had turned cold, a pall settling over the homestead. Even the dog was despondent, lying on his rug in the doghouse with his food untouched, head between his paws.

She tried to call him, but he wouldn't pick up, reinforcing the anger. She was supposed to wait for him to call her at his convenience. What was she? An eighteenth-century woman pacing a widow walk?

She replayed their conversations in her head, the signs she missed which now seemed so obvious, the cryptic goodbye and lingering kiss. Why had she been so easily duped? Anger collapsed into humiliation and self-loathing.

Exhausted by the recriminations, she sleep-walked through the afternoon, coming to a reconciliation of sorts. Of course, he couldn't answer his phone on a motorcycle, and she understood the innate need he'd been struggling with for weeks to be at his brother's side. Not only to assist with whatever he was caught up in, but to get himself out from under the harassment he'd been subjected to here. She couldn't imagine what that was like, but knew it had taken a toll. Joachim was a known commodity, an intriguing figure, everything she imagined an older brother to be, while she was a supporting character. Important but not key to the story.

He said he would call and inferred he'd be back. Of course, she would wait—a bitter thought—that's what women do.

She found herself in front of the bookshelf searching for the dog-eared book of poems belonging to her mother.

Retreating to the stable—her childhood haven—she leaned against a bale of hay and read to the horses, finally embracing the wisdom of acceptance. They were lulled into contentment, but with dusk coming on, she brooded over the shadows. Everything had lost color, life bleeding definition. She lingered over the scoop in the grain, the pages in the book, and the knots in a coil of baling twine, a meditative unraveling.

A shadow crossed the doorway. Abby, tall with resolve, stood in the door of the stable.

"What're you doing here?"

She handed Sadie a printout of a map. "I found this on Stefan's floor behind the door."

Sadie's eyes fell down the page. There were pencil notations in the margins.

"I suspect he meant to take it." She studied Sadie's face. "He's either an idiot, or was in an awful hurry."

Sadie looked at the circled X in Canada. Sure enough, in Manitoba. "I don't understand." She frowned at Abby. "Why Manitoba?"

"Who knows with Joachim? And if he's with those other two. . ." She shrugged. "Stefan obviously thinks he's in trouble and thinks he can help." She made a face, *as if.*

"Did you show this to your mother?"

"No. I wanted you to have it. He can explain himself to her when he calls." She motioned at the map. "That's where he's going. I just thought you'd like to know." She turned abruptly and left the stable. The gravel crunched under her feet, and Sadie was alone again with the horses and the doves, alone with her unraveling life and the gathering night.

CHAPTER 37

Joachim fled the Narrows with Savior and Bobby under cover of dark. They split up five miles out to take separate routes with a plan to reunite in Manitoba when they crossed the border and made the town of Mafeking.

"Turn your phones off until we get past Portage," Bobby said.

Savior tipped the brim of his Stetson. "Yessir. Anything else?"

"Keep to the speed limit, no hot-dogging. Remember . . ." He looked back and forth between them, "the gas station outside of Mafeking. My cousin says there's only one. If you beat me, try not to look like you're loitering."

"Well, hell," Joachim drawled, "they got a bar where we can loiter without it looking bad?"

Bobby dismissed them with a wave over his shoulder. "See you in Manitoba."

They were within fifty miles of that border when the flashing lights of a problem appeared ahead.

"Shit, what's this?" Savior hit the clutch and downshifted.

Joachim hadn't been able to get comfortable. He'd fashioned a sling out of his spare flannel to support his shoulder, but he felt every jag in the road, and he needed to piss. He squinted at the lights. "Looks like an accident."

The Mounties were on the scene, and Savior was signaled into a line of waiting vehicles. Joachim rolled down his window. "What's going on?"

An RCMP officer stooped to the window and looked them over. "Washout ahead, car in the river."

A wrecker blocked the entrance to the bridge span, and figures moved in the shadows.

"What's the wait time?"

He studied Joachim, eyes lingering on the makeshift sling and the bandana wrapped tight around his head. "You boys in a hurry?"

Joachim set the satchel on the floor and swung his legs out of the truck. "I take it there's time to take a leak and have a smoke?" He placed a cigarette in the corner of his mouth. "Want a smoke?"

The man settled his law enforcement gaze on him, and Joachim regretted calling attention to himself. He should've kept his mouth shut, could never keep his mouth shut. He stepped away and struck a light. *Quit staring at me.* "You aren't gonna watch me piss, are you?" he called sarcastically over his shoulder.

There I go, just can't stop myself.

The officer's radio was talking to him, and he walked away with it in his ear.

Joachim walked to the edge of the embankment into the shadows. Their nosiness irked him, brought out the worst in him. He hunched his shoulders against the night and smoked his cigarette. Smokestacks in the distance spewed black smoke against the night sky. They waited until dark to turn the burners on. He blew out a stream of his own smoke and took another draw. The smokes might be aggravating his problem, but the nicotine kick was good, countered the ache in his shoulder, and the one in his chest that had reemerged like a dormant virus.

He lit another off the butt of the first and unzipped to relieve himself. He wasn't going to die in some white man's jail or in a sterile hospital room. He made that promise to himself after a visit to Sonny's cell, reinforcing it beside the hospital bed they transferred him to at the end. After it was too late.

"Jac!" Savior was leaning out the window. "Let's go." Traffic was moving.

Joachim ground the cigarette out under his boot and hefted himself into the cab, favoring his injured shoulder. The officer glanced his way, and Joachim threw him a wave.

"You shouldn't have said anything to him," Savior said. "He kept staring at me."

"He wasn't paying any attention to you. C'mon, let's get out of here."

When they were across the bridge and back on two lanes, Savior stepped on the gas. Joachim downed two pain pills, laid the seat back, and let the numb of the narcotic wash over him.

They made their rendezvous point in the predawn hour as a flock of geese on the move honked overhead in an arrowhead formation.

Bobby was waiting, having had no traffic tie-ups to contend with.

They pulled alongside and rolled down their windows. "I need some shut-eye," Bobby said. "There's a motel up there." He pointed at the blinking *Vacancy* sign.

They had to ring the bell to wake the desk clerk. Joachim scanned the lobby for wanted posters as the clerk took their information and gave them the room keys.

He took a hot shower, turning the small bars of soap over in his hand, and smelling them. He washed his hair with the motel's complimentary shampoo, emptying the bottle on his head. It was the first shower he'd had in a month, and he stood under the spray long after the soap and grime had drained away.

CHAPTER 38

Sadie held the map to the light to better see Stefan's circled X's and shorthand margin notes. Abby was pretty devious, leaving all this in her lap.

The sound of the van's engine turning over jolted her to action. She jumped to her feet and ran outside, motioning for Abby to stop.

She rolled down the window. "What?"

She held up the map. "What am I supposed to do with this?"

Abby looked at her shrewdly. "I thought it would come in handy."

Sadie raised an eyebrow. "Oh?"

"You *are* going after him, aren't you?"

"Are you crazy? I'm *not* going after him. How would I even do that?"

"He obviously meant to take that with him. It's an omen that he left it for you."

"He didn't leave it for me."

"It's providence. My brothers are always talking about *providence.* Don't you see? He has a shitty phone, Sadie. You know that, right? It doesn't even hold a charge. You should go."

"I don't think he'd like that. He obviously didn't want me to go with him—" Her voice broke. "He never said a word about leaving, just let me make all my stupid plans."

"He's an impulsive idiot and Mother is tearing her hair out. He needs that." She nodded at the map in Sadie's hand. "You need to go after him. See that he comes back."

"He says he will."

"Like he said he was buying a boat and taking me out next weekend to show me how to fish the way our dad did?" Abby drummed her fingers on the steering wheel. "I hate to call him a liar, impulsive is maybe better. I'm surprised he hasn't called and asked me to take a picture of that and send it to him. Can you imagine, trying to decipher that mess on the screen of a shitty phone with a cracked screen?"

Sadie looked at the mess. His abbreviated margin notes were indecipherable to her, but obviously important to him. How far did he get before he realized he didn't have it? At least he had his shitty phone. But everyone knew GPS could put you on a circuitous route to nowhere.

"I've been checking the weather," Abby squinted at Abby with a calculating eye. "There's a big storm moving across the U.P. He's probably holed up under an overpass soaking wet." She revved the engine. "Keep the map, Sadie, and think about it, but not for too long."

She thought about it. Walking circles in the stable to Two Socks' soft whinny of understanding—*a horse knows what you're about*—she couldn't stop thinking about it. One little nudge and she was entertaining the impossible. But with each pass around the stable, the certainty grew—there was nothing left for her here.

That night she couldn't sleep—*he's probably soaking wet under an overpass*—and she hunted through the medicine cabinet until she found her mother's expired sleeping pills. She downed two with a glass of water.

They might have been expired, but two were too many, and she woke in the morning feeling groggy and sluggish with a dull ache behind her eyes. She took two anti-inflammatory capsules to help counter the side effect of the sleepers.

Stefan's map was lying on her bedside table. The idea planted by Abby had morphed into possibility and saturated her drug-laden dreams with Stefan hunkered under a windy viaduct. Along with the headache was the growing feeling of dread that harm would befall him without her ever having told him she loved him. She loved him, and she needed to tell him.

She only had one life. What was she going to do with it?

There was one straight route across the Upper Peninsula, through Wisconsin, and on up to the Canadian border, but Manitoba was a big place, and his route from there to the point circled in red was a zigzagged maze. But at least it was a map, a map he didn't have.

He had a jump on her, but she could drive faster and harder than he could on a motorcycle, and when he called from his halfway point— because she knew he would, probably to get his notes off the map—she could be close. They could travel on together. It would be safer. Who rides a motorcycle north with winter coming on? Her mind was taking her on an implausible mission, but once it was made up, she moved fast.

She threw a few things in a bag and left her own note on the counter by the coffee pot she emptied into a thermos.

There was a knock on the door. It was Abby again, this time with a backpack.

She frowned, needing to get out of the house without drawing her nosy grandfather's attention. Simon Wixom II was always underfoot. He needed to find a woman too. Maybe from the Altar Society.

"What are you doing here?"

Abby glanced at her bag. "I knew you'd do the right thing, and I'm going with you."

"No, you aren't."

"Please, I won't be any trouble."

"Abby, *no*. Go home. Your mother will need you. Besides, Sam would be worried." She played an underhand card. "He really likes you, you know. He would kill me, not to mention what your mom would do to me."

Abby chewed on the corner of her mouth. "I'm so afraid he won't come back."

"We'll be back. Here," Sadie took her phone out. "Give me your number. I promise I'll call you."

"Promise?"

"Promise."

She waited until Abby disappeared over the hill, then drove out the opposite way, and headed for the interstate. She had never been to Manitoba, looked forward to seeing it, and meeting this brother he

278

would do anything for. She was doing something wild with her one precious life.

CHAPTER 39

One minute Stefan was riding through pockets of sunshine and warm air, and the next he was caught in the squall that blew off Lake Michigan without warning. He pulled off on the shoulder of the sandy roadside and put on his rain gear.

The further away from Sadie he'd rode, the worse he'd felt, the anticipation of the road home fading in incremental miles. The pelting rain that soaked his jeans before he got the rain suit on added to his misery.

The sandy bluffs did little to buffer the wind off the lake, and there was nothing to do but keep going until he found shelter. Many establishments had already closed for the season, and he passed several discouraging *Closed* signs before coming to a motel and restaurant with the lights on. He parked in front of the motel and stood dripping in the foyer, a long way from his imagined midway stopping point, and checked the radar on his phone. A solid patch of green filled the screen, the angry squall a precursor to an all-day event.

He checked into a room and stripped off the wet clothes for a dry pair of jeans before heading to the bar for something to eat. The bartender eyed him suspiciously, much as the clerk at the front desk had done when he asked for a room.

"You work at the casino?" The bartender asked as he gave him a menu and a frothy glass of beer.

Stefan raised his glass to sip his beer and fastened his eyes on him. "Never been in one."

The bartender snorted his disbelief.

"Have you?"

"Do I look like I can afford to gamble?"

"I wouldn't know."

"You aren't from 'round here then?"

"I'll take a hamburger, the half-pounder. And extra onions." Stefan pushed the menu away. "Can you fry those up on the side?"

The bartender shrugged. "I can't, but maybe our fry guy can."

Stefan's lip curled in a smile. "Fry guy . . . I like that."

The television behind the bar was on, and he watched it without seeing it. He glanced at the phone sitting at his right hand, tempting him to call Sadie. It would be so easy.

He regretted sneaking off without a proper goodbye, but he couldn't handle a proper goodbye. He couldn't handle explaining himself. He was on the fly.

The onions were done up right, and after a second beer, he paid his tab at the register.

"That your bike out there?" The bartender nodded at the door.

Stefan followed his gaze through the glass at rain pelting the motorcycle.

"There's an overhang around back. You can park it up against the side of the building."

"That right?" Stefan considered him afresh. "Maybe I will. Thanks."

Having realized he'd forgotten the map he printed off at the library with the additional directions he scrawled in the margins, he picked up what maps he could find in the lobby. The GPS directions on his phone were incomplete and service was spotty. He needed information off that map. Debating who to call, he fell asleep with the Upper Peninsula tenting his chest and rain drumming the metal roof over his head.

Thus, Sadie got ahead of him on the road, driving past his hotel the next morning, and straight through to Ironwood with her wipers slapping sheets of rain. She paid cash for dinner and a room in a historic roadside inn in the once-booming town turned quiet. It was gradually climbing back to prosperity, but the ghosts of desertion lingered in the hallway and in the tiny room with its standing, tube-style radiator hissing and clanking. But it was warm and dry, and she settled in, waiting for his call.

The foolhardiness of the venture nagged at her consciousness, kept at bay by rereading his note, recalling Abby's confidence, and composing her own end to the story, denying the fact that the ending was dependent on him. Or dumb luck.

She propped herself against the headboard on the sagging mattress and played Words With Friends on her phone, her only contact with some of them. The internet was as slow as the system moving across the peninsula, and it occurred to her that she could have outpaced him. He was either ahead of the storm or holed up somewhere. He wouldn't ride in this.

She rang him up for the umpteenth time and it went directly to voicemail.

"Hey Stef," she breathed into the phone. "I'm sitting in this ghost town called Ironwood. Maybe we can ride the rest of the way together. If you want out of the rain . . . if you want to get to Manitoba before the snow flies, why don't you call me back? And what's this about Manitoba anyway? By the way, I have something you might need. Call me."

She hung up with a satisfied smile, secretly hoping the rain would never stop.

But in the morning, the sun was shining through trees past their peak of color and losing leaves outside her window. She unplugged her phone from the wall, made a cup of weak complimentary coffee, and tried calling him again. Why would he not pick up? *Where is he?* She took a quick shower and braided her hair all the while wondering, was he ahead of her, or behind her? Deliberating her move, she walked down the town's main street, passing storefronts that encompassed a trace of the town's mining past with its future as an up-and-coming tourist destination. But the tourist season was over, and winter lurked a few miles out in the waters of Lake Superior that touched the Canadian shore, the rivers and inlets from the far north emptying into Thunder Bay and feeding the frigid, if pristine, waters of Hiawatha fame.

She bought a headband and a beaded necklace, and found an old-fashioned diner where she ordered a coffee and an omelet. She listened to the clipped accents around her talking of an early winter and hunting season, wondering how long before Stefan gave in and answered his phone. He didn't even have it on, calls going directly to voice mail telling her to *leave a message*. She wanted to climb through it and wring his neck.

She drove to the gas station on the edge of town, nothing but open road winding into the woods ahead, and as the pump clicked the gallons, she rang her father and left a message on the house answering machine, apologizing for leaving without saying goodbye. She topped off her coolant and pumped air in her tires, just for him.

After a late lunch outside of Ashland, she lingered over several cups of coffee before continuing on into Wisconsin, passing signs for the Apostle Islands and Iron River—Iron this and Iron that—obsessively checking her phone with self-doubt creeping in. *What the hell am I doing?* And why hadn't he called her?

She entered a desolate stretch of highway and started looking for a motel. She was in unfamiliar territory and didn't want to go any further by herself, but she couldn't live with the defeat of turning back. By her calculations, it was almost further now to turn back than to keep going.

She was driving through a heavily wooded area where trees overhung the roadway to further diminish what daylight was left when a full-bodied buck jumped the ditch and lunged at her car. It crashed into the side and flipped onto the hood with a sickening thud.

The car skidded to a halt, and the metallic rendering of the collision echoed in the silence that followed, a silence that took on a sound of its own. She loosened the seatbelt that was cutting into her chest and blinked at what looked like a small tree stuck in her windshield. The glass was a spiderweb of cracks and made a kaleidoscope of the lifeless eye of the deer, and she realized the tree was actually a prodigious rack belonging to the animal sprawled across the hood of her car.

Steam rose off the engine block in a rising hiss of urgency, and she fumbled for the door handle, frantic to get out of the car. The door was jammed. She climbed over the seat, flung the back door open, and fell out on the pavement in a tangle of arms and legs.

She staggered to her feet and walked around the wreckage. The front wheel well was crumpled and the tire was flat. The hood was crushed and fluids were pooling under the front end.

"Shit!" She kicked the flat tire. Her nose was bleeding, and she wiped it on her sleeve. She needed a tissue; she needed her phone.

She climbed back in the car and grabbed her purse off the seat, but her phone wasn't there. She searched the floor and under the seat.

A car pulled alongside and honked the horn.

"Anyone in there?"

Sadie climbed out the back, held a tissue folded in on itself against her nose, and looked at the two men who had pulled up in a late model Mustang.

"Hey there." The one talking climbed out of the passenger side and whistled. "Look at the rack on this baby, Sid." He turned to the driver who was rounding the front of the car.

Sid was clothed in camouflage and knee boots, and the only sound he made came from the broken glass crunching under his heels as he made his way around the car. He took hold of a hoof to heft the buck's hind quarter, and then settled an appraising gaze on Sadie with eyes so dark they looked black. "You all right?" he said.

"I'm fine." She rubbed her arms. "Just a little shaky."

"I imagine. You two did a number on each other." He looked from the buck's broken neck to her crumpled front end. "But you just got yourself a freezer full of meat."

Sadie opened her mouth and closed it again, uncomprehending.

"Don't you want it?" he said.

She made a face. "Are you kidding?"

A calculating expression settled over his face. "Then we'll take it." He looked at his companion. "We'll have to go back and get your truck."

"Should we give her a lift?"

284

Sadie looked at their car. They had a police type antenna mounted on the roof, and the rear window was plastered with Confederate flags, NRA and Remington decals. "No," she said. "Go ahead. I have Triple A. I'll give them a call."

"Screw Triple A. You're in northern Wisconsin, baby. We have our own wrecker service, don't we, Sid?"

Sid was eyeing the carcass, parceling it out. "We have to get him gutted." He dropped a hand to the empty sheath in his belt. "I didn't bring my knife, Billy. You got yours?"

Billy shook his head.

He looked at Sadie. "You got a knife—what's your name?"

"Sadie."

"You got a knife, Sadie? No? Figures. Get in the car. We'll take you into town."

She crossed her arms. How stupid did they think she was? "I'll stay here until the wrecker comes; make sure nobody else takes off with your freezer full of meat."

The two men exchanged a look.

"She could be right, Billy," Sid said. "You can stay, and I'll take her into town."

"No!" Sadie steeled her voice. "I stay with the car. You do what you need to do."

The camouflaged hunter shrugged. "Suit yourself, but you might want to stay *in* your car. Black bears are active this time of year, storing up food for winter." He cast a look back at her. "They'll be attracted to your smell, so I'd advise you to stay inside. We'll be back in twenty minutes."

She watched them drive away and then climbed back in the car to find her phone. She didn't have Triple A, but she had a smartphone. She would line up her own wrecker, not some flimflam outfit, hopefully within twenty minutes, hopefully before night fell fast and complete.

The phone had fallen between the seat and the passenger door. She turned it on and waited for a signal. Nothing. She climbed out of the car with a quick glance around and walked to the center of the road with the phone stretched out.

Nothing.

She walked as far as a bend in the highway.

Nothing.

Shadows lengthened across the road as she walked further into the dead zone. It wasn't that she minded being in the open with night coming on, but these woods weren't the fields of home, the swales, low spots and headlands she knew like the palm of her hand, the open pasture where she could see what was coming.

Crickets chirped from the ditch and she sensed the stirring of things coming. They didn't have bears downstate, and she didn't plan to make their acquaintance anytime soon. She looked back at the lonely wreck of her car in the distance, a distance she couldn't remember walking.

Cricket sound was drowned out by breaking brush and snapping branches. Was that a grunt? She turned her ear. *Don't run.* Her encounters with vicious dogs while reading meters taught her well. Don't look them in the eye, don't show fear, but most of all, do not run.

She started for the car, resisting the urge, but the faster she walked, the further that distance stretched out before her. Suddenly the far-off sound of a muscle engine drifted through the trees. She stared at the silver ribbon of highway that curled into the woods in front of her as the distinctive sound of a motorcycle filled the air like a low-flying tomahawk.

It was Stefan rounding a curve, laying it low and kissing the asphalt. She held her breath for a heartbeat and then ran.

CHAPTER 40

Stefan swerved to avoid the spray of broken glass and skidded to a stop next to the wrecked car blocking the center of the road. The largest whitetail he'd ever seen was draped across the hood dwarfing the crushed vehicle.

He parked the bike and stared at the car. *Jesus.* It looked just like Sadie's. He tried the driver's side door, but it was jammed. He shaded his eyes to look inside. Poor sucker. There was blood on the steering wheel and glass on the dash.

He looked in the rear window. There was a backpack on the seat. He went to open the door when he heard the sound of running footsteps. He squinted at the distant figure coming towards him, arms pumping. It was Sadie.

She ran into his arms, almost knocking him off his feet. She hugged his neck, and he couldn't think. The disarray of her hair brushed his face with the smell of autumn and damp earth. He breathed in the scent of her. She was perspiration and familiarity, frustration and desire. He ran his fingers along the side of her face, taking it in. There was dried blood around her nose and down the front of her shirt.

"Are you hurt?" He choked the words out.

She shook her head. "No," she breathed.

"What the hell are you doing here, Sadie? What happened?"

"It came out of nowhere. I never even saw it until it was too late." She glanced over his shoulder. "Look what he did to my car!"

287

He looked at the wrecked car silently leaking fluids and then back at her, a baffling complication. He had never been so surprised in his life.

"I'm so happy to see you," she said in a rush. "I didn't know what I was going to do. Two guys stopped and wanted to give me a lift, and they're coming back for the deer, but they gave me the creeps and, oh—" she drew in a breath— "I'm so glad *you're* here."

Wisps of hair had escaped the green headband that framed her face, her bloodied nose, the broken glass in her hair.

"Hold still," he said. "There's glass in your hair." He loosened the headband and worked the shards free from the tangles at the crown of her head.

"There." He stepped back and looked at her. She had come after him—a girl from back home would *never* have done that—and his thoughts were as tangled as her hair.

She gingerly felt her scalp with her fingertips, and then pulled the headband back in place.

"I can't believe this," he said. "What were you thinking?"

"You didn't say goodbye."

"I *couldn't* say goodbye. I told you I'd call you when I was halfway. Didn't you get my letter?"

"Yeah, a letter. We could've talked about it."

"No, we couldn't. Talk complicates things. This was something I needed to do by myself."

She chewed on her bottom lip. "I'll get a rental car and go home."

"Don't be ridiculous."

"I have a credit card."

He exhaled through pursed lips. "You aren't old enough to rent a car."

"No problem. I'll hitchhike."

"You think?" Stefan cracked his neck and looked at the wreck of her car.

"You're mad."

"I'm thinking."

"Yeah." She kicked the heel of one sneaker against the toe of the other. "I am too. I'm thinking I can hitchhike."

"I'm not mad, Sadie, but this complicates things."

"I called you a dozen times! What happened to the call you promised me?"

"I wasn't halfway."

"Sheesh."

"Besides, I never dreamed you do something this crazy. And you aren't hitchhiking."

They walked back to the car and stood in front of it.

"Do you think it's totaled?" Sadie said.

"It's definitely totaled."

She grabbed her backpack off the seat and unzipped it. "I have something for you."

He looked at his map, astonished. "Where'd you find that?"

"You need it, right?"

"Yeah, I do. But where—"

"Abby found it. She's the one convinced me to come after you."

He shook his head. "I'll be damned. An Abby idea. So, you came all this way to give me a map I could pull up on my phone?"

She gestured at the scrawled handwriting. "You'd find *that* on your phone?"

"Probably not." He smiled in spite of himself. "My GPS won't update, but if it hadn't been for the storm, you never would've caught me."

"And you would've been lost. A lot of help to your brother then."

He looked at her looking at him and tucked the map in the inside pocket of his motorcycle jacket.

"I'd have caught you, Stefan," she said softly.

"By blowing your motor?"

"I won't be any trouble, promise."

"Get your things, only what you absolutely need."

She looked at the bulging saddlebags.

"I'll make room," he said.

She rearranged her backpack and emptied the glove box into it while he made room in the saddlebags for her purse and toiletry bag. She double-layered a sweater, and changed her shoes for boots. He shook his head at the tennis shoes. "Leave them." He helped her zip the jacket and stepped back. She was smart to braid her hair. One smart thing.

He handed her a do-rag. "Put this on. We'll get you a helmet as soon as we can."

"I thought we didn't need helmets."

"We do in Canada." He looked away for a second then fixed his gaze back on her. "To be honest, I don't know what I'm getting into, and if you'd really rather rent a car than ride into it with me, there must be ways, or a bus, something."

"Is that what you want?"

He looked at her. The braid and bandana suited her. What he wanted wasn't clear cut. But even with the joke of a map in his pocket, he didn't know what he was getting into. "Honestly," he said quietly, "even with the map, it'll be rough going. I've never been to Manitoba."

Sadie pulled the bandana-type scarf over her ears and knotted it under her braid at the back of her neck. "I'll go there with you."

The headlights of an approaching vehicle flashed through the trees and a pickup on over-sized tires rocked to a halt in front of them as a wrecker with flashing yellow lights pulled up behind it.

Sid climbed out of the truck; black eyes shiny with suspicion. He looked from Sadie to Stefan. "Who's this?"

"A friend."

He gave Stefan a once-over. "You have friends from off the reservation?"

Sadie made a noise in the back of her throat. "That's rude. He's from Canada."

"Whatever. We're back for the deer." The black eyes issued Stefan a challenge.

"I have no interest in the deer," Stefan said.

"I wouldn't think so given you can hunt anything you want, anytime, anywhere while we have to settle for roadkill."

Stefan pinched his lips together. He wouldn't be drawn into conversation with this one.

The hunter shrugged. "C'mon, Billy," he said to his companion. "Let's gut our roadkill."

They gutted the carcass on the slope of the ditch, and then loaded it onto the bed of the pickup while the driver of the wrecker hitched up her car. Freed of its bloody cargo, the full damage to the Duster was on display.

"How much is she going to get for it?" Stefan asked him.

The driver threw his gloves in the truck and took out a clipboard. "Maybe a hundred bucks, if she's lucky, but she owes me ninety."

They looked at the sad wreck of a car—tufts of hair stuck in the quarter panel, blood smeared across the crumpled hood and cracked windshield.

"I bought that with my own money," Sadie said wistfully.

"Give me your number, Miss. I'll be in touch if I get more."

She shrugged. "Keep it, the hundred, whatever."

Stefan strapped on his helmet and threw a leg over the seat, balancing the bike as she climbed on behind him.

He revved the throttle. "You ready?"

Her thighs gripped his, arms around his middle.

"Hang on. We're out of here."

Before he was out of second gear, he knew he hadn't needed to tell her to hang on. She tightened her hold as the flashing lights of the wrecker faded in the side mirrors, and the road rushed under their feet. In defiance of the odds, which had never been in his favor, hurtling through the night with her arms fastened around him, body warm against his, he felt an imperceptible shift in the balance of favor.

CHAPTER 41

After another shower to loosen his muscles and inspect his healing gunshot wounds, Joachim stashed the remaining soap and little bottles of shampoo in his bag, lifted a washcloth and a roll of toilet paper, and went looking for Bobby and Savior.

Savior was in the hotel's breakfast room by himself.

"Where's Bobby?"

"He wants to ditch us."

"He said that?"

"He didn't have to."

Joachim drummed his knuckles on the table, glanced around the room, and then back at Savior. "Maybe we should split up. We could find this place if he gives us an address."

"Maybe the place doesn't have an address."

"Appears his record's clean, can't blame him for wanting it to stay that way."

"I think it's the girl. She's a problem." Savior stirred his coffee absently with a spoon. "I don't like driving with her plate. That was a dumb idea. I should've stayed in Luca, helped those people with their qualifier. I know dogs."

"And I know horses. What of it?"

"She liked my name, said it suited me."

Joachim rolled his eyes, poured himself a cup of coffee at the self-serve station, and inspected the tray of day-old donuts and croissants. He was having his own concerns about Bobby and where he was taking them. Other than Yellowknife in the Northwest Territory, he had never been outside of the province. He'd been as far north as Lake Athabasca and Uranium City—why would anyone name their town that? —but never into the neighboring provinces. He had traveled one time into North Dakota with his father and older brother for a summer meeting with tribes south when he was a teenager, and had a brief fling with a girl from South Dakota before his father whisked him back over the border. Now it felt like they were being herded onto one of those reserves where their grandparents had never wanted to be confined.

They found Bobby in a poolroom at the back of a garage converted into a tavern, but the game wasn't good. Bobby was on edge, kept checking his phone, stepping outside with it to come back in and flub a bank shot, chalking the nub off his cue, and furtively texting like a teenager. But he wouldn't confide in them, denied he had any worries, a mask of concealment in place. It wasn't the Bobby they grew up with and exchanged secrets with.

They were back on the road again at dusk. "Stay back a little bit," Bobby said. "I don't want you riding my ass."

They were standing outside the dry goods store where Joachim had bought a change of clothes and another hat to replace the one blown off his head by a high-powered rifle.

"It's trunk highway most the way, should take us about four hours, keeping to the speed limit." Bobby chewed the corner of his mouth. "I figure we can stop for coffee at one of those all-night truck stops and still make our fishing hole by dawn. Poles in the water by sun-up."

Joachim adjusted the band on his hat and pulled it low over his eyes, the way he liked it. *Eddie* had three more messages on his phone from Josie, each one angrier than the last, but at least there had been no more wanted posters crediting him with things he hadn't done.

"Just to be clear," he said, "your cousin's place has running water and electricity?"

"Would I be taking us to a place like Savior's? I can't believe Josie left you there."

"It was my idea."

"Don't be disparaging my cabin," Savior said.

"There you go again . . . *disparaging*?" Bobby looked at Joachim. "Josie keeps harassing me because you won't pick up, and between her and Camille—" He bit the sentence off on the *-ille*.

Joachim held his gaze. "You been talking to the little thief?"

Bobby tossed his keys from one hand to the other.

"What's to talk about, Bobby?" Joachim pressed. "Getting our money back? You working on that?"

The mask fell back into place.

"So, that's a no?" Joachim threw his bag of old clothes disgustedly behind the seat. He caught himself in the side mirror and adjusted his hat. It wasn't Jake's, but it fit.

Savior cranked the engine. "Are you done admiring yourself so we can hit the road?"

Bobby looked at them for a second, as if there were something else to say. Then he backed away, threw a wave over his shoulder, and pulled out of the lot ahead of them.

Driving through deforested land with earthmovers and bulldozers parked alongside the road, it was good to be traveling after dark. The bulky shapes figuratively spewed fumes even when they weren't, reminding him of everything taken in exchange for beads, blankets, and color TV with a middling share of royalties promised over a white man's handshake, but the land was fouled, the fish tasted bad, and the animals had left.

Passing the alien behemoths reeking of oil and crowding the berm, it was good to be traveling after dark.

CHAPTER 42

Sadie and Stefan rode through a lunar landscape along a desolate highway on a wend through the forest. Moonlight flickered in the ditches and glanced through the trees. It reflected off the asphalt and the chrome of the bike, and Sadie rested her chin against his shoulder as the astral globe slid behind a cumulus canopy. The sky was an inverted bowl of fleece formations and they rode through cold pockets of air and then warm, like the mercurial nature of a human relationship.

The vacancy sign blinked through the trees, and they got off the road, into a room, and cranked up the heat. Sadie took inventory of her scant belongings while Stefan stripped and turned the shower on.

Ever since they'd checked in, his eyes had gone opaque, mouth set in that damnable, blank expression, and she was unsure of this man she thought she knew. His myriad moods—passionate one minute, aloof the next, secret yet open, prideful yet demure—the many complexities of loving a man with a past as dissimilar as his, yet one with surprising similarities as well. Just as the hurdles her father and grandfather alluded to were of no consequence one minute but insurmountable the next.

"Mind if I go first?" he asked, hand under the spray.

Steam billowed around his straight-backed figure, and she was struck by the intimacy of the moment. *How about save water, shower together?* She looked away. That was from another era, and with his taciturn expression in place, she doubted he would be receptive to the idea.

"Go ahead, but save me some of that hot water."

He saved her some. She wrapped a towel around her wet hair and sat cross-legged in front of the pizza he had ordered from a to-go joint. She stacked excess pieces of crust in the corner while Stefan turned to his phone.

"Any news from your brother?"

He shook his head.

"His girlfriend?"

The light from his mobile glanced off his face, distant and withdrawn, and she felt the burden of her presence in the shake of his head, in the shoulder turned her way. She might as well have been Abby, an annoying little sister. He set the phone aside and pored over his map, worn thin at the creases, as she propped pillows behind her back and thumbed through the channels with the remote control.

He hadn't spoken a handful of words since they left the scene of the accident and now he was engrossed in his map with his thoughts, retreating into his reticent nature. And so, they sat there, together in a small room with one bed, but as far apart as if in a hostel filled with strangers, each with a private corner, a few square feet of privacy. He was holding tight to his. She had made a mistake and now he was stuck with her.

Stefan knew the second she fell asleep by the subtle change in her breathing pattern. He sensed it the way one senses a shadow crossing their path, a breath of air in a dead calm, the innate sensation of companionship versus the solitude of an empty room. She was asleep, and he was alone.

He eased the remote from her grasp, pulled the covers around her shoulders, and then turned the television off and sat in the dark. He opened the drapes to let the moon in. It was the same wherever you went, following its path across the sky, growing smaller as the Earth turned and the night drew on. The path of its beam slid slowly across the bed to light the familiar contours of her face, and still she slept.

He had received a disturbing call from Josie hinting at Jac's ignoring the advice of some doctor called *Murphy.* She had abruptly changed the subject, an uncharacteristic slip of the tongue he could almost see her biting.

The moon was gone from his window when he finally undressed and slid into the warmth on Sadie's side of the bed. He tucked his knees into the crook of hers, his chin into the warm pocket under her shoulder, and closed his eyes.

When he woke up, Sadie was braiding her hair in the morning sun. He drew a cup of coffee from the small pot and rearranged his saddle bags, culling the contents, combining toiletries, ditching hair product.

There was a cycle shop down the street, and after sharing a couple of day-old donuts and black coffee from the lobby continental, he helped her pick out a helmet with a shield; *a helmet that doesn't fit right is worse than no helmet at all,* and she bought leather gloves and a wool scarf.

He took the Duluth bypass and headed across Minnesota. They slept over in North Dakota with the Canadian border on the horizon.

And then there was Customs.

The border crossing was easier for Stefan than it was for her.

"How long are you staying and where in Canada are you staying and what is the purpose of your visit?" The Canadian agent exuded animus towards her, asking for additional ID and whether she was bringing in contraband: drugs, liquor, excessive amounts of money.

Sadie laughed at that and the border agent said something to Stefan she didn't catch, a brief back-and-forth between them, and then he turned to confer with a counterpart behind a partition. Sadie shifted nervously on the seat, wondering what was wrong, having never been on the wrong side of Customs. Stefan sat ramrod in front of her, not saying a word.

"What's wrong?" she whispered.

He gave her a quick shake of the head.

The agent finally handed back her passport with a word to Stefan who passed it over his shoulder before lifting his feet to the pedals and gassing the throttle.

They stopped south of Winnipeg for the night. They had crossed extensive prairie farmland before entering the outskirts of a small town. The border crossing had unnerved her, she felt like a cigarette, or a drink, and she wanted Stefan back on her side.

She could only see one way to achieve that. "Look, Stefan," she said when they were settled into their room, another four walls with a desk, a lamp, a bed with two pillows, and picture on the wall of a pastoral scene. "I'll get out of your hair at the next town. I'll get a rental car or hop a bus."

He turned to her and blinked.

"I made a mistake. This isn't going to work. I know that now. I know you don't want me with you, don't even want to be seen with me."

He stripped beside the bed and pulled the sheet over his legs, folded his arms behind his head and stared at the ceiling.

She rose on an elbow. "I get it, I'll go back." Her voice rose. "Say something, dammit!" She punched him in the shoulder. "I can't take this anymore."

He rubbed his shoulder and looked at her askance. "You say enough for both of us. I can't think and talk at the same time."

"Bullshit."

"Your cousin never shut up. Every thought had to be out there in the open. My sister is getting just as bad. And you . . . well, we're different, that's all, but just 'cause I'm not talking doesn't mean what you think it means." He looked out the window, drapes thrown open to the night. "Mom always said she could tell when Dad was anxious because he became less talkative. And he was never much of a talker to begin with. So, I guess that's me."

"I get it, you're anxious. Well, so am I."

"Maybe I haven't been good company, but I don't want you to leave." He propped himself on his elbow. "I had another message from Josie. She's trying to catch up with Jac. He's on the run, and it doesn't sound good, and, yes, I'm worried about having you with me, but if you

298

left—" he brushed her hair back with the side of his hand— "how would that help me? It would only be something else to worry about. I don't want you to leave, baby. I like you in my hair, so no more talk about leaving, okay?"

She turned her face into the palm of his hand, a swelling in her heart. She was okay with that.

He wrapped his arm around her, but there was something else bothering her. "That border agent, Stefan—" she paused. "Why was he so hateful towards me?"

He looked at her. "Hateful? I wouldn't say *hateful*, but there's prejudice on both sides and a lot of mistrust, something about us together . . . well, next time, don't talk so much. And don't laugh."

"Will there be a next time?"

He shrugged the question aside. "Let's not worry about that now." He took her face between his hands and kissed her the way he hadn't since the night he left Michigan, and then reached over and turned off the light.

CHAPTER 43

Joachim exited the diner with Savior to find Bobby gone. He turned in a puzzled circle, searching the perimeter. He and Savior had lingered over their coffee while Bobby was supposedly checking fluids and pumping air. The air pump was off to the side but there was nobody there. The adjoining pull-out by the drive-through lane that snaked around back was also empty.

Bobby was gone, and part of him wasn't surprised.

There was a note under their windshield wiper.

This is a trap. Turn back and get off the highway. My advice—get into the Lake District, Indian Reserve Land, contact Legal Aid and Josie. You can beat this thing, Jac. I'm sorry about Camille, but she found out the rewards are doubled if you're apprehended together. She guessed where we were heading, but she misread me.

Sorry for sneaking off, but I didn't want an argument and this way I can lead them away from you. Hurry. There might not be much time. See you back home when this is behind us.

Bobby

He sat for a minute with the note dangling from his hand and a toothpick in the corner of his mouth. What home? Where was home? The house where they would soon need a rowboat to approach the stoop? He handed Savior the letter and moved the toothpick to the other side of his mouth.

"Well, son of a bitch." Savior threw it on the dash where it fluttered against the windshield in the air from the defrost. "Son of a bitch," he said again. "I knew something was wrong."

"But did he have to sneak off like this?"

They sat silently, pondering the news.

"It's just like him," Savior said. "Never wants an argument."

"It's not a bad plan." Joachim motioned at the note. "I never liked the idea of heading this far south. Never liked it, Savior." He chewed on his toothpick.

They studied the map and then turned around, and Joachim guided Savior in a new direction, heading back north, a direction he was more comfortable with, the Lake District and yes, Josie.

But Bobby had waited too long to direct them into a better direction and tribal authority. Joachim was taking a turn at the wheel when the flashing lights came out of the dark behind them. He pulled off the road, and watched the two policemen in his rearview mirror as they climbed slowly out of their squad car, radio crackling.

"Give me my satchel, Savior."

"Be cool, Jac."

"They run the plate, it won't be cool."

"I knew that was a stupid idea."

"She's your girlfriend, so get your story ready."

The provincial police officers double-teamed them in their classic flanking maneuver, flashlights bouncing off chrome and brass.

Joachim rolled down his window. "Is there a problem?"

"Step out of the truck, please, and let us see your hands." Painfully polite, they were.

Joachim climbed dutifully out of the truck and showed his hands.

"Step away from the vehicle. Both of you, back of the vehicle."

"What are you stopping us for?" Joachim said.

"Whose truck is this?"

"My girlfriend's," Savior said, kicking a tire, resisting the urge to elaborate.

"Didn't think either of you look like a Camille."

"She let us borrow it. Is that a problem?"

The first officer aimed the beam of his flashlight at Savior. "That depends." He turned the light on Joachim. "What happened to your arm?"

Joachim adjusted the sling, taking his time. They were getting out of this, one way or the other. "My bursitis is acting up," he said.

"That right? Bursitis?"

His partner laughed. "Just when you think you've heard it all, they come up with a new one. Suppose you're on disability for that bursitis?

Weren't they a nosy pair?

"We need some ID," the first officer said.

"Not on me." Joachim patted his empty pockets.

Savior took out his wallet.

The officer peered at the laminated ID in the beam of his flashlight. "Savior Hastinghorse? For real?"

One-thousand percent Indian, Savior lifted his chin with a straight-on stare at the man.

"Yeah, right." The man dropped his gaze. "So—" he shone his light on Joachim— "I'm betting that makes you the wanted Joachim Montegrand."

Joachim stood motionless. "Don't know what you're talking about."

"Our report, *Mr. Montegrand*, doesn't say anything about bursitis. It says you took a bullet, arm in a sling, and you—" he glanced at Savior— "what's his name again, Charlie?"

"Savior Hastinghorse," Charlie smirked.

"You, Mr. *Hastinghorse*, are wanted back in Saskatchewan for aiding and abetting your friend here in several instances of criminal activity."

"Bullshit!" Savior kicked at the tire with his worn-out boot. "I don't know what you're talking about. You got no business harassing us. We are on official tribal business and within our rights to travel freely amongst the provinces and territories of our beloved Canada, and you, sirs, are out of line and owe us an apology."

Joachim's mouth twitched. Savior coming through, the aggrieved party in need of apology.

"Exactly what official tribal business?"

"I'm not at liberty to say."

"Hmph. We're taking you clowns in. Charlie, call the tow for *Camille's* pickup. I'm sure she'll be happy to hear it's been recovered."

Joachim held his free hand up, palm out. "The truck is not stolen," he said evenly. "And you have the wrong guys. You think we all look alike, but there are a hundred Hastinghorses, like your Pearsons and your Petersons, who all look alike to us, and we are innocent victims of mistaken identity. Do you want that on your record?"

The one in charge thumbed the button on his radio. "You're the right guy, and I'm taking you in."

Joachim dropped his hand to the door, thoughts racing.

"Keep your hands where I can see them!"

"My ID is in the truck," he said calmly. "Let me get it, keep you from making an embarrassing mistake."

The officer hesitated, and Joachim opened the door and reached slowly for his satchel with the other hand in the air. "Right here, officer, my wallet's right in here."

They didn't stop him. His heart was about to jump out of his chest, but his hands were steady as he dropped the sling, drew his pistol, and spun, leveling the barrel at the first officer. "You aren't taking me anywhere. Do as I say, nobody gets hurt."

The cop in his sights raised his hands, but his partner, Charlie, snaked a hand to his holster.

"Don't do it!" Joachim barked. He fired a round between his feet. Gravel and dust flew, and the echo from the gunshot reverberated in the clearing. "I have seven more of those, but I only need two. My father always said you only need a single shot. My father was always right, didn't deserve what you people handed him."

"What the fuck are you talking about?"

He held the gun steady, shoulder pain forgotten as adrenaline coursed from his glands to the tips of his fingers. "Unarm them, Savior."

Savior swallowed. "Shit, man . . ."

"Do it. I have you covered." But as Savior stepped forward, the first officer drew down and fired two shots. Savior reeled and his hat flew.

Joachim fired his weapon, and the firing officer fell backwards. His partner pulled his weapon, but before it cleared the holster, Joachim shot him in the hand. He yelped, and Joachim struck him across the face with the barrel of his revolver, kicking the weapon out of reach. He darted a look at Savior.

Blood dripped down the side of his face, and his Stetson was in the dirt.

The two policemen were on the ground. The first reached for the gun lying out of reach and Joachim kicked it back with the other one. He trained his weapon on them, wondering what he was going to do with them. Blood was pumping in his ears, but the whole world was quiet—what he would remember for the rest of his life—shocked stillness in the aftermath of gunfire, four men just breathing. *What was he going to do with them?*

Savior wiped the blood off his cheek and looked at his fingers dumbly. "Motherfucker shot me."

The headlamps from the cruiser cast them in a surreal light, and the red and blue flashers circled slowly in the swelling silence. Savior swayed on his feet, naked without his hat.

Joachim wet his lips. "Are you okay?"

Savior hesitated, gripping his side, confusion blanketing his face.

"Savior?"

"Yeah." He blinked. "Yeah."

"Toss asshole here his radio." Joachim looked at the first policeman. "Sit up. You're gonna call in your mistake. You got the wrong guys, nothing to report. Do it right, you walk out of here. Do it wrong . . ." He aimed the revolver at his partner. "I finish him."

The man struggled to sit up, holding his arm and groaning.

Joachim pulled him upright. "I'll hold it, you talk. Mess up, I break it over your head and finish him." *Was that him talking?* He wiped the sweat from his eyes. "Ready?" He thumbed the talk button and Dispatch was live.

The policeman looked Joachim in the eye and called it in clean and slow.

Static crackled from the speaker, and Joachim released the button.

"Good job, Peterson. I'm gonna remember you." He hooked the radio on his belt and looked at Savior. "Drive their car off the road. Make sure there isn't another radio."

"Then what?"

"Then we get the hell out of here."

"We need medical assistance," the officer said. "You can't just leave us without a radio."

"And keep the keys, Savior," he called after him.

"I need a doctor." The partner was on his knees, holding his jaw. "I think you broke my jaw."

"Then quit talking." Joachim still had his pistol trained on them, but the adrenaline was dissipating, and his shoulder burned. His heart was beating in his palms, and the firearm was taking on weight. He changed hands.

Savior drove the squad car off the road, killed the engine which killed the flashers, and a subterranean darkness settled over the scene.

Joachim waited, one eye on the two policemen, one out for Savior. Finally, a door slammed, and his shadowy figure limped around the squad car, then slumped against the rear panel.

Joachim peered through the darkness. "Savior? What're you doing?"

"I gotta sit down."

Joachim wiped the sweat out of his eyes, couldn't see a damn thing, and the gun was taking on weight. Savior was hurt. They needed to get out of here and get help. *Think.* He needed to think. "Get in the truck, bud," he said. "I'll wrap this up, get us out of here."

He watched his shadow disappear into the truck. He wanted to drop the gun. He'd never held anything so heavy. The burn in his shoulder had sunk into his chest, and he put his elbow back in the sling, then turned his attention back to the two policemen.

"You guys have a backup radio?"

"No. We should, but we don't."

Joachim considered him for a second. "You lyin', Peterson?"

Peterson shook his head. "Look, we need medical attention."

"Cameras?"

"I need a doctor!"

"Get up." He walked them across the road by the beam of the mag light and through the thicket lining the ditch where Savior had parked the car. "Get in the car. They'll find you soon enough. Flesh wounds don't need medical attention. Trust me, I've seen worse. And a message for your bosses. Tell them to stop wasting their time and resources trying to find us."

Joachim aimed the revolver at the tires, then thought better of it, and put the gun in his belt. He raised the hood and disabled the motor.

He climbed in the cab of the pickup, engaged the clutch, and flipped on the headlights. Savior was hunched against the door, teeth chattering. Joachim turned the heat on, leaned across the seat, and took his arm. "Savior, it's over. We're okay, we've got their radio and we're out of here—find Josie and disappear. Right, bud? She'll patch you up." He shook him. "Right?"

Savior groaned and clenched his middle. "He got me," he whispered. In the light of the instrument panel, Joachim saw the spreading wetness that had darkened the front of his shirt. He pried Savior's hand away from his stomach. It was wet and sticky.

"Jesus. You're gut shot."

"No shit."

"Why didn't you say something?"

"It didn't hurt. Swear I didn't feel a thing until I tried to walk."

There was blood on the seat and on his hands. Blood everywhere. He lifted Savior's arm.

"Arghh!" He flinched.

"What?" Joachim was alarmed. "You said it didn't hurt."

He gasped a lungful of air. "It hurts."

Joachim yanked his sling off, folded it into a rough compress, and pressed it against Savior's stomach. "Hold this." He placed Savior's hand over the makeshift bandage. "Hold it tight. We gotta stop the bleeding." His mind raced with what Josie would do. "Just breathe, nice and slow." His words echoed hers at the cabin in the woods. "Keep the pressure on. That's important. Got it? Pressure." Savior closed his eyes and took a shallow breath. He said something so soft Joachim had to lean in close to hear.

"I have it," he whispered. "You drive."

Joachim gunned the engine and peeled out on the road, steering with one hand and thumbing a number on his cell with the other.

Come on, Josie. Pick up. Pick up. Tell me where you are. Tell me what to do.

Savior was shivering, bleeding color and life, and Joachim knew they didn't have much time.

He thought of his first kill, the doe eyeing his approach as he knelt beside her, the eyes open and seeing, then a spasm and the glass-over as she bled out, his dad slapping him on the back, congratulating him on a clean shot, but he had only wanted to close that glassy eye.

CHAPTER 44

Through sporadic cell service with Savior fading in and out of consciousness, Joachim met Josie on First Nation reserve land at a group of rustic cabins that her midwife contact for the region promised would have firewood and water.

He parked alongside her in the gravel pull-out and pried his hands off the wheel.

"He's shot bad, Josie."

"Is he conscious?"

"I think he's in shock."

"Help me get him inside."

Together they got him in the cabin and on a bunk. "Grab my backpack, Jac, and then get a fire going and draw water."

She rolled her sleeves, pinned her hair up, and felt for a pulse.

Savior opened his eyes and smiled wanly. "Hi, beautiful."

"Shh, don't talk."

"It hurts, Josie."

"I know, sweetie. I have to cut your shirt off. Don't move." She rested her hand on his forehead. "And don't talk, okay?"

She worked quietly and efficiently, and Jac was reminded of their stay in her cabin when she was taking care of him.

He shifted his weight from one foot to the other. "Is there anything I can do?"

"Get him some water. He's dehydrated."

He held the bottle to his mouth and Savior drank, spat, coughed, and pushed it away. He urged more on him until it ran down his chin. "Enough," Savior rasped.

Josie had his shirt off and was holding a compress over the wound. Savior moaned in pain, and Joachim looked away. He couldn't handle it. He needed air.

"Jac, how's the gas in Savior's truck?"

He looked back at her in surprise. "Gas? Why?"

"He needs a hospital. The closest one is in Le Pas, but it's over a hundred miles north of here. I'm near empty, and nothing's open this time of night. If we can make it there in Savior's truck, I'll try to stabilize him, and we'll head out. Otherwise, we'll have to wait until morning."

Joachim was already out the door.

He turned the key in the ignition and watched the gauge settle. Less than a quarter of a tank. The thing was a gas hog, and when was the last time they thought to check the gas?

He tried to light a cigarette. He should have filled up at the truck stop. He shouldn't have pulled the gun. His thumb kept slipping on the wheel of the lighter, and the should-haves and shouldn't-haves mounted in his head. The wheel finally struck the flint, and he steered the cigarette into the flame, sucking in smoke. His hand was shaking and he rested it on the steering wheel.

He walked back to the cabin but hesitated at the door. He couldn't go in there. He sat on the stoop and lit another cigarette off the butt of the first—*fuck the malfunctioning lighter, get a book of matches*. Anyone could strike a match, even a dropout Indian with sweaty hands and a bad aim. He dropped the dead butt at his feet.

Josie stepped out and sat beside him. "Well?" she said.

The hair around her brow was damp and there was blood on her shirt.

"We have a quarter of a tank," he said.

She took a drag off his cigarette.

"He gonna be okay until morning?"

She knocked the ash off the cigarette with the tip of her finger and handed it back. "He's lost a lot of blood. Right now, he's semi-conscious. I don't think feeling a lot of pain."

"You sure?"

"I have something I can give him if he needs it."

"But he's gonna make it, right?"

"The bullet is still in him. I can't tell if it hit a vital organ, but I think there's internal bleeding. I cleaned the wound and dressed it, as best I could."

"Don't suppose we can call an ambulance." He placed the cigarette in the corner of his mouth, drew on it, left it there. It wasn't a question.

She made a noise in the back of her throat.

"Isn't there anyone else you can call?" Another rhetorical question.

She took the cigarette from him. "We'll leave at dawn. I have something for fever—" she drew on the cigarette and handed it back—"and a vial of morphine to keep him comfortable. If he needs it."

"I can't stand seeing him like this." He brushed a hand over his eyes. "I swear, I feel it too."

She looked at him for a minute. "Have you had anything to eat, Jac?"

"No." The thought of food made him sick. He climbed to his feet.

"Why are you limping?"

"Am I?" He looked down at himself and shrugged. If he was, he wasn't aware. "I need some air."

He walked to the edge of the clearing, sucked air into his lungs, then left the pool of light in the clearing for the dark of the wood. He paused, listening, then stepped further through the trees to follow the sound—the distinctive call of the Eskimo curlew, presumably extinct, but his father claimed to have spotted one the year before he died. He mimicked the call for Joachim; he had a knack for things like that. A legend, his friends said.

Sonny, you're gaming a legend.

It wasn't a legend; it was a curlew, and he went deeper into the woods because it was calling to him; he and Savior together in the woods as boys, gaming their own legends, a future that stretched out before them unhampered by the concerns of adulthood, skipping school, and whittling sticks in the forest to fend off make-believe enemies, tenting, or sleeping on the ground and shooting squirrels out of trees with their slingshots. Then it was his father, talking him through it—the ways of the world, the death of family, friends, and a bird gone extinct.

Savior's fever flared in the night, and they took turns sitting with him. He didn't know them, mumbling about the girl with the red ribbon in her hair—he was stuck on that ribbon—and then he thought Josie was her. Even wounded and delirious, Savior was strong, and Joachim had to restrain him. He thought it was Bobby holding him down and fought against him, then his face slackened as he collapsed back on the bed.

In and out of consciousness, his breathing was shallow and raspy. Josie checked his pulse and tried to get him to drink more water. She placed the vial of morphine beside the bed.

It was Joachim's turn to sit with him. Savior had calmed, hands unclenched and facial muscles relaxed. Joachim watched the rise and fall of his chest. He closed his eyes. Soon it would be morning, an hour, maybe two. His last thought as he dozed off in a chair by the window was getting Savior into the arms of a nurse with peppermint breath.

He jerked himself awake to a deathly silence with no sense of the time that had passed. It was still dark, but he could hear leaves falling on the roof with the *drip drip drip* of the rain that came in the night. But from Savior's bed, an awful stillness.

Joachim dropped his head to Savior's chest.

"No, no, no . . ." He pounded on his chest. "Wake up, Savior. Wake up!" He dropped his head to Savior's heart, listening desperately for a heartbeat. He tried compressions. One, two three—*Is this how they do it?* — One, two, three, counting to himself. He shook him by the shoulders. "Don't do this to me!" He pounded on his chest. He didn't know how to do it.

Josie came up behind him and felt for a pulse. She grabbed his hand. "Jac, stop. *Jac!* He's gone."

"No! No, he isn't."

Josie tried to pull him off, but he wasn't letting go.

"It's okay. You can let him go."

He shook her off. "Leave us," he said. "Please."

She rested her hand on Savior's chest for a long moment, then on Joachim's back, and then she was gone.

He collapsed across Savior's body, head over his heart, and closed his eyes.

He was still warm. He couldn't get over how warm he was. How could he be dead and be so warm?

He held him as the warmth seeped out of him and the dark retreated in the face of the rising sun. It broke the surface of the earth and rose through the woodlands of Manitoba. It glanced off the porch, streamed through the windows, and across the bed. The first birdsong drifted through the walls of the cabin, life stirring all around, but he had never been so alone.

He didn't know how much time had passed when the door creaked open and he felt her presence, the hand on his shoulder.

"I fell asleep," he whispered. "I didn't mean to fall asleep. When I woke up—"

"I'm so sorry, Jac."

"I didn't mean to."

"He wasn't in pain. I made sure of that."

"Yeah?" A hint of suspicion furrowed his brow. "What if you hadn't given him any painkiller? Was it the morphine did it?"

"It was a bullet did it, Jac, a bullet to the stomach. His lungs were filling with blood. The morphine made it bearable."

He sat quietly, mulling it over.

"I know what you're thinking. Don't go there."

"Where?"

"It's not your fault."

"But it is. We both know it is." He went back to looking at whatever it was he'd been looking at before. "I wasn't going to let them take us," he added softly.

"Tell me what happened."

And he did, as best he could remember.

"I wasn't going to let them take us, Josie. All I could think of was that cell Dad was in."

"You're sure they weren't badly injured?"

"Fuck them. Who cares about them?"

She considered him for a minute. "Because there's other news. I would've told you earlier but, well, with everything—" She waved a hand to encompass everything. She took a breath. "They found the person responsible for the firebombing at that storage facility."

He stared at her.

"It wasn't even a native; they just tried to make it look like it was—the judge was livid about that—so you're in the clear there, and it looks like the evidence regarding the detour signs you and Savior supposedly erected will be thrown out. Luckily that case is coming before the same judge, something about the fingerprints and no credible eyewitness."

Joachim rocked back and forth on the balls of his feet and rubbed the stubble on his chin, processing the development—a coin flipped his way—but without Savior to share the news, it was tarnished luck.

"Jac?"

"It doesn't matter, Josie. Not now." He ran a hand through his hair. "They killed Savior." He sounded it in his head, seeing how it felt in his mouth. "They killed him because of me."

"Don't, Jac."

"If I'd known—" he looked at her for a minute— "if I'd known the other charges were going to be dropped—"

"How could you know? They obviously didn't."

He crossed his arms, rocking himself and looking out the window at the unfamiliar surroundings. He couldn't even say for sure where he was. He and Savior had come so far, the two of them together, shared so much. Who would've thought they'd end up here in the godforsaken middle of nowhere? A party of two reduced to one.

He knew what he had to do. This wasn't home. It was no place to bury a friend.

"I'm taking him home," he said bluntly.

She took a deep breath. "Stefan's coming here, Jac."

"*What?*"

"We've been in contact."

"Are you crazy?!"

"There was no stopping him," she reasoned. "He's coming on a motorcycle. I figured I might as well guide him in the right direction."

"What motorcycle?"

She shrugged. "That's what he said."

"Jesus." He ran his hands through his hair in what he knew was a habitual gesture, giving himself a minute, wondering what else she was going to come up with. *Any other bombshells, Josephine?*

He looked at her with the unspoken question, but she was evidently out of bombshells.

"Could there be a worse time?" he asked.

There was no answer to the question.

"I wanted to keep him out of this," he said finally.

"We always knew he'd come back."

"But not now. Not to this." He looked at Savior, death settling over him, rigor mortis creeping along his limbs. He should have stayed with the girl with the red ribbon in her hair.

He paced the room, came up against the doorway and glanced back at Josie. "Do you remember who the sexton is at the burial grounds?"

She frowned and shook her head. "I can talk to Avery at the Council House. We need to be careful. The prosecutor at White Lake will be looking for any excuse to nail you, been gunning for you since before your father died, and with what just happened—"

"How will he know I'm back in the area? I'll take my chances and Stef—where did you say he was?

"Southern Manitoba, last I knew."

"Christ." He rubbed his eyes and paced the floor, pacing the varnish off the boards. He felt a sudden urgency to get Savior back home on familiar ground. They should never have let themselves be run off.

"He has the directions I gave you. He can't be far now."

Winter coming. Snow on the horizon. Savior dead. Stefan on a motorcycle. What more could go wrong? And how long could they afford to wait?

CHAPTER 45

They didn't have to wait long. The rumble of the motorcycle carried through the quiet of the forest from a mile away.

There were two of them, and Joachim's first thought was that Abby had coerced Stefan into letting her come along.

But the long-legged girl with flaming hair hanging out below her helmet wasn't Abby.

Stefan tucked his helmet under his arm and strode across the clearing.

Joachim pulled him into a one-armed hug. "What—" he choked, "are you doing, little brother?"

"Good to see you too." Stefan stepped back and eyed the sling that Josie had refashioned. "What's with the sling?"

"Josie's orders."

Stefan looked at her with a small smile. "You are the only one he'd ever listen to."

"He is hard to handle," she said, taking his hand solemnly.

Joachim looked at the slim girl standing by the bike rubbing her tailbone. She had hair the color of a slow burn. She reminded him of pictures at the boarding school he ran away from where the angels were always white with auburn hair and angelic features. "Maybe you should introduce us," he said.

"Sadie!" Stefan beckoned to her. "Come on, meet the rest of my family."

The bond between the two of them was obvious as Stefan looped an arm around her waist and she looked up at him with an emotion that gave Joachim a fresh ache. They were in deep.

"It's so nice to finally meet you," she said. "Stefan has told me so much about you. I feel like I already know you." She had a musical voice and a firm handshake.

"I see why Stefan was beguiled."

"Beguiled?" She laughed nervously.

"This is Josephine." Stefan steered her in that direction. "Joachim's woman." He smiled. "She tries to keep him on the straight."

"As if that were possible." Josie took Sadie's hand. "Call me Josie," she said with a slight smile.

"It's nice to meet you, Josie."

The two young women locked eyes for a second. Sadie looked away first. "It's beautiful up here." She gestured at the surrounding area. "Unspoiled, just like Stefan said."

"That's because it's Indian land," Joachim said.

"But for how long?" Stefan said.

Joachim studied him. "You've changed."

"Bobby said I looked too much like you. Like this." He thrust a crumpled poster at him and Joachim was looking at the unflattering likeness.

"How'd you run into Bobby?"

"He was where *you* were supposed to be. Told me he warned you off and that I needed to do the same, on the double—really worked up about a trap of some sort—and that's when I got the call from Josie guiding me here." He glanced around. "Where is Savior? How is he? Josie said he was shot."

Stefan looked from one to the other, settling his gaze on Josie. "You said it wasn't serious."

"He didn't make it," she said. "He died early this morning."

Stefan's face blanched. "You said it wasn't serious!"

"He took a bullet to the stomach; that's always serious."

"Why didn't you say so?"

"Over a phone? There wasn't anything you could do." Josie went on the defensive. "I didn't want to—over the phone—you never know, he could've pulled through. I've made mistakes before."

Stefan ran a hand over his eyes. "I knew you were in trouble. I should've—"

"No, you *shouldn't* have." Joachim spat in the dirt.

Stefan studied him. "What happened?" he asked.

Joachim looked away. How had it happened? And when had it all turned wrong?

"You're on the run, is that it? You shoot someone, Jac? What more are you wanted for? How long can you stay here—" he gestured at the cabin— "hiding?"

"I'm not *hiding*. I'm taking him home."

"Home? You're going home with a reward on your head?"

"I told him," Josie said quickly. "Let's go inside. They must be hungry." She took Sadie's hand. "Come inside. We can talk there."

Josie did the talking. There was roasted duck and air-dried venison she brought with her, along with a jug of home brew from the council house, but nobody was eating.

As she continued explaining things to Stefan and his girlfriend, Joachim paced the living room. Her matter-of-factness was bothering him. Maybe that was her strength, her ability to be practical in the face of calamity, setting out food and drink because someone needed to do it.

Since early morning and a letting go, he had avoided looking at the still form on the pallet. That wasn't Savior. He had the image of Savior in his mind he wanted to retain. Yet a ghostly presence filled the cabin. It drew him reluctantly back to the foot of the bed, to the husk of a man he had thought of as a brother. His eyes were closed; he could be sleeping.

Wind wisped through the boughs of the white pine forest and seeped through the chinks in the logs of the cabin. A tree branch scraped the window, and he wanted to say something. *I'm sorry, man, so sorry.* Something more, a prayer he didn't know. He touched his foot through the sheeting. There was no warmth. This wasn't sleeping.

He walked back to the kitchen and poured a glass of beer.

"You need to eat something, Jac," Josie said.

"Not hungry." He kicked a chair back and sat down. The table was silent.

Stefan looked at him "So, you could be in the clear but for what just happened?"

"That's true," Josie said. "But it did happen and even if the policemen only suffered superficial injuries, as you say—" she looked pointedly at Joachim— "that's enough to haul him back inside."

"Inside prison?" Sadie said.

"Yes," Josie said, "prison. If he's recognized, if he draws the *wrong* kind of attention." Her eyes rested on Sadie who shifted nervously in her seat.

"I'll take my chances," Joachim said firmly.

"The prosecutor would like nothing better than to flip that judge."

"We're going back. It's the least I can do."

Josie crossed her arms and stared at a spot on the wall.

Joachim topped off his glass of coffee-colored beer and motioned Stefan to a chair beside him. "Here's to the poor man's solace." He sized up his brother over the rim of the glass. He'd put on weight and capability. "What about you? What was the trouble you had yourself in?"

"I committed rape, according to a jacked-up girl and a local lawman."

Joachim choked. "Rape?"

"I know. Ridiculous, right?"

"No brother of mine would do that." Joachim lit a cigarette and tossed the lighter on the table. "So, tell me what happened. And how you came by this motorcycle."

Stefan and Joachim were conversing softly, and Sadie helped Josie clear the rest of the dishes, sensing herself on the wrong side of Joachim's girlfriend.

It was good to see Stefan with his brother, the man she had heard so much about for so long, and though Joachim's hair was longer, his brow darker with deep-set eyes which made one wonder what he was thinking, there was a striking resemblance in their features and mannerisms. They could be twins.

She watched as Joachim wrapped an arm around Stefan's shoulders, forehead to forehead in a private moment.

"So, Sadie, what do you do?" Josie asked.

She blinked and looked at her. She had to think for a minute.

"I was going to college, but I needed a break."

"What were you going to school for?"

"I wanted to be an investigative reporter, you know, win a Pulitzer Prize, like the guys at the Washington Post." She laughed. "I'm kidding."

"Journalism is a fading art."

"You think?"

"*Investigative* journalism? Let's just say I don't see any of that here. We get reporters up here once and a while, but the story is always slanted to the other side." She shrugged an *oh well* and asked, "So why take a break?"

Sadie shrugged. "I needed some time off, time to be at home, help my dad and grandpa and figure things out."

Josie nodded. "I get that. Family is important. So, they were okay with all this?"

Sadie made a face. "Not exactly."

Josie raised an eyebrow, and Sadie felt like she was back explaining a broken curfew.

"I mean they know—I assume they know I'm with Stefan. I left a message on the house phone." She shrugged. "I guess I haven't thought too much about it."

Josie dried a glass with a flour sack towel, disapproval etched on her face as she rubbed it to a shine and started on another. "Joachim is set on taking Savior back home. It's a risk, but you can see how stubborn he is. We can get in quietly enough, I'm confident of that. The burial grounds are remote, and the shaman will conduct a discrete ceremony, but if we draw attention to ourselves—even in close-knit native communities, people talk—and last I checked he's still on the RCMP fugitive watch list."

Sadie nodded, wondering what that was and where this was going.

Josie leaned on the counter and gazed at her, opened her mouth to say more, but seemed to think better of it and turned back to the sink

"What were you going to say?"

"I'm just surprised is all. Stefan never said a word about bringing someone with him." She paused, letting that sink in. "We figured he'd be back; he has ties here—I wonder he hasn't told you—and there was a good bit of argument about him leaving, but Jac was intent on his sister and mother leaving the province. After his dad died, I think she wanted to leave, and she wanted Abby to go to college, not some residential boarding school." She broke off with another shrug. "I don't know why I'm telling you all of this, but family . . . well, I have my own regrets, things I wish I'd done and said while my parents were alive. And resentment, like regret, doesn't die, Sadie. It settles in our DNA. Believe me."

Stefan came up behind them and put an arm around Sadie. "Regret what?" He gathered her hair in his hand and lifted it off the nape of her neck. "What're you two talking about?" He smiled. "Genealogy?"

Sadie swallowed. "Nothing."

"Family. Jac," Josie said bluntly. "She regrets leaving her family without letting them know."

This was something she and Stefan hadn't talked about, and Sadie felt a twinge of resentment at what seemed an underhanded meddling.

Stefan frowned. "You didn't tell them?"

"Of course, I did." She challenged Josie with a look. She didn't need an enemy, but Josie needed to mind her own business. "I called Dad. He knows I'm with you."

"Well…" Josie wiped her hands on the towel and hung it on the sink. "I have some calls of my own to make. And I need to check Jac's shoulder, make sure he's not out of that sling."

Stefan draped an arm around Sadie's shoulder and she turned her face into the collar of his shirt, the smell of flannel. Josie was wrong. She had nothing to regret.

"What's wrong, baby?" Stefan murmured. "You seem upset."

She hesitated. Josie's words were troubling, and there was backstory she had only dipped a finger in. "I just don't want to be a bother, be in the way."

"What a silly thing to say." He tilted her chin and kissed her on the mouth.

"I want to stay with you," she whispered, "ride with you."

"Of course. Why are you crying?"

"I'm not." She blinked her eyes dry. "I'm not."

"We'll leave first thing in the morning, drive straight through to the burial grounds north of the Narrows. A place called Black Bay.

"And then?"

"Jac wants to go back to Josie's place. He feels it's safe. He wants to cut wood, get over that cough."

"It sounds like bronchitis."

"He probably just needs to quit smoking."

"What about us? What are we going to do?"

"Are you homesick?"

Sadie made a face. "No, it's just that with the motorcycle, well, it limits us, doesn't it?"

"Of course." He hesitated and a look of uncertainty crossed his face. He leaned against the sink and crossed one booted foot over the other. "I need to get you back before serious winter hits these parts. That or we chop some wood and stay through until spring. If I remember right, Josie's neighbor has horses."

"I don't want you to change your plans on account of me. What had you planned to do?"

"My concern was to see Jac safe, you know, in a good place, see for myself what was going on, and figure out this money problem he seems to have."

"Josie doesn't like me."

"What? That's nuts, Sadie. She hardly knows you."

Sadie didn't say anything, wanted it refuted, wanted a case to be made.

"My people, Sadie, we aren't like you. I've told you. It'll take time to get to know her. Don't prejudge her, please."

He was displeased, not even trying to hide it. "I'm sorry," Sadie said. "You're right. Forget I said anything."

"I hadn't thought things through," he continued after a moment, "just knew I had to get up here. As it is, I guess you could say I was too late."

"About Savior?"

"About everything." His eyes were hooded, and she wondered what else he was hiding, the ties Josie alluded to. There were so many things she didn't know about him, his family, and their life up here. It was hauntingly beautiful yet forbidding in the very things that made it so.

They joined Joachim and Josie in front of the fireplace, and she sat at Stefan's feet. They were talking about burial plans, and her eyes were drawn to the cooling body on the cot in the next room. The fire cast shadows around the room, but none more starkly than the ones that played across that shrouded form.

The fire popped and sent sparks flying. An ember landed at Sadie's feet, and she snuffed it out with her foot. "At least," she hesitated, "at least you've been able to spend some time, have closure."

Joachim stared at her.

"Closure is part of the grieving process, this is true," Josie said.

"You know something of this?" Joachim said.

Sadie nodded. "My mother was in a closed casket. It's not like I didn't know she was in it but there was no, as they say, closure. I felt so disconnected. That closed casket somehow made it impossible to say goodbye."

"This closed casket is something your people do?" Joachim seemed confused by the concept.

Sadie nodded. "To protect me, they said." The bitterness welled up in her voice.

"I didn't know this," Stefan said.

322

"And her wedding ring . . . why bury it with her? If we believe the spirit ascends beyond worldly needs and goods, why bury precious belongings in the ground with that which is no longer there? I have a stupid sarong. That's what I have."

They were all silent.

"There's an old tradition of sending the dead into the hereafter with things to sustain them on their journey." Joachim stared into the flames as if therein lay the basis for tradition.

"I'm surprised your dad didn't think of that," Stefan said. "That you'd want it."

"He was a mess. I don't blame him. He's still a mess." She shrugged. "But I think he might have a girlfriend." She looked up with a small smile.

"That's good," Josie said. "You're wise to be supportive. But your father will still need you." She leveled her gaze. "No woman ever takes the place of a daughter."

Sadie met her gaze with a clear understanding of her solid footing on Josie's wrong side.

They let the fire die, and Joachim directed them to the loft. He and Josie were staying in the room with Savior, which Sadie found macabre, but she had learned to guard her opinion.

She and Stefan climbed the ladder to the nook under the rafters. There was a sleeping pallet under a tiny window that looked out on treetops and stars. It felt like a treehouse, a place where they could see and not be seen.

Sadie shook out the pillows, ignoring the dust that billowed softly in the air. Stefan dropped his boots in the corner and leaned on the windowsill, gazing out at the night, shoulders slumped.

"I wish you could've met him, Sadie," he said softly. "He was so full of life, one of those people who just light up a room."

She rested her hand on his and followed his gaze out the window. The muted light of the hunter's moon cast ghostly shadows across the clearing, but his eyes were far away.

"I'm sorry, Stefan." It was all she could think to say.

He heaved a sigh, gathered himself with a quick glance around the tiny room, and at the pallet on the floor. "Well, this is it. We should try to get some sleep. Think you can sleep on that?"

They undressed beside the makeshift bed, and he wrapped a blanket around them. Alone at last in the certainty of his embrace, the lingering doubts of the road and of her place in his world were dispelled. But it was a long time before she fell asleep.

CHAPTER 46

The operatic warble of a meadowlark outside their window brought them awake. Stefan sifted through the pile of clothes on the floor for his shorts. "I gotta pee," he said.

Sadie stretched and watched him climb barefoot down the ladder to relieve himself. Reluctant to get up, she leaned on the sill of the little window over the sleeping pallet and watched him as he peed off the stoop, taking aim at the quarreling red squirrels—notorious thieves of the woodlands—scolding him. She laughed to herself. They were too clever by far to be hit by a stream of piss. He gave himself a shake and left her line of sight.

The others were stirring downstairs and she smelled coffee.

Stefan brought her up a cup, and she sat cross-legged on the sleeping pad and braided her hair in a single plait as he quickly dressed. She took a final glance around the room and followed him down the ladder.

There was little time for talk as they all busied themselves for departure. Joachim and Stefan wrapped Savior in a blanket, and arranged his body in the back of the jeep.

Sadie tucked the braid inside her helmet and watched Joachim as he shut the hatchback, secured the latch with a nudge, and walked around the vehicle, trailing a finger on an invisible racing stripe. His movements were Stefan's, his stature and manner of speaking were Stefan's. He climbed inside the jeep with one foot on the running board, resting his hand on the dash. Was the bullet still in there? Fragments of bone, shelved in blood? She imagined him slumped over the wheel in a blood-soaked shirt. What little Stefan had told her of that night was embellished like goldleaf in her mind, a night of pain and exhaustion, and what that must have done to him.

The disembodied voice of a weather forecaster drifted across the clearing from the radio, warning of a weather system heading inland from the Pacific, crossing British Columbia, and heading their way. An early winter storm, the voice intoned.

Stefan revved the engine and motioned her on.

She threw her leg over the seatback and settled herself behind him. The weather wouldn't matter as long as he was at the controls.

They pulled out of the clearing in the mid-morning hour and drove until noon, stopping at a small diner for lunch.

Sadie immediately sensed the disparity between herself and everyone else. The diner was crowded with men and women of various ages and dress, coppery-colored, quiet, dignified denizens of the community.

There were nods for Joachim and the others, and sparks of lingering curiosity for her. Stefan led them to a table in the center of the room. The others slung their coats over the backs of their chairs and ordered coffee.

"And you?" Sadie realized the waitress was talking to her.

"Coffee's fine," she said.

The room had taken on a chill, and the talk had reduced to whispers and murmurs. She imagined everyone looking at her.

She picked at her food. Joachim and Stefan seemed to know everyone, which was, of course, impossible, but their commonality knit them like a sweater, from the waitress to the cook to the man wiping down tables. Stefan was relaxed as he had never been back home, easy and affable. Ever since meeting up with Joachim, he was a changed person.

"Eat." He nodded at her plate. "We won't be stopping again."

"There's a weather system moving in," Joachim explained. "We need to get you two clear of it."

Joachim and Stefan paid at the counter, and Sadie and Josie went to the bathroom, washing up at adjacent sinks. Josie looked at her in the mirror.

"You can ride with us for a spell," she said, applying lip balm.

And where would she sit? Beside a dead man?

When they stepped outside, they could see their breath. Stefan zipped his jacket and secured his flaps, then helped her buckle the strap under her chin. He flipped the visor down over her eyes and smiled. "My mysterious woman. If people don't stop staring, I might have to knock a few heads together."

So, it hadn't been her imagination.

"If it gets nasty, I'll signal Joachim, and you can hop in with them."

"No. I'm staying with you. I don't care about the weather."

"I was hoping you'd say that." He tightened the strap under his chin. "You keep me warm." He threw a leg over the saddle. "No more stops until we're in Saskatchewan."

Over the rev of the throttle, she thought she heard an added *until I'm home.*

The posted speed limits and road signs were in kilometers, and Sadie lost track of the miles, but Joachim was setting an arduous pace.

She would have missed the sign for Saskatchewan if Stefan hadn't thrown an arm out and pointed. Tucked back off the road, one with the terrain, *Saskatchewan, Naturally* welcomed them. They had been traveling due west, but after crossing the border, they veered northwest, and twilight time accelerated in the face of the heavy cloud cover descending over the distant mountains.

Joachim signaled and pulled off the road ahead of them.

It was time for a bathroom break, and Sadie thought of the first time she and Stefan did this in the open—a different time zone, a different world.

Waiting for him, she warmed her hands and walked off a cramp. "How much further is it?"

"Actually—" he zipped himself up and lit a cigarette— "I'm not sure."

He handed it over and she took a puff. "It's getting dark and cold, and I'm hungry."

He looked at the menacing sky. "Let me check with them."

Joachim was studying a map spread out on the hood and Josie was on her phone.

"How much further is it? Sadie's cold and we're both hungry."

"I told her she could ride with us," Josie said.

He shrugged.

"If your brother would've listened to me, we'd already be there."

"Your GPS makes up roads."

She rolled her eyes. "You and your maps . . . at this point we might as well stay at my place for the night. I'm telling you—"

"What's the radar look like?" Stefan interrupted.

"There's a front moving in." She scrolled through her phone. "Looks like snow."

"Oh, great," Stefan groaned. An early November blow. He looked back at Sadie sitting patiently astride the bike. "So, where are we?"

Joachim smoothed the map out with the flat of his hand and drew a circle with the pen stuck behind his ear. "Right about here," he said. "And here is the cemetery and Black Bay. And there—" he drew another line in a zigzagged direction, "is Josie's place."

"But first, Murphy," she said as their eyes locked.

"Who's this Murphy?" Stefan broke in.

"A doc we know," Joachim said.

"A friend," Josie added.

He looked back and forth between them. "Oh, yeah, the doctor. You got other issues besides a bum shoulder?"

"Naw." Joachim's face closed like a book. "Only issue is getting Savior back."

"Okay, let's do it."

Sadie slid back on the seat to make room for him.

"Well?"

"We're close."

"Thank God." She tugged the helmet back in place and threaded the strap tab through the loops. "I need a hot bath."

He gassed the throttle, and they were on Joachim's tail, warmed by the thought of feet on the ground, hot water to be had, and a room of their own.

Joachim was right. Wapawekka Lake, which fed the tributary where the burial grounds were situated, shimmered through the trees on a bend in the road, and street lamps shone ahead in the gloom of twilight.

They parked in front of a two-story brick hotel with window boxes, and Sadie slid gratefully off the bike. They hung their helmets on the bike and she shook out her hair, working through the tangles.

Stefan took her hand. "Come on, let's see about that shower."

The front desk was flanked by two potted plants clinging to life, and a staircase with an old wooden banister led to the upper floor. The others were discussing the particulars of a room when Sadie's eyes fell on the "Wanted" poster tacked up on the far wall.

Drawn across the room, as if on a plumb line, she stood in front of it. The likeness was disturbingly accurate. She touched it with her finger, the heavy brow and dark eyes, aristocratic nose and square chin. It could be Stefan.

CHAPTER 47

Dolphus Hastinghorse washed his son's body to prepare it for burial, then Joachim helped clothe him in traditional garments. Savior's father had agreed to forgo the normal four-day mourning period, but there was still ritual to adhere to.

Joachim stepped back while the elder man tied an eagle feather in Savior's hair with a muttered incantation and attached a sacred feather to his shirt. He ran a hand across his eyelids and smoothed his hair back from his brow. Together, they opened the burial cloth and wrapped the body in it.

The bulk of the family had scattered after the troubles, so only his father, resplendent in native garb, his sister, two silent nephews, and a cousin with a guitar joined the shaman and the four of them at the cemetery.

There was a white clapboard fence around the perimeter, and small fence enclosures protected each grave to keep out trespassers.

As Sadie stepped through the gate with Stefan and followed the path of softly padded grass, the meaning of hallowed ground enveloped her like a vision. It was a quiet place, yet the air was heavy with presence, as though watchful souls were guarding the gate.

They followed the procession to the prepared site. He had explained that native burial traditions were deeply spiritual and celebratory, one of their own returned to the earth. But she wasn't prepared for the visceral physicality of the ceremony. Or for the sister.

The black-haired girl ran out of nowhere and clasped Stefan's hands between her own. She wore a long leather skirt with leggings underneath and a pair of mukluks, as if winter had already arrived.

Her name was Aiyana, Stefan told her later.

She was short and stocky with glowing charcoal eyes and a round face, and Sadie knew she was no relative.

"I'm sorry about Savior," Stefan said. "He was like a brother to me."

"He and your brother . . ." she sighed. "They were always in trouble."

Stefan took Sadie's hand. "Sadie, this is Savior's sister."

Sadie smiled, but Aiyana didn't smile back.

"Nice to meet you," Sadie said to fill the awkward void.

With a slight movement of her head, the girl managed to dismiss the lie, and Sadie just as fast.

Stefan said something in a soft voice and she looked up at him with a serene smile, and Sadie wondered if this girl had been his first. With that thought finding purchase, they moved to the gravesite where the ceremony was underway.

The shaman lifted his arms and raised his voice in a hypnotic chant, and the guitar player bent over his instrument. He had Band-Aids wrapped around his fingers and held the notes with a quiver. The shaman bowed deeply to the earth, to the father, and then moved around the circle swinging a metal censer that released fragrant plumes of burning sage and sweetgrass. His voice rose on a crescendo, and the guitar player strummed a rhythmic tune.

Someone came forward with a drum and set it at the head of the grave. It was made from moose skin stretched taut across an engraved hollow of cedar. There was a brushstroke of red paint across the center and feathers tied around the outer edge. An aura of mysticism surrounded the drum and permeated the air.

Sound seeped from it even before the drummer sat in front of it, a low thrum, like thunder echoing through the ground from miles away, a tingling up through the soles of her feet.

Sadie felt dizzy. Did no one else feel it? Hear it?

A flock of crows darkened the sky and settled in the trees along the fence. Their feathers gave off a purplish sheen in the sunlight, and their eyes were intelligent. Stefan told her later that to First Nation peoples, a crow was a harbinger which could guide the soul to the afterlife. An entire flock was a powerful symbol.

The drummer began to accompany the guitar, and as the low decibel beat reverberated in her chest, Sadie found herself swaying with the others to the shaman's chant. The solemnity of the ceremony intensified, and all the crows were silent.

The shaman deferred to Savior's father who had placed no blame and hid his sorrow. Savior's mother had died years earlier in an epidemic. He and his sister were raised by their grandmother, and a father who would show no grief in public.

He stepped straight-backed to the edge of the grave and dropped a handful of dirt on the canvas-wrapped body. The dull thud resonated like a twenty-one-gun salute. Each of the mourners did the same, and Sadie inched backwards, wanting to get out of the way, feeling more of an outsider than ever, but Stefan motioned her forward.

"You should participate," he whispered. "It is expected."

She dropped a handful of damp clay in the hole, then quickly stepped back from the edge, seized by an ingrained horror of falling in. She thought they only did this in movies.

The groundskeeper and Joachim started shoveling dirt into the grave. At home, all this was done after mourners were safely in their cars and out of sight. At home, people had to be protected from the final internment. Here things were more organic, more complete. There would be no lingering questions.

The hole was only half-filled when Joachim collapsed over his shovel, shoulders heaving. Stefan eased the shovel from his grasp and bent his back to the earth.

They sat around the table in the father's house and shared a fish stew prepared by Aiyana which she served with gritty cornmeal biscuits.

Stefan was seated at the end of the table between the girl and her father, and Sadie found herself at the opposite end next to the guitar player.

Up close, his fingers were calloused, the nails clipped short, and she remarked on his playing and he thanked her in a quiet voice. But neither were given to small talk, and they ate in silence.

She glanced at Stefan, but he was absorbed in conversation with Aiyana, heads together, arms touching, and what was going on under the table? Every time the girl got up for something, she leaned over him, taking personal requests—whispering, smiling, touching. It was with obvious cunning design that she, Sadie, was seated at the opposite end of the table between a mute guitar player and the sullen cousin.

She concentrated on the food in front of her, getting through it, and her thoughts turned back to her encounter with a police officer after they had left the burial grounds.

She had waited outside the gate as Stefan and Joachim had smoothed the mound of dirt, tamping down the clumps of upended sod and saying goodbye. They left the cemetery with a plan to meet the others for dinner, but Stefan had stopped abruptly in front of the hotel.

"Give me a minute," he said. "I want to wash up, change my shirt." His palms were creased with grime, and his face had taken on the lines of his brother's, his hands their burden.

Sadie knew he needed time alone. "Take your time, Stef. I'll stay with the bike." He nodded, and she watched him disappear through the door. She inched forward on the seat, grasped the handlebars, wondering what it would be like to be at the controls.

A police cruiser pulled up silently beside her. There was a bold blue stripe down the side of the sedan and POLICE was stamped across the quarter panel.

The officer climbed out and adjusted his shoulder mic. "Hello, miss."

"Hi. Is something the matter?" Sadie asked with an impassive face, but her thoughts circled back to the wanted poster she had destroyed in the hotel lobby. Did they have security cameras? Was he here to bust her?

He walked admiringly around the front of the bike. "This is quite the bike. Don't see many of these up here."

"It's not mine."

"I didn't think so." He glanced at the plate. "You ride all the way from Michigan?"

"Yeah. Visiting family."

"Is that right? What's their name? I might know them."

"It's my boyfriend's. I'm not sure." She shrugged ignorance and gave him her best empty-headed smile. "We're getting ready to head back before the weather breaks."

"You'll be cutting it close. Do you have helmets?" He settled his guilty-until-proven-otherwise gaze on her.

"Of course."

"They're mandatory here, so just checking. Wouldn't want you to get a ticket. They can be costly, ruin a vacation."

She wanted to ask him outright what the hell he wanted, but found herself rattling nonsense. "He went to get them, goggles and what all. He's taking care of things, room and stuff you know." She was digging a hole, but couldn't seem to stop. "Guess I better go check on him."

She pointedly took the key out of the ignition and swung her leg over the saddle with a little finger wave. "Nice talking to you."

He touched the bill of his cap with his finger. "You be careful now. Make sure your boyfriend drives with his lights on."

She stood inside the door and watched the *Peace Officer* pull away; the designation etched in large letters across his trunk.

Stefan came down the stairs. He had changed his shirt, and his hair was damp.

"What's the matter?"

"They call cops *peace officers* up here?"

He frowned. "What do you mean?"

"One was just out front, admiring your bike. That's what it said on his car. He told me to make sure you drive with your lights on."

"Really? Nice of him. That it?"

Laughter from the other end of the table brought her back to the present. Now what was Aiyana doing? Buttering Stefan's biscuit for him?

Suddenly Joachim pushed his chair back. He was pale, and his bowl of stew was still half full.

"Look, I'm sorry, everyone, but I'm very tired. My apologies." He bowed slightly to Savior's father. "I'm going back to the room."

Josie dropped her napkin and followed him out.

That night he was sick, and Josie confined him to bed and wouldn't even let Stefan in the room. "Not now, Stefan. He needs rest." She stepped into the hall, leading him by the elbow. "No talk. Not now."

"When?"

"We'll see how he is come morning."

"Tell me about this Murphy."

She looked at the door from where behind, the coughing had not stopped. "As we said, he's a good friend."

"Is he a real doctor?"

"Of course, he's real. He's the best, and he knows someone who can help." She settled a cool gaze on him. "Someone who has studied chronic lung infections."

Stefan frowned. "He has a chronic lung infection? What's that mean?"

"Antibiotic-resistant. Jac has periods of stability interrupted by periods of exacerbation."

"He was fine last I saw him."

"Maybe he seemed so. Your brother can be very . . . private, shall I say? That combined with his distrust of hospitals makes him a difficult patient."

"How did he get this? He's never sick."

"Bacterial fungal infections are often soil-based. With what he's been doing for the last couple of years, who knows what he's come in contact with?"

Stefan sensed she was holding something back. "How difficult, Josie?"

"If he doesn't get appropriate treatment, he could die."

His brow darkened. "Then why haven't you insisted he get it? Why are we standing here talking about it?"

"He was hard to pin down, never in one place more than a day or two. He made lots of promises; they were hard to keep. Then he got shot and, well—" She put her hands in the air. "Here we are."

Stefan dropped his arms to his sides and looked at the closed door, a spell of quiet. He moistened his lips and focused his gaze back on her. "Did he know? Before I left, did he know?"

"He was in denial."

"What about you?"

"This isn't about me."

"Oh, I think it is."

"It was important to him that you and Abby leave. I wasn't going to get in the middle."

Stefan shoved his hands in his pockets and looked at the ceiling, rocking himself.

"Look, we all need to get some sleep."

Stefan nodded numbly. He could never win an argument with her. He went to leave and then turned back. "Another thing, Sadie ran into a copper earlier today. She was waiting for me by the bike outside the hotel when he stopped." The encounter had nagged at him and there'd been enough secrecy. "He started to ask questions, curious, I guess. She pretended ignorance, which evidently played well. But she said the encounter seemed odd."

Josie's eyes narrowed, and her chicken pox scars stood out like freckles.

"What is it?"

"Why didn't you say something earlier?"

"I just thought about it."

"Did they run the plate? It's in your name, right?"

"Why would they do that?"

"Because that's what cops do."

He thought for a second. "Sadie saw a wanted poster in the lobby. Said it looked like me."

Her lips, bitten white, all but disappeared.

336

"Why are those still up, Josie? I don't like that. She ripped it down, says nobody saw her do it."

"I'm getting him out of here first thing in the morning."

"I'm going with him."

"What about Sadie?"

"What about her? She'll ride with me."

"In the snow?"

"We'll ride with you, then. I can store the bike."

"There isn't room, Stefan. It's a long drive; Jac will need to lie down." A calculating look crossed her face. "Sadie can ride with us. You can meet us at my place."

"I don't follow."

"There's a storm coming. Do you really want her on the back of that bike? You can get to my place, store it in the garage. There's a key to the house on a hook inside the garage door. I need to find a pharmacy to get some prescriptions refilled. It'll take time because they'll need to be transferred. You can feed the cats—" she attempted a smile— "park that bike out of sight and lay low."

Stefan frowned. "I don't think—"

"Snow moving in, wouldn't you be better off on that bike by yourself?"

He couldn't deny the logic of that.

"You can travel faster by yourself. Am I right?" She didn't wait for an answer. "I'll send directions to your phone. You can turn on the water, open things up; you know how to do all that.

Call me if you see anything suspicious. We'll be a couple of hours behind you, drop Sadie off, and rest a bit before taking on the rest of the trip."

He didn't argue. The plan sounded okay to him.

A fit of coughing resumed from behind the door adding a further sense of urgency.

"You think you can get him out of this, this—what you call it—pattern of exacerbation?"

"We're going to try. Like I said, Murphy is in touch with a colleague who's conducting experimental studies on soil-based bacteria."

It all sounded foreign to him, but plausible. He gave her a quick nod. "Okay."

"Go to your room and get some sleep." She hesitated a second. "Tell Sadie to meet me downstairs in the morning. Okay? Give us some time alone. I'd like to talk to her about arrangements, get on the same page, and we'll have breakfast."

He nodded agreement and they said good night.

CHAPTER 48

Sadie hadn't liked the plan and put up an argument, but he played the weather card, and she gave in. The new travel arrangements were sensible, and it would be easier for him.

"What does she want again?" She had asked Stefan the next morning as she pulled on a pair of wrinkled jeans from the day before.

He propped himself up on an elbow and watched her dress. "To talk arrangements, she said."

Josie had more to talk about than arrangements and didn't waste any time, starting in while Sadie was still stirring a dollop of cream into her coffee.

"You may not realize it, but you have drawn attention to us, attention we cannot afford."

Sadie froze with her spoon in the air. "No, I haven't. I haven't said a word."

"You don't have to."

"What then?"

"Your hair, your face, your, your everything. Look in the mirror, for God's sake. You stick out like a sore thumb. Just look at yourself."

Sadie looked down at herself. A sour thumb. *She couldn't think of a better analogy?* That old feeling of smug superiority inched upwards, but then she remembered the border crossing, the cross words from the agent and the glare directed her way filled with something more complicated than simple dislike.

"What about the cop out front of the hotel? Stefan told me about that."

"He was just looking at the bike."

"Right, the bike. The two of you on a motorcycle. Heavens, announcing you to everyone for miles around, bad enough he's on that thing by himself. We have to assume they ran the plate. Montegrand is an unusual name."

Sadie thought of the wanted poster she had ripped off the wall.

"To be blunt, Sadie, why are you even here?"

Sadie looked past her shoulder at the waitress setting out fresh coffee, shocked by the question.

She met Josie's gaze. *Why are you so rude?* "What do you want, Josie?"

"I'm just trying to help you understand the situation. Stefan would never leave Jac now. I always questioned his leaving in the first place. He has ties here, but it was important for his sister and mother to go. She never really fit in, and after their dad died . . ." Her voice trailed off, letting the thought drift between them.

She spread jam over their toast, offered Sadie a piece, and continued nonchalantly, as though they were talking about a simple matter. "Maybe someday, if this dies down and Jac can stay out of trouble, and if things don't work out for Stefan—a lot of ifs—" She paused for maximum effect, "maybe *then,* you could come back."

What things? Sadie stared at the toast. *Come back?* The full ramification of what she was saying hit her like a slap. She lifted her chin stubbornly. "You're wrong. I couldn't possibly leave him. He wouldn't want me to. You've got it all wrong."

"Have I? Jac is seriously ill. Stefan doesn't realize how serious, so now I've told you something I shouldn't have."

"What's wrong?"

"He has a bacterial lung infection. There's a specialist that's been recommended to us but all this—" she waved her arm to encompass much— "has interfered. He of course thinks he's invincible."

Sadie frowned. "But he doesn't—"

"Look it? He hides it well. But it's why Stefan needed to come. We always knew he would be back, but he never said he wasn't coming alone. Look—" Josie rested her palms down on the table— "Jac has to get treatment. He's already put it off too long. If he goes to prison, he'll die." She paused and took a deep breath. "If we can arrest the infection, there'll be a period of recuperation, and he'll need comfortable, dry surroundings. Not a damp prison cell."

"And you think I could be the cause of that?"

"I'm sorry, but yes, I do."

"You're overreacting. I'm nobody."

"No, Sadie, you aren't. People talk. A guy on a motorcycle up here with a white girl seals the memory of the traveling companion with a limp and an arm in a sling. Two plus two." She threw a hand in the air. "Talk, talk, talk. I can hear it if you can't, all the innuendo and prying questions that dig up trouble."

Josie talked with her hands and Sadie tried to keep up.

"You underestimate the impression you leave behind," Josie added softly.

It wasn't a compliment. Sadie took a sip of her coffee gone cold in the cup.

"The attention it brings on your companions."

"What do you expect me to do?"

"I can have someone from my office meet us and arrange transport to Saskatoon. From there, it will be easy for you to rent a car —we can help with that— and get back over the border. Go home. Go back to school. Or—" she brushed the crumbs off her fingers— "you could convince Stefan to take you back. After all, he's the one who brought you here."

Sadie swallowed. If she only knew.

"If you want to do that," Josie continued. "But in the long run, given what you now know, don't you think he'd come to resent that?"

Sadie was silent. What she resented was Josie spelling it out.

But Josie was far from done.

She looked Sadie in the eye. "This has gone on long enough. It's time you knew. Stefan has a prior commitment, a pledge to Aiyana. It's true—" she held up her hand— "and I'm sorry to be so blunt, Sadie, but the two of you are *not* meant to be. Aiyana is his intended, while you are, frankly, just another fling.

Another fling? Sadie felt her insides hollow out, Josie taking a shovel to them. Her voice receded, as if from a great distance, the words garbled and distorted like an echo through a tunnel. The tunnel closing in on her, taking her air.

"I'm sure he didn't want to hurt you—"

Was she still talking?

"And probably didn't mean for it to go this far. He's like his brother—all the Montegrands—tight-lipped, but you deserve to know the truth." She took a breath and moistened her lips. "An arrangement was made between Aiyana's grandmother and Stefan's when they were only children."

"An arrangement?" Sadie spat the word. "That's archaic!" She found her voice and refuge in denial. "And medieval."

"Of course, it's not binding," she said, plowing ahead in the face of Sadie's shocked outburst. "We don't hold with arranged marriages anymore, but you saw them together, didn't you? Sometimes the elders know best."

"Why wouldn't he have said something?"

"Maybe he didn't think it important you know."

Breakfast was over.

She set her coffee cup on the sideboard with a thud. Why hadn't Stefan told her how sick Jac was? Had he even known? And what the fuck was this thing with Aiyana? Maybe he didn't think it important she know?

When she climbed the stairs to their room, Stefan was on his way down with his satchel over one shoulder and an elbow linked through Joachim's.

He gave her a nod, a *see you downstairs*. She numbly went up to gather her belongings and braid her hair.

With each turn of the plaiting, Josie's parting words settled in her psyche, like the braid tightening between her fingers. With each twist of a strand, *it wasn't important she know.*

She tucked her headband behind her ears, straightened her shoulders, and looked at herself in the mirror. It couldn't be true, so why would it have been important?

Joachim and Stefan shared a last cup of coffee while Josie loaded the jeep. The first snow was falling in sharp pellets, half sleet and half hail. Joachim was hunched over his mug and had a scarf wrapped around his neck.

"Dad rode his all winter," he replied to Stefan's question. "I think he was actually addicted to riding in snow, but that man had layers of steel." He reached across the table and squeezed Stefan's bicep. "I have hand weights in Josie's closet. In between cat detail, you should pump iron."

"I have a full-face shield, overpants, and good boots." Stefan had heard enough about the cats. "What else would Dad never be without, can you remember?"

"Good quality winter gloves. If your fingers get cold, you won't be able to work the levers. Other than that, well, it's not going to be zero cold, so you'll be okay." He took a sip of his coffee. "Dad used to layer newspaper between his inner and outer garments."

"Newspaper?"

"It's a great insulator." He shook his head sadly. "So much you don't know."

"Do you even know where you're going?"

"Josie knows. Don't worry. We'll be in touch."

"At Josie's, right?"

Joachim studied Stefan's face. "I'm glad you came, Stefan, but I'm sorry you got caught in this weather. I know you both wanted to get back."

"About that, I'm not sure what we're doing."

Joachim eyed him over the rim of the mug. "What do you mean?"

"I talked to Mother yesterday to give her an update. She might take a teaching position at Abby's school. Abby is upset about that." He stifled a smile. "I think she's decided to settle there. I made her a co-signer on the account before I left. She didn't have to agree to it," he added in a rush. "You know how that works."

"I never wanted the money. You understand, don't you?"

"Not really."

"This way, should anything happen to me, it won't be tied up in court."

"Why would anything happen to you? You just need the right antibiotic. Right?"

Joachim cradled his coffee cup in his hands, and his eyes took on a distant look. "They never should have signed those treaties," he said. "They were full of tricks."

"They didn't know what they were signing. Dad always maintained Grandfather thought he was signing treaties of peace and friendship. What a joke."

"And the settlement with Hydro—" Joachim continued as though Stefan hadn't spoken, "when they first came in and offered compensation, we didn't know we would be flooded, so how were we to discuss compensation? How do you flood someone just a *little bit?*"

"Water under the bridge," Stefan made a face. "No pun intended."

"We were betrayed, brother."

The door to the lobby opened, and Savior's father and sister came in with a gust of wind. One of the nephews Stefan recognized from the ceremony stepped in behind them, his sullen countenance still in place, and he wondered what his issue was.

"You weren't leaving again without saying goodbye, were you?" Aiyana asked Stefan.

"Of course not." He looked at her father who appeared older in the morning light and smaller of stature without his fur and beaded leggings.

"I come to give you this." Adolphus handed Joachim a leather pouch. "He would want you to have it."

Joachim hesitated, hands clasped, and stared at it.

The pouch took the shape of what it contained and Stefan knew what it was. Joachim had told him the story how he, Bobby, and Savior, mere boys, were following their father's trap lines along the banks of rushing water. They had stopped on a rocky bluff above the river to eat their lunch of dried fish wrapped in paper when a bald eagle with a wingspan that threw a shadow like a hydroplane swooped over their heads and dropped something at the edge of the water.

It sparkled like a spray of blue diamonds.

Savior had scrambled down the rocky bank to the water's edge and held the shiny object aloft. The sun caught it like a prism, and from that moment they thought of it as a gift from a reincarnated ancestor.

Savior later showed it to a petrologist at the Council House. He told him it was likely forged from flecks of gold and tanzanite deposited in the Canadian Shield by a glacier on its slow passage south.

They assumed it was lucky.

Stefan looked from the leather pouch to Savior's father, gone as white as that eagle. He doubted it was lucky, but Jac had no choice but to take it.

Joachim palmed the amulet, pushed his chair back, and then walked the older man to the door.

Stefan followed them out with Aiyana. "What's with him?" He nodded at her cousin. "He acts like we're the enemy."

"He blames your brother for what happened."

"He wasn't there. If you ask me, there's no point in placing blame."

"I agree." She rested a hand on his arm. "Father says a guilty conscious needs no accuser."

"You think he's guilty?"

"It doesn't matter what I think."

He looked at the hand on his arm and waited for old feelings to resurface. He stepped away and opened the door for her. "It was nice to see you again, Aiyana."

She looked over his shoulder and her eyes hardened. "I wonder what your grandmother would say about you with a white girl."

Stefan turned to see Sadie step off the staircase and lean against the banister. Her backpack was slung over one shoulder, and her face was devoid of expression.

"She's not here either, is she?"

"I waited for you. I still wait." She rose on her tiptoes, kissed him on the lips, and whispered against his mouth, "When you tire of her, Stefan Montegrand, I'll be here."

Stefan didn't move, hiding his surprise at the uncharacteristic public show of affection. He gently removed her hand from his neck. "I won't, Aiyana, and I'm sorry if I led you to believe otherwise." He motioned her out. "I'm sorry about everything, but I have to say goodbye."

She lifted her chin with a final show of defiant pride. "We'll see," she said and walked stiffly to the waiting car.

He let the door close softly on its own.

Sadie hadn't mentioned her conversation with Josie to Stefan. When had there been time? She was about to make time when she walked downstairs to witness the two of them together. Josie's final statement— after which she had no appetite for breakfast— was still ringing in her ears and she misread the interaction. As the two of them walked away arm-in-arm in an obvious intimate moment, she leaned against the banister for balance. The ringing in her ears turned into an angry buzz of jealousy to override her reason and set her up for the kiss Aiyana planted for her benefit. There was no misreading that. He'd been playing her, had never wanted her here in the first place.

Body language doesn't lie, and what if Josie was right, and by her mere presence she was a danger to those she loved? Loved but didn't belong with?

Stefan turned and looked at her, and a deceitful smile spread over his handsome face.

He didn't think it important she know.

She had been played and felt a flush of anger as it all became suddenly clear. Josie was right on many levels.

Her insecurity had never been obliterated; it had only retreated to await revival. Cultural differences couldn't be alleviated in a mere few days or even weeks, could, in fact, take months to untangle and years to integrate. It was something that even Stefan's mother had never been able to completely accomplish.

Josie didn't have to further convince Sadie of the right thing to do during the ride ahead. She had already convinced herself well before Stefan drove out of the lot with an arm thrust into the air in a gesture of goodbye.

It was better to forgo drawn-out goodbyes.

CHAPTER 49

The key was where Josie said it would be, and after fumbling in the cold, Stefan got the door open. His fingers were numb, and Joachim was right: for the last several miles, he'd had trouble with the levers. It had started snowing hard when he was only halfway, and he had to stop twice to warm up. The last time, he was tempted to ask the bartender for some newspaper.

The fuse box was in the basement. He found a flashlight and stooped to descend the narrow steps. He flipped the switches, and the water pump gave a gurgle and a hiss of air, and the furnace kicked on above his head. He crawled back up the stairs, kicked his boots off, and put on a warm pair of socks. He hung his coat over the register, then opened a bag of Josie's jerky and a jar of home-canned plums. The kitchen was in a state of clutter and there were dishes in the sink. It was obvious she left in a hurry and a wonder she remembered to turn anything off.

He chewed thoughtfully on a piece of jerky and spooned plums into a bowl, sucking on the stones and spitting them back out. The events of the past two days had been draining and Aiyana's presence had taken him by surprise, even though it shouldn't have.

He set his bowl in the sink and ran the hot water. The pipes banged and clanked, then spit out a geyser on a rush of air. He stepped back as the flow settled. He wasn't much for plumbing and took note of the bucket set handily in the corner next to the gas stove.

He'd only been here once before and what stood out in his mind was the neighbor's string of horses. He hadn't had to worry about pipes, fuses, and what was for dinner.

His phone beeped and he grabbed it. It was a text from Josie.

Are you there? We're having trouble with a pharmacy, won't arrive before dark. Everything okay?

He texted back:

Good. Heats on. How's Jac?

Sleeping.

Sadie?

Sleeping.

He drummed his fingers on the table. Their goodbye had been strained and was nagging at him. He had replayed it in his head across the miles, trying to put a finger on it. She had turned distant and aloof, more so than after the episode with Nan, turning her cheek when he tried to kiss her goodbye. At the time, he attributed it to shyness in front of the others, but after sixty miles of thinking, he wondered.

A blur of movement from the living room caught the corner of his eye. He stared at the shadowy shapes and the darkened hallway that led to the rear of the cabin. A sudden high-pitched howl bolted him to his feet as a streak of fur spitting green fire leapt across the floor and landed on the table, swinging its tail like a bobcat.

"Damn!" He breathed, heart racing. He'd forgotten about the cats. There were two. He looked around suspiciously, not wanting to be ambushed. "Where's your buddy?" he addressed the one sprawled out on the table, calmly licking his balls. One was presumably shy and never came out of hiding unless Josie was alone. Jac had joked that there was really only one, and the other was buried somewhere in the yard.

"Which are you? Casper?" The cat flipped his tail back and forth indolently, staking his claim. "I suppose you think I'm going to feed you?"

He searched the cupboards, admiring Josie's stash of canned goods with handwritten labels. He found the bag of cat food beside the washing machine. Something had been gnawing at the bag and he looked at the cat door. What was to keep every rodent and skunk a mile around from entering the house? He didn't understand people and their cats, but Casper had taken a liking to him and wrapped his body around Stefan's legs. He filled the dish and set the bag of food in the mop pail. He washed his hands again at the sink and glanced outside. It was still snowing.

The quiet was getting to him. He turned on the kitchen radio, and walked through the living room, switching on lights. There was a small television in the corner next to a bookshelf and an end table stacked with board games, a cribbage board, and checkers. Everything took two people.

He went back in the kitchen, checked his phone, and sent a text to Sadie. The thermostat was set at sixty degrees. He left it alone and found an oversized sweater in the closet.

Josie's driveway was long, but the road out front was visible through the denuded trees where a car was passing slowly by. He shut the lights back off and sat at the table with nervous energy. He got up and paced the room, peering out the windows, looking half-heartedly for the other cat, and checking his phone.

There was beer in the fridge. He cracked one open with the magnet on the door and drank from the bottle.

He took another into the living room along with his phone, stretched out on the couch and turned the TV on, flipping through the local channels. He muted the sound and drank his beer.

He awoke to static from the radio that had lost its station. It was pitch black and the television was off, though he didn't remember doing it. The empty bottle had rolled down between his back and the cushion, and he dug it out, realizing with a start that both cats were lying across his feet, keeping them warm. "So, you're good for something." His voice echoed in the eerie quiet of midnight, and he concluded that cats could be good company.

He heard a car engine and sat up with a jerk, dislodging his company. Lights swept the front of the house and turned into the drive.

He jumped to his feet and rushed to the kitchen window. It was them. He ran his hands through his hair, tucked his shirt in, and turned on the outside light.

Joachim shuffled in first. He was out of breath from the simple trek from the garage.

Stefan helped him off with his coat.

"Took you guys forever. I fell asleep on the couch. Did you get your prescriptions? Did you get some sleep in the car?" The questions kept coming, but Joachim just shook his head. There were dark circles under his eyes and his breathing was labored. "Talk to Josie. I'm going to bed."

He kicked off his boots, and walked down the hallway, knowing the way.

Stefan followed him with his eyes, then hung the coat on the back of a chair, picked up the boots, and set them heel-to-heel out of the way.

Josie came through the door with her arms loaded down. He took a bag of groceries from her. "Good, you picked up some food." He rummaged through the bag as she set several white pharmacy sacks on the table and unwound her scarf, identical circles under her eyes.

"Rough drive?" He looked towards the door, waiting.

She shut it without looking at him and started to sort the prescription bottles.

"Where's Sadie?" He frowned at her back. What was wrong with her? He opened the door and leapt the two steps to the garage floor.

It only took a matter of seconds for him to realize that the jeep was empty. He opened the hatch and stared dumbly at the interior. There was no trace. He stood motionless for a sliver of time, narrowing the possibilities.

He went back in the house, closed the door, and leaned against it.

Josie was at the table with the pill bottles lined up in front of her. She motioned him to a chair. "Sit down, Stefan."

"Where is she?"

"I don't want an argument. Jac took a turn for the worse on the drive. I'm going to let him sleep for a while, but as soon as he wakes, we're heading out. I bought enough food for you but if you need anything, you can take my jeep. It should have gas."

"Where the *fuck* is Sadie?"

"She decided to go back. Her grandpa isn't well."

"Go back? What do you mean, go back?"

"Home. She wanted to go home."

"Bullshit! Without telling me? Without saying goodbye? What bullshit is this, Josephine?"

"Calm down."

"Don't tell me to calm down. You and Jac conjure this up? Here I've been telling her to give you a chance."

"Leave him out of it."

"Okay. So, where'd you dump her?"

"We didn't *dump* her. She decided to rent a car and go home."

"She wouldn't do that. Besides, I thought you had to be twenty-five to rent a car."

"We arranged it."

"Sweet," he said sarcastically.

"She said she would call you later and explain."

"No, you're going to explain. Or I'm getting back on the bike and getting the hell out of here."

"Wouldn't that be smart?"

He pulled a chair out with his foot, sat with his legs spread, and motioned with his hands for her to get on with it.

"It wasn't a matter of giving either of us a chance. This is about your brother and his situation. I'm getting him into treatment in a secure clinic where there is anonymity and discretion, and we don't need any more run-ins with cops. We don't need any more attention."

"What's that got to do with Sadie?"

"It has everything to do with Sadie. She doesn't fit. Not when you are trying to travel under the radar." She paused and studied him for a second. "I think that's what went wrong at Murphy's clinic. Someone couldn't keep their mouth shut, and here we are."

"And to think Sadie wasn't with you," he retorted. "There's no connection. What's the real reason?"

"Murphy was in contact with a colleague. He was waiting for culture results. He might have gotten Jac started on the right antibiotic then, but we had to leave in a rush; the cops were closing in because someone blabbed."

"You and Jac had a lot of problems that predate me and Sadie. Look, I would do anything for Jac, you know that, but—"

"But?"

"I need to know what happened with Sadie. Where is she?"

"They were going to a twenty-four-hour car rental in Saskatoon. If she left there straight away, she'd be past Regina by now, close to the border."

"They?"

"A colleague of mine."

"You dumped her with a stranger?"

She pursed her lips. "A colleague is not a stranger."

Stefan pushed his chair back. "What's wrong with her grandfather? Something else you've made up?"

"She didn't elaborate."

He walked into the living room and stood listening at the top of the hallway. He could hear his brother breathing. He was sleeping, and a measure of calm settled over him. He walked back into the kitchen.

"You've taken a lot on yourself, Josie. But you aren't my mother and, frankly, with regards to me and Sadie, you're way out of line."

"Am I? She wanted to go home. Maybe after seeing you and Aiyana together, she sensed there wasn't anything here for her. Maybe you were doing her a disservice leading her on, parading her around."

Stefan stared at her. "That's a lousy thing to say. And what does Aiyana have to do with it?"

"It was always expected that you would marry. It was your grandparents' wish."

"Who said anything about marriage?" He threw his hands up in exasperation. "God Almighty. So that's it. You filled her head with the out-of-touch wishes of dead people!"

"That's disrespectful."

"And you're worse than an old woman."

"No reason to get nasty, Stefan."

"I didn't mean any disrespect, but I don't love Aiyana. I love Sadie." There, he said it. It felt good to finally say it. "I'm leaving in the morning. I'll see Jac off, talk with him in the morning, and then I'm out of here."

"I need you to stay here, wrap up some loose ends for us, and keep an eye on things. She doesn't want you following her. She said as much. When she's ready to talk to you, she'll call you. This will make sense in the morning." She gathered up the pill bottles and started down the hallway, looking back at him over her shoulder. "You didn't come all this way to leave now when he might need you the most."

He stood motionless, and his arms hung limply at his side as she walked confidently into the shadows not waiting for a reply. *Josie in the night*, knowing what was best. Knowing everyone inside out.

There was no way he would leave Jac now, and she knew it.

"Sleep on it," Josie added from the bedroom door, a slant of light crossing the threshold. "Trust me; things will look better in the morning. They always do."

CHAPTER 50

Things didn't look better in the morning. Joachim's condition had worsened, and Sadie wasn't responding to his text messages.

While Josie left Post-It notes around the kitchen with last minute instructions, from the care of her cats to the trick with the water pump, Stefan helped Joachim dress.

"Thanks, man. I know you didn't sign up for this," Jac mumbled as Stefan helped him lace his boots. "Taking care of an invalid."

"Don't be stupid." Stefan gave the laces a yank and a double knot.

"You can take off now. We'll be fine. Take my jeep."

"I'm not doing that."

"I'm sorry about Sadie."

Stefan stiffened. "Not your fault."

"I know this isn't what you signed up for," he said again.

"How far is this clinic?"

"I don't know."

"An hour," Josie said. "If we don't run into any problems." She was standing in the doorway, arms crossed. "We need to go, Jac. Car's running."

He stood up and then sat back down. A sheen of sweat lined his brow.

Stefan bent over him. "Take my arm," he said.

He got him in the car and reclined the seat, while Josie placed a pillow behind his head and a throw over his lap. She tucked it under his legs, shut the door, then motioned Stefan around the front of the vehicle.

"If anyone comes around, gets nosy, tell them you're house sitting, that I was called away on an emergency. I'll call you when we get there." She hesitated for a second. "One more thing, I need you to check for any of Jac's stuff, personal items, in case they show up with a warrant."

"What am I supposed to do with it?"

"There's a shed across the road the neighbor lets me use when sap is running. He's gone for the winter. Put it there. Just in case there's anything that shouldn't be here. One more thing, Stefan, and this is important. If any mail comes addressed to him, especially from insurance, anything with the NIHB insignia on the envelope, hide it."

"You want me to *hide* it?"

"Or put it with his other belongings. Be smart about it. The post was being held, but they would only do that for a week." She rested a hand on his arm. "Thanks for helping this morning. I knew you'd do the right thing."

"Stef!" Joachim rolled his window down and motioned him back to his side of the jeep.

"I have some papers in a folder in the bottom of my dresser. There's a manila envelope in there too with old letters from Bobby and Savior."

"Letters?"

"We didn't always have cell phones. Pictures too. Burn them."

"Burn them?"

"I shouldn't have kept them. They might incriminate Bobby."

Stefan swallowed. *Jesus.* His head was spinning. "Everything?"

"Everything." He clasped Stefan's arm with a reserve of strength. "In the burn barrel, soon as it's dark. Got it?"

Stefan licked his lips and nodded.

"Thanks." He dropped his head back on the pillow. "I'm sorry to put you in a jam."

"It's not a jam. I can start a fire. I'll take care of things. Get better, and I'll be over to see you as soon as Josie lets me."

"Say goodbye, Stef. We gotta go." She threw the jeep into reverse and the tires rocked.

He stepped back with a wave and watched as they disappeared on the road, thinking about his new responsibilities.

Back inside, he looked around the kitchen, larger and emptier than before. He poured a cup of coffee and took to familiarizing himself with Josie's cupboards, the meat in the freezer, and the near empty vegetable tray in which a lone rutabaga nestled in the corner.

He turned his phone on. His text messages to Sadie that night appeared to have gone through, but there was no way to know for sure until she replied. He opened the weather app and thumbed down the page. Colder temperatures were settling across the area. He pulled up the forecast for Northern Michigan, wondering if she had made it home. Wondering about her grandfather, wondering about the unease that had a firm hold on his heart as he scrolled through meaningless information and finished his coffee.

He set his cup in the sink and rinsed out the pot. He should find the papers Jac was worried about, but before tackling all of that, he needed some exercise.

He pulled a sock hat over his ears, grabbed his gloves, and walked back across the yard. It had been snowing lightly all morning and the tire tracks in the driveway were already filling in.

He swung by the mailbox and then looked across the road for the neighbor's shed.

A small structure stood next to the road an eighth of a mile down. He approached it with one ear out for traffic. It was a simple ten by twelve structure with a metal roof and a stovepipe jutting out at a crooked angle. He kicked snow away from the door and was wedging it open when he heard the sound of an approaching vehicle.

The utter silence of the woods made the harsh noise of combustion all the more shocking. With a sudden instinct to hide, he slammed the door shut and flattened himself against the rear of the shed. For a heart-pounding second, he thought the engine was slowing, but then it accelerated and moved off into the distance.

Shit. He peeked around the corner to assure himself the coast was clear. Why did he feel like a crook? All the clandestine tasks he was assigned had him sneaking around like one.

He ran the eighth of a mile back to the cabin and kicked his boots off at the door. Having had enough exercise and excitement for one morning, he sat at the table with his phone. Nothing new.

Josie had not messaged him yet like she said she would, and it'd been well over an hour. Maybe it wasn't Sadie's phone. Maybe it was his, piece of shit. He tossed it on the table.

Remembering what Joachim asked him to do, he went through his dresser. He found the manila envelope and papers he had referenced and dumped everything in a paper sack to burn.

There was little traffic on the road, but for the rest of the day, every time he heard a vehicle, his heart raced. Peering out windows, tiptoeing about the premises like a cat burglar, he looked for anything that was pure Joachim. Feeling the weight of responsibility, by mid-afternoon he was ready for a beer and happy for the company of two felines.

He turned the television on low and heated up a hunk of cornbread from the freezer with something that looked like gravy, ignoring the rutabaga, with his phone sitting dormant on the corner of the table. Was her number on roaming? SMS accidently deactivated? Conflicting apps? Just plain shut off? There was no way for him to know until she got back with him.

He waited until dark before dumping the contents of the paper bag in the burn barrel and striking a match. He watched the fire shape and shift the contents, pictures of a grinning Bobby and Savior in his Stetson curling inwards and turning black.

When he got up the next morning, there was a text waiting from Josie. They had arrived safely. The timestamp was from the night before. It took the cellular service here twelve hours to deliver a message from sixty miles away.

He fried a skillet full of venison sausage, and then went back to sorting Joachim's belongings; from their dad's wallet and tobacco pouch—he opened it and smelled it—to snow shoes, long johns, and pieces of mail with forward stamps. He found a couple of boxes in a back closet, and was emptying the contents on the floor to make room for Jac's things when he heard someone pull in the driveway.

He peered through the slats in the window blind. The car was unmarked but clearly law enforcement. He was surprised it had taken them so long.

He glanced at the burn barrel behind the cabin. Was that a thin trail of stubborn smoke wafting from the ashes? He hadn't lit the match until well after midnight, mixing Joachim's papers in with the kitchen trash, and warming his hands over the fire as it consumed any evidence of wrongdoing.

He made a mental note to stir the ashes and make sure there was no evidence left uncharred.

He darted to the other window with a view of the front stoop. The men had climbed out of the sedan and were approaching the door. Plainclothes to match their plain car, but he recognized the walk, the spread-leg stance, and authoritative knocking.

Their patience was admirable, shading their eyes at the window and quietly conferring. They disappeared around the corner of the cabin and resumed knocking on the back door. He slid down to a crouch with his back against the wall, holding his breath.

If they had a warrant, he was screwed.

They finally left, and when quiet returned to the clearing, he went back to boxing up Joachim's belongings and loaded them in the back of his jeep. After dark, he drove across the road to the neighbor's sugar shack.

Everything he was doing had to be done after dark.

The second time they came, Stefan was in the shed changing the oil in the jeep. He had it on ramps with an oil pan under the front end.

He heard the car's approach and slid out from underneath the engine block. He wiped his hands on the rag in his back pocket and walked warily to the corner of the shed. Crows were jabbering from the tree line, calling him out. Obstructing justice, he imagined himself back in jail on the wrong side of the law. Once you landed there, it was a hard cycle to break. The shed was only a stone's throw from the front porch, and Stefan almost welcomed the jabbering crows which surely masked any sound of his labored breathing.

The same two men and the same vehicle, trying again. This time they didn't linger. After a few sharp knocks and a look around, they walked back to their car. Losing interest? They sat in the drive on their phones, engine running. He waited them out, and after they pulled away and the sound of their engine was long gone, he crawled back under the jeep.

Amazed at the steadiness of his hand, he gave the wrench a decisive turn. Born to the life of a bounder? Was that in his blood too? He had quickly adapted. Well, shit, one couldn't help what they were born with.

The third time he couldn't avoid the knock on the door. It was an unseasonably warm day and he had the inside door open to let in the sun, which even now barely cleared the treetops. He was cleaning Josie's garden tools, anything to keep busy while awaiting further word from the hospital, something from Sadie, anything to jumpstart his bottomed-out life.

It was a different vehicle in the driveway and different men on the stoop. He opened the screen, story ready, but they only wanted to talk to Joachim, talked right through his feigned ignorance, and handed him a business card. "Have him call us—it's Stefan, you say?" *Had he given his name?* "We need to talk to him."

They knew exactly who he was. Stefan turned the card over in his hand, at a loss for words.

"Stefan—can I call you Stefan?—he might be interested in what we have to say."

The guy doing the talking wore a wired earpiece. Who was on the other end?

"Look, to be straight with you, we know he's on the run, and we know you know where he is."

"I *don't* know where he is. They didn't want me to know."

"They?"

Stefan crossed his arms. It was a standoff, the three of them.

The officer adjusted his earpiece and said, "Aiding and abetting is no small matter."

Stefan didn't budge, in stance or facial expression. He wasn't a snitch.

"Okay, maybe you don't know where he is, but if he gets in touch, tell him this. More evidence has come in about the altercation in Manitoba, and given the fact that the two police officers weren't seriously injured and your brother's friend was killed, along with other extenuating circumstances, their department has agreed to turn the matter over to us."

Stefan palmed the business card weighing their words. *How do they know that?*

The one doing all the talking hooked his thumbs in his belt. "I can't go into detail with you, but there's a new initiative that just came down that requires maximum involvement of Indigenous peoples with implementation of *their* guidance and *their* ideas.

Stefan snorted disbelief. "*What* new initiative? More smoke and mirrors?"

A look passed between the two men. A shift in stance and acknowledgment of Stefan's standing.

"Look, we know what you're thinking, but this is different. There might be something in it for him. Something in it for you."

What the hell does that mean?

"Give him that," the man said, nodding at the card. "We need to talk."

They had had their say, and Stefan showed them off the porch.

He sat at the kitchen window and watched them drive away. He looked at the business card. *Ministère des Ressources Naturelles.* Now, why on Earth did the Ministry of Natural Resources want to talk to Joachim? What was up their sleeve? What new initiative? It sounded fishy to him. He tapped the edge of the laminated card on the table and then stood it against the sugar bowl.

His phone was upside down on the table and he turned it over. His last message to Sadie—*Whatever Josie told you about me and Aiyana isn't true*—had gone unanswered. Delivery to numbers that were roaming was not guaranteed. Was she roaming? His mouth turned down on the word.

He couldn't figure it out. She wouldn't have given up so easily, not after all they'd been through. He toyed with sending another, but the list of *sent* messages were already stacked up like dominoes. Was that not in itself a message?

He needed to talk with Josie again, find out more about that so-called *colleague*. Get a number, one that wasn't roaming. Maybe this time she would let him talk to Jac so he could pick his brain about this new development. This Ministry of Natural Resources development.

He heated up a can of soup and mulled things over.

The following day, Bobby showed. Bobby with a plan, unconsciously stepping into Savior's shoes. He had a plan and needed a place to stay.

He parked his truck behind the shed, settled his gear in a back room, and they reacquainted themselves over a beer. Stefan showed him the business card, but Bobby was as flummoxed by it as Stefan.

"They must have the wrong guy, Stef. Makes no sense to me. What'd you tell them?"

"Nothing."

"I haven't heard anything about any new initiative that involves us. Could be a ploy."

"It wasn't the first time someone's come around, but these guys seemed different."

Bobby squished up his mouth and tossed the card back on the table. "Different how?"

Stefan shrugged. "Just different." He thought for a minute. "Jac had me burn some papers."

"What papers?" he said suspiciously.

"Letters and stuff he said incriminated you."

"Shit."

"A picture of you and Savior at your crossbones marker and some at the roadblock."

"He kept *those*?"

"I burned them. All of them."

"Are you sure?"

"Absolutely."

362

Bobby fished in his pocket for his cigarettes. "I'll be dammed. He's the one insisted we read and destroy. And no pictures, all the old guys harping on that, and here all along—" he struck a match, blew out a puff of smoke— "he kept those." He eyed Stefan over the burning tip of the menthol cigarette. "What do you think? Your brother have a sentimental side?"

"I think he just forgot about them."

"Yeah, well, don't think he didn't have one."

They sat quietly for a minute considering each other, what had transpired, and what might yet come.

Stefan picked up the business card and flipped it back and forth between his fingers.

"So, Bobby, tell me more about this plan of yours."

CHAPTER 51

Sadie had reclaimed her place. It was as if she'd never left—grooming the horses, wrapping heat tape around the water pipes, and throwing hay down for the cattle as shadows lengthened through the slats in the sideboards of the mow.

In her absence, Margie had all but moved in, but Margie had no interest in the horses, the barn, or the hours Sadie kept.

There were two new calves to bottle-feed that were birthed to cows bred out of season when the bull broke through the pasture gate, and she discovered a new batch of kittens in the haymow. Their eyes weren't open and she left them alone, secretly checking on them periodically to make sure the mother cat hadn't moved them. By the time they opened their eyes, they each had a name.

Simon Wixom had broken ground on his house plans, but then slipped and sprained his ankle. He still hoped to have his house framed in by spring. In a subtle twist of the knife, he used the funds received from the suit against Maxwell Bolton for his building permits, and a Hadrian-inspired stonemason's wall along their shared border.

She had received her acceptance for winter semester and put in a request for the only dorm that had not transitioned to co-ed. She was waitlisted for Investigative Techniques 101 and Gendering Migration, which focused on women crossing borders. The next time she crossed one, she wouldn't be caught flat-footed. If they both opened up, she would have a full load.

She leafed through the catalog with her tentative schedule highlighted in yellow and felt a twinge of anticipation. A moving forward.

"Good morning." Henry poured a cup of coffee and pulled out a chair.

"Morning," Sadie replied without looking up.

He studied her for a minute. "Margie would like to have the kids over for Thanksgiving dinner. I told her it was up to you," He was still trying to include her in their new arrangement. "You'll be home, right?"

"I'm not sure, Dad." The thought of coming home to "the kids" made her want to study abroad. "My advisor says I need a math class, which is ridiculous, and I'm going to see if I can test out of it. There's a tutoring session I need to check into."

Henry dropped a spoonful of brown sugar in his coffee, part of his *after* routine. "Can't you do that online? Margie would like you to be here. Her son will be home from college."

That information had already been volunteered, but she had no interest in reacquainting herself with Margie's son. He was a weight-lifting wrestler in high school obsessed with looking at himself in a mirror. People didn't change that much. "No, Dad. I can't." She set her coffee cup in the sink, tucked her jeans into her riding boots, and grabbed a pair of gloves, escaping the overheated kitchen before Margie could join in the assault.

She'd been home over a week, and after obsessively checking her phone for text messages the first couple of days, she broke the habit and let the device die in a drawer. After the first confusing message from him the night she left—*still sleeping?* —there had been nothing. Sleeping? She hadn't slept for a week.

Halfway to Saskatoon in the company of the mother of all midwives who wore a size eleven boot and had the girth of a black bear, she realized she had accidently hit *chat* instead of *text* when she replied to *still sleeping?* so she resent it, but there'd been nothing more from him. Why would there be when he was busy making plans with Aiyana? That girl could cling, and why not? She would be hard pressed to do better than him. *Him*—making plans for marriage while fooling around with her.

Thank God she'd the sense to get on the pill. She'd flushed the rest of them down the toilet, then regretted it. The responsible thing would have been to toss them in the burn barrel.

She had sent him one last message asking about Jac. She liked that guy.

Dead cyber silence.

She had taken the boomerang off the shelf and unwrapped it from the frayed towel, remembering the way he handled it. She even went so far as to carry it outside thinking to throw it, but she was afraid it wouldn't come back.

She worked her fingers into the riding gloves as she crossed the drive. Wolf ran alongside slapping her leg with his tail, and she dropped an affectionate hand on his head. He had met her joyfully the day she returned, giddy as a puppy peeing himself. But he kept looking over her shoulder and at the road with his head cocked.

The boomerang was back on a shelf in her closet, but in the recesses of her mind, there was a niche of hope that he'd be back for it. That had obviously been his intent—she would give him that—but now that he was home with his *intended,* the game was over, and it was more likely he'd ask her to mail it.

Two Socks and Lucy were waiting with heads hung over their adjacent gates.

It had felt good to get back in the saddle, the best part about coming home. The worst part was showing up in a rental car.

"Hey, boy." She stroked Two Socks' long face. "Not your turn this morning." He would always be her favorite, though Lucy had her admirable moments, none more so than when she carried her out of Clem's clutches.

She threw a blanket over the mare's back, rocked the saddle into place, and tightened the cinch under her belly. As she rode out of the stable bay, like a mirage, Stefan was in front of her, straight-backed with knees tucked. He threw a look over his shoulder and tipped his hat.

She kicked Lucy into a gallop and rode her hard down the lane to outpace the shimmering illusion, wind buffeting her face and neck, faster and harder. They reached the bend at the end of the lane, and she turned the mare into the path alongside the fencerow that led to the creek, mercilessly kneeing her into a gallop, leaning over her neck to urge her on. She was all heart, and kicked up a swirl of leaves and corn husks, hooves throwing clods of clay that reminded her of Savior's burial, the dreams that plagued her since coming home. The family she had wanted to be a part of versus the one she had.

She didn't have anything against Margie. She wasn't trying to be a mother, but she wanted to be friends, and Sadie wasn't there yet.

When they reached the creek, she reined the horse in and ducked through the low-hanging branches that lined the bank. They flushed a rabbit and two ring-neck pheasants at the same time as a flock of sparrows fled to the treetops. Lucy side-stepped at the commotion.

"Whoa, girl." She patted her neck. "You don't want to throw me, do you?" The mare was still easily spooked but hadn't thrown her since that day on Bolton property. That wasn't the horse's fault, but she hadn't used the hackamore bridle since nor ridden bareback again. She slid off her back, dropped the reins, and led her through the underbrush. The mare high-stepped over a fallen log and caught her hoof on a protruding branch. The same hoof, always getting caught on something, like a sore toe you kept stubbing in the night. Sadie reined her in, glanced at the leg, and there he was again, leaning against the horse, tapping the front of her leg until she lifted the foot, probing the wall of the hoof with his pocketknife and knocking out a stone. Born to it.

Sadie pulled the horse out of his ghostly reach. "Get out of my head, damn you!" She jumped back in the saddle. "You and that girl," she muttered to herself. "Didn't think I needed to know about her? Made a fool out of me, traipsing after you like a damn fool! Come on, Lucy." She clucked her tongue. "Let's get out of here." She steered her towards a low-water area, and they forded the creek and headed for the trail through state land where there would be nobody, not even him.

He was a specter in the night when the floorboards in the old house settled and creaked with release from the weight of passing feet, when the nails shifted in their rusty groves to replicate footsteps. First it was her mother walking the hallway, now it was Stefan Montegrand, and whenever she heard the low throttle of a motorcycle, her heart leapt.

Maybe she should take up with Margie's son. He wasn't a bad sort. Maybe he would help her forget someone else's intended.

It was state land but the presence of another person, whether on whispering skis in winter or a hiker in summer, was an affront. Fortunately, it was remote enough that meeting up with anyone was rare. A bizarre murder when she was in middle school had branded the area dangerous, and the reputation had stuck.

The woods were dark and empty of birds. The songbirds of summer long since departed and the wintering juncos, pine siskins, and snow buntings not yet arrived. She came to a fork in the trail and took the one untrampled. The trees narrowed over the unused trail, and she had to lean over the horse's neck to clear low-hanging branches. She and her mother had snowshoed through here once in virgin snow, breaking trail. Jenny was on a birding kick, adding entries to her life list. She consulted her pocket Birds of North America and pointed out the hardy snow bunting, the last arriving passerine and the first to depart. She called them snowflakes, rousing Sadie from the breakfast table to stand at the window, as a newly arrived flock swirled through the air like snowflakes to settle in the field where she had lost the boomerang. *And did she know there were eight species of woodpeckers in these woods?*

She scanned the tops of the hemlocks, the bare branches of the maples and oaks. She stilled the horse and listened for the rhythmic drumming, the rat-a-tat-tat she once mistook for a ringing phone when it was just a woodpecker hammering for insects outside her bedroom window.

At first the distant hoof beats sounded like a giant woodpecker, or that hallowed drum that made a noise all on its own—another unwanted dredging of the past. She checked her impulse to flee and only yanked Lucy back from the trail.

She glimpsed the approaching rider through a break in the trees before he disappeared in a heavy stand of pine, coming hard and fast like a rough rider. She thought to hide, but too late, he was upon her.

She recognized Two Socks before she recognized Stefan. He wore a fur hat with ear flaps, and an oilskin duster draped the saddle and covered his legs.

He pulled up beside her, the horse stomping and lathered. She stared, speechless.

"Hi," he said, holding the reins high in one hand and tucking his knees in tight. Two Socks whinnied and nosed Lucy in horse recognition.

"Who said you could ride my horse?" she blurted.

He grinned. "I think I can handle him."

"What are you doing here?"

"Wanted to ride this horse again."

"How'd you find me?"

"Your dad gave me a hint. I think he was happy to see me."

Her heart was hammering like a woodpecker. She backed Lucy up, maintaining her distance.

"Plus, I could hear you from a mile away."

"You should've let me know you were coming."

"I wanted to surprise you."

"You think you can just show up? You're lucky I was home. I wasn't waiting around, you know."

"You weren't?" He kneed Two Socks forward and grabbed the pommel of her saddle, self-confidence overflowing like the smile playing his lips.

It was too much. His smile and his confidence, being taken unawares, caught flat-footed. She yanked the mare free and kicked her into a gallop.

But she should have known the mare could never outrun Two Socks.

Stefan cut her off at the fork in the trail, grabbed her reins, and pulled Lucy around snorting and stomping.

"Stop it!" she screamed, fighting to keep her seat and control of the bridle. "What do you want?!"

"I want to talk. What'd you do with your phone? Drop it in the toilet?"

"Why are you here, Stefan? I'm over it."

"You're lying."

It was a standoff, and they stared each other down.

369

"Nobody throws away something that good without an explanation. And a damn good reason."

"You're the one who never picks up, or answers messages."

He shook his head. "See? That's why I had to see you."

Their breath mingled in a confusion of angry vapor, and then she realized why he looked different.

"You cut your hair."

"I cut it after you left to stop myself from doing something worse."

Her heart lodged in her throat and choked off her voice.

He still had a hold on the reins and the horses were jostling each other as they turned in a slow circle. "Josie said your grandpa was sick, but he looked ornery as ever to me. He still doesn't like me, but he let me in." He turned serious. "I think I know why you left, and I'm sorry I didn't come back sooner, but I couldn't. Let's talk, okay?"

The creak of harness. The breathing of the horses. The steadfastness of his gaze.

She swallowed. "How'd you get here? Surely not on the bike."

"I have Jac's jeep. He was the one suggested it."

Sadie wrapped her fingers in the mare's mane to stop their trembling and heard herself ask, "How is he?"

"He took a turn for the worse after you left. Everything went to hell, then the Mounties showed up—he wasn't there, but they had me on edge and kept coming around. Then the specialist Josie took him to discovered that the infection in his lungs wasn't bacterial but fungal, which explained why the antibiotics wouldn't work. He prescribed a miracle anti-fungal drug. I was with him when he took a turn for the better—appetite back, wind back—and he told me to take off. He knew where I wanted to be."

"What about the Mounties?" She thought of the *wanted* poster she had ripped off the wall.

"I didn't know it was them at first, but then these guys from the Department of Natural Resources showed up, polite as could be, left calling cards. If he showed up, could I please notify them—there'd be something in it for us."

"Natural Resources? What—"

"Something in it for me."

"They expected his brother to turn on him?"

"A relative is usually a fugitive's downfall."

Sadie didn't know what to say.

"Bobby was back, sick about what had happened, blaming himself. He stayed with me at Josie's for a week, making plans to go to Yellowknife to work for some outfitter. He was pulling Jac one way, Josie the other, and then a registered letter came to the house for Jac, in care of Josie. Don't think Ottawa can't find you if they want to. Turns out they only wanted him to come in to discuss a plea bargain."

Sadie sat back on the horse. "A plea deal?"

"Yeah. You remember how some of the charges were dropped? Well, they offered a reduced sentence on the other, community service and a fine. Community service meaning he would agree to join an undercover operation in the Northwest Territory tracking poachers. They received orders to involve the Indigenous population behind the push to eradicate what's been going on for a long time, and nobody is better than Joachim when it comes to reading the signs of illegal hunting and fishing."

"He agreed?"

A smile touched his lips. "He won't have to wear a tie. Josie is bringing in a lawyer to draw up the legal paperwork, make sure there's nothing underhanded about it. No *gotcha* moments."

"I could never see him in a tie." She thought for a second. "I like your brother. He never seemed to have any ulterior motives."

"He likes you too, told me I shouldn't let you get away. I told him I didn't intend to. If all goes well, he'll be heading up with Bobby in the spring when the doc and Josie give the okay." He smiled. "And I'm here."

Yes, he was, and ridiculous looking in that fur hat and worn oilskin. Where on earth did he find that? Salvation Army? What else? His jeans were dirty and his face looked haggard. She wasn't letting him back in. There was too much unresolved, too many raw emotions. She picked at the scab.

"What about Aiyana?" she said. The girl from the north was the heart of the matter. She stood between them, even from a distance, the brick and mortar between them. "Josie said you were going to get married."

He snorted. "And you believed that?"

"Not at first. Then I saw you together that last morning and realized she was right. I was the one out of place. What did I know about your family? Your upbringing and your culture? I knew nothing. I'll tell you what it looked like to me—you were making plans to get married while having fun with me under the table."

He shook his head. "You thought so little of me?"

"Sex. It was just about the sex, but you didn't want me up *there*. Admit it."

"I admit it was pretty damn good. But it was on the table, not under it."

"Joke. All you can do is joke."

"Look, Aiyana and I are *not* getting married. I should have cleared this up before I left. I knew something was wrong." The horses were restless, and he shifted the reins in his hand. "Let's walk the horses so we can talk. Come on, Sadie. You're the one always wants to talk."

"No. I need to think. Now let go!"

She tried to yank the bridle reins out of his hand, but he grabbed her around the waist and pulled her out of the saddle. She struggled against him, and the cape attached to his duster swirled around them as they slid off Two Socks' back, landing on the ground in a heap.

"Let go of me. Are you crazy?" She struggled to get up, but he had her pinned.

He straddled her with eyes shot through with emotion. "Tell me you don't want me anymore. C'mon, baby," he whispered, "tell me. Tell me we had nothing special, and I'll let you go."

His breath smelled like peppermint and tobacco, and his weight was a blanket.

She couldn't tell him that.

His eyes had the same magnetism, but his face had aged, and the truth of what he said was plain to see in the lines around his mouth, the

372

exposed nape of his neck. "You shouldn't have cut your hair," she managed a whisper. "I liked it."

He lowered his mouth to hers, and they clutched each other.

"It's true," he whispered. "I have fun with you." He tugged on her lower lip with his teeth, finding her tongue. "I love you, Sadie Wixom," he rasped, "with all my heart."

The dappled light moved across his earnest and complicated face, and she ran her hand through his cropped hair. "You broke mine, Montegrand. Don't do it again." She kissed the smooth skin inside the neck of his tunic. "I love you," she murmured. "I've loved you from the first moment I saw you."

The horses moved away with their noses in the carpet of pine needles, looking for something worth eating, inured to the humans and their strange behaviors. The canopy overhead filtered the fading light that moved across the forest floor as the day grew long.

Cushioned by a thousand years of decaying leaves, pine needles, and feathers from molting song birds, they lay together until the cool of the earth seeped through the layers of vegetation and dampened his coat. Stefan pulled her to her feet, and they fastened their clothes and brushed each other off. He shrugged the duster back on, and she shook the debris from her hair, overcome by an incredible buoyancy of spirit.

He gathered the reins out from under the horses' feet and they led them out of the forest into a patch of sunshine.

A rush of wing overhead drew their attention to the field in front of them.

"Look, Stefan!" Sadie pointed at the flock of snow buntings that dropped out of the sky, settling in what sunshine was left of the day to forage in their winter home. "It's Mom's snowflakes. They've come back."

They stood together and watched the migrating flock sing the song of the tundra as they explored the fallow field for sustenance, having endured the long journey south.

"How do you know they're the same ones?" he said softly.

"All creatures pass on memory. Robins return to nest in the same tree; monarchs follow the same route year after year, owls mate for life. Why can't they be hers? Some things always come back."

"The boomerang, Sadie, do you still have it?"

"What a silly question."

He took her hand. "Let's go throw it. See what happens."

They stabled the horses, and with light enough to see and the dog circling, she handed him the boomerang. He unwrapped it, widened his stance in the throwing position, tested the wind against his cheek, smiled, and threw.

The End

Acknowledgments

I'd like to first thank creative writing teacher, Cathryn Essinger, for encouraging me to reach outside my comfort zone and write a novel, which gave me the courage to write this one. I'd like to thank all my readers, especially those who read through multiple drafts. I owe a debt of gratitude to authors Hugh McCullum and Karmel Taylor McCullum for their collaborative effort in writing *This Land Is Not For Sale*. I relied on their knowledge, interest in, and love for the North, its peoples, and their struggles while writing the parts of this novel for which I had no firsthand experience. Finally, to all the folks at Unsolicited Press who believed in the story, thank you.

About the Author

Yvonne Osborne is a fifth generation Michigander who grew up on the family farm founded by her great-great-grandfather. Her poetry and short stories have appeared in the *Midwest Review, Slippery Elm Literary Journal, Full of Crow, Third Coast Review, Airline Reading, Great Lakes Review,* and elsewhere.

About the Press

Unsolicited Press is based out of Portland, Oregon and focuses on the works of the unsung and underrepresented. As a womxn-owned, all-volunteer small publisher that doesn't worry about profits as much as championing exceptional literature, we have the privilege of partnering with authors skirting the fringes of the lit world. We've worked with emerging and award-winning authors such as Shann Ray, Amy Shimshon-Santo, Brook Bhagat, Kris Amos, and John W. Bateman.

Learn more at unsolicitedpress.com. Find us on twitter and instagram.